30TH STATE

ALAN GEMMELL

BLOOMSBURY
NEW DELHI • LONDON • OXFORD • NEW YORK • SYDNEY

BLOOMSBURY INDIA
Bloomsbury Publishing India Pvt. Ltd
Second Floor, LSC Building No. 4, DDA Complex, Pocket C – 6 & 7,
Vasant Kunj, New Delhi, 110070

BLOOMSBURY, BLOOMSBURY INDIA and the Diana logo
are trademarks of Bloomsbury Publishing Plc

First published in India 2025

ISBN: PB: 978-93-61315-42-8; eBook: 978-93-61316-03-6
2 4 6 8 10 9 7 5 3 1

Typeset in Minion Pro by Manipal Technologies Limited
Printed and bound in India by Thomson Press India Ltd

MIX
Paper | Supporting responsible forestry
FSC® C010615
FSC www.fsc.org

To find out more about our authors and books visit www.bloomsbury.com and sign up for our newsletters

For sale in the Indian subcontinent only

Advance Praise for *30th State*

'A provocative, sharply satirical thriller that flips history on its head. Gemmell masterfully explores power, politics, and empire in a future where England becomes India's newest colony'

Vikas Swarup, former Indian High Commissioner of Canada and author of *Slumdog Millionaire*

'It is 2027, and the beleaguered Kingdom of Britain—no longer "United" or "Great", politically rudderless, financially bankrupt and without any allies—finds itself being sucked into the orbit of its most coveted former colony, the jewel in its long-lost crown, India, becoming in the process its thirtieth state.

This saga of reverse colonisation—where India is nearly imagined as the swaggering hero of a retro "masala" Bollywood movie, reincarnating to exact revenge on former tormentors—may seem outlandish. But in fact, it is a cautionary tale, grippingly told, which could serve to awaken Britain to the perils of historical amnesia: of glossing over the horrific realities of Empire to yearn for that mythical age long gone.

As audacious as it is astute in its searing examination of modern Britain's political and social fault lines, sumptuously rich in detail and brilliantly executed, Alan Gemmell's *30th State* is a triumph of insight and imagination'

Shashi Tharoor, Member of Parliament and author of *Inglorious Empire: What the British Did to India*

For justice, liberty, equality and fraternity

Acknowledgements

Many people helped me write my first novel. I particularly want to thank:

Damien, my husband, for letting *30th State* eat up our evenings, holidays and weekends;

my mum, who was determined to give me the best possible start;

Sivapriya and the brilliant Bloomsbury team for taking a chance on a first-time author;

Charles, Diana, Sheetal, Susan, Toby and Usha whose comments and encouragement considerably improved what you read;

my wonderful P7 teacher at Annick Primary, Girdle Toll, who shared the first spark of what became *30th State*;

the inspiring people I met and worked with in India and with whom I had the most magical time;

and those who voted for me to become the member of parliament for the place where I grew up: the greatest privilege of my life.

Most of all, thank you, dear reader, for giving *30th State* your time.

One

Thursday, 12 August 2027
London

The leader of the opposition was exhausted. Khalid Khan had watched the continual destruction of his country every day of the last four years. His shoes were worn out campaigning from Carlisle to Cardiff. Finally, something was about to change. MPs and ambitious young staff had convinced him to expect the announcement today. An election would bring a jolt back to this lifeless legislature.

The Kingdom of Britain was burnt out. The square outside parliament—its one-time amphitheatre of democratic excess—was silent. An army of homeless people slept where protests had been staged, flags flown and rights fought for. The government, which Khalid despised, had placed what was left of the former united kingdom in a state of constant despair.

Westminster was spent. Khalid kept one eye on the crumbling masonry as he dodged workers beginning their daily battle with victorian steam pipes and hundreds of miles of fraying cables just to keep the lights on. He shuddered when he remembered the great men and women who'd walked this medieval hall. What would they think about the state of it now? A visible sign of national atrophy. He caught his tired reflection in the tarnished brass plaque whose barely visible words marked Charles the First's trial by another rump parliament.

The marbled politicians of St Stephen's Hall stared down at all who hurried by as if to say, there are no great statesmen left. This place was once a sign of England's ability to rise like a colossus above its greatest struggles and fashion them into a new national myth. The original protean state—one that could leap to the next opportunity way ahead of the rest. A nation-building blacksmith who, by embracing impurities, forged ever stronger alloys ready for whatever the world threw at it.

Fire had once rent this ancient palace asunder. Buoyed by the vast riches of England's colonial enterprise and its global domination, clever architects with an imperial state of mind had created the apogee of victorian-gothic theatre in its stead. For some two hundred years, the world's political stage had been set on the banks of the Thames. The words recited in the once-great House of Commons reverberated around the globe. Kings and kingdoms had followed the pronouncements of this mother of democracy as if made by God himself. Khalid, above all others, knew this was no longer the state of play.

He stopped to take in the shimmering, pixelated saints of central lobby, parliament's beating heart. A quartet of gilded mosaics high above him, each catching the day's light, positing a story about what Britain once was in the world. He paused to remember the message hidden in their placement. St George, the patron saint of the English atop the way to the Lords—parliament had always been English first. 'And the English lord over all of us,' Khalid's father had reminded him every morning as he read the latest news from Lahore and whatever that day's *Morning Star* was peddling. St David marked the way to the commons—a reminder of the great Welsh orators who have shone in the chamber, as well as those who love the sound of their own voice on the green baize benches. St Patrick stood astride the exit. The Irish had always been searching for a way out of an enforced union. 'And, to this day, that's why exits around the world are green,' Khalid, with a gleam in his eye, whispered to anyone on a tour with him. And for the Scots? He'd chuckle. St Andrew sent you off to Stranger's, at one time the most notable, if not notorious, pub in the country. Parliament was, after all, a riparian boozer with some offices attached. Like the Kingdom of Britain, the great chandelier high above him, and this once iridescent hagiography, had long since lost its lustre; but this parliament now had much more to worry about than the decaying state of its bricks and mortar.

Khalid marched to members' lobby, nodding at the police. The doors opened just ahead of him. 'At least some things continue like clockwork.' Khalid smiled gratefully at Harry, one of the indefatigable doorkeepers in black, long-tailed coat, white bow tie and shiny badge of office dangling from his waistcoat.

'We're in some state, sir.'

Khalid raised his eyebrows.

The ornate doors to the House of Commons were directly ahead of him. Khalid's colleagues were running in and out. They'd called him to join them early. They were expecting an explosive performance. He hoped it would be terminal for his opponents. Their shouts and jeers seeped out like children in the playground on the last day of school. When at its most intense, the temperature and temperament of the 591 souls in the chamber leached through the whole building like high-voltage current. Churchill cowered over Khalid, who turned to Harry. 'At least you're both still here—watching over England and the poor sods in there.'

The din, the sweat, the cheap colognes of the 591 representatives of the parliament of Britain hit him. The chamber was charged as if lightning had struck. This heady mix unleashed the unmistakable metallic taste in his mouth. Like an actor waiting in the wings. Or a boxer for the fight to start. It gripped him the exact same way every time he rose to speak at the despatch box opposite people who had become his sworn enemies. His father's words would ring in his ears, 'Every time, ev-very time you go into that place, you think about the best you can do for our people.' His father had benefited from an England that reluctantly welcomed migrants like himself. In time, as Khalid's children had benefited from that England it had become 'your people'. Recently, it was 'the people', a command from Khalid's father that he prepare himself for government. Both he and Khalid were tired of watching from the sidelines as a corrupt and ineffective administration pulled the country from its knees on to the floor and into a state of perpetual despondency and despair.

Khalid heard an unmistakable cough. He'd been blankly staring at madam speaker, neither bowing to acknowledge the office nor making his way to his seat. With a gleam in her eye, she winked and nodded at him.

The cheer from his own team brought Khalid back to his senses. Like the roar of a crowd for their favourite football player. Or the throng he imagined you heard and saw at the colosseum. He winked back as he made his way to madam speaker's left. The shouting and banging continued as he sat down surrounded by his supporters and the ones who'd launched the coup that led to him becoming their leader. They were always directly behind, staring out from over his shoulder like the bullies who commandeered the back seat of the school bus. He could sense them salivating for what would come next, like a pack of fighting dogs on one of the many lost housing estates that now littered the country.

Of course, Khalid had been flattered when they'd asked him to be the first Asian leader of the labour party. Like them, he wanted to win. To change the course of his country's history. He'd known it would take at least two elections to finally turn around the party's fortunes. But how many years would it take to turn the country's around? His plan had relied on the government keeping the union together. But that was not to be.

Prime minister Richardson's predecessor wrongly convinced himself that a ragtag Scottish coalition for secession would never rally enough people to rescind the 300-year-old act of union between England and Scotland. Like so many fights in those years, it was taken on by pushy and overconfident posh English ministers. Their hubris and heritage assured only one thing: rapid and vapid agreement on the problem and its solution. Khalid had seen it all too often. Their good breeding led to inbreeding in decision-making. So they did the only thing they knew to do, pour English pounds down Scottish throats. The canny Scots took the promised gold and left the union anyway. The posh boys' campaign fizzled out like the cheap fireworks Khalid tried to set off each new year. His miserly celebrations had become a thing of legend. In a battle between bumbling buffoons and future-focused freedom fighters, the union was the principal casualty. An independent Scotland appointed its first prime minister. Khalid's country took its diminution badly. A shortened name. A reduced role in the world. A chastened course ahead. This painful birth for both was a lifeline for Khalid. It was a death sentence for an ailing conservative government. And the epilogue to a state of English greatness, which had started with Sir Thomas Roe's first audience with Jahangir.

The shock of the loss of Scotland had sent the once United Kingdom into democratic turpitude. With the creation of the Kingdom of Britain, it was great no longer. The conservative party hung on to Mark Richardson. He'd taken them through the 2023 election with a simple promise to be 'better than the last guy'. Richardson's steady state campaign—bolstered by a predictably boring life, a wife and two kids, a successful and straightforward career—was welcome relief. In sharp contrast to a run of predecessors. But the Richardson administration had failed in office and flailed in all directions.

Khalid had known all along that Richardson was irrelevant. It was the chancellor whom he really worried about. If anyone could beat Khalid to the koh-i-noor in the crown as first asian prime minister, it would be Karan Puri. In many ways he should have been Khalid's chancellor. Another successful, hard-working ethnic minority from a provincial town in the north of England. Karan's parents were labour voters. His father had been a campaigner in the party's glory years. But unlike Khalid's party, it was clear Karan still had problems choosing a British-Asian leader. What to most was an inevitable consequence of three hundred years of colonising the countries, if not the minds, of the British empire, was too much to bear for many of the people on the benches opposite. Plus, Khalid could only imagine how the Puri family had coped with the advent of Isha, Karan's rich Indian wife. Her father's vast wealth shot Karan into the stratosphere of bollywood superstars and punjabi billionaires. Even Khalid's long-standing labour-voting constituents were enthralled by the glitz and glam of Karan and Isha's impeccably designed world. Politics was notoriety as much as it was anything.

Madam speaker's 'Order! Order!' silenced the house.

* * *

In Buckingham Palace, the king was in his private study at a desk freighted with history, littered with gilded trinkets, laden with framed photos of his majesty and the leaders of his realms, and peppered with the occasional picture of his much-trimmed royal family.

A submission from the all-too-dashing Canadian prime minister caught his eye. 'Oh dear, more trouble with his cabinet, I see,' the king proclaimed aloud. 'Such factionalism. These poor elected representatives live in a state of extended uncertainty.'

The door opened. 'Sir.' Lord Banerjee bowed. 'The prime minister is on his feet.'

The king nodded as Banerjee uncovered a television carefully obscured behind some louise xiv vases.

'Banerjee, this note from the prime minister about my new order of chivalry for public service?' The king leafed through another of the many important documents from his red box.

'Yes, sir?'

'I really think we should review the badge and ribbon. Have we settled on my profile? To the right or the left?'

Banerjee looked over as the king continued, 'Yes, I think we should revert to the left. It's much my better side. And the royal blue with what shade of green, did you recommend?'

'Oh, I think the ballater green, sir. There is a sample in the box, I believe.'

'Yes, excellent choice.'

* * *

Karan picked up the draft of the prime minister's statement from the sleek gunmetal desk Isha had requested for his office as chancellor of his majesty's treasury. 'This is the latest version?' he asked.

Oliver nodded.

Karan continued, 'I still think I should be in there,' pointing at the scenes on the television.

'One minute, pitaji.' Isha broke off the call with her father. 'He heard you and says you should stay out of it.'

Karan watched them both. His oldest friend and closest political ally. His most ambitious partner. Most days he didn't know which was which. 'Well, here's a good question, if I'm not in there, where am I?'

'I'm currently reading hundreds of comments about our prime minister,' Oliver replied.

'*Current* prime minister,' Isha added, a wide smile forming. 'Pitaji says you can thank him for the relentless trolling of your soon-to-be immediate predecessor.'

Oliver scoffed, 'Your father has done well with these fake social media accounts. There must be thousands of them.'

Isha beamed. 'Yes, he says the Chinese ones were much cheaper than the Indians. And totally untraceable. So he doubled the spend.'

'They need to find a better default attack than piss-poor performance from a pint-sized politico.' Glancing at Karan, Oliver added, 'That might be a little close to home. Anyway, Isha says you're recovering from emergency dental surgery.'

Isha's index finger jumped from Oliver to the screen. 'He'd have had you sitting beside Richardson and his fuckwit friends. Then you'd be smeared with his incompetence. We needed some distance from their self-imposed shit show.'

Karan replied, 'Either way, I'm glad I'm not in there with that poor bastard. It's a suicide mission.'

'He was never going to beat pitaji,' Isha sat the phone on the table. 'It's all going like clockwork. Will you announce Karan's coronation the minute he sits down?'

Oliver shook his head. 'Let's see the reactions first. We will need to convince people Karan is the right guy to replace him.'

Isha glared at Karan. 'Fuck's sake. You've had weeks to do one job. Neither of you are any good at sticking the knife in.' Picking up her mobile, 'No, pitaji, that was Karan's secretary. She uses such terrible language.'

* * *

'Shit.' Molly was searching for her pass. 'It's only day two. How can I have fucked this up so badly?' She looked at her shoes. 'And what the fuck was I thinking buying these? I look like a high-class hooker.'

'Do you want to change your destination?'

'Eh, no. In fact, I can probably get out here.' It still felt weird to talk to a screen. But how else should you address a driverless cab?

She glanced at the red-soled shoes one final time. Her mother's voice ringing in her ears from this morning's call, 'It's what you look like on your second day that really counts for something.'

She dragged her feet along the pavement. And checked them again. The scuff marks convincing her, at least, that they were not brand new. Her mother's voice again, 'And don't let the bastards grind you down.' 'Well, she was of Irish heritage,' Molly thought.

Molly walked over London Bridge, wary of the enhanced police presence. The homeless had been cleared away following requests from the various city financial institutions that they were bad for business. Most days it was only twenty-something graduates, like her, and junior managers, that made their way into work. Everyone else had made enough money to issue orders from a converted-shed-office in a large garden somewhere in the south-east. She made her way along the broody, moody side of the Bank of Britain—a daft name change the current government had introduced to try to curry favour with increasingly populist ideas.

Merchant's bank had been at lothbury for almost two hundred years. Their understated edwardian portico was a relatively recent addition funded by a burst of early-twentieth-century exuberance. Inside what was once the marble banking hall, the optimistic architecture continued with reliefs, filigree and pediments, each and every stone a reminder of the bank's role as buccaneering enabler of the zenith of British empire. Throughout the recruitment process for the job, Molly had been repeatedly told the bank had happily shorn itself of its final imperial vestiges. All its promotional material confidently confirmed it delivered a substantially pleasing return from global investments through its greater-than-average risk appetite mitigated by insight and intelligence from its long-nurtured relationships.

A squat, round reception desk was anchored in the centre of the vast temple to global ambition and money.

'No pass? Not to worry.' The receptionist issued a giant temporary pass. 'We're just lucky you've come back for a second day,' he chuckled. 'They're like foxes in the hen house up there. Or bull elephants in mating season. I can feel it down here. All that musth! Make sure and keep your wits about you. Oh, and some hand sanitiser!' From the corner of her eye, Molly could see the tight-fitting trousers of younger traders running along the mezzanine like well-tailored zombies on speed.

In the bank's penthouse boardroom, city grandees, retired permanent secretaries, a former intelligence chief and an Oxbridge vice-chancellor had assembled, watched over by regency paintings and Mughal miniatures. For over a hundred and fifty years, the Merchant's bank boardroom had been a place to make the good great and the great rich. Its directors always managed to be miles ahead of their neighbours and light years ahead of their members of parliament. Usually, they'd back more than one horse in the race—and then buy the stadium with their winnings.

* * *

In the commons chamber, the prime minister was on his feet. He'd drained his first glass of water in one gulp. A colleague was refilling it, but he hadn't the energy to look round to thank them.

'Madam speaker, I regret to inform the house that without further assistance, England will be unable to meet its international financial obligations—and our debts have been called in.' Richardson took a moment. He could feel his words jar with the self-serving political brains in front of, and, more importantly, behind him. He wasn't yet prepared for the inevitable disregard for his statement, his leadership and himself. He reached for the glass. He stared down at it as it approached his mouth—the water shaking like the storm inside him.

Cries of 'Shame! Shame!' brought him to his senses with all the pungency of asafoetida.

'Sterling is suffering enormous international speculation. The Bank of Britain has already spent almost 50 billion pounds today to maintain the value of sterling at $1.40. But we continue to suffer attacks from global actors.'

Richardson felt the sharp intake of breath across the chamber from the ashen faces of the many hundreds of legislators.

'We believe this pressure on the pound is being coordinated, and I have tasked the UK's intelligence agencies with identifying the sources. And swiftly bringing their actions to an end and the individuals to justice, wherever they are.'

'Don't just catch the bastards. Bomb them,' someone shouted.

A note was being passed along the government benches. Richardson saw it out of the corner of his eye. He picked it up.

'I am reading this aloud. I understand the prime minister of India has given a media interview in New Delhi to say that she will cease all bilateral cooperation with England.'

Khalid sat his papers down. This wasn't in his version of the prime minister's statement. The government's chief whip had called to say things were bad but not apocalyptic.

The house now sat in silence as if listening to their collective last rites. Their stillness gave Richardson the strength to keep going, 'Her statement continued, British banks, which rely on data held in India, will be unable to trade. British energy companies, which rely on Indian software and workers, will cease to function.'

Richardson knew he was reciting his own political death warrant. Knives were being sharpened on all sides. He could hear them and was resigned to his fate. 'Just so long as it isn't that bunch of bastards in front of me,' he thought. He'd told Karan's team to keep him out of the chamber, telling him he needed a clear run at the imminent leadership election the statement would launch. Or had they told him?

'Madam speaker, data from sitara—the anglo-indian satellite company—will be withheld: meaning that all mobile communications will stop; our naval and armed forces will be unable to operate.'

The uneasy quiet broke. There were murmurings. Then, from up behind Khalid came a low, guttural, 'Resign!' A starting pistol had been fired. It set off a cacophony of sound coming from all sides. 'Resign.' 'Shame.' 'Disgrace.' 'Call it quits and call an election.' It was as if a pressure valve had been opened. Anger flew out like the sewage that needed parliament's victorian steam-pipe network to expel it from its bowels deep below the chamber. Like the sewage, the abuse couldn't be stopped once it had got going. Khalid turned to the particular troublemaker who had initiated this wall of shit and gave him a nod. It was always better to have the wolves at your neighbour's door. But if they only knew how bad it truly was, they'd not waste their time with sedentary interventions.

The noise grew to unheard-of levels. Richardson struggled on as if he were running through water. 'Order, order.' Madam speaker shouted and then stood, 'Mis-ter Jen-ner,' hitting every syllable, 'I think we've heard enough from you for one day. One more injudicious grumble and you'll be out.'

Richardson caught her eye. The chortle she generated was sufficient for him to plough on. His head was bowed, and eyes transfixed on the large-type, double-spaced statement in front of him. He knew by the timbre of the voice from whom and from where it had come. It took what was the last reserve of all of his energy to bring his chin up and fix his stare.

'They shout, "Resign". They call for elections. That's all they know. But there is nothing the party opposite can do. We are at a moment of national calamity. And, fast approaching the limits of this house. Maybe even this country.'

Khalid's backbenchers screamed at Richardson. Some called, 'Point of order!' Others jeered, 'Resign! Where's the chancellor!' The overexcited cries of Khalid's troops could be heard like the piccolos atop an orchestra. His wolves were pushing him to get to his feet.

'Order!' Madam speaker leaned forward in her chair. Her feet lifted off their footrest. This slight gesture was sufficient to convey extreme discomfiture to her 591 charges.

In this final crucible of English parliamentary democracy, it was Khalid's moment. The wolves now running alongside him. Eyes trained on the prey opposite. They'd been chasing the fatally wounded animal for many miles. Richardson's end was now in their sights. 'Madam speaker, the prime minister has told this house the country is hurtling towards bankruptcy. He lost Scotland.' Khalid pointed at him. 'Killed our united kingdom. Now his incompetence alone will lead to the death of all that we have left. A litany of losses. He should be ashamed to stand at that government despatch box. It is time for a new government. A new prime minister and a new plan for this great country. He must call an election!'

'What's the plan?' the wolves continued to chant as Khalid sat back down. 'Even your chancellor's given up on you. Where is he?'

Richardson smiled. He knew Karan's absence would draw fire. Misdirection with Khalid's clowns was as easy as being a magician at a five-year-old's birthday party. 'Madam speaker, my right honourable friend the chancellor is working on a rescue package as we speak—with assistance from our international partners.'

'Which international partners do you have left?' someone shouted from high up in the labour benches.

'His father-in-law?' Another hollered, 'How much will it cost him to get you out of the shit this time!'

Khalid was up and bouncing on his feet as if in a parliamentary boxing ring. 'Madam speaker, it is time for the prime minister to have an audience with his majesty, hand over the seals of office and go! The country needs fresh momentum. For that we need a new government. And that government needs a new leader.'

Khalid had promised his team he'd never miss an opportunity to punch the privileged arses of the party opposite. He knew the public weren't tired of politics. They were tired of the piss-poor politicians forced on them time after time.

'For God's sake, go!' the wolves could sense fear and taste blood. 'And give us a chance to run this country. You've run it into the ground!'

Richardson shook his head, 'As ever, the leader of the opposition focuses on self-advancement when selfless service is what's needed. Well, madam speaker, I am able to speak for England—no, thank you. Not today. Not ever! No matter how dire and desperate, madam speaker, I could never advise his majesty to appoint as the king's first minister someone who believes in neither king nor country—but only in himself.'

Richardson knew it was his last act in this particular parliamentary circus. He was out of time. Out of energy. Out of luck. Soon he'd be an audience member again and watch them tear down all that he'd built. His shoulders hunched. He fixated on the thick wooden table that separated him from the barbarians opposite. But his real enemies were behind him. His throat dry. Forehead moist. Back sodden. This fresh sweat joined the fetid scent emanating from his jacket. The cries of 'What's the plan?' and 'Resign' continued unabated. Madam speaker had given up any semblance of refereeing.

He closed the binder and rubbed off what was left of its government gold crest. Another note was slowly making its way to him. He read it, then took off his reading glasses and with little ceremony put them in his inner pocket. If he wasn't reading, they knew he was making it up as he was going along. It was all he'd had left. The final throw of the prime-ministerial dice, like putting the last of your chips on black and waiting to see where the ball landed. 'Of course there is a plan, madam speaker. But thanks to the right honourable member's exhortations in this chamber, the spivs and speculators are continuing to do their best to bring the pound, the government and the country to their knees. I will be instructing the governor of the Bank of Britain to use all of the bank's reserves to maintain sterling at 1 dollar 15. If needed, I will also raise interest rates to 10 per cent this afternoon. The markets can expect a statement from the bank governor imminently.'

The wolves screamed, 'Resign! Resign! Resign!'

Richardson blurted, 'That should give us a few days' grace,' and fell back into his seat. The silence on his own side was as if they'd been told the cancer was back and this time it was inoperable.

* * *

Karan, Isha and Oliver were staring at the screen. Karan blurted, 'No, he fucking won't,' and shouted to his private office, 'get me the governor.'

Isha fumed at Oliver. 'You ignored what I told you to say?'

With a loud crunch, Karan started on an apple from a silvery, designer fruit bowl in front of him. 'I thought we didn't want a rescue plan?'

Oliver continued to scan social media on his phone. 'We don't. But this is why you're not around. We want everyone to think you're trying to craft one.'

Isha made to storm out. 'And I think a plan that doesn't work damages Karan's reputation.'

The phone on Karan's desk rang. Oliver walked over. 'This is his mess,' he said, putting the handset down, 'but if we play it right, it's your moment. You know Ranjan Bhai won't make a statement. He was at your fucking wedding!'

Isha turned around, smiling. 'This I agree with.'

Oliver continued, 'Let him blow up the bank. Then there's only India's offer left on the table.'

They watched Isha walk past Karan's private office staff. Oliver added, 'We won't need a plan. Your father-in-law has another card to play.'

* * *

Lord Banerjee returned to the king's private office with the rushed afternoon edition of the *Evening Standard*, whose front cover asked, 'Can Britain Survive?' His majesty continued to read his government papers, ferreting each from the open red box on the desk in front of him with the glee of a child fishing christmas presents out of their stocking. Without acknowledging Banerjee, he added, 'I assume we will have an audience of the prime minister this evening.'

'And, a resignation, sir?' Banerjee asked.

'Yes. I should speak to the Indian prime minister now to see where all this is going. Don't you think?'

Banerjee nodded and made to leave. 'I'll speak to her office.'

'No, do it through Sunil.' The king's squeaky scribbling stopped. 'Have you had any contact with his daughter?'

Banerjee turned. 'You mean with the chancellor's wife?'

The king nodded. Banerjee shook his head. 'No, not yet. I felt it better to wait.'

His majesty nodded again and returned to his tall pile of letters. The room was filled with the gloom of his extended apprenticeship. The promises of global relevance and striding the world stage as titular head of a top-tier country had not materialised. And now they never would. Throughout his brief reign, Britain's downward spiral had continued as power drained from the North Atlantic to the Indian Ocean. The waters were swirling faster than ever. And someone had just pulled the plug. Banerjee looked at him. That which was left of his kingdom was disappearing before his eyes. Yet he sat there, untroubled. In a state of calm, maybe even bliss.

* * *

Molly headed to the lifts at the back of the hall, catching the screaming news updates on the screens around her.

'Following unbelievable scenes in the British house of commons,' the American newsreader sneered, 'the British pound, a one-time reserve currency, is experiencing unbearable international pressure. Its collapse now appears inevitable, as does the failure of the Richardson administration. And of the country itself.' Molly was immobile, gaping at the television.

'News just in. Ranjan Chakrabarti, governor of Britain's reserve bank, has issued a statement to say the bank will do all it can to support the British pound. Due to elevated levels of volatility driven by AI trading platforms, the bank is suspending online trading of sterling and requiring all trades to be made through accredited brokers on calls.'

The lift opened on to Merchant's trading floor. It was pandemonium. Traders screaming down their phones for an open line to the bank. 'We're going old-school,' one shouted as she walked through them. They were high. More like peacocks than kites. Every one of them was betting against Richardson.

Jonathan, Molly's boss, was a forty-something veteran of Merchant's trading floor. He had the body of a football-playing gym junkie battling heavy sessions of drink and the occasional class a drug. He was one of the last working-class kids from east London to join the bank straight from school. Taking the mobile away from his mouth, he shouted, 'Where the fuck have you been?'

Molly's cheeks reddened. 'Did I miss the start of world war three?'

Jonathan motioned for her to be quiet. He switched between calls and pointed for her to watch. On the monitors she could see records of him buying hundreds of millions of pounds from international dealers and selling to the bank for tens of millions profit. 'It's fucking christmas, hanukkah and diwali rolled into one. We're making a fucking mint. Macau levels of gambling going on here. You cannot lose today. Unless you're the fucking government. People have been buying pounds betting on this moment for days. Richardson's mental attempt to save sterling has lit up the trading floor like pouring kerosene on fire. Look around. Traders are dumping whatever they can to sink him.'

Pointing at the screen, he carried on, 'I can't find sterling fast enough. This clever little AI platform scours the world for tanking pounds, and, thanks to an innumerate prime minister, the bank has its mucky hands all over me, like a drunk undergraduate at a strip club.'

Molly watched the profits accumulate. 'Charming. And everyone is doing this?'

Jonathan's eyes didn't leave the screen, 'Every fucker in London.' His hands moved between screens and keyboards like he was playing Chopin on the piano. 'This shit show is going to cost at least 100 billion pounds.'

'How long can they keep it up?' Molly asked.

'A day if they're lucky, like ...'

She turned to him. 'Like a drunk undergraduate at a strip club.'

'You're learning.'

She walked away and he asked, 'Molly, did you get in okay?'

She nodded. But then she headed to the toilet. She took out her mini-notepad and wrote down everything he had told her word for word. She took photos of the notes and texted them.

* * *

Richardson squeezed along the front bench between his MPs to leave. He tried to catch madam speaker's eye but she remained in detailed discussion with her clerks. He was unsurprised to see his own backbenchers were studying their order papers and deep in conversation with one another. 'Fuckers, 'he thought. 'You're only here because of me.'

The doorkeeper grabbed his arm, telling him, 'You'll get us through. Could be worse. Chelsea could've won last night.' The heavy victorian carpets and ornate wood panelling of the narrow corridor to his office behind the chamber closed in on him. He undid his tie and felt the sweat on his shirt. His police protection officers had raced ahead. He was grateful for their decisiveness. Meaning he didn't need to think for a minute or two.

'Well?' he asked of the aides and civil servants following behind.

'Not terminal yet,' one ventured.

'You'll fix it, PM,' an ambitious, oily young tory MP squeezed by, going in the opposite direction. Close enough to see the sweat on Richardson's brow.

'Not fucking likely,' Richardson thought. 'Probably sent by the chief to keep my spirits up,' he shared with no one in particular. 'Wonder what they promised him? A rung up the ladder in Karan's government?' In the courtyard he slumped into the back seat of the waiting car, staring at the display panel in the front.

'Was that always there?' he grunted and pointed.

'What?' His aide was at a loss. But it was better to continue with whatever this distraction was than focus on his recent performance. Or on what he would do next.

'That flag. Right there,' he pointed. 'Have we always had the Indian fucking flag on the dashboard? Have I been receiving the kind compliments of the Indian government every time my arse was in this car?' Richardson's aide focused on her inbox and let the question hang in the air. He looked out the window at the empty faces in the square. A collective state of despair.

The Downing Street press were shouting, 'When will you resign, prime minister?' Richardson ignored them. Once in Number 10, an aide passed him a new folder. 'We've set up the call. She's ready for you but the chief wants to see you first.'

He stormed round, almost knocking down a Henry Moore. 'If the chief whip wants to recommend that I stand down, then he can wait in fucking line.'

The aide whispered, 'The chief of MI6 is in your study.' And opened the door.

'Dame Rebecca, nice to see you,' Richardson extended his hand and watched the sixty-something, stick-thin head of his intelligence agency walk towards him. He was always intrigued by her tailored jackets and short skirts.

'Prime minister,' Dame Rebecca had the deepest public-school voice of anyone Richardson knew. Her father had been in intelligence, and he assumed she'd attended some impressive college at the taxpayers' expense. Whenever her piercing eyes narrowed at him, he was sure she had authorised assassinations. Whatever she told him, he believed.

'Prime minister, we've tracked a large proportion of the currency speculation. You won't like what we've uncovered.'

'Go on.' He sat down and was momentarily distracted by the ease with which she did too.

'It seems Sunil Grover has taken a globally significant short position on sterling.' Dame Rebecca handed him a folder marked 'secret'.

'Karan's father-in-law?'

'Yes. He used three of his hedge funds to borrow billions of pounds, selling for a basket of foreign currencies, Euros, dollars, rupees and RMB. His actions alone have created a global run on the pound, which neither we nor the bank will be able to stop.'

'I never liked him. I don't think Karan did either.' Richardson snapped the folder shut and added, 'I'm sure he had nothing to do with this.'

'Are you sure, prime minister? His wife appears to have been in direct contact with her father ahead of many of the most significant trades.' Dame Rebecca handed over a note marked 'top secret.

'Oh, come now.' Richardson was going through it. 'That's merely circumstantial. You know what a daddy's girl she is. She is insufferable about the father, but she agreed to all the vetting. You signed off on his appointment.'

'We did, prime minister. But the interesting part is just how many of the loans have come from Indian public banks in Isha's name.' Dame Rebecca took back the note and highlighted the individual transactions.

'Well, what can you do now?'

She took a deep breath. 'I'm afraid nothing, prime minister. None of our allies want to confront India in this fight. My international colleagues are too busy fighting populists in their own countries. No one wants to take on the Indian prime minister. They feel you, and your government, are collateral damage in the new great game. They are almost as beholden to India as we are. I imagine they will start to reduce their reliance in the next few days.'

'So, what happens next?'

'That all depends on what you can negotiate directly with the Indian prime minister. But we are on our own. You are on your own.'

'Don't you have any assets in India you could press into service for us?'

She shook her head. 'None that we can call into action quickly. And we have become much more squeamish than the Indians have.'

Richardson got up, shook her hand and walked through to the boat-shaped table that filled the vast cabinet room. His team were nose-deep in their notes. A large screen opposite had the imposing image of the Indian prime minister.

He opened the folder in front of him, and smiled. 'Good afternoon, prime minister. Can we return to your offer to the chancellor to renegotiate our loans?'

Usha Sachdev shifted in her seat. The fifty-six-year-old Indian prime minister's immaculate turquoise sari shimmered down the screen at him. She took a slow, deep breath and clasped her palms together. She checked her aides, then rested her chin on her hands. After a moment she told him, 'The time for renegotiation has passed, prime minister. Now we have to protect India's interests. Our national security is threatened. Our currency is threatened. Our people are threatened.' Usha paused. 'The lights go out at midnight.'

Richardson's most senior aides were off-camera. One, sitting nearest him, was frantically drafting a reply. Before he could receive it, Richardson blurted out, 'Usha, these are not the actions of an ally. And certainly not one of our oldest friends. I hear sterling is undergoing an extreme attack orchestrated by Indian speculators close to your party.' The aides in the cabinet room gasped.

She drew herself to her full height. 'We are gravely concerned about the safety and security of our citizens. Who knows to whom a desperate, bankrupt England would turn? And we are concerned about the many tens of billions of rupees invested in England as well as our much-valued intellectual property, which your administration is trashing every hour it remains in office.'

She purposefully straightened her sari before crossing her arms in front. 'You should be aware we have given orders to the commander of our carrier strike group to head to the North Atlantic and anchor in international waters outside the channel. We have dispatched subsea drones to monitor your cable traffic with Europe, the US and India. If you fail to follow our request, and those of our allies, we will cut these cables and dislocate England from the global economy.'

The cabinet room was silent. Richardson watched one face after another. These were some of the smartest people in the entire country. But they hadn't seen this coming. They'd formed their bonds throughout the two-year fight with Scotland. Through some of the most painful political choices he thought he'd ever have to make. How could they not have foreseen this tsunami?

He'd hoped for an opportunity to bring England back together after the shock of a new border in Great Britain. No one had really cared for Scotland by the time that second referendum came. If they really wanted to leave so badly, if England had become some kind of abusive partner, then they could and should just go. He'd done his duty and fought valiantly, but in vain. All he'd really wanted was these last few years to put the country back together. They'd felt the loss of Scotland. The loss of purpose was greater. Where they once had pride of place in the world, now they struggled to get by. This couldn't really be happening. 'What you're outlining is an act of war,' he told her.

Usha waited. She looked at her team. She, and they, understood the English far better than they knew themselves. She turned back to the camera. 'We won't be lectured on acts of war by an English prime minister. We here know well how England acts to protect its own interests. Colonising. Enslaving men, women and children. And all too often a navy used to exert domination over free peoples. To turn five thousand years of Indian civilisation into a state of subjugation. Now you are the despairing state, prime minister, and you have to realise it.'

He felt the sweat on his brow and back. And he could smell it too. It stung his eyes. His face reddened. His pulse quickened. Thoughts flooded his mind. 'When had it happened? This new India. This shift in dynamics. The global south not just leading the global north but denigrating it? Was it just her drive and determination? Was she bluffing? Was there any way to charm her out of this?' Finally, he pulled his crumpled self up. 'Usha, that was almost three hundred years ago. I cannot let you do this.'

'You will not have to, prime minister,' she replied. 'I have spoken to the king. He agrees the situation in which England finds itself—as a bankrupt nuclear power without a friend to turn to—requires action in both our national interest. England will come under the temporary protection of India. Tomorrow, the king will sign this instrument of accession,' she held the document aloft, 'and you will resign. The carrier strike group is merely an invitation to treat.' She smirked. Finally, those Delhi law classes were of use to her.

Richardson's mouth was open. But he had nothing to say. Could she really have spoken to the king? Would he have given up his prime minister so readily? And his kingdom? 'Usha, I need time to speak to his majesty. He can't. You can't. We won't.'

Usha had never tasted a sweeter moment than this. Sitting at the feet of her grandfather she'd learnt to run successful election campaigns. She hadn't been guaranteed the power base he'd built in Ludhiana. It was clear her father had wanted it to go to her brother. But her grandfather had seen something in her and repeatedly told her that her day would come. A day that would allow her to make good the losses the British had visited on her family and all of India.

'Prime minister, your king has waited a lifetime to be a head of state. It turns out he wanted to be head of any state. After our recent decision on Jammu and Kashmir, he is to be head of our thirtieth state. He is not going to give that up as easily as your country has given up on you. He and I have come to an arrangement: be our appointee or become a civilian in a pedestrian life. It seems he would rather have the trappings of power than power itself.'

'Usha, I need time. My office will be in touch with yours.' Richardson ended the call and asked, 'What the fuck are we going to do?'

His aide replied, 'I think you're going to see the king and resign, prime minister.'

* * *

Oliver left Karan's treasury office when Richardson stopped speaking in the chamber. He sprinted across the road but had been held outside as the current boss exited. He watched Richardson stare resolutely ahead and thought, 'I wonder if the poor sod knows how quickly this will all fall.'

In every room in westminster, gossip had replaced the silence after Richardson's last utterance. In some quarters panic had already broken out, with tory MPs sure of a snap election asking their teams to pack up offices. Communications officers were tasked with finding arrays of photos of MPs for campaign material that most assumed would be needed in a few days' time.

In the rich crimson-red, gold and green of the Pugin Room, among the paintings of parliament's architects and designers, underneath the optimistic embrace of an elaborate chandelier, tory loyalists sat next to the plotters and those totalling their retirement pay-off and pension emoluments. Right at the back overlooking the Thames were Sir Dennis and the grandest of grandees.

'Oliver Benjamin, I think we had better have a word.' Sir Dennis knew this would suck the air in the room towards him like a gas-turbine engine and force Oliver to weave his way through the whole damn lot of them.

Oliver suggested, 'Shall we have the 2019 brouilly?'

The room pretended to return to their own conversations. When the bottle arrived, Sir Dennis scanned it approvingly. 'They don't give us the 2019.'

Oliver leant towards them. 'You saw him today. We all know Richardson's finished. We need someone with Karan's financial brains and connections if we are to have any hope of getting through this.'

Sir Dennis's family had been in and around parliament since the fourteenth century. With rich, arable land in Norfolk, they'd paid obeisance to every English monarch. They'd generally been on the right side of history up to, and including, Cromwell's commonwealth. 'England lost,' he cried. 'I feel like the fourteenth earl. He also supped with the devil. As one of the fifty-nine.'

Oliver topped up the shire knight's glass. 'You're drinking decidedly better plonk, Dennis. And they decapitated a king. We are merely paying for some cosmetic surgery.'

Sir Dennis snorted. 'A constitutional nose job by the Indians? I hardly think that's accurate. You're giving the cadaver up for medical research. And who knows what state she will come back in?'

Sir William Lewis peered over his drink, 'Mutilated. Most probably unrecognisable,' and drained his glass. He pointed for Oliver to fill it up. 'So, it's come to this, has it?' Sir William's knighthood rewarded thirty-five years' political service. Never once had he been anything but reactionary.

Oliver poured himself what was left in the bottle. 'Just enough for a toast, gentlemen. If you mean we elect the smartest politician in his generation to lead the party and save the country, then yes.'

Lord Winston, a Northern Irish peer, finished a long draught and checked the now-empty bottle. 'What's left of the country? England under foreign occupation for the first time in a thousand years. It's so thoroughly European. And an Indian leading the conservative party. Churchill will be turning in his grave.'

Oliver snapped, 'Churchill filled the graveyards in Bengal. Karan's from Bradford.' Oliver paused. 'And we need him. You need him. Unlike the regicides, you don't want to be on the wrong side of history this time. Integration is a temporary international fillip. It will all be over by christmas.'

Sir William swatted this away. 'You mean an international fuck-up. What's in it for you? Chancellor?'

Oliver breathed in to fashion an answer, but Lord Winston's Northern Irish brogue interrupted before he could reply, 'Deputy PM?'

Sir Dennis added, 'Both, I'd have thought.'

Lifting his glass, and checking to see who else was watching, Oliver asked, 'Does Karan have your support? We will no doubt need a new speaker, Sir Dennis?'

Glasses chinked and Oliver summoned for a second bottle. As he walked to central lobby, a journalist shouted from across the corridor, 'Anything on the record yet, minister? A promotion perhaps?'

Oliver turned back. 'Maybe later, Sally. Keep up the excellent work.'

* * *

The day's trading was over, and the early-evening August sky was still bright outside Jonathan's favourite private members' club. Molly nodded to the doorman. 'Back again?' She smirked as she passed the punters littering the ground-floor restaurants in another converted banking hall. They told themselves they were enjoying the same privileges as the plutocrats who partied many floors above. But the truth is they were subsidising them.

A lift took Molly to an exclusive rooftop with a Lutyens' stupa marrying English, buddhist and hindu styles. The design was a ghostly echo, an architectural palimpsest of the syncretism Lutyens had deployed to make the capital of British India the seat of the greatest empire the world had ever seen. Setting the ball rolling for the events that were now in play.

Molly surveyed the bacchanalian scene unfolding around a rooftop pool high above what had once been the city of the world. Her priapic tableau shared a history with the romans who worshipped at the nearby temple of mithras and the medieval Londoners who toasted successes and drowned their sorrows at the inns of borough market. All around Molly newly rich, and plastered, bankers were doing their utmost to channel this ancient heritage of excess, celebrating the only way they could, popping bottles of inordinately expensive champagne and downing eighteen-year-old whisky as if it were water. A twenty-first-century state of excess rarely seen. Like the hordes of cicadas that appear in prime-number years to outwit their predators, creating a feast so gluttonous thousands still survive. Three-figure cocktails were ferried around the room by staff with perfect smiles and clothes wrapped round them as tightly as a second skin. Long-married traders tipped excessively and flirted to the point of sexual incontinence before returning home to kiss their ordinary lives and wives goodnight. If this was the end of excess, it was going out with one hell of a bang.

'Molly, over here.' Jonathan caught her eye. He was a founder member of the party of outrageous consumption. 'You must be our lucky charm. We haven't had it this good since the 1980s.' He handed her a whisky and a champagne.

Above the bar a US news channel was blaring, 'It's clear that the UK has only one option. Secede to Indian demands. This will bring stability, certainty, liquidity. A much-needed state of calm to a volatile twenty-four hours. Eventually, the markets will price in this change, and we'll all go about our business.' The anchor continued, 'What's most surprising about this turn of events is how few world leaders are reacting to it. We haven't heard the US veto the Indians. The Chinese don't appear to be concerned about Indian access to British nuclear weapons. And the Pakistanis aren't bothered about this first act of Indian hegemony. It seems Britain doesn't have a friend left in the world.'

Molly asked, 'How long can all this last?' Jonathan ignored her as another round of mind-numbing whisky cocktails arrived. She headed back to the toilet while one set of bankers were unwrapping little silver packets and another unwrapping the waiting staff. She texted her notes. Turned off her phone. Let down her hair and returned to the party.

* * *

Late that night, Oliver was sitting under a Bridget Riley print in Karan's office. 'We have the numbers for your coronation.'

Karan was once again trying to work out if Bridget's multicoloured stripes were going up or down. The fizz of Isha's champagne bottle interrupted his train of thought as she poured them both glasses.

'No.' Oliver stopped her. 'If anyone sees us. If this gets out. That.'

‘That what?’ Isha demanded to know. ‘That we are about to save the tory party from rack and ruin? And this shitty little country. That India will finally have the kind of recognition it deserves from broken and washed-up Britain?’

Oliver stepped back. The hair on his neck was charged. ‘No, that we kept the lights on when everyone else was turning them off. It’s too early to celebrate. It’s not a celebration for him.’ Oliver poured some sparkling water. ‘It’s a wake. And it’s work.’ Each offered their glasses to Karan.

Karan sighed. ‘Does it always have to end with me choosing one of two extreme options?’ He took the water.

Isha cackled as she downed her glass and gulped on a second. ‘Of course you’ll always do what he tells you.’

Karan turned to Oliver. ‘The party doesn’t want this. And they certainly don’t want me, do they? Do we even want integration with India?’

Oliver made to reply but Isha interrupted, ‘The party doesn’t know what to fucking think. We just need to keep telling them it’s temporary integration. India helps us back on our feet. And you lead us to freedom. All over by christmas. You’re the saviour.’ She had drunk half the second glass before adding, ‘Pitaji has spent more than money making this happen. We can’t let him down now.’

Ignoring her, Oliver added, ‘You have to let Richardson announce it all on his own. Let him shovel the shit right up to his resignation. Then you save the day.’

Karan asked, ‘Now who has the messiah complex? We have no idea what state the country will be in at the end of this.’

* * *

Just after Noon on Friday 13th, Richardson walked to his waiting car. ‘Leaving for the last time, are we?’ one of the journalists shouted over the throng of the thousands of protesters who’d gathered in

Trafalgar Square and were marching towards them. As the gates of Downing Street opened, additional police officers pushed against the first wave of marchers whose posters and banners showed Richardson with blood on his hands. He read them as they drove out, 'Death of England' on one, '1,000 years of history RIP' on another. Children held a banner saying, 'Humare future kahan hai? Aapka future khatam hai.'

He'd asked to go in via the members' cloakroom. The few MPs inside focused on placing their coats on their individually named hangers, each with a little pink ribbon for members' non-existent swords. His protection officers raced ahead. Richardson stopped. These stairs were his favourite part of the palace. He waited for the team to disappear from view, then held his pass against the door beside him. With a click he entered the tudor cloister and the last surviving part of the medieval palace. He looked up to see the carved pomegranates and tudor rose marking the badge of Catherine of Aragon alongside Henry the Eight's coat of arms. He walked along the corridor looking for Cardinal Wolsey's. He stopped at a delicate arched doorway surrounded by tiny diamond-like glass panels and turned to his private secretary, 'The victorians called this the Cromwell room. It's where they believed he signed Charles the First's death warrant. I'm about to sign my own upstairs.' Richardson fell silent.

The door clicked again and the cough of one of his protection officers forced Richardson out of the 1600s and into the last act of his own premiership. They walked up the members' steps, and he took what he knew would be a final look at the victorian tiles and vaulted ceilings. 'Such optimists,' he thought. But for once it left him with nothing.

He headed through the division lobby and waited in the corridor behind the speaker's chair. The mood was bleak. His civil servants kept their distance. He had the shakes of a man who hadn't slept in weeks as he tried to open a bottle of pills. A secretary took them from him and handed him two. As he swallowed them, Karan bounded by, telling him, 'I'll go in and get your seat ready.'

Richardson followed. MPs had squeezed into every available seat and space. 'My word,' he uttered as he peered out at an unrelenting sea of sombre faces. No cheer. No jeer. Not one sound from his own side. It was all so different from the heady days.

As Richardson stood, one of Khalid's wolves shouted, 'Ten rupees for England's freedom—cheap at half the price. You should be ashamed.'

The words echoed for what seemed like an eternity. Richardson could see the mason carving them into his gravestone as he heard the smack of lips in the press gallery above him. He motioned as if to fall into his seat. Karan nudged Richardson upright and back to the despatch box like a prompter for an aged actor.

'Madam speaker, I regret to inform the house that the government's policy to save the pound has failed and, with the near exhaustion of the Bank of Britain's reserves, the country now balances on the precipice of self-destruction.' He took the glass of water and waited.

The wolves had nothing to say. Nor did his own side.

Whether it was the pills or not, Richardson's hand wasn't shaking as he put the glass back down on the table. 'Madam speaker, when one becomes prime minister, one's first act is to give instructions to the commanders of our nuclear submarines on the action to take following a catastrophic attack on these islands.

'Mine have been: head for a friendly nation, seek temporary succour and shelter and take instruction from a like-minded government. At this moment of national catastrophe, I make a similar recommendation to his majesty and that friend indeed is India.'

Richardson picked up the papers in front of him. 'I have an audience with the king this afternoon at which his majesty will sign this instrument of accession. England will come under the temporary mandate and protection of the Republic of India. We will be India's thirtieth state, and I, madam speaker, for the moment, will be the last prime minister of England.'

Richardson could feel the sickness in his stomach make its way upwards. The doctor had convinced him the pills would get him to the end of this speech. He visualised them making their way through his system and pushed the bitter bile back down. 'I recommend only one person succeed me. Someone uniquely placed in ability, skills and temperament to lead this great nation back on course—and back to freedom—my right honourable friend the chancellor.'

He sat down. Then for those few seconds, nothing. The affirmations didn't come. Richardson wondered if he was facing a mutiny as well as this mauling. Either way he could sense the powers of his prime ministership had left him the moment Khalid stood up to reply.

The chamber was silent. 'So, it ends today. One thousand years of English freedom. The country that gave the world Locke and liberty. That taught countries like my father's about Adam Smith and free trade. The people who repelled a dictator and saved Europe.'

Khalid took a sip of water and let the words sink in. 'But it ends today. Public-school-educated, oxbridge-polished braggarts delivered this fatal blow. Beaten by the groundswell of populist nationalism. Broken promises of trade deals in far-off places. Pretending we have others to rely on than our nearest neighbours right here in the North Atlantic. And what friends do we have left now? Not one.

'And finally, the lie of all lies. They could pull up the drawbridge and release the portcullis of sovereignty to stop the foreigners from coming here. From taking our jobs. Taking our ideas. Well, now they've sold us all down river, and Indian populists have come to take our country and our future. And no one will fight for us. Not one.

'I don't trust the Indians after what they did to my family. We were all Indian until they decided we weren't. Then they took whatever we had and forced my great-grandfather to march out of his country. He watched muslims beat hindus and hindus beat muslims. Muslims rape hindus and hindus rape muslims. And muslims kill hindus and hindus kill muslims. And they were all

Indians. Well, I don't want Indians coming this way. My party doesn't trust them. And I think this country doesn't trust them. So, they had better be ready for a fight.'

Richardson heard the speaker say, 'Father of the house, Sir Dennis Butler.'

Sir William let out a supportive 'Hear, hear' as Sir Dennis stood.

'I cannot believe I am to speak about the end of a thousand years of England. Our freedom. Our democracy. The essence of what it is to be English. And this pitiable state of affairs to have come about under a conservative government. I am ashamed to sit on these benches today and find myself in the unhappy position of being in direct agreement with the leader of the opposition who, it seems to me, is prepared to fight for this land in a way my own party is unwilling and unable.'

Richardson could not bring himself to turn round.

'If I can barely fathom what is going on, what does my right honourable friend think people out there—and around this country—are asking themselves? They are asking if they should be fighting on the streets. The shallow charlatans and high priests of populism have used many recruiting sergeants these last few years. But what is being outlined today in this mother of parliaments will not merely lead to the end of English sovereignty, it will lead to all-out war up and down the country. And I may yet join the freedom fighters, whom our overlords will no doubt call terrorists.'

Two

An hour later the king was whistling down the corridor; Banerjee, smaller and much wider was struggling to keep up. He'd rarely heard his majesty whistle. The king stopped to look at the many trinkets on the sideboards, running his finger along the edges to check for dust. He waited for Banerjee to open the door to the yellow drawing room in which Mark Richardson was waiting.

'Sorry for my delay, prime minister,' the king said. 'So many phone calls from our realms. I've been reassuring them on your behalf.'

'I don't see how you can, your majesty. It's a national calamity.'

'Shall we sit, prime minister?' The king took his usual side on one of the long, golden-yellow sofas. 'I'll ring now for chai.' Richardson's face screwed up as the king pressed the underside of a table lamp. 'I watched your statement in parliament, prime minister. So I am aware of the recommendation for your successor.'

Richardson nodded. 'This is my last act as the first lord of your majesty's treasury.'

A footman brought in the steaming masala. The king nodded to Banerjee to serve as Richardson continued, 'I'm joining a long list of failed prime ministers, sir.'

Richardson held the cup to his nose and sniffed. As he sipped his first mouthful, the king stood, forcing him to swallow the boiling hot peppery chai, cough then clatter his cup on the table between them. The king was looking at the many images of himself. One of his first tasks had been the redecoration of his state rooms. He'd hung the portrait of himself in his coronation robes opposite one when he was a young and dashing prince. On every other surface of the lemon-yellow room were silver, framed photos with world leaders interspersed with five-high piles of books on eastern philosophy and the occasional copy of *The Meditations of Marcus Aurelius*. The king caught himself in the rococo mirror above the fireplace. 'Some might say, thankfully for England, we have had a far shorter list of failed monarchs. Or who knows where we would have ended up?'

Richardson replied, 'More German, sir. I'd have imagined.'

His majesty ignored this and declared, 'I have asked Lord Banerjee to witness the occasion, prime minister. I trust that will be in order.'

The king moved to a desk at the opposite side of the room overlooking the Mall. He ran his hand over the gilded crest on his red box, with 'reader number one' embossed above it. The delivery mechanism his government used to ensure he had first sight of the most significant official documents. With little hint of the ceremony he lived for, he opened it and reviewed its solitary contents. Banerjee removed the box and switched on the table lamp, ensuring the miniature stage was set.

The king inspected the instrument of accession for some time. He gazed briefly at Richardson, smiled and signed the top. A legal conceit that his majesty did not have the time to review the contents of the business his ministers and privy council sent him.

'Done. And quite painless. Now, what do we offer you?'

'Sorry, sir?' Richardson wasn't sure if he was about to endure a fresh form of torture.

'My new award. Yes, that would be most fitting. Lord Banerjee and I have just confirmed its badge and ribbon. I suggested we appoint you the first knight of the order of Britain.

Banerjee procured a little leather box from a drawer in the occasional table beside him.

'Most gracious, Your majesty. And unexpected.' Richardson reviewed the box. 'But is there any way people might shorten this to "K-N-O-B"?'

The king furrowed his brow, 'Well, we couldn't offer you the garter. Or thistle. Those are orders of chivalry. And there is nothing chivalrous about the state you leave the country in. But we do need both to know what we call you and to thank you.'

'Sorry, sir? What you call me?'

'Yes, you are no longer our prime minister.'

'I think "Sir Mark" will be fine, your majesty. I will have his appointment gazetted tonight,' Banerjee added.

'Now, Sir Mark. If you'd be so kind.' The king motioned for Richardson to come forward. Banerjee handed the contents to the king.

'I decided to do away with swords for this order of knighthood. Something more befitting of the modern age. So in placing this collar on you, I happily appoint you our first K N O B.'

'Thank you, your majesty.' Richardson took a moment to survey the room. Had he also just witnessed the end of the king's British realm?

'If Sir Mark would follow me.' Banerjee's greasy vowels were a fitting conclusion to the makeshift ceremony.

The king extended his arm. 'Yes, thank you, Sir Mark.' They shook hands briefly. 'I'm sure Lord Banerjee can sort out the collar and accoutrements. I believe you can even buy a pin badge from a shop on the Strand.'

Sir Mark bowed his head and walked backwards, trying to take it all in. The king, at the window, was dappled by the sun. Could it be a halo—a corona—signifying the constant national reassurance of a hereditary monarch. Or a neon sign from the dodgy honours shop he was in the process of establishing. It was surreal. Perhaps they were all in some state of drug-induced euphoria. Before an almighty morning-after crash.

The king, uninterested in Richardson's departure, was focused on his soon-to-be new first lord of the treasury. His maxim had been: always the future, never the past. And now they were to be that future, together.

'Banerjee, I imagine the prime minister will want me to address the nation this evening. Our age and experience will be needed to settle the national nerve.' He would advise his new prime minister. He was the only one to be counted upon to guide a young and naïve politician in this most delicate of transitions. It was time for a seasoned monarch to play a far more active constitutional role than the one he had inherited. From a powerless figurehead—with the right merely to be consulted, to encourage and to warn—to a player of the global game. This Indian gambit would need all of their combined expertise and insight. A twin-headed hydra to fight back the Indian serpent. He was sure he could convince an unschooled Karan Puri of this.

The king continued, 'I think my first audience with our new prime minister should be in the white drawing room. And I should be in military dress uniform, do you agree, Banerjee?'

'Yes, sir.'

'Our new prime minister seems so insubstantial. Such tiny hips, don't you think?'

Banerjee tittered and left.

* * *

In the car on the mall, Isha was distracted, 'Where are the flags? We should have vast, enormous Union Jacks. And a military band?' She searched from side to side. 'Where is all the pomp and ceremony? We will fix this country now you're in charge.'

'I'm not in charge yet. And there's much more to worry about than flags. What on earth will the king be thinking? The state of the country we are handing over. And, right at this moment, he has to appoint an Indian as his prime minister.'

Isha grabbed him. 'Not this again. You're as British as anyone else in your miserable little party. We've saved them. Time and time again. Whose money kept the conferences afloat? Whose friends funded the last election campaign? My fucking father's. We did all this for you. For this moment. We believe in you. Even when you don't.'

'I wish my dad had been alive to see this, don't you?' Karan asked as Isha squeezed his hand. He went quiet. Like he always did when he felt the thing he was about to do was bigger than himself. 'I know you and your father believed in me more than mine did. He never believed the nasty tory party would elect me leader.'

'I suppose he was right, you know.'

'Huh?'

'I mean, they didn't elect you leader so much as the Indian prime minister just appointed you. You're swamped right now. Thinking it's bigger than you and me.' She moved her hand up his trousers and leant into him. 'Want me to help take your mind off it?'

'No.' He grabbed her hand, sniggering. 'Umesh doesn't need the distraction!'

'Master?' Umesh, Karan's long-standing driver, turned round.

'Nothing, Umesh. Drive straight into the palace like we did last time.'

'Pitaji has so much he wants you to achieve.' Isha glanced at him. 'He has a list. You know he does because he's told you about it. He wants you to fix England. And, you know he's impatient for you to succeed.'

'Not yet, darling.' Karan sighed. 'At least let the king appoint me before your dad starts VAT-free shopping. I assume this list is as much about the places he wants to acquire as the policies he wants me to change.'

Karan scanned the wide-open pavements of the Mall into St James's Park. It was mid-August in central London. No tourists. No cheering crowds. No adoring young conservatives. 'You're right. Where is everyone?'

Ignoring him, Isha asked, 'What am I going to do while you and your boyfriend run the country?'

'You'll be dressing every woman in England. Your designs will be on every runway in the world.'

Isha smiled. 'Yes, they will, won't they?'

Umesh drove round the glistening Victoria memorial, and the gates opened. The car scrunched across the gravel. Karan felt for the Welsh guards, roasting in their bearskins and red uniform, as they progressed through the narrow archway and headed for the vip entrance.

He and Isha had last been there together at what was the best party in London: his majesty's diplomatic reception. The entire diplomatic corps assembled with that year's great and good. At the exactly appointed hour, state trumpeters of the household cavalry heralded the arrival of the royal party. There had been a notable increase in flummery when the king took over hosting duties from his mother, with much more talk of the king's garter than his wife's tiara. The king's ministers had to wear their dress privy counsellor uniform, which they paid for themselves. The queen entered the room wearing an emerald necklace and one of Isha's off-white satin gowns. 'We are still waiting for them to fucking pay,' was all Isha muttered whenever he mentioned it.

Umesh slowed as they arrived at the colonnaded portico where a gush of footmen were waiting. He turned to Karan with tears in his eyes. 'Congratulations, prime minister.' Karan beamed. He'd broken the rules to hire Umesh. He'd been one of Isha's drivers. The one Karan liked the most. Umesh had travelled the world with the family and helped Karan navigate the Grovers when Sunil had decided Karan would marry Isha. He drove Karan to collect the engagement and wedding rings Isha had chosen and Sunil had paid for. And Umesh had taken Karan to every hospital visit for his father up to the night he died. In return, Karan was Umesh's greatest champion. He demanded that Umesh join him in government, paying him a real salary from his own pocket. And after many months of being Karan's official driver, Umesh had finally been given a place on the mandatory government training course. The right-wing newspapers loved it. Karan sharing the taxpayers' burden. Umesh had briefly been the most popular driver in London.

Karan's door was opened by one of the many red-liveried staff of the king's household. Banerjee, escorting Richardson down the palace steps, spotted Karan's shiny brogues and uttered, 'Oh, this is a slight breach of protocol. I do hope his majesty doesn't see.'

Richardson extended his hand. 'Karan, the country owes you a debt of gratitude. As do I. I'm handing over an unconscionable mess. But up there,' Richardson pointed over his left shoulder, 'up there is a steadying hand on which I have always relied. And on which you can too. Keep our king safe and you keep England safe.'

Karan nodded. 'I hope to do you both proud. And the country.' Isha's twitching hand signalled he needed to wrap it up.

'Chancellor? His majesty is waiting for you,' Banerjee interrupted and swept Karan up the red-carpeted stairs past yet more regal footmen. Inside, Banerjee pointed out Karan's route, 'Mrs Puri will wait in the chinese drawing room.'

A nervous equerry quickly handed Karan a protocol sheet, which he read bounding up the stairs behind. Karan stopped halfway to reread the instructions. He gaped at the palace aide, who grimaced. He spotted Isha. She winked and blew him a kiss. Karan continued re-checking the note while trying to grab the young footman's attention.

He was well ahead of Karan, racing past Titians and Canalettos. The king had brought the Leonardo sketches out of storage and hung them liberally around. At the end of the corridor the equerry turned and cheerily added, 'Good luck.' Before Karan could answer, he knocked on the door of the elaborate white drawing room and entered, 'The chancellor, sir.'

Karan bowed his head and walked slowly past the trappings of hundreds of years of hereditary privilege. The bronzes, rococo vases, gilded mirrors, and, at the end of it all, the king, stood in front of a portrait of his much-younger self.

He tutted at the paper shaking in Karan's hand. 'No need for a prompt, chancellor; I have done this before. I haven't yet had a message from New Delhi, but I think we can proceed. The country needs a leader. Mr Puri, the former prime ...'

Karan interrupted, 'Sir, I have directions from New Delhi, here.'

His majesty's shoulders tightened. 'Directions?'

'In fact, orders.' Karan handed over the flimsy note. 'Set out in this protocol sheet.'

The king flicked it, then scanned the document as Karan continued, 'The Indian prime minister has appointed me her first minister.'

Karan heard the king spit back, 'Her?'

He continued, 'Yes. Having signed the instrument of accession, you are no longer king of England or hrh.'

'What?' His majesty's eyes narrowed.

'From this point, you will be Albert, governor of our thirtieth state. Addressed as "your excellency".'

The newly named governor collapsed into one of the pair of blue and gold silk chairs he had taken from the 1844 room. He was grateful for his own foresight; this would not have been a moment to drop into floral sofas. He grabbed the gilded armrests, seeming to hang on for dear life, his back firmly pressed against the finely upholstered seat, 'This isn't ...'

'Sir,' Karan continued, 'Delhi has appointed a governor-general who arrives tomorrow. He will confirm my cabinet.'

'This isn't how it was meant to ... Not at all ...' He toyed with the tassels. Momentarily distracted by the exquisite nineteenth-century craftsmanship, the artistry he had been trying to reintroduce to communities across England's poorest areas. 'Am I to remain head of the commonwealth?'

Karan nodded, 'Yes, head of the Indian imperial commonwealth. The protocol sheet instructs you to celebrate integration day, your excellency.'

Breathing in slowly, Albert stood up, 'I think you mean Indian independence day. I have already listened to enough directions for one day. You might want to be aware we have already done this.'

Karan took back the flimsy sheet of paper, marvelling at its power to denude both of them. 'This protocol sheet is quite clear: 14 August will be from here on marked as integration day in the thirtieth state of the Republic of India only. The state governor should officiate at a flag-raising with the Indian standard in the senior position. It lists the specifications for the flag if you would like to review them, sir.'

Albert swatted away Karan's paper. He pressed another button obscured from view.

Banerjee entered. 'The first minister's wife, your excellency.'

'Not now, Banerjee. I must call.'

Karan turned his head to Isha, who strode forward and, without bowing, proffered her hand with a wide grin. 'Your excellency, it's a pleasure to meet the first governor of our thirtieth state. I have just been speaking to my father who sends his best regards. Shall we sit down? I have a few further requests from the prime minister.'

Albert winced. The coronation portrait hung above them all. He could feel the heavy weight of those robes press on his chest. He breathed out with a grumbling low hum, almost a deathly rattle, as if whatever divine power had been transmitted on coronation day was leaving one temporary earthly host in search of its successor.

'The prime minister was keen to clarify the order of precedence in person. Protocol for the new thirtieth state will go: president of the Republic of India, prime minister, governor-general, first minister, and finally governor.' Isha smiled, continuing, 'My father says that we should expect a visit from the prime minister in the coming months. She will no doubt expect to have the best rooms here. We understand you continue to stay at clarence house. This will now be known as the governor's residence. We will decide what to do with this building, which pitaji has been calling Buckingham Mahal in the longer term once the governor-general has arrived.'

Albert flinched at Banerjee. 'Well, thank you, Mrs Puri, for this additional and extremely useful information. I'm sure it will be conveyed to us in the normal way too. I'm sure you and the prime—'

'First minister, governor.' Isha waved her finger in front of Albert. 'We must adhere to the new protocol.'

'First minister,' Albert corrected himself. 'I'm sure you and the first minister have much to do.'

Albert stood up and waited as Isha gathered her things. Finally, she and Karan stood. 'Thank you, governor, for a most delightful afternoon.'

* * *

In India's new parliamentary complex, a rare joint session had been called. The red dholpur rajasthani stone and makrana marble glistened, as Usha's sari billowed down the main corridor. It was as if the building itself knew it would hear a speech that would echo down the centuries. This new chamber built by Indians for Indians in time to swallow up England's pride.

Inside, over one thousand members of India's Lok Sabha and Rajya Sabha were celebrating. Her words would ring as loudly as Nehru's had some eighty years ago on the night of India's freedom. This time, one and a half billion Indians would see and hear what it meant to be not only a self-reliant India but a world reliant on India.

A panoply of parliamentarians and personages surrounded the Indian prime minister. Handing her updated speaking notes, which she made clear she had no need for. This speech would be from memory.

'Message of congratulations from the US president, prime minister,' an aide handed her the printout.

'This from the UN secretary general.' Another tried to outdo his colleague.

'The governor of the RBI thinks we will be able to reduce interest rates by a point.' Usha smiled as she heard this. 'Markets are reacting well.'

'The Chinese prime minister has described this as a delightful turn of events.'

'Anything from the Pakistanis?'

'Do they even have email?' Sunil added. He knew how to make her roar.

'That stupid Pakistani Labour politician always talking about Kashmir. We must sort him out.'

Ahead of her an excited crush of junior parliamentarians waited, each holding aloft their individual, prized copy of the instrument of accession. Pens ready. She signed every one, relishing their devotion. She asked Sunil, 'It's done?'

He nodded. 'Karan will do us proud.'

She fixed her rich green sari in a matter-of-fact way. 'Sunil bhai, I don't need him to do me proud. I need him to do what he's told. Are you sure he knows that?'

Sunil nodded. She was the most powerful person in India. Maybe in the world, for this one day. She'd beaten Indian politicians with her political brain and guile. But mainly with constant, gruelling, arduous work. And now she'd beaten the feckless English. With much less effort than she had once thought. She knew looks and sexual charm counted too. Men still needed to be flattered. Even the most impotent of them. 'Sunil Bhai.' She moved towards him and stroked his arm. 'This cannot be my project alone. When the problems come, and they will come, we will need someone to take the blame.'

Sunil was enthralled. Waiting on her every utterance. He whispered, 'Can't we find a role for Rahul Bhai's son?'

Usha smiled. This was exactly the reason she'd had Sunil at her side for twenty years. Two punjabis. They thought the same way. They spoke the language of power. They understood how to make things happen. He'd started off raising money when she was campaigning for her father, then a cabinet minister in the last congress government. Sunil and Usha both knew her father did not have it in him to lead the country. Slowly, Sunil shifted increasingly more of his resources to her: money, time, networks. In 2019 she took her grandfather's Ludhiana constituency. He had first won it in 1971. That day Sunil told her it was the only seat for her, from where she would become prime minister.

She and Sunil had worked hard to rebuild the party through the doldrums of the 2020s. Each time they felt they had an opposition capable of winning, fate conspired against them. She had thrown out all the old, dead wood and replaced them with younger candidates for a new India. Female candidates, internationally minded, US-minded, free-market liberals. Now fifty-six, she knew exactly what she wanted to do.

She nodded to have the door opened. One of the many young men around her grabbed it and a conversation delayed by two hundred years concluded: 1947 gave India its freedom. Today it claimed a scalp for almost two centuries of British dominion in this land. A delicious act of familial revenge. Bringing England to its knees and India to its triumph. That was the party she was about to felicitate.

She marched in without a moment's notice or a second glance at Sunil. Inside, the whooping, shouting, jeering, cheering of over a thousand people almost brought her to tears. But she checked herself. They did not want a weak woman to lead them. She let a smile form. Not enough to gloat. Just sufficient to acknowledge others' recognition of what she had done for them. For their country. A score settled. A wrong righted.

She stopped to speak with every politician she could. They knew this was her moment. The apogee of her power and infamy. A little feminine charm went an extraordinarily long way in what was still the male-dominated world around her. They all knew her to be ruthless and that the 2030s were to be her decade.

She stood, casting her gaze in all directions, and waited for them to settle. 'At the stroke of midnight, our tryst with destiny takes a Bara North Atlantic Yatra.' The cheers, whoops and screams of elated elected representatives filled the cavernous hall. And for that split-second she allowed herself a broad, and genuine, grin.

For this moment, the country itself stopped. Lakhs and crores of Indians sat in awe-struck silence. Families gathered round any screen they could find, from the biggest cities to the smallest towns. Grandchildren took phones to grandparents and watched them wipe the tears from their eyes, asking themselves, 'Could this new India, their India, really be about to take over the coloniser?'

In Arunachal's Tawang, some 10,000 feet above sea level, monks brought students and families to watch together in the shadow of the mountains of the Eastern Himalayas. People assembled outside the famous monastery once a well worn stop off on the trail that had taken the buddha's teachings, and his followers, to and from Tibet. A few miles away, over a contested border, Chinese army soldiers were watching the same broadcast, celebrating this attack on capitalist privilege. Around the world tens of millions of the great global diaspora were partying as if it were some record-breaking desi wedding. In the US, Indian-American tech titans and investors were searching for a quick killing. Notes were sent to the White House to tell the Hinkle administration to let the Indians ride this out.

'England's story with India was written in centuries. The connection ran as deep as layers of sedimentary rock. And for a time we knew each other as brothers. Throughout the twentieth century, self-proclaimed English indophiles described our colonial inheritance as the foundation of our entrepreneurialism, our commerce and our distinct ability to trade in all markets at all times. How wrong they were. This inheritance had merely delayed our rightful place at the world's top tables.'

She glanced around the room. Heads were nodding.

'Such a relationship was not deep but shallow. It had always been one-sided and voracious. And then became brittle. The indophiles wanted their own people to forget about the violence. The theft. And that they put no price on the five thousand years of civilisation that had gone before colonialism.'

Her parliamentarians applauded.

'Colonisation is part of our history, and defeating it has played some considerable part in the formation of our contemporary identity. Yet it has played none in England's. Decades of hidden regret and remorse had transformed into an almost ahistorical failure to acknowledge their colonial responsibilities. Well, no longer. We call this day many things. Integration day. But also, a day of international reparations.

'All countries have their original sin alongside an origin myth. America's combines slavery and freedom. Ours the birth of civilisation alongside the caste system. England's free trade, the free exchange of ideas and people—and the filthy stain of colonialism. Placing free peoples and their lands into a state of perpetual subjugation.

'But England has been lost for these last few years. As a younger sibling we wanted to warn them. Their lack of history became a failure to believe in themselves. A country which once ruled the waves became ungovernable. With the loss of empire, that foundational myth became the cause of fighting fascism in the 1940s, conveniently forgetting that some of their leaders conspired with it only the decade prior. But unlike our story of national renewal and revival, poor old England failed time and again to find a compelling contemporary mission. Instead, the populists infected the common man with grievance and injustice, and in so doing, confined themselves to this path of national suicide.

'Whereas our 2020s redefined India—our commerce, our culture, our confidence all grew. And now we have our rightful place at the top table. Of course we will be assuming that seat at the UN security council. Not given it as an afterthought but claiming in our own right.' Usha knew that today for one and a half billion fellow citizens of the Republic of India, and many hundreds of millions more around the world, beating England would taste sweeter than any other victory. 'We have already received a message of congratulations from the prime minister of Scotland. Another colonised people late to be liberated. We will do all we can to develop the Scottish economy. As partner and friend.'

Usha continued, 'For the duration of the project, Britain's international affairs will be overseen by our ambassadors around the world. We will send a governor-general to oversee our thirtieth state as well as a resident commissioner to supercharge exports from continental India to the new jewel in the Indian imperial crown. Every Indian family will benefit from integration.'

The chamber sat in silence at Usha's majesty. She knew the awesome power of what she'd told them. 'Not only has our country become the most populous in the world, but today we become a great power too. Integration will bring prosperity to our businesses and our one and a half billion citizens. It will bring as much security to the world as it does to our republic.'

* * *

'You'll note, your excellency,' Banerjee pointed, 'the Indian flag's staff has been placed in front of the Union Jack. I believe that is the senior position?' Albert was staring at the crossed flagpoles in the throne room as his forebears' portraits cast a long shadow over the day's proceedings. On the dais ahead of him, framed with plush red curtains, were the eponymous, gilded thrones built for his coronation.

Albert tutted, 'Yes, you have it right, Banerjee. Play the damn national anthem. So I can get out of here and watch what that infernal woman has said about us in the Indian parliament. Though I'm not sure we can call a room almost literally built yesterday a parliament. Or at least, not one to rival what we had here.'

'A state assembly now, sir?'

'A what?' Albert turned round.

'Yes, well, states in India mostly have assemblies. I assume what we now have is the assembly of the thirtieth state of India.'

Albert huffed, 'Not yet, Banerjee. Now just get the band to play.'

Albert stood to attention and saluted to the rattle of the snare. The drum was too loud and too fast for 'God save the king.' Albert lowered his hand as his string quartet played the first bars of 'Jana Gana Mana'. Banerjee saw a twitch. Even he had expected the national anthem. So he had no idea what Albert was thinking. After a lifetime of singing it for his mother, and then listening to others sing it for him, it was an earworm for a sovereign already consigned to national irrelevance. Only some hours ago he was king of a once-great nation. An island which had told itself that from the days of pangaea it had stood alone. The formation of continents had taken place around it, and then slowly it had shaped the modern world. Banerjee had no idea if this were true. Perhaps the Indian prime minister was right. It had never quite overcome its nineteenth-century hubris—not in the twentieth century, never mind the twenty-first. And now its king was subservient to Indian overlords.

Part-way through, Albert spat out, 'I think we've had quite enough of that, don't you, Banerjee?'

Banerjee motioned to the musicians to pause. When they finally stopped, Albert had already left.

* * *

Isha was struggling with the cork of the champagne bottle when it ricocheted off the corner of Karan's favourite painting. 'You've done it, my darling.' She poured him a glass.

'Oliver did it,' Karan said matter-of-factly, pushing his glass to the side. 'Thanks, but I won't have any right now. I have to give my statement. I'll drink with you after.'

Isha moved to sit beside him. 'But he's not the first minister, is he? Pitaji says you have to listen to us now. Delhi doesn't want you to be led by a junior batchmate any longer.'

Karan slammed the table. 'What else has your father told you?'

'That Ushaji wants you to succeed.' Isha raised her glass to toast. 'And that we are the guests of honour at the party he is paying Banerjee to host tonight for integration day.'

'Integration day?' Karan asked. 'Is that really what we are going to call it?'

'Pitaji says the prime minister loves it.'

'Does your first official event have to be both Indians only and with Banerjee? There is something so slimy about his unctuousness around Albert.' Karan made a retching sound.

Isha was looking at her adverts in the glossy fashion magazines in Karan's office. Without missing a beat, she replied, 'Yes.'

Seb walked in. Karan asked, 'He's in the car?' Seb nodded as Karan kissed Isha.

'Showtime?' she asked.

'Yes, wish me luck.'

'Well, my dad paid for you to get here,' she took another sip of champagne, 'the Indian prime minister has appointed you and told everyone she wants you to succeed. And the entire room will be full of people who now depend on you for their continued employment. I think you'll be fine.'

Karan walked out as Isha instructed Seb, 'Now, can you have all the things I've just had delivered installed in the flat tonight?'

Sitting in the car, Karan pointed, 'They've moved fast.'

'What?' Oliver asked. 'Shouldn't you be rehearsing your speech? Biggest fucking moment of your political life and you're worried about the flags. Are you sure you're not the gay one?'

Karan teased, 'You're gay enough for both of us. In fact, for the whole fucking parliament. By the way, I'm worried about that thing you have for Indian men.'

'What the fuck are you talking about?' Oliver was peering out of the window. 'First you're on about fucking flags and now about fucking fags! I can say that by the way. You still can't.'

'I remember you at our wedding. Even if you can't. Isha's cousin remembers too. What did he call himself?' Karan waited for Oliver.

'Sam. He called himself Sam.'

'That's right. The poor boy had only just come out to her. You were like a homing pigeon. In fact, a homo-ing pigeon.'

'He was five years younger than you; I'll have you know. But a body ten years younger. And he knew how to use it. Anyway, what were you moaning about?'

Karan pointed to the flagpoles. 'Indian flags as far as the fucking eye can see. Every flaming flagpole and I assume round the fucking corner outside parliament too?'

Oliver nodded.

'You're moving too fast. Just like with Sam. Take time or the Indians will fuck you over.'

'Just like—'

‘Don’t say it.’ Karan put his hand over Oliver’s mouth. ‘Umesh doesn’t need to hear your filthy ways.’

They both laughed as the car turned into parliament square. Indian flags fluttered triumphantly from every pole. This square was once the fulcrum of the English constitution: three of its sides bringing together politics, church and law. Each able to take exuberant, wild and costly flights of fancy. It was not by chance that the fourth side tempered all: the rational spendthrifts of what had been his majesty’s treasury.

‘We received a protocol sheet from the Indians,’ Oliver could see Karan was worried, ‘which I assumed you’d approved. There isn’t a flagpole in central London that hasn’t been changed.’

Karan shook his head. ‘Remember, we need to give our people time to adjust.’

‘Don’t worry. You’re in charge now. Okay, maybe less orthodox than we had planned. But you’re going to do remarkable things for our country. I know it. My advice, for what it’s worth, is let’s do the easy things quickly. The intractable issues will come thick and fast. I know what it’s like just ordering takeout with you and Isha. Never mind dining out when Sunil is in town.’

‘We couldn’t even have kept a Union Jack above Churchill. He’s standing unhappily beneath the orange stripe of the flag. This isn’t going to end well. Not at all.’

Oliver replied, ‘Look, we’re in it now. Let’s pull out as fast as we can.’

Karan smiled. ‘I bet that’s what Sam told you.’

As they waited for parliament’s black iron gates to open, Oliver jumped out. ‘You’ve got this. Remember to smile for the photographers.’ He pointed to the gaggle of cameras in the shadow of Big Ben. ‘I’ll be getting our side ready.’

As Oliver entered the chamber, it went silent. He spoke to each member of Richardson’s cabinet, making sure they knew who would decide on their immediate futures. Sir Dennis led the cheers as Karan stopped at the speaker’s chair to thank her for refereeing what was about to happen. Oliver mouthed, ‘Speaker in the making for sure,' and winked at the grandest grandee in his best three-piece suit. The speaker had always been kind to Karan: from his maiden speech to his most recent budget, he remained her favourite. Karan was pleased that at least she was unaffected by what he was about to say. She rose and waited for silence, 'Now, before we hear from the first minister, we know that tempers are likely to be high and that some billions of people are watching us today. So I urge honourable members on all sides to be their best selves. Statement from the first minister.'

Karan stood. He surveyed the chamber, full to the gunwales. It was so vastly different from his first speech in this place. When a leg-shakingly nervous young Karan Puri, with his much more experienced best friend beside him, extolled the virtues and expunged the vicissitudes of being the newly elected member of parliament for Bradford.

He had wanted to be prime minister from his first campaigning session with Oliver. A thankless task became an oft-repeated mission, scouring the streets of northern England to uncover shy Tory voters and grow their number. In those days, people were simply unwilling to answer the door to an Indian with a tory rosette. Through it all, Oliver had been there. Right beside him. He'd guided Karan in the weird and wonderful world of tory politics. Whenever Karan had been let down by another selection panel, Oliver was there. By his side. Convincing him to keep going. Telling Karan that he would be leader of the party one day and the country soon after. All Oliver had ever wanted was to be by Karan's side. But he'd made it abundantly clear it was to be as chancellor and deputy prime minister. Nothing was free and no one completely altruistic. 'Not even Mother Teresa,' he would always say, before adding, 'I'm sure she was a tory too.'

Karan took a deep breath. 'Thank you, madam speaker.' He punched out the words, conscious of the thud of his beating heart. He inhaled slowly. 'Our great nation has weathered many storms, and, in time, all have passed. And so it will be for the period of our temporary integration with India.' He scanned to see if anyone on the other side of the chamber was nodding. Khalid's Labour colleagues were inscrutable.

'Madam speaker, I know we do not have the support of the right honourable leader of the opposition, nor his party, but as I undertake my duties as the first first minister of Britain and of India's thirtieth state, I will work for everyone regardless of whether they feel we have taken the right decisions. That work starts immediately, madam speaker. I am closing the banks, suspending the stock exchange, and pausing all currency trading for the next seventy-two hours. The government will issue a new currency—the digital sterling rupee—and we will rebase all sterling obligations. We will not start our new life in more debt than is our fair share.'

Oliver smirked as he watched the shock grip Khalid's face.

Karan continued, 'I have a further message for the banking buccaneers, the spivs and speculators: I am levelling a windfall tax on excess profits made in the last twenty-four hours—all as a result of people trying to benefit from the calamitous decisions of the previous administration.'

'That was your own side!' one of Khalid's MPs shouted. 'We know who's doing your bidding,' he continued.

Oliver now turned behind him to see his own MPs who were warming to Karan's decisiveness and judgement and were ready to protect him from further attacks.

Karan was in his stride. Khalid diminished, for now. Karan continued, 'Madam speaker, integration marks a new journey for India as well as England. In what could have been our darkest hour, our friend extended a hand and—with a magnanimous gesture—turned that into a "namaste".' Karan raised his palms together on his chest.

Karan continued, 'The economies of England and India have been intertwined since that initial letter from Elizabeth the First to Akbar the Great in 1585. Indians have risen to prominence in every field of English life. Our language is rich with Indian words; passion for cricket and football as high in Bradford as Bangalore.'

Karan had walked this tightrope in every public speech he'd given. It was mandatory. To say something about Britain's inevitable Indianness without going too far. Nodding to your heritage without losing votes. Always worrying about courting the populists in his own party. This time it didn't matter. So he'd tell them the whole truth. 'Indian food is loved up and down this country, but it is the Indian finance that built Britain over the last twenty years which I love. Our cars, our steel, our power and much, much more is already Indian. So, people shouldn't be worried about temporary integration. Our daily lives will feel much the same. The digital rupee on our phone will feel like the pound in our pocket. Our freedoms are guaranteed. Temporary integration is about getting us back on our feet—not about stamping us out of existence. We can quietly celebrate this next and brief chapter in England's story at midnight tonight: Integration day. Jai Hind. Jai England. God save our governor.'

* * *

In Wyke, Karan's eighty-year-old mother repeated, 'Jai Hind.' A pride radiated from her that was almost perceptible to family and friends around her. Photos of her son's successes jumped out from every available ledge. The small front room hadn't changed since it had been Karan's home. There had been great plans to build a conservatory. A new kitchen. But after his father died, his mother had simply lost interest. She wanted to preserve things as they were. Perhaps, Karan thought, so that on those days she forgot he was dead, she could sit and wait for him to come through the door. Beaming, she grabbed the hands and arms, elbows and legs of her nearest and dearest as her son became the Indian leader she could not have dreamed were possible. Mrs Puri's eponymous samosas were being passed around with steaming hot chai.

'Aunty, aunty,' one of the many children asked her, 'when will Karan uncle come to visit?'

'Soon,' she replied with a huge smile.

Out of her front window and across the garden she could see tens of photographers and tv crews. A few brave individuals had made their way to her front door. 'Mrs Puri?' 'Mrs Puri!' they were shouting. 'What can you tell us about our new first minister?'

Mrs Puri leapt up, grabbed a bowl of samosas and went to the door. With a flourish she replied, 'He loves his mother's cooking. My son hasn't changed a bit. And this is his favourite dish. Secret ingredient: Worcestershire sauce! Try some.' The photographers snapped as she offered them with the proud grin of a delighted mother.

* * *

The mood on the trading floor at Merchant's could not have shifted more quickly from the celebrations of yesterday's highs to the wake now enveloping Molly and each of her colleagues. 'He's cancelled christmas for the next three years,' Jonathan wailed, ripping up the lists of luxuries he was going to buy with his unbanked bonus. Molly focused on a spot on the carpet. 'All right for you, Molls,' Jonathan added. 'You didn't put a ten grand drinks bill on your credit card!'

A clipped English 'Good morning' interrupted them.

'Morning, we don't often see you down here, Sir John.' Jonathan had stood up in a very formal fashion.

'Who's that?' Molly whispered.

Sir John Merchant had been with the bank for over fifty years. His gray hair and wiry frame concealed a steely businessman. He had predicted all the great highs and lows of the British economy for the last forty years. He coughed to get their attention, 'You had great fun yesterday, and now comes the reckoning. The bank alone made over 3 billion pounds from your successes and excesses. But our new first minister has tried his damnedest to rip that from us. I'm delighted to say he does not yet fully appreciate the benefits of the federal Indian banking system. Overnight, Merchant's was acquired by a Mr Sunil Grover, who had rather a lot of sterling sitting in our vaults, making us the foreign wing of his domestic Indian bank. Profits had already been repatriated ahead of Mr Puri's announcement. It's almost as if Sunilji knew what was about to occur.'

The traders cheered and Jonathan visibly sighed as he thought about his credit card bill and the new top-of-the-range car he had on order.

* * *

In his office beside the Tower of London, ambassador Lu Quan set down his papers and walked through to his private inner sanctum. This dark wood–panelled room on the top floor of the former British royal mint had been his one stipulation. Its balcony let him look down on the city and across time. For almost 800 years the currency of England, of the united kingdom, and of the British empire had come from this site and the citadel opposite. The impenetrable strength of both had symbolised the global dependability of sterling as a reserve currency and England's place in the world. There was no greater sign of the decline of anglo-centric capitalism than the sale of the royal mint to almost-communist China. A decision the Richardson administration was keen to rush through and explain away as part of the natural development of anglo-sino relations. On completion of the deal, Lu Quan projected his influence round London with the same effect as the coinage that had once been sent to all corners of Britain's empire.

Lu Quan put his whisky down on the ledge of the table. A lit cigarette was gently smouldering on an ashtray beside it. He was turning his cue into the light-green chalk. Lu's aide was waiting for him to break and smiled at the crisp clink as the cue ball split the reds, scattering them across the table, potting one, as usual, in the far-left corner pocket.

Lu looked over and in a strained English accent told his assistant, 'You know, I first learnt to play this infernal game on that initial visit to Oxford in the seventies.' Lu's aide nodded as his boss sunk the black. 'I had no idea what on earth it was. But I was hooked.' He added a red. 'Collect the note from my desk.' Lu was sinking a red-black double when the aide returned. 'You know my highest break in all that time?' The aide could see a little bead of sweat form on Lu's brow. 'Thirty-eight. I feel today could be the day.' A third red straight into the right middle pocket. 'I like being the deus ex machina.' Lu potted the black followed by the white. 'Today was not to be the day.'

He took the cigarette from the side of the table and read the note again, inhaling deeply. 'I agree, a slight correction to the markets should be acceptable to Beijing. But any further attempt to manipulate the currency and the many tens of billions India now owes us will become an immediate problem. Now we wait to see if this Indian England has potential or creates problem for our masters back in China.'

Lu signed the note and started to reset the table. 'Have the note couriered via tonight's government flight to Beijing.' The aide nodded. 'Let me know the minute the courier returns with the reply.'

* * *

Sunil poured Usha some chai. She asked, 'Can your daughter be trusted to do exactly what we want?'

Sunil replied, 'My daughter has never let me down.'

Usha was deep in thought. After a while she responded, 'My grandfather was thrown out of Kashmir with only what he could carry. I made him two promises: that we would never lose the state of J&K and that someday the English would be humiliated. Making right the grubby little deal between Mountbatten, Nehru and Jinnah. It would all fall to me.'

Sunil placed his cup on the table. 'Prime minister, integration will have costs.'

'You mean empires are not cheap,' Usha fired back at him, cackling. 'The English should pay for all of it—and more. They have to make up for two hundred years of misadventure. Not one Indian family will pay a single rupee for England's mishap.'

'I was thinking the same thing,' Sunil answered. 'I'd like to start with the banks and the airports.'

'How much will you make for us tomorrow?' She sniggered.

* * *

Rolls-Royces were queuing like cabs at a taxi rank. Banerjee came out of his and handed the uniformed doorman a fifty-pound note. 'How many?'

'Twenty-five and counting, Lord Banerjee!'

'These silver beasts are to Indians what tigers are to the Sundarbans,' Banerjee scoffed, knowing the doorman had no idea what he was talking about. 'Natural habitat!' Banerjee pulled himself up to his full five and a half feet. He peered down at his Italian leather shoes and regretted not doubling the insoles.

Inside one of Mayfair's signature art-deco hotels, enterprising British Indians, glittering almost as much as the 1930s chandeliers, were eating, drinking and dissecting the events of the last twenty-four hours. Banerjee smiled and waved in every direction. They wanted favours from the incoming regime. And Banerjee was poised and primed to help. For twenty years he'd been there to facilitate Indian business engagement with every hue of British government. Part catalyst, part conductor. Total salesman. He knew, and confidently dismissed, the many charges against him. There was only room for one at the pediment of this temple. He had had to trample on the less fortunate. They would have done the same to him.

'I hope you're pleased with our modest decorations.' The hotel manager swept beside Banerjee to marvel at flags, ganeshas and unremitting saffron on every corner and cornice. An extra layer on the ornate thirties décor.

'Yes, you've done an excellent job, Philippe,' Banerjee tittered, 'and with only three hours' notice—about as much as his majesty had!' Then, whispering, 'Please do keep that to yourself. Has the chef been able to prepare the hilsa? I had it flown in and sent to you this morning.'

Philippe nodded. 'Yes, it will come out soon. With the mustard sauce you requested. But it came from a Bangladeshi courier.'

Banerjee leant in. 'Don't tell them here, but we Bengalis know the best hilsa comes from there.'

'And it appears to be half the price, too,' Philippe replied.

Banerjee winked and launched himself at his crowd of well-wishers. 'Isha, my dear!'

Isha was already holding court in a room fizzing with unbridled opportunism—money and reputations were about to be made. And Isha was a surefire route to success.

Out of her earshot, Abdul and Zarin, an attractive thirty-something couple, drank Banerjee's champagne. Every rich Indian in London had responded to the demand from Banerjee's office. Failing to part with the 2,000-pound sponsorship fee would be like giving up your child's place at one of the many English boarding schools now solely kept afloat with the children of successful Indian billionaires. Pointing the rim of his glass at Isha, Abdul groaned, 'She's going to be beyond insufferable.'

Lifting her glass to cover her lips, Zarin replied, 'The whole family will be. Her father has been dependent on corrupt politicians since he almost lost the family business. Now they'll run this country into the ground.'

'I imagine he's got a list like the properties on a *monopoly* board for her.'

Zarin replied, 'Don't we need one too?'

Isha, touring the crowd, was stopped by Archana, her oldest friend and business partner. 'So, your dad chose well with Karan after all?'

After checking out the interesting faces in the crowd, Isha replied, 'Yes, but I put the work in. We wouldn't be here if I hadn't convinced pitaji to push and position Karan at every turn. These English boys are too polite to screw someone the way we do back home.'

Archana nodded. 'They don't know what's about to hit them. There will be a long shopping list from this lot too.'

Toasting Archana, Isha smiled. 'And we'll charge a high price.'

Banerjee made sure every eye at the party watched him escort Isha to the hotel's front door. Philippe was waiting for them. 'I trust you had a pleasant evening, Mrs Puri, and you too, Lord Banerjee?'

'Isha darling, Philippe is the finest frenchmen in London.' Banerjee shook his hand vigorously as he walked out. 'My office will sort out the bills tomorrow. I'll hope for the usual discount.' Philippe winced.

As he opened the door of his Silver Shadow Banerjee gushed, 'All electric. I'm sure they don't have a car like this for the wife of the first minister, darling. Please treat this one as your own. It's the least I can do.'

* * *

Karan was finishing a meeting with party donors and grandees in his office at the house.

'Have you any idea what we've done?' Lord Winston asked. 'Or how we get out of it? The Indians are fiendish negotiators.'

'I understand the nervousness, but it's only temporary,' Karan replied.

'How on earth do you know that for sure?' Sir Dennis asked. 'And how did you let us get into this mess? You were the chancellor, after all. You promised us all those deals with the Indians would stand us in good stead. Knock-down prices meant lots of investment. You sold us down the river. They were waiting for this day to happen.

I found myself in total agreement with the odious leader of the opposition.'

'Well, don't be,' Oliver replied. 'We are all responsible for how we got here. Even saintly Khalid. A series of self-inflicted semi-fatal blows. You know that as well as I do.'

Sir Dennis rolled his eyes and the grandees left.

'I don't think we convinced them.' Karan breathed out, shutting the door.

Oliver replied, 'I wouldn't worry. They haven't been convinced by a tory leader since Thatcher. That lot in particular have deep nanny issues. You've earned points by showing decisiveness on the banks. But it will take time to prove to them you aren't a sleeper.'

Karan, 'Am I? Have we done the right thing?'

Oliver, 'We've done the only thing possible. Integration is temporary. What did your dad say, "Don't let those bloody punjabis in. Worse than the tories."'

Karan smiled. 'I've been thinking about him today. He'd have told me what a huge mistake I'm making.'

Oliver was searching in the cupboard behind his desk. 'He would have.' And then in the desk drawers. 'But he said that about your best friend.' Oliver continued to rummage. 'And about your university and about your politics. So, he'd have come late to the party, like he always did, proud of his son.' He handed Karan a bottle of champagne. 'Anyway, we'll be free of them by christmas.'

Karan examined the dusty bottle and spotted his and Oliver's signatures, 'You kept the bottle of champagne we failed to sneak into the comedy club?'

'Well, we managed to sneak it in. They told us, in no uncertain terms, it was remaining unopened and coming back out with us. After you met Isha and abandoned me, I brought it back home for a special occasion.'

'That was twenty years ago.' Karan felt queasy turning the bottle in his hand. 'It wasn't the best champagne back then!'

‘I knew to keep it to toast when you became the leader of our country.’

Karan put the bottle down. ‘But I’m not, though, am I? I’m a sort of locum. And maybe even worse than that. Millions of people think we’ve sold out.’ Spotting Oliver’s crestfallen face, he added, ‘We agreed I didn’t abandon you. I hadn’t had sex in about three years!’ Karan was staring at the bottle again. ‘You’re incredible. I know you got me here.’ He pushed it over to Oliver. ‘But I don’t think we have anything to celebrate yet. We’ve given up on the ambitions and dreams of some pretty native twenty-somethings. Anyway, I have to go to Banerjee’s Indians-only party.’

‘I haven’t. This was my dream. Our plan. You leading the country. I think you becoming first first minister merits the only bottle of champagne we could afford with the last of my student loan.’ Oliver opened it. A twenty-year delay resulted in a puff of air like a balloon deflating.

‘Anyway, from that night, Isha swept into your life and swept me out.’

‘Now who’s feeling sorry for themselves,’ Karan said. ‘Let’s drink this shitty champagne then. Who was on that night? You had convinced yourself it was going to be a celebrity. Didn’t you get into a conversation with them?’

‘I didn’t think you would remember.’

‘I remember,’ Karan paused. ‘We’ve come a long way since then.’

They held their glasses up and drank.

‘That’s far from the finest champagne.’

‘It’s fucking terrible is what it is. Here, let’s drink this instead.’ Oliver opened another bottle from the mini fridge.

Karan smelled it. ‘Much better. Have you seen the list of cabinet appointments?’

Oliver shook his head.

Karan continued, ‘I’ll have them sent over and confirm your appointment as chancellor and my deputy with the governor-general tomorrow.’

Oliver asked, 'How was the king?'

'You mean the governor,' Karan replied. 'It was strange.'

'In what way?'

'It was as if he knew how all of this was going to pan out. Did you speak to his office?'

'No. He can't have. He does have that arse-licker Banerjee. He'll have filled his head with nonsense and false promises.'

Karan finished his champagne. 'No, it felt like more than that. I'd told him that he was no longer an hrh.'

Oliver poured more into their glasses. 'Well, that alone must have fucking stung.'

Karan smirked. 'Yeah, and now he's hoisting an Indian flag as we speak.'

Oliver added, 'I wouldn't be surprised if the flagpole is sticking out of Banerjee's arse.'

* * *

It was 8.30 p.m. on a particularly hot and sweaty monsoon night in Mumbai. Outside the Deshmukh family compound, near the green-grass loop of the Mahalaxmi racecourse, electric buses were silently taking tens of thousands of mumbaikars home. Taxis plied their wares and drivers sounded their horns in all directions. Arun was turning his car and waved to the state police as he drove in. Officers used whistles and bare arms to part the sea of people waiting for their chief minister, chanting, 'Aaj England humara desh hai!'

Arun laughed, thinking, 'How on earth could England be ours!' Like most rich mumbaikars, and a certain type of Indian politician, Arun spent the summer in London. It was his city as much as anybody's. Walking in the parks. Anonymous coffees in little hole-in-the-wall cafes. Shopping. Clean pavements. No security. 'God, I hope we don't ruin it,' he thought.

Rahul, Arun's father, was chief minister, having only recently returned to political success following a decision to align with Usha's grand coalition. Rahul was well into his seventies. Everyone knew the big decisions were now being taken by Arun, himself a prominent minister in the Deshmukh administration, having been given the industry, innovation and investment portfolios after increasing his margin by 80,000 votes in a gruelling election.

Party workers milled around wishing for jobs and to be granted favours. Arun raced to his office and changed his t-shirt, checking how his gym classes were working out in the mirror, and put on a formal blue shirt. He sprinted to his father's office past what must have been a hundred people waiting in rooms, along the corridors and down the stairs. A few had made it through to their actual waiting rooms. They carried flowers and gifts. Arun stopped to exchange greetings with some of his father's oldest friends and longest-serving allies, apologising for rushing off.

Rahul was at his desk, waiting. Arun's grandfather's picture hung prominently behind him. The walls were littered with posters and party slogans. On the desk between Arun and Rahul were photos of the pair of them with members of his father's cabinet; with party workers; of Arun addressing lakhs of people during the most recent election campaign; and, most importantly, with his mother. Phones rang constantly—on the desk, in the corner of the room, and in the outer office from where secretaries shuffled incessantly with papers for Rahul to review. A television in the corner was distracting them. 'Aaj England humara desh hai!' was being chanted by crowds across India.

Arun sat down. 'This is crazy, pitaji. You know my work is just starting. For the people. For our people.'

A chaiwallah came in and searched for a space on the desk between them to place his tray of cups and nuts. Rahul waited until he left. 'Beta, you've been asked to serve our country. There is no greater honour.'

Arun had listened to his father get increasingly excited on the phone as he drove home. Ever since the prime minister had called him, Rahul had been plotting. 'You don't understand what this means for our party. For our family.'

Arun tried again. 'Pitaji, my work is needed here now. To support you, build up the party. Prepare for the election.'

Rahul avoided responding and grimaced. He sipped his tea with a loud slurp and let Arun continue.

'Pitaji, we've been told to support this PM's crazy plan. It's aggrandisement. It's from another century. This is 2027. Our people don't want to become a colonial power. What would grandfather say? He didn't fight the British to become them.'

This roused his father. 'What do you know of fighting? Of what your grandfather had to do. All of this,' he pointed, 'did not come easy. And it can be lost in an instant.' He clicked his fingers. 'In the flick of a switch. The blink of an eye.' He took another slurp of his chai. 'Ushaji has appointed you her resident commissioner. You will accept this and get on your way to London tonight.'

Arun gazed at the ceiling. 'A coloniser. You want to make me a coloniser. You want to make us all colonisers. Jobs from 1827. Governor-general. Resident commissioner. We are already giving out the trinkets and baubles. Soon it will be knighthoods and peerages. I await the star of India!'

Rahul waved and tutted. 'You have been listening to too many of your comedians. This time we will be in charge. It will be good for our people, good for you, and good for us.'

Arun pleaded, 'Pitaji, you know these English MPs. Not one of them is able to lead their country. Least of all Sunil's damaad. He was the only one they could find to take Isha.'

Rahul sneered, 'Selling your country so that Sunil Bhai can add a few London squares to his property portfolio. It's vulgar. But Sunil has already made 3 billion pounds and has a bank in his name.'

'Already?' Arun's eyes widened. 'Those parliamentarians aren't in India's league any more. Living in tiny, rented flats. Worrying about expenses.'

The chaiwallah returned with fresh chai, vada pav and some mithai. Arun took his drink but left the sweets on the table. 'I will have to deal with these English boys every day.'

Rahul was now more interested in the sweets and tea. 'And most of them are gay.' He offered some laddu. 'These used to be your favourite.'

Arun placed the sweets back on the table. 'You know I am trying to keep fit, pitaji!'

When the last sweet was eaten, Arun knew the discussion was over. Rahul barked, 'Enough talk. You'll have the flat in St James's and the party, and the prime minister's support. If this works, you'll bring many jobs and much investment to Maharashtra. If it doesn't, you'll bring down the government, Ushaji and her chief petty officer. Paving the way for us to take her place. You leave in a few hours.'

* * *

Bleary-eyed, Karan yawned and searched for his phone from deep in the sofa. 'Are you coming, darling?'

'What's that? I've just woken up.' Shouting, he added, 'I can barely hear you.'

'It's in full swing here. And you're the guest of honour. Please hurry the fuck up!' She hung up.

'What the fuck have we done?' Karan was looking out the window down on to the Downing Street garden. He felt sick but couldn't work out if it was like waiting for the declaration at his first count or when his father told him he only had weeks to live. Either way he was sure he knew what was coming and couldn't do anything about it.

He poured a coffee from his little student stovetop coffee maker. Isha hated it. He constantly found it in the kitchen bin or at the back of a cupboard in the bedroom. It had been his first adult birthday present from Oliver and was as reliable as he was. Isha had been in charge of the redecoration of this flat and made it clear the coffee pot had to go. She wanted sleek surfaces, brass trims on plush coffee tables and designer kitchenware. There were pinks and blues and greens. Whenever Karan suggested it was too busy, she told him he had no taste whatsoever. The one concession they'd both agreed on was that the many books could be arranged by colour rather than subject. His phone rang. 'Yes, switch?' he asked.

'Your wife has been back on the line, first minister. She erm ...'

'Go on. She was probably insolent if not seditious. Please read it out quickly. It will be better for both of us.'

'She asked me to tell you to get your cute little arse into the car pronto.'

Karan smiled. 'Thanks.'

A knock at the door was followed by, 'May I come in, prime minister?'

'Yes, Seb. But it's first minister.' Seb was Karan's principal private secretary. A thirty-something treasury high-flyer. Karan had asked him to come with him saying he needed someone he trusted who was smarter than Oliver.

'The car is waiting downstairs and I think your wife might take a contract out on me if you don't leave soon!'

Karan grabbed his jacket, and they walked downstairs together. 'How have the markets reacted?'

'Things have pretty much stabilised at 1 dollar 12.' Karan cringed as Seb continued, 'Today's cost us over 100 billion pounds. Well, the Indians actually. We've had some interesting messages from the Indian prime minister's office about how they intend to recapitalise our banks and have us pay for the cost of the integration.'

'Do you want me to look at that now?' Karan asked hopefully.

'No, first minister.' Seb frowned. 'You have to join your wife at Lord Banerjee's. But you may also want to know your father-in-law has just bought himself Merchant's.'

'What did you say?' Karan stopped on the stairs. Ramrod straight. 'Sunil has already bought a bank?'

'Yes, and he appeared to be a considerable proportion of the global shorting of sterling. Much of his profit sitting with Merchant's.'

'Merchant's,' Karan interrupted Seb. Karan's face tightened. 'Thanks for this, Seb. Tell me anything else you hear. See you tomorrow. Go home now, please. You all deserve to see your families.'

'We'll be staying late tonight. Just in case.'

Karan turned to him. 'Tell the team thank you for today please.'

The police motorbikes were pulling onto Whitehall as Karan got into the car. A small group of Indians had gathered. 'At last,' Karan thought, 'some hindus who might be happy with what I've done.' He watched them as he drove by. They'd lit candles and were holding placards with posters of people who had been brutally beaten. On them was written: 'Usha Sachdev. Indian PM. Wanted for Murder.'

Karan was grateful for the police protection when he saw thousands of people in parliament square. All the flags had been pulled down. Some set alight. Others had been draped around a giant makeshift coffin under an oversized poster announcing, 'Here lies England. 927–2027. RIP.' Another announced, 'Karan Puri, coward wanted for the murder of our freedom.'

In St James's Park, people were coalescing around a giant yurt. Karan peered over the top. 'It can't be, can it?'

He took his phone out to call Oliver as they turned into the Mall.

'Have you changed your mind?' Oliver asked.

'What is the fucking Indian flag doing flying over the palace?'

'We didn't ask for it. Let me check.'

While waiting for Oliver to reply, Karan realised why they were going at such speed. The roads weren't just quiet. They were desolate. No buses. No traffic. Only police cars careening in either direction. Then he saw the police on the streets.

'Are you still there?' Oliver asked. 'Instructions direct from the Indian prime minister's office.'

'Shit. So it really has begun,' Karan replied. 'Did you order the police on the streets? It looks like they've closed the roads.'

'Yes, while we wait for your cabinet to be appointed, we took the decision to close the roads in central London and shut down the tube. The police and the security service are worried about the groups in Westminster and in the city.'

Karan sat in silence.

'Don't worry. The police know what they are doing. Go enjoy your time with Banerjee.'

They had turned into a square off Knightsbridge. 'Stop, please Umesh.' Karan got out and looked at row upon row of some of the most expensive flats and four-storey townhouses in London. Tea lights flickered at every window. Indian flags fluttered from every balcony.

He stood staring, 'It's…' He turned round on the spot. In every window a spark of hope. Belief in him. In his community. In what they could achieve together for the country they love. 'It's magical. It's little fucking India.' He heard himself laugh out loud. His cheeks were moist. His eyes were welling up. He hadn't cried since his father died.

'First minister?' Banerjee's shouting forced Karan to quickly wipe the tears away.

'First minister, are you enjoying the decorations for our street mela?' Banerjee was walking over to Karan, arms outstretched. 'You did it, my boy. You did it.' He hugged Karan like a proud parent and led him to the door of twenty-two. 'Look at this,' pointing at the windows, 'look what you've achieved. I know your father would have been exceptionally proud to see all this. As is every successful Indian in London. I should know. They are all inside—dying to see you.'

Through the hubbub of chat and clinking of champagne flutes, Karan heard the tunes of his youth. Just as he was starting to enjoy it the music stopped. All eyes turned to him, and Banerjee announced, 'Ladies and gentlemen, our first minister.' Like the compere on a cruise ship he continued, 'And, I'm delighted our first, first minister has chosen to host his first official function in our humble home.'

‘Speech,’ someone shouted from the back. The room was pregnant with hope and expectation. All pinned on him. He spotted Isha at the back blowing him a kiss. ‘Thank you, as ever, Lord Banerjee, your generous hospitality is far from humble. It’s Indian. And we all know the transformational things we Indians can do for our wonderful country.’ Karan smiled as they applauded.

He scanned the room. Bankers, founders, venture capitalists mixed with Isha’s media, design and fashion crowd, all of them bright young British Indians. ‘We’ve got a lot to do.’ He continued, ‘Our fathers and grandfathers are staring down at us. I hope we can live up to their expectations. And, thank you, Lord Banerjee, for taking such excellent care of my wife while I was otherwise engaged this evening.’

Banerjee asked loudly, ‘But first, time for a little celebration?’

Karan replied, ‘If you mean a little night-club dancing, Lord Banerjee, then yes.’

The crowd laughed and the music restarted.

Banerjee led Karan into an immaculate back garden and lit a cigar. ‘I stayed with the governor after you left, first minister. He is in some state of considerable shock.’

Karan replied, ‘I think we all are.’

Banerjee waited. ‘Do you know who our new governor-general will be?’

Karan smiled. ‘You mean my new boss? No, not at all.’

Across the party, Abdul and Zarin were watching Banerjee in action. ‘Banerjee is almost as insufferable as Isha. He’s spent his whole life ingratiating himself to the white British elite,’ Abdul added. ‘Wiping the king’s arse for a peerage and to be commander of the british empire. God knows how much he will make out of all of this.’

Zarin added, ‘And, now he’s seamlessly shifting to the new overlords.’

Abdul nodded. ‘Such a fucking chamcha. He’ll get burnt this time. We’re never as polite as the English. Everyone here expects to get even richer even quicker under Karan’s lacklustre government.’

Karan took a moment's gap in another Banerjee monologue as Isha came out to see them, 'Lord Banerjee, I am so indebted to you.' He grabbed his hand. 'But I'm afraid I have to go.'

Isha was surprised. 'Aren't we partying tonight?'

Karan took her hand and put it in Banerjee's, 'You definitely are. And probably enough for both of us. I have to go back. It's a big day tomorrow. Okay to leave you here?'

Banerjee interjected, 'She'll be in excellent company, first minister. We'll look after her.'

Isha shrugged. 'I'll be late.'

Karan shouted back, 'No change there then', and headed for the door. In the car he said, 'Umesh, you are a godsend.'

'Home, sir?' Umesh asked.

* * *

In Mumbai, Arun was under the sea, marvelling at the engineering. 'If we can build this,' he smiled, 'then maybe we can run England.'

They surfaced on to Marine Drive and his friend added, 'England is crazy, bhai. They're saying your father has agreed you'll go.'

As they exited the tunnel into the humid night air, Arun replied, 'Let's not talk about it tonight.' He parked outside his favourite comedy club in south Mumbai. The poster by the door announced, 'Bombay favourite Raksha Chowdree.' Arun walked in and found his friends watching the young female comedian. He'd asked them for a seat near the back row and told them he wanted to be inconspicuous. They had chosen a table so far forward they could have been her agents.

Raksha was midway through her set. 'So we're an empire again. Some people are asking is this legal. Others are asking if they still get tax-free shopping. Malabar Hill kids are asking if Selfridges will deliver.

'I think the whole thing is so we can have one shit-hot olympics team in Los Angeles. We are going to kick some Chinese ass next year. Namaste to third-place Beijing.'

The comedian scanned the front row. 'I see we have the new resident commissioner in tonight. How are you, sir? Flying business or first tonight? Think of those air miles.'

Arun shouted, 'Yaha! Magar, keep me out of it!'

* * *

Oliver, Alessandra, his private secretary, and team were huddled round a table in his office on Waterloo Bridge. Behind them was a grand sweep of the Thames. The twinkling lights of London interspersed with protestors' fireworks. 'Have we reviewed the papers for my meeting with the resident commissioner whenever he gets here?'

Holding the printouts in her hand, Alessandra replied, 'Yes, but …'

Oliver stopped, 'But what?'

'They already have a comprehensive list of assets they would like Indianised. And a few are concerning.' Oliver rechecked the file.

'When do we send it to Karan, I mean, the first minister's office?'

'As soon as you sign them off,' she replied.

Oliver continued to review the file. 'Have we received the final list of cabinet appointments?'

She checked the papers in front of her. 'Not in this bundle. Aren't you celebrating tonight, boss?'

Oliver smiled, 'Someone has to do the dirty work. But you should go. You should all go. It's not every night you remake a constitution.' They started to pack up as Oliver asked, 'Do we know anything about the new resident commissioner?'

Karan walked in with a magnum of champagne followed by one of Oliver's team carrying pizza. 'He's apparently young and handsome like you used to be.'

Oliver looked at Karan with the kind of pride reserved solely for a best friend's best days. 'Banerjee left this monster in the car. I can't think of anyone else I'd rather drink it with—than all of you.' Karan handed it to Alessandra, who was embarrassed that their boss's boss had arrived. 'Well, will you open this and eat the pizza I've brought too, please?'

In Oliver's office, Karan asked, 'Why did we banish you over here?'

'You told me it made sense to keep me away from the press, remember?'

'Ah, yes. But I remember you had worked out this office had the best view in London.'

Alessandra brought in champagne and pizza. Oliver turned on the tv, asking, 'You think we can get some Indian comedy on this thing?'

Karan flicked between the channels with a remote. 'How can you still want to watch Indian comedy? You don't even understand Hindi.' In between bites he added, 'I think we need to keep your office safely away from Downing Street regardless of what comes next.'

Oliver nodded. 'I'm already being asked repeatedly if we really know what we've done or what we're doing.'

They streamed Raksha live from Mumbai, 'Seventy million temporary Indian citizens; fifty-six countries in the Indian imperial commonwealth; and we hear all this is because the British prime minister's sasur didn't get one visa extension last year! That is an expensive complaint. Is it true, sir?'

Karan dissolved into laughter as she continued, 'I know one thing, there's gonna be some mighty shit to clean up after all this.'

* * *

Lu Quan called an assistant into his office. 'Have we received instructions from Beijing yet?'

The assistant nodded his head. 'Yes, the flight landed at Beijing–London airport thirty minutes ago, ambassador.'

Ambassador Lu read, 'Tens of billions of pounds down on our British investments. But hundreds of billions of assets will be made available to Beijing by the governor-general.' He smiled.

Three

It was Saturday and Karan was lounging in the four-poster bed Isha had demanded for them. A streak of summer sun was warming his big toe while the Royal Marines band rehearsed beside their garden.

His body was limp. Relaxed for the first time in months. Isha had finally come home late and merry. Karan woke up as she climbed on top of him. She walked in now with a half-open dressing gown, forcing him to stare; he loved how beautiful she was and she knew it.

'I haven't had sex with a prime minister before,' she teased, giving him a glass of orange juice. 'I've had lots of sex with a chancellor. That was ten a penny. Easy cum easy go, in fact.'

'Thanks to your dad, I'm merely first minister, remember? Anyway, I hope my diminutive status was sufficient.'

'It still makes the point!' Isha was staring out of the window. 'What's that fucking racket?'

'The band is rehearsing for the formal welcome of our new overlord. But if you mean next door, they are packing up Richardson's things. Ready for Oliver to move in.'

'I've been thinking about that.' Isha was now on the bed beside him, starting to play with him under the covers.

Karan laid his head on the pillow and shut his eyes. 'Go on, but maybe talk less?'

'This apartment is too small for us. I think we should take next door too. I could have a little design studio. And we can knock through the main room. I've already had someone look at it. And now we don't need to stick to the miserly renovation budget Richardson gave you.'

'You keep going and you can have whatever you want.'

'Great.' Isha jumped out of bed. 'Coffee?'

'I have a question for you first.' Karan pulled himself up. 'Why did your dad buy the bank before I had even been appointed?'

Karan heard the kettle go on. Then the radio. He jumped out of bed, found his pants and favourite dressing gown and walked into the kitchen. 'You know I'm right—a typical play by your dad: take-take-take.'

'Don't.' She slammed the coffee pot on to the counter and pointed her finger in his face. 'Pitaji knows what he's doing. He got you here, didn't he?' She turned the tap on full and splashed water everywhere, her eyes narrowing. 'You have something from all this. Pitaji has something. Oliver has something.'

He peered out again at the lorry being filled with items. 'They've been at it since yesterday afternoon. How can he have that much stuff? They never came over as interesting enough to have interests. Did they?'

Isha poured them both coffee. 'What do I get out of all of this?'

Giving up, Karan watched the delivery men load box after box of Richardson's belongings. 'I didn't think he had stuff. He never talked to me about anything other than the kids and how we lost Scotland.' For the two years of the formal secession negotiations, Karan and Richardson had chatted to one another long into the wee hours. Reviewing that day's trials and traumas. Night after night. Every morning started with them in the den strategising with their top advisors agreeing that session's red lines. They'd meet the four-person delegation, headed by the Scottish first minister, in the cabinet room for three or four days of unremitting torture. On almost every issue, the Scots were implacable. If Karan had to listen to the words 'sov-errreign-tee' and 'dignitee' ever again he promised to kill himself. The Scots barely cracked a smile. Each night Karan offered to take them for a drink. And each time, for the whole two fucking years he'd been told, politely, to fuck off.

He and Richardson had tried every possible avenue to keep the union together. History and tradition. Promises of a federation. Moving the fucking capital to Edinburgh. Glasgow. Even fucking Wick. But it always came down to more money and dignity. Not one of their red lines was ever kept. Threats to cut an independent

Scotland out of common defence and security arrangements; ending the common travel area; limiting health services across the border; and, denying access to the UK's freshly minted trade deal with the US. Scotland got it all. They were simply better at holding out. Finally, Richardson concluded it was over. The Scottish first minister had even managed to convince English voters and the media that the deal was in their interests. 'Soon,' she trumpeted constantly, 'England would have enough money to invest in Berwick as well as Berkshire.'

Karan and Richardson were jointly and severally liable for a deal that ended 300 years of the union. A deal that, for many, began the path to today's ignominy. Oliver had made sure it was deemed another of Richardson's stumbles. The loss of Scotland had been the beginning of the end for him. It also sounded the death knell for that idea of England forged in the mid-twentieth century from the embers of the previous hundred years.

Karan smiled at Isha. 'Sounds like you're going to get Richardson's apartment. Once they get rid of all their shit.' He had returned from showering with a choice of ties.

She knew he wanted the navy blue one with green polka dots. 'That's your special tie. The one with all the good energy in it. Feeling nervous?'

He was wearing his standard, tailored navy blue suit and a tight-fitting shirt. As he knotted the tie he told her, 'Yup, first meeting with the governor-general. He arrived overnight from Delhi. He requested, no, demanded, that no one greet him on the tarmac. And none of the usual rigmarole outside. Told us quite directly no one, not even the Indian high commissioner. And it was made crystal clear that Albert was definitely not welcome.'

Isha was leafing through a glossy magazine. 'You know I know all this. Pitaji says Ushaji chose him because he knew how to get under the skins of English politicians when he was here last here.'

'Your father doesn't think I get briefings?' Karan was redoing his tie. 'Or that I have any memory?'

'And pitaji says to remember Manish is a fan of a good eighteen-year-old whisky.'

'Well, at least that should make tonight's reception go quickly.'

Isha asked, 'What was that?'

'Didn't know that, did you?' He handed her an embossed card. 'There's to be a reception to mark his arrival tonight. First time there's been a diplomatic reception on a Saturday since William IV or something. And a great faff about whether these invitation cards need to be hand-delivered today.'

'Great.' Isha slammed the magazine on the tabletop. 'They'll all want dress fittings this morning. I'll have to work some magic to hide some aunty ankles!'

'Thank your father when you speak to him for the advice, won't you?'

Isha was already on her mobile. 'Yes, I need all of you in the shop now. No! In the fucking shop now. I'll see you there in twenty minutes. I don't care about childcare. No, you can't bring them in with you. Oh, I don't know. Get a fucking taxi.'

Karan leant over and kissed her. 'I was thinking maybe I'd buy you something special to mark this thing we're doing now.'

Isha stopped. 'You have my attention, I'm listening.'

Karan smiled. 'I was thinking of having a ring designed. From the jewellers you like off Bond Street.'

Isha was walking into the shower, 'The jewellers I like is on Bond Street. Daddy says he wants you to give him Heathrow. Can we start there, please?'

Karan stared blankly.

* * *

Sally was on the television in Oliver's office. 'It's understood that the new governor-general arrived in the early hours of this morning. Yes, that's right, Henry, we are in completely new constitutional territory. The first minister will have his cabinet confirmed by the governor-general on behalf of the Indian prime minister.'

Oliver checked out Alessandra and the team around her. Each had dark circles under their eyes and the sallow skin of students cramming for finals. 'I thought I told you to go home last night. Can someone turn this shit off?'

Sally added, 'But we are seeing signs of rebellion here in the capital and across the city.'

'Hold on.' Oliver raised his hand.

'Yes, that's right,' she continued, 'we don't know if London is still a capital city.'

'Of course it fucking is,' Oliver tutted.

'The labour leader of the opposition has been out meeting protesters in their makeshift camps in the city's parks and squares. I have him here now. Mr Khan, what do you think is going on?'

'Well, the truth is, Sally,' Khalid replied, 'No one has a bloody idea. Least of all our clueless, gormless and spineless new first minister. I don't want to be a colony of India, and nor do tens of millions of people in this country.'

'But you do accept, do you, that India has saved us from—'

'Saved us from what, Sally? From ourselves? No, let's get one thing straight. They held us to bloody ransom. And I for one am not taking it. The promise is this will all be over by christmas. These brave people here—and my party will stand with them—these brave people here are fighting for our freedom.'

Alessandra put down her coffee as Oliver came over. The team had steadfastly refused to eat the croissants he'd brought them. She was holding back tears when he said, 'He's an idiot. India is only helping us out. This will be over by christmas. And all of you are on the side of the angels. You've kept the lights on. Kept the wheels of government turning. Kept our army and our military functioning. Yes, there are going to be teething troubles. But we can trust Karan to get us through this. So, what's this?' Oliver grabbed a pile of papers inches thick.

Their silence continued until Alessandra broke it. 'That's the too-difficult pile.'

Oliver grabbed a croissant. 'Okay, what else do we have?'

The team ignored the question. One took a deep fascination in the cover page of the file in front of him. Another doodled. Oliver knew they had spent most of the last twelve hours wanting to have this conversation. He could tell they had urged Alessandra to start it. 'So we're going to give them the country bit by bit? Look at what they're asking for. We know what they plan to do. And we will have facilitated it.'

'Look,' Oliver replied. 'Those people on the streets think they are doing something. But they are simply making noise. Khalid is a bandwagon-jumping gobshite. He was a jumped-up arsehole before all this started and he still is one today. What you're doing is difficult and it's necessary. You're uncomfortable with it.'

Alessandra sighed. 'You can say that again.'

'I'm uncomfortable with it too. But the boss needs us to begin the process of Indianisation. I mean integration. He's convinced we need to start quickly. He says let's find the easy things we can be seen to do quickly. Our job is to deliver this for him.' He picked up another pile of papers. 'What about telecoms?'

* * *

Molly was in the back of an auto-taxi texting photos of her notes when Jonathan called, 'Where the fuck are you?'

'I'm getting out of the cab now. All bridges have been closed down by protesters or the police.'

'Are you fucking kidding me? You should be in reception. I told you we all needed to be in by 8.45.'

'Well, it's Saturday. You don't pay me overtime. And I'm getting to you as fast as I can.'

'Well, hurry the fuck up. We have some cleaning up to do before the new owners arrive on Monday.'

'Wait, what?'

'You heard.'

Molly's cab froze where the encampment started. Tents were littered across this main route into the city. Bonfires were blazing. The air, thick with smoke, stank of petrol and cannabis. People were as high as they were angry.

At the far end of the bridge militant groups had gathered to burn Indian and English flags. They'd set up posters and placards saying, 'Fuck You, India.' And had overwritten on one '~~Karma~~ Karan is a Bitch!' and on another, 'The colonised becomes the coloniser.'

By the look of the dazed commuters walking along with her, Merchant's/Grover's wasn't the only bank to call its teams in on a Saturday. Panic was contagious. Pandemonium too. Police sirens were going off all around. Barricades were being pulled down. Businesses had already been smashed up. A few protesters were sporting brand new leather handbags with their security tags still attached.

At the opposite side of the bridge, police were checking those coming and going. One gruffly asked to see Molly's pass. Protesters were throwing bricks at the Bank of Britain. Immediately ahead of her a young man lobbed a bottle at the officers. Three heavily armed men proceeded to beat him, and they didn't want to give up. Molly turned away at the crunch of a broken bone. This wasn't a London she recognised. Blood was pouring from the boy's face. He struggled and fought against being repeatedly struck.

Finally, one officer shouted, 'Taser, Taser, Taser!'

Molly heard the young man scream when 50,000 volts entered his body. He was rolling and writhing on the ground as if having a seizure.

'Stop,' she heard herself scream. One of the men glowered at her. She tried not to catch his gaze and made straight for Merchant's.

More heavily armed officers, with their faces concealed under dark glasses and masks, shouted, 'Stand to the side,' and another pushed Molly into the thick stone wall beside her. She watched them raid the protesters, dragging them back to be arrested, beaten and interrogated. More officers followed with snarling dogs. Behind them others were setting up barriers to keep some of the road and pavement clear. Molly knew these masked raiders weren't ordinary policemen. They were carrying the kinds of kit and weapons she'd only ever seen on television. She caught her breath standing against the bank and took out her notebook.

* * *

Umesh was driving Karan down the eerily quiet Mall. 'What's the flag on the front of the car?' Karan saw heavily armed officers every 20 yards.

Umesh replied, 'It was changed overnight.'

Karan looked intently at the flags on either side of the main route to what had been the head of state. They'd been changed too. It was a Union Jack of sorts but what would have been the blue of the St Andrew's cross had been replaced with the colours of the Indian flag. Four saffron triangles suffocated the top of the cross of St George and four green triangles smothered it from below. A brilliant indigo-blue ashoka chakra had been imposed in the centre atop everything else. Each flagpole was being protected by heavily armed police. Five-foot-high barricades had been erected to keep protesters in the parks and to limit any more from joining them. Frighteningly armed officers were manning the entry and exits. Karan called Seb, 'What are these flags?'

'The new anglo-indian standard? I'm told they were brought over on a plane that landed at the Beijing–London city airport. They told me they had been made by an ngo in southern India. The only one with the licence to make them. But I'm sure they have come from sweatshops in China. We received a protocol order that all these flags had to be up by 0930 hours this morning. I think we've made it.'

'But who authorised that we would have a new flag?'

'Well,' Seb stalled, 'I assumed you had been briefed on this. The protocol order came direct from the Indian prime minister's office. Can't we say this is a temporary one to welcome the GG into his new place?'

'I can't believe we've let ourselves move so quickly. When you give an inch, they will take a mile and sell the land from under our feet. I know my wife's family pretty well, I'm afraid, Seb. And did the request for such a heavy military presence come from the Indian prime minister's office too?'

'Yes, we received a formal military assistance request overnight. The chancellor of the duchy of Lancaster signed it off.'

'Oliver?'

'Yes. Tell him we need to have a cobra meeting when I'm back. This will all get rapidly out of hand.'

* * *

Albert was peering from the top-floor window. Banerjee knocked. 'I thought you would like to know, sir. The first minister is on his way to buckingham palace.'

'What are those damned flags, Banerjee?'

'What, sir?'

'The flags that look like the love child of a bollywood movie and a west end show. They may as well have lights underneath them and cabaret dancers.'

'That's the new standard of the thirtieth state of the Republic of India, sir. Did you hear that the first minister is on his way to the palace?'

'Yes, I didn't see we had an audience in the diary. Are we already dropping our standards as they raise the Indian one, Banerjee? I assume you will tell me when he is coming here?'

'No, sir. Number 10 told me there's no time before the cabinet is confirmed. And, err ...'

'Go on, Banerjee.'

‘The governor-general’s office has made it clear you will no longer have a formal audience with the first minister.’

‘I’m already a relic, Banerjee,’ he wailed. ‘Like our dear old Union Jack. Both of us not merely demoted but superfluous.’

Banerjee stood silent.

‘Something else?’ Albert asked.

‘Yes, about tonight’s reception, sir.’ Banerjee paused. ‘The GG’s office have been in touch about that too. Your attendance is not required, sir.’

Albert grabbed Banerjee’s hand and displayed a look Banerjee had only ever seen on dogs, ‘I need you to attend.’ Banerjee detected the slightest wail as he continued, ‘I need to know what is going on. Please see this as one of your special missions.’ He’d sent Banerjee on missions before. Usually to find donors for some of his most important projects. ‘The hare-brained unfundables,’ his wife called them. Banerjee had always delivered, and Albert trusted him implicitly. Seizing one of his many framed photos, he added, ‘At this rate I’ll be neither use nor ornament.’ Banerjee left Albert staring at the flags.

* * *

The growing queue of women outside Isha’s eponymous store was the who’s-married-to-whom of the new Indian polity. She had been unbending with her father—there was only one street in London on which his daughter could set up her fashion empire. He’d agreed to a ten-year lease and the promise that she’d turn a profit before then. The location was a dream for both of them. Directly beside Britain’s best designers and midway between Sunil’s favourite gentlemen’s clubs.

Isha came out to meet the many wives of the rich and connected. ‘Ladies, we are busier than usual today. I suggest you take a table round the corner. We all know Vijay uncle owns a nice five-star hotel on the square. We’ll call them when we are ready for each and every one of you.’ Much to Isha’s relief, the smart, sexy Indian women were happy to chatter round the corner and patronise uncle's hotel. 'And he has the champagne on ice waiting for you!' She smiled and waved.

Inside Isha's boutique, the high-spending women of the new Indian elite had their credit cards out and were paying obeisance. Isha knew the game they were playing. These ruthless businesswomen, and in some cases their cuckolded husbands, were betting Isha was the priority lane to vast riches. Isha knew she would deliver. A well-cut five-figure dress was a worthwhile investment if it meant Sunil Bhai's daughter put in a good word for you, a feckless husband or a spoilt child.

Pins in her mouth, Isha was fixing the hem of a dress belonging to a particularly difficult fifty-something, who told her, 'Darling Isha, we are in charge now. You can take it up a little higher. Let's show these English boys what's been right under their noses.' There were cackles and murmurs of approval in between never-ending champagne, canapés and macaroons. Archana nodded at Isha before gushing, 'Of course.'

The woman continued, 'My husband says Karan is already gift-wrapping England like a good gujju.'

Another replied, 'It's a good thing they didn't put my punjabi in-laws in charge; we'd only be selling the tractors and the fields.'

Isha handed the final alterations to Archana. She smiled at the thought of the sales about to go through the till and the scores of women waiting for her attention. For too long she'd been forced to listen to their generic stories about how successful their sons and daughters were. Who'd married into extreme wealth. Who'd IPO'd, become a tech investor or hedge-fund manager. The poorer ones still celebrated their doctors, lawyers and engineers. Then they'd tilt their heads and ask Isha forlornly if Karan had made it to the top of politics yet. In India their families had gloated over her father's disgrace. He had worked hard to win back their respect. In some cases, he'd bought it. Now they would buy Isha's. 'Pitaji does have a long list and Karan is working through it.'

Two women were going through Isha's prêt-à-porter line, bemused.

Isha continued, 'If you want to add to it, you only have to ask.'

One whispered, 'She's gauche. The nouveau riche are definitely now in charge. God help this poor little country. It has no idea what's about to hit it.'

'And the price of these dresses,' her friend replied, holding a tag. 'I swear they've gone up 35 per cent in twenty-four hours!'

'Well, she is her father's daughter. But it's all so unnecessary. I hear it's the same in Delhi. He hangs around the PMO like a stray dog. Desperately waiting for her to throw him some crumbs.' Picking up one of Isha's many figure-hugging creations, she added, 'These dresses are our scraps now.'

The other one replied, 'Maybe we are the scraps.'

Isha rolled her eyes at Archana going through the order book. Archana covered her mouth with her hand. 'Don't lose it, okay. They are your customers, after all. Every fat fucker in here.'

Isha breathed out slowly. 'These women.'

Archana smiled. 'Focus on the sales.'

Isha replied, 'And not the fankles.'

Archana was pointing at the order book. 'We are missing this one, for Sunita Ma'am.' Isha checked over Archana's shoulder, 'It's still at Christian Street,' and picked up her mobile. 'We are still waiting for one dress. You told me it would be here yesterday. Get those lazy fucking women off their arses and on to the machines. And get it here before lunchtime.'

* * *

Umesh drove through the palace portico into a traffic jam. The usually pristine quadrangle was speckled with all manner of luxury vehicles. Most were ten times what Karan's government-issue car cost. 'The new Indian elite have beaten us to it, eh, Umesh?' Karan asked.

A liveried footman appeared and pointed to lower the window. 'I'm sorry, first minister, we appear to be inundated this morning. I'm afraid you'll have to walk.' Karan taunted Umesh as he attempted a three-point turn in the tiniest of spaces. It was as if his father was back in one of the many free car parks he managed to find, miles from wherever the family intended to be. Karan tried to spot which elaborate part of the private apartments the governor-general had arrogated for himself.

Stepping inside, Karan heard an Indian flutist somewhere from the far back of the hall. A television had been installed, playing Hindi news on loop, which mainly consisted of images of the people he could see all around him waving enthusiastically as they entered earlier that morning. Every Indian artefact and trinket from the stores had been cleaned and polished and was now in pride of place on the corridors, mantelpieces and ledges that led to the governor-general's office. Where once the entrance been a quiet sanctuary, a place for someone to gather their thoughts before a careful and considered audience with the king, it was now a walkway at Delhi's chandni chowk. Karan heard, 'First minister, over here,' from all angles. A sea of hands was outstretched. He tried to speak to as many people as possible. Strangers filled the hallway. Grand and elderly Indians were sitting on chairs stacked against the walls. Karan watched delicate negotiations and avoided requests to lobby the governor-general. The smell of fresh flowers and Indian snacks hit him as if they were at one of Isha's cousin's weddings. Above the throng, one asked, 'Many congratulations, first minister. I'm here from Delhi News. Are you here to have your cabinet confirmed?' Karan smiled and pushed through.

Another grabbed him by the waist and whispered, 'Do you remember I donated to your first campaign? I hope you have some good punjabis on your list.' He slapped Karan's back. 'Now, I have a little investment opportunity in Lahore.'

Karan nodded blankly.

'Well, I'm hoping his excellency might invite the chief minister over. And put him up here!' He waved his hand around like it was the new five-star Indian hotel of choice.

Karan saw the man's staff juggling giant hampers.

'Luxury of course,' he added proudly.

Karan counted every kind of opportunist. Some were holding letters of introduction. One or two had bottles of horrendously expensive whisky. Karan stopped at the archbishop of canterbury who had also been kept in this diplomatic holding pen. 'Archbishop, I wasn't expecting to see you here!'

England's first female archbishop was a canny cleric. 'No, first minister. My staff recommended an early outing. Established church and all that.'

'And maybe a bit of competition for that title now, Archbishop?'

'Yes, would you mind terribly helping explain what it is we do when you see him, first minister. It will no doubt be as alien to him as—' She cut herself off.

'Of course, archbishop.' Looking around, he added. 'This must all feel peculiar to you. It does to me too. It's more the outer office of an ambitious Indian cabinet minister than the home of our head of state.'

The equerry found Karan and ushered him upstairs. Karan couldn't help but say, 'It's all so, so Indian—all of a sudden. You are letting this happen too quickly.' Before the equerry could reply, Karan spotted an image of Lord Vishnu. 'He's beautiful. My grandmother had a copy of this in her house.' The God was depicted in his eighth avatar of Krishna. The God of protection, compassion, tenderness and love. A conch, a discus, a lotus and his mace in each of his four arms. Karan prayed, adding, 'In all this noise, destruction and rebirth, he is both peaceful and powerful.' A conspicuous brass plaque had been added to the wall outside Albert's audience room. It read, 'Manish Pahlkiwala, Governor-General of Britain, 30th State of the Republic of India.'

Karan shook his head as the equerry turned to him. 'Now, no need to bow. We've done away with all that.' He knocked and entered, 'The first minister, your excellency.' Banerjee was deep in conversation with the new boss.

'Well, Manish, your next appointment is here.' Pointing at Karan, Banerjee added, 'He's exactly what we all need. Smart, seasoned in politics, but still young enough to be able to learn a thing or two from an old professional like you!'

'First minister, you know Lord Banerjee.' Karan nodded as the governor-general continued, 'He and I met when I was last in London. He continues to support Albert, as you know, and will update me from time to time.'

Banerjee winked as Karan walked forward to shake the governor-general's hand. 'Thank you, your excellency. And welcome back to London. My father-in-law sends you his best regards. I'm sure you have fond memories here from your time as high commissioner?'

'We have too much to do, first minister, to reminisce. Though I was high commissioner when you were probably still in short pants. If they wore those at your school.' Karan could feel his face warm as the governor-general picked up a brown paper file. 'Though this file doesn't make clear if you made it to private school, which suggests you may be one of the few conservative leaders not to.'

Karan's face reddened further. 'Yes.'

'Oh, don't be embarrassed, first minister. Of course, most top Indian bureaucrats and politicians will have gone to our private schools. I had a marvellous time at mine. And, as you know, our businesspeople flood your public schools here, keeping them afloat. But we do also pride ourselves on the Indians who pull themselves up from the bottom.'

'Yes, sir. You'll have seen my cabinet appointments. Many of them have a similar story to mine. Ready to serve this country. Our country.'

'Yes, yes, we'll come to those shortly.' The governor-general pointed at another file under a sheaf of papers. 'You have this list of assets for the first wave of integration?'

Karan nodded. 'I have my people working on it right now. Things will move more quickly when you approve my cabinet, particularly chancellor. Oliver Benjamin will play a critical role in speeding up the programme of integration.' The governor-general continued to leaf through the papers rather than look at Karan.

Karan continued, 'But if I may, governor-general, I noticed troops on the street last night and this morning. I have asked my office—'

The governor-general interrupted, 'Yes, first minister. I requested them, then instructed your office to do it. For our own safety and security. Transitions are dangerous times. New allegiances. Alluring opportunities. We have all read Shakespeare, first minister, and I assume some English children still do. Though not in the numbers they do in India. Really quite remarkable. Here, though, we require a show of government strength to allay any misplaced fortitude.'

Karan paused. This was to be a joust. A battle. But he did not yet have all of his brigadiers in position. He examined what had been the king's pride and joy. His audience room. Designed to startle and surprise. His seat of power. Framed pictures of the Indian prime minister had replaced Albert's many photos with world leaders. The governor-general watched Karan take it all in. 'Yes, I like to have the prime minister's eyes on my work. I will be issuing a copy of this photo of her.' The governor-general took a picture of Usha out of his shirt breast pocket. 'I keep her here. So she knows I am doing her work twenty-four seven. We hope your senior officials will proudly display it on their desks too.'

'I'm not sure that will be necessary, your excellency.'

'We shall see.' He had returned to his papers. 'Hon'ble prime minister believes her image helps good public servants make excellent decisions.' The governor-general focused on Karan. 'These are new customs for you and your people, first minister. They will take time. But that is the one thing we do not have. India has saved your country, but it cannot afford to run it at a loss. No Indian family will pay for English errors. Nor can the prime minister afford any political failure. Her future and England's future are now enmeshed.

Entangled. Both must succeed. And for that to happen, we need you to make the right choices.'

Karan smiled and continued to scan the room. The portraits of Albert had gone. Replaced with mughal paintings and Indian textiles. One was familiar to him.

'Yes, it's the Krishna in the garden of Assam. We will be returning it to Guwahati when the prime minister arrives. Something I failed to achieve as lowly high commissioner. But I could not fail to see it up close. It's majestic, isn't it?'

Karan and the governor-general were staring at the saffron and red scenes inspired by the life of Krishna. 'I should have requested the troops on the street, governor-general. And our system prefers to use police for those tasks.'

'Your system is our system now, first minister. Anyway, it is done.' The governor-general asked him to sit. 'But let us talk about more important matters. You made the correct decision, first minister, to pause trading on the markets, but you should have sought this office's approval first.'

'That's not how the English system works, sir.'

'It is now, first minister. I repeat, your system is our system. And our system is my system.'

'We do still have a constitution with rules, governor-general.'

'We are making new constitutional rules every day. We,' he pointed to himself, 'are in fact a new constitutional norm. But no matter,' the governor-general continued, 'while the markets are paused, please effect this instruction.' He handed another file to Karan. 'It has come direct from the PMO.'

'PMO?' Karan asked.

'The prime minister's office. You should know this, first minister.'

Karan reviewed the contents slowly. 'Sir, I'm unable to do this.' He placed the file on the table between them. 'It's privately owned.'

The governor-general looked through Karan. 'What was owned by whom pre-integration no longer matters. Anyway, Heathrow will make a fine gift from a daughter to her father. Please see that this is done today.' He pushed the file back to Karan.

'You have seen the new anglo-indian flag, first minister?'

Karan nodded. 'Parliament will have been expected to be consulted, your excellency.'

The governor-general sat upright in his chair. 'Matters of state and union protocol are for this office alone. We have learnt in our most difficult transitions from union territory to statehood that symbols matter and that they must quickly be introduced to give people confidence. Confidence in the rule of law. In the security of the state. Confidence in their leaders. We have achieved this in our twenty-ninth state, Jammu and Kashmir. We will do so here too.' All the while the governor-general's eyes had narrowed and focused directly on Karan. 'Please see that what will become the state assembly receives a briefing sheet on protocol. We do not want them confused, like you are, on their role. Our parliament is in Delhi now.' The governor-general watched as Karan took it all in before confirming, 'One final thing, first minister, your government will follow the standards of our government in relation to flags from this point forward.'

'Of course,' Karan replied distractedly.

'You do understand you have wrongly crossed flags all over this palace. The Indian flag's staff should be in front of the flag of the state of Britain. I have had my office send you the relevant excerpt from the flag code of India. I can fix the mess here but please make sure your offices are following this too. I do not want to be embarrassed on an unscheduled visit.'

Karan nodded as if back at school.

The governor-general picked up another file from the table in front of him. 'Now we come to your cabinet. All fine except the chancellor. We cannot leave such an important office to chance.'

'Oliver's appointment isn't chance, your excellency. He's the only one I trust to balance our books while also delivering Indianisation.'

The governor-general replied, 'You mean integration. But he is not the only one I trust. Your chancellor must be one of us.'

Karan tried again, 'Whatever one of us is. He is that. He's a fully signed-up member of this project. He's also the only one with the skills to renegotiate our Chinese loans.'

The governor-general was unimpressed. 'You know exactly what we mean. England's bad debts are not the concern of the government, first minister. We have some suggestions here.' He handed Karan a sheet of paper.

Karan read it. 'I must have space to make my own cabinet choices, governor-general. This will not work without that. These names are not a patch on Oliver.' Karan stopped himself. He took a breath and continued, 'If you are set against my choice, then I suggest we remove the office of chancellor from my cabinet for the time being. I will do both jobs.'

The governor-general nodded. 'As you wish. We think that the chancellor of the duchy of Lancaster can focus on the continued integration of the two economies. And we are pleased if you wish to give him the unofficial title of your deputy. Will he meet the resident commissioner before tonight's reception?'

Karan nodded. 'Yes, as soon as the commissioner is ready.' Karan reviewed the list. 'I think you are making a mistake in not appointing Oliver.'

'First minister, my government does not make mistakes in its states and now in its colonies. Your administration will be well served to remember this.' The governor-general's hand was searching under the table. 'Such an ingenious little device. Now, if we have concluded our business, I have some old friends to reconnect with. My wife and I look forward to seeing Isha and you later.'

* * *

In his riverside office, Oliver was making the last-minute adjustiments, pointing at Alessandra to shift the flowers on the table. 'So I have a clear view of the enemy.' They repositioned the nameplates and confirmed where they would both sit. She and

Oliver would have their backs to the window to give their guests the distraction of the London skyline.

Alessandra interrupted his final checks. 'They're almost here.'

'Right, I'll go down.'

Alessandra furrowed her brow.

Oliver continued, 'I didn't agree to the departmental bigwigs' plan to stay up here. Your permanent secretary might have been trained at some snooty, tight-arse diplomatic academy.' Oliver was walking out of the door with Alessandra trailing. 'But Karan and I are from Yorkshire. We are polite to our guests.' Oliver paused. 'Well, at least initially.' Oliver made it to the front door of his department as a cavalcade of cars with blacked-out windows appeared. Waterloo Bridge was deserted. Closed to all traffic and pedestrians by the soldiers at either end.

'Resident commissioner.' Oliver held out his hand but was struck speechless by the handsome thirty-something Indian politician who got out of the car. He felt a rush of blood to the head and turned round to Alessandra, 'Can you call the lift, please?' Alessandra saw him blush and couldn't quite understand what he was doing. The interlude had given Oliver enough time to turn back and ask, 'I suppose you're horribly jet-lagged coming in on an overnight flight?'

'Ah.' Arun smiled. It was a genuine, honest smile. The smile, Oliver sensed, of a friend. 'Ah, that's what you hope. So you can beat us into submission, minister? No, I'm fine. We took the prime minister's jet—India Force One or something, she calls it. I spent the night watching reruns of comedy shows.'

'You'll be surprised to know the first minister and I watched a Mumbai show last night. Raksha—'

'Chowdree? No! I was there last night. Kya aapka Hindi bol sakte?

'Nahi, commissioner.'

'Arun, please.'

'No. But Karan, I mean the first minister, and I are old friends. And there is probably not an Indian comedian he and I haven't watched together.'

‘Well, minister, that is unexpected. The governor-general will be disappointed we already have a common interest.’ Arun chuckled.

The lift doors opened, ‘Oliver, please, we are going to spend rather a great deal of time together, I fear.’ Oliver could see how happy his team were and how Arun’s were not. Arun turned to see them too and quietened himself down.

Sitting down, Arun introduced the many officials he had been sent with. ‘My colleagues from the office of the governor-general are keen that we make considerable progress on integration. They will be assisting me in these, and all, meetings. And will, of course, ensure the governor-general is fully aware of the state of all ongoing negotiations.’ Arun winked at Oliver.

Oliver was sure no one had noticed. His pulse had definitely increased, and it was nothing to do with the process of integration. He was probably fifteen years older than Arun and about to start some of the most significant negotiations in the history of his country. It didn’t help, he supposed, to have someone pretty to look at. ‘Well, thank you, commissioner. Shall we begin? I know our teams have taken the discussions as far as they feel they can. I’m told your officials are fiendish negotiators and mine believe we have given all we can at this stage.’ Oliver glanced over and was happy to see smiles on the faces of Arun’s overseers from his faint praise.

Arun had opened the folder in front of him and was reviewing its contents. He turned to his speaking notes with a large, double-spaced font and began to read a stilted English, ‘We had expected that more progress would have been made than this, minister.’ His officials had returned to their resting faces, a mixture of inscrutability and indifference.

‘Commissioner, I assure you our teams have made excellent progress. We have examined bank liabilities, new asset classes, an early assessment of the first-year costs of integration, based on our current spending rate. If you are willing for us to offer the increased settlements we have suggested to the companies being expropriated, we believe we will clear many of the legal hurdles we have identified. We will make much more rapid progress now you are in position—and once we are clear about your priorities for integration as well as the strategy for avoiding challenge.'

Arun closed his folder. 'Minister, the beauty for us of integration that the legal issues are for your state government to worry about. My government cannot be held liable in England's courts for the first minister's administration.' Arun was enjoying this little rush of power over an Englishman. Albeit a more attractive one than he had expected. 'How can your businesses be expropriated when the legal basis for their continued operation has fundamentally ceased? They do not have an operating environment in which to work. We have not, as I understand it,' Arun was watching his team, who were nodding pre-emptively, and thumbing through his papers, 'yet agreed the mobile spectrum English companies will be able to use; similarly the subsidies for your green energy sector have yet to be approved by the Indian cabinet; nor have they determined what your critical national infrastructure is. Or how the UK will support Indian industry through preferential purchasing, never mind our defence commitments. In these circumstances, I would have thought that some soon-to-be-loss-making enterprises would be happy to relinquish their liabilities for the promise of more lucrative business in the months to come. Much like Merchant's.'

'Poor Merchant's, some might say,' Oliver replied.

'Lucky bastards, I would say, minister. They got out and back in fast. So many more British companies will see the benefit of integration soon enough. There are prizes for being first in this race.'

Oliver closed the file in front of him. 'Commissioner, this isn't how we run government in England.'

'Minister, it is now. I've been sent here to onshore business to continental India. And that's what our teams must deliver. Now, have you effected the transfer of the telecom businesses?'

Oliver watched his team. One nodded.

Arun focused on Oliver and asked, 'All of them?'

The aide replied, 'Yes, commissioner.'

Arun asked, 'And you've, I hope, kept the debts in the residual English business?'

Oliver nodded reluctantly.

'Thank you for this. I have this additional list from the prime minister's office.'

Oliver interrupted, 'You mean first minister's office? I am making that mistake at the moment too.'

'No,' Arun replied. 'My officials take their orders directly from the Indian prime minister—as your first minister does.' Arun handed over the list.

Oliver's eyes widened. 'We cannot give Isha's father Heathrow airport. It would be illegal.'

Arun replied, 'I'm trying to make clear to you, minister, the people in this room make the laws now. So how can this be illegal? Can your officials make this happen? It has been made abundantly clear to me this is a singular priority for our prime minister.'

Oliver inspected his team along the table. None wanted to catch his eye. Alessandra gave the tiniest bob. In turn, Oliver nodded.

Arun smiled, 'Great work. A particularly good first session, I think?' It was a question of sorts. Arun's team nodded enthusiastically while Oliver's put him in mind of a herd of gazelle trying to signal the risks of the predators all around them. Arun stood, forcing his team to do the same. As they made their way out, He asked Oliver, 'May we speak privately, minister?' Arun's most senior official made to stay with him, but Arun shuffled him out of the doorway.

Oliver noticed this manoeuvre and replied, 'Of course. In fact, why don't my colleagues give yours a tour of the building? There are some excellent views of central London from the other side of the office.' Once they left, Oliver shut the door firmly.

Arun was marvelling at the view from Oliver's office. 'My family have had a home here for over fifty years. Most of my favourite memories are in this city. We love London. I love it.' Arun moved closer to Oliver. 'I don't think either of us particularly wants to be here doing this. Let's make it as painless as possible.' Oliver gazed far down the Thames. He was unsure how to respond and unsure whether to look at Arun. Arun grabbed his elbow. 'There are more important things in life to worry about, are there not?' and smiled at Oliver, who found himself admiring that open, genuine smile once again. Arun continued to look out over the Thames. 'How far along the river can we see?'

* * *

When the lift doors opened, Molly was hit by the unremitting shrieks of paper being shredded. At every cubicle, and in every office, a mixture of secretarial staff and managers were busy chucking paper down the greedy throats of the machines.

'Molly,' Jonathan shouted, 'we have a bit of emergency admin to do. Can you dump the shredded paper in the bins, please. Someone from the team will help you.' Leaning in he told her, 'For God's sake make sure that the stuff they are destroying is unreadable, will you?'

'What's going on?' she whispered.

Jonathan walked her to the windows. 'Let's say some of Merchant's buccaneering spirit wasn't too successful. Or necessarily wholeheartedly legal. And that we've had to fund some of our intelligence-led expansion across southeast Asia from less than wholesome sources.'

Molly tried to look surprised. 'What, Russia? China? Iran?'

'Do any of us care? But yes, something like that. Now we have a chance with a new owner and a new regimen to clean up the books. Make sure none of this stuff ever makes the light of day, will you?' Jonathan walked her back. 'These bags,' he was pointing at some unremarkable grey sacks, 'have some of our most sensitive documents. Take these downstairs to the super-shredder yourself, would you?'

'Super-shredder?' Molly asked.

'You'll see. Basement three. Asked Kenny to let you in.'

Molly pushed the trolley laden with the bags into the lift and watched the frenzied staff delete, destroy, deny whatever it was that Merchant's had been up to. In the basement Kenny gave her a pass. 'Super-shredder is in there. No cameras, by the way.' Kenny winked and left her.

Molly turned on the massive machine. It hummed and beeped and begged her for some lubricating oil, which she dosed liberally along its teeth. A poster on the wall warned that it should only be used by authorised individuals and that 'cross-cutting shredding was for only the most sensitive documents'. Molly pulled a handful out and read them. This first bunch was a series of ledgers with funding flowing into the bank in the tens of millions. All from nameless Iranian and Russian accounts. Molly took photos of the most interesting files and began to shred. The next bundle were emails following the financial crash with the bank asking for further extensions on their loan period and agreeing to aggressive, and definitely unprofitable, interest rates. Molly took more photos. And shredded. A final bunch was the bank's senior managers agreeing to evade sanctions and regulatory rules with money from the same countries as well as China and India. One name, Sunil Grover, was prominent on many documents, showing that Sunil had been betting against the pound for a long time. She took more images and reluctantly shredded the documents. She was sure she was committing a series of crimes in most jurisdictions around the world. Finished, she forwarded the images and deleted them from her phone.

Back on the trading floor, work had stopped. People were watching the rolling news coverage of the protests across London. 'If the Indians thought they would easily take over England, then Londoners are sending them a message. Across the city's parks, and in the city itself, tens of thousands of people are coming together to protest the loss of freedom and their country. The substantial risk for the police is that these groups shift from protest to violence. We are already seeing pockets of aggression across the capital.' The coverage shifted to show groups of individuals breaking into shops and businesses across the city. It continued, 'We are seeing large numbers of heavily armed police, and some people say military personnel, on the streets today. It's clear the first minister wants to begin his administration with a show of strength. It's a big gamble, but probably the only strategy he can adopt in these early days.'

The news had live coverage of businesses across London's square mile being trashed. Glass-fronted head offices were easy targets. A thick cordon of officers continued to protect the Bank of Britain as well as inhibit new protesters from entering the city. Much of which was already overrun with angry activists. Their temporary headquarters were being set up directly round the corner from Merchant's. One group had managed to break into one of the shimmering towers of mammon and unfurl a banner from the twenty-fifth floor, 'Indians Out. Karan Out. England for the English.'

Molly and her colleagues were now receiving regular text updates from the police as well as Merchant's own security team. They had hoped that Merchant's relatively underwhelming offices would go unnoticed by the majority of the protesters but a small and determined group had started to gather outside and sprayed, 'All bankers are cunts,' on the white Portland stone. Reading the message, Jonathan added, 'It's hardly Banksy. I should know; I have two in the house in Chichester.' All of the updates reassured the bank's staff that the police were in control of the situation. The bridges had been secured. They were told it would take some time to remove all the most violent activists, 'staff should remain in their offices and await a further update.'

Molly made herself and Jonathan a cup of tea and sat down to watch the news reports. 'We understand that a large number of self-described anarchists have been able to evade the police and join the protests in the city since the cordons have been set up. These individuals are solely intent on causing as much damage as possible under the cover of legitimate protest.'

'What the actual fuck is legitimate about that?' Jonathan pointed out of the window to the acrid black smoke billowing towards them and the hundreds of people charging the police and running away when mounted officers charged back. 'Someone's going to get killed out there,' he continued. 'But check this out,' he showed Molly his phone, 'someone's bought Heathrow airport.'

* * *

Isha was watching Karan fiddle with his black tie in the back of the car. Finally, she knew her father had made the right decision after all. So many of her friends had found men who became successful businessmen and gave them a life of luxury. They'd spend their days chairing the company foundation, joining glamorous international advisory boards of this museum or that. But not Isha. She and Karan had to work. She, in particular, had to work. Her diligence was a stipulation in her father's considerable allowance for the pair. But checking out her successful husband, tonight as handsome as when they first met, she knew they'd made the right decision.

Karan spotted her examining the bottle-green velvet dress she'd made herself. 'Yes, you're gorgeous. And all eyes will be on you tonight!'

'All eyes will be on both of us, my darling.' She kissed him, then wiped off the lipstick. 'Why are we going so fast all of a sudden?'

'Manishji has closed the roads around St James's Park. Government traffic only.'

'Excellent. One day of the Indians in charge and we are all in the vip lane. You watch, they'll be charging us for this, like the Mumbai toll. I don't know why your government didn't close these roads off to the plebs sooner. We will never need to worry about traffic again.'

Karan's mind was on the even greater numbers of troops lining the roads. 'Where have they all come from?' he thought. 'What should they be guarding?' At least the settlement that was now becoming permanent inside St James's Park didn't appear to be violent. 'What traffic problems did we have? Umesh is always good at finding a rat run.' Umesh smiled and caught Karan's eye in the rear-view mirror. 'Now we're limiting the rights of English citizens—Londoners—to drive in the centre of their own city.'

'I don't think there are any English citizens any more—haven't you made us all Indian, and pretty much overnight?' While Karan thought about it, she continued, 'Pitaji asked me to thank you for his gift.'

'What gift? What have you bought him now?'

'Heathrow.'

'Are you fucking kidding? I didn't agree to it. In fact, I expressly told Oliver not to accede to that. It's all too fast.' Karan grabbed his phone. 'How did that happen? And what will he ask for next?'

Isha took the phone off him. 'Calm the fuck down. Pause. Remember how we got here. Everyone has to pay the piper eventually.'

'More like puppet master.'

'Please, Karan. Pitaji deserves it. So do we. All those years I've been waiting for you to be seen to be successful in their eyes. And boom. You've done it. Do you know how many women have been forced into my designs tonight?'

'I hope there's scaffolding round them,' Karan teased. 'The pressure in some of those dresses will be like a small nuclear reactor.'

'We even had a rush order from Manishji's wife. I sent one of the seamstresses from christian street to stitch her into it. I hope she hasn't fucked it up. You know they can't speak much English.'

'You told me they can't speak any English. And that's why you pay them almost nothing.'

Umesh had put on the blue lights and pushed to the front of the long queue of super cars. All the Mayfair showrooms had emptied for the night, and all the playboys were out in them.

Isha waved to the women sporting her latest creations. 'Look there's another one, Karan!' Karan tried to look neither interested nor embarrassed. 'The thing is,' she continued, 'Pitaji's airport is merely the start. The girls' husbands have all sent Delhi a list of favours as thick as one of your college textbooks. They'll pay over the odds for them. I want to know what we will get out of all this.' Karan's lacklustre reply was drowned out by Umesh winding down the window to let them hear the band play bollywood hits. 'Tum se hi!' Isha shouted. 'My favourite!'

Karan turned to her. 'Like the song says, I don't know what's happening. But I hope we get our country back in one piece someday.'

A red-coated liveryman came to collect them, forcing Isha into silence. 'First minister, Mrs Puri, would you care to follow me.'

The quadrangle, now clear of that day's cars, was filled with performers and flaming braziers. Above them, acrobats were shooting from one side of the square to another on bicycles over undetectable high wires. Thousands of drones where high in the evening sky, morphing from the tiranga to the new anglo-indian standard of Britain. Every now and again they would attempt the face of the Indian prime minister. Though she appeared to be scowling down at them. In the now-red-and-gold foyers, bharatanatyam dancers were accompanied by a celebrated English tabla player. Karan glanced around. 'The only white faces are the waiting staff.'

'Wonderful, isn't it,' she sneered. 'It's liberating. Finally equal at last.'

'I'm not sure that's what the people outside feel.'

'Ah, but you're the insider's insider now.' Isha grabbed a glass of champagne and milled around the pre-reception, smiling at women judging how many calories Isha's designs would allow them to consume.

The aide returned and escorted them up the stairs, past another set of performers. From Odisha,' he told Karan. 'His excellency had them flown in specially.'

Karan studied the young cloakroom attendants waiting patiently for some customers. Tonight's crowd could buy and sell the palace for staff. No doubt some tens of people were waiting outside to minister to each individual guest's whim the minute they left. More Indian miniatures from what had been the royal collection erased any sense of Britishness from the artwork on display. The aide left them at the base of the horseshoe-shaped grand staircase under its glass-domed roof. He whispered, 'The first minister' to a disinterested, lanky member of staff who in turn handed Karan's presentation card to a colleague manning the flimsy red cord, which restricted access to the most distinguished dignitaries. Mere vips formed a lengthy procession on the opposite side. Framed by old masters, they were more interested in calculating why they had not been given vvip treatment. For most it was a repeat visit. For everyone, it was the first visit under new management. Oliver and Arun were at the top of the stairs. Isha shouted, 'Arun Bhai. I didn't know they were sending you.'

Arun waved, excused himself from Oliver and headed down. He planted a big kiss on her cheek and leant into her left ear. 'It's like ghungroo all over again.'

She replied, 'Where's that awful boy you always went home with?' Isha guffawed, forcing both sides of the horseshoe to look at the pair of them as Arun shook Karan's hand and added, 'It's a pleasure to meet you, first minister.'

Karan replied, 'And you, commissioner. I see you know my wife pretty well.'

Isha's arms were around Arun's waist as she shouted, 'He was a keen participant in my misspent youth in Delhi.' Grabbing his hand, she pulled Arun up the stairs and away from Karan and Oliver. 'Let's go in together and leave those two. They haven't spoken in about four hours so they've no doubt much to gossip about. You don't mind, do you, darling?'

Karan watched Isha push her way to the top of the stairs. He stopped Oliver. 'Look, I can't make you chancellor, you're blocked.'

Oliver peered at his shoes. 'Is it the gay thing?

Karan continued, 'No. At best he's a typical alpha-male delhiwallah dickhead. Don't be downcast. I owe all this to you. We have agreed you'll be my deputy. My eyes and ears. God knows I need it.'

'You know I'll do whatever is needed,' Oliver replied. 'I assume he had some other candidates he has forced you to take?'

'Yes, he wanted a sycophant. He gave me a list of five to choose from. I told him in that case I won't appoint a chancellor. I'd do both jobs and needed you as my deputy.'

'Five!' Oliver whispered. 'I couldn't find you two people from our party today I'd trust to run a bath, never mind the integration of our economy with a sadly, much larger, Indian one.'

'Don't overthink this. I'm not appointing a chancellor. It will have to be you and me. We'll sideline all of his appointments. Isha has commandeered both apartments above Downing Street so that's gone, I'm afraid. You can have anything else you want.'

Oliver pulled Karan into a niche at the top of the staircase. 'Okay. But why did you put troops on the street? It's completely the wrong message. I'm taking a lot of flak from the party and I'm struggling to justify it. I agreed to it when it came in last night as I was told it came from you. But I told the team to leave implementing it until we spoke.'

'Who told you that?' Karan whispered. 'One day in, and we are not in control of this situation.' Oliver nodded. Karan continued, 'We can't let anyone know that things are already out of hand. I don't know who formally put the troops on the streets. I assume that the order came from here. But how did they get into the army chain of command? I asked my team if I had missed anything in Richardson's final acts. You know he wet the bed getting his knighthood. It's all the poor bastard had ever wanted.'

Oliver grabbed two glasses of champagne. 'Nor do I know how the transfer of Heathrow went through. I thought we'd agreed to sit on it for as long as we could.'

'Me either.' Karan sipped the drink. 'He's serving the decent stuff tonight. Not like one of Albert's cheap nights in. I need you to find out what the fuck is going on and slow down as much of the madness as you can. Stay out of ten downing and away from as many of them as possible.' Karan pointed over at where Arun had been. 'That appeared cosy. You also moving fast on day one? On a date?'

Oliver smiled. 'Maybe. I'm not sure. He was a surprise, to say the least. And we've had some useful side chats. I don't think he's completely on board with their project. And anyway, you are taken.'

Karan pointed to his heart. 'Only here.' Discreetly gesturing to Arun, he added, 'Yes, I think he will be helpful. Sunil has always been cagey about Rahul Bhai and his family. They are far more than competitors. They're bitter rivals. So I can't quite work out why he's been sent to us.'

'I assume he's here so one of Usha's main rivals is deeper in the blood and mire of all of this.' Oliver walked over to Isha and Arun, who were deep in Delhi gupshup.

Karan teased, 'I'd no idea my wife was going to reintegrate as part of this process. The pair of you look like you have been talking down most of the people in here. I don't know you well enough, resident commissioner, but I'm willing to ask my wife, whose reputation have you been traducing?'

Arun smiled. 'You know me too well, first minister. Isha and I were reminiscing about our misspent youth. She made me party twice as hard as I studied.'

'But we got through.'

'By the skin of our teeth,' Arun reminded her. 'Don't you have formal duties to undertake tonight, first minister?'

'No, in fact, quite the opposite. I'm pretty much a common or garden guest here. My predecessor always complained about attending commonwealth summits. A vast collection of prime ministers waiting for Albert to appear following yet another costume change.'

They laughed and Isha asked, 'Can you hear the trumpets? I think we should shuffle to the white drawing room.' Isha led them to the crowd as a wall-size mirror opened.

'Had someone cracked it, that would be decidedly inauspicious,' Arun told her.

'Hold on,' and as if by magic the governor-general appeared from behind the mirror, accompanied by his wife in shimmering jewels and a dress designed by Isha.

'That's not?' Isha asked.

'It can't be,' Karan replied.

'Haha. It's the fucking koh-i-noor! She's hit the jackpot!' Oliver replied.

'Shhhh,' Karan told them as people turned round.

An aide came over. 'First minister, the governor-general asks if you and Mrs Puri might join him at the unveiling.'

'The what?' Karan asked.

'The governor-general has confirmed a few final tweaks to his personal standard and is unveiling it tonight.'

'That fucking man.' Arun said to Karan. 'He has some fetish for symbols of power. It's why Ushaji has chosen him. Wherever he has been posted, his first question is about the flags.'

Drums and trumpets sounded the start of 'Jana Gana Mana,' allowing the crowd to separate like the parting of a stage curtain. At the far end of the gallery the grandiloquent governor-general and his wife were standing by their own blue-liveried equerries.

Karan asked, 'What are we being shown?'

The aide replied, 'You can see the new anglo-indian standard. Beside it is a deep-blue one adorned with the gold crest of India.'

'And what is that?'

'That's the governor-general's personal standard. He will have all of us in that deep-blue uniform over the next few days.'

Isha whispered, 'Do you think I should fit out the palace staff too?'

Karan gaped at her. 'No, I fucking don't. This is beyond ridiculous. Here we are debating personal standards, and the city is about to catch fire.'

* * *

Merchant's Saturday staff were glued to the televisions in the bank's groundfloor reception area. Molly watched the eldest members pace from side to side. She moaned to Jonathan, 'They've abandoned us here. They've bloody left us here like sitting ducks. The police will never get this under control. We could be here all night.' Pointing at Jonathan's phone, she asked, 'Anything on there from them?'

'Nothing, I think they've given up and clocked off for dinner.'

'Fuck this.' Molly stood up and checked her phone again. 'I have places to go even if you don't. I'm taking my chances.' She grabbed her bag and started to make her way across Merchant's marble floor to the front door.

'Hold up,' Jonathan shouted. 'I'm coming with you. But we'll need to go out the back way. I think there's a fire exit. The front's been secured—by us and them.' Jonathan and Molly slipped out on to an empty back street. Round the corner the main entrance to the bank had been barricaded by their security company and was being bombarded by activists and protesters. The disconnected and dissonant chants and drums of the different groups of protesters hit Molly loudly and forcefully, like waves crashing against her. Molly's heart was racing. She stopped to catch her breath. 'You okay?' Jonathan asked.

She put her hand in his pocket. 'I think it might be better if we look like we're a couple in the wrong place at the wrong time rather than a pair of wanker bankers.' Jonathan put his arm around her and squeezed. She smiled. At the end of the lane Molly looked at Jonathan.

He paused, 'It's 50-50 kid,' adding, 'both look pretty shitty. But either way ends with you buying me a large and exceedingly fucking expensive drink.'

She squeezed back and giggled, then nodded her head left. The crashing rhythm of the drums was getting louder and louder, like they were about to find a whole orchestral percussion section round the corner. Molly saw one particularly proficient and angry young man smashing drumsticks against upturned plastic buckets.

He'd lit a fire in a metal bin beside him and was drinking liberally from a bottle of vodka. Another bottle had a bit of cloth sticking out the top of it. The drummer glared through them. He was high and ready to fight.

Handfuls of terrified people like Molly and Jonathan were trying to make their way across the city to the nearest and safest exit. They all walked like they were in some combination of open prison and grim reality television show. 'Brave souls?' Molly asked.

'Idiots, more like,' Jonathan replied, adding, 'Let's keep our heads down.' Molly walked over to the ring of officers around the private members' club they'd been to.

'I'm going to ask them the best way out of here.' She came back frowning. 'Not one of those fuckers would speak to me. They look weird to me. Police should each have an identifiable number. None of them do. Nor can I tell you what these guys are. And the guns aren't standard police issue either. Those are assault weapons. Stuff our soldiers use on actual battlefields. Not common or garden city bobbies.'

Jonathan watched her closely. 'How do you know that?

'I try to do my homework. I admit it doesn't look like that today. His earpiece crackled into life when I was speaking to him, and it sounded like the best way out would be to head east and try to get on the tube at Whitechapel. I think more protesters are coming over the bridges.'

'They're not protesters. They're fucking animals.' Jonathan pointed at the smashed buildings all around them. 'They've started so many fires even the air is black. It's like a war zone.'

* * *

The hubbub of the rich and connected was drowning out the string quartet Arun was pointing up at. 'Classical music from a fucking minstrel's gallery, no less. Manishji really has settled himself right in.'

'And he appears to have an eye for Albert's premier cru wines.' Oliver was reviewing the menu card as Arun gawped at the footman's knee-high black breeches and reached for one of the anglo-indian fusion canapés. 'A state of pure luxurious excess.'

'I think we call it diplomacy over here. But yes, I'm sure we're both happy that none of our constituents can see us in action. Much better to keep all this out of sight.' Arun had walked them over to Victoria's golden piano.

'Is that all you keep out of sight?' Arun had a twinkle in his eye. 'Do you have a wife or partner?'

'I'm sure you've done your homework on me and know I'm gay.' Arun raised his hand to his open mouth, then smiled, as Oliver continued, 'But I know nothing about you. I didn't even know you liked to drink. In fact, I think your media profile says you are a teetotaller.'

Arun took a long swig. 'You need to do some primary research then. Every good hindu politician will have that added to their profile somewhere. Let's say we are all more layered than you would expect.'

Karan joined them. 'I've had an inspection of the governor-general's new standard. He's opted for viceroy Mountbatten's blue and added India's lions.'

Arun spat out some whisky as he coughed, 'The Ashoka lions? He is shameless. And lucky for you, I don't think he has the wisdom of Ashoka.'

Oliver nodded when Karan added, 'I'm being asked to attend a briefing on the situation in the city. Do you want to join me?'

Arun downed the last of his drink. 'By the look on your face, I think I should come too.' Karan paused and turned to Oliver, who shrugged his shoulders.

Seb appeared at Karan's side and escorted them from the reception. 'A backstage tour,' Arun said expectantly. Seb squeezed the four of them into a creaky 1930s lift around which a red-carpeted staircase spiralled. As the lift approached the third floor, Karan could see an unmistakable, tight fitting tailored skirt.

'Dame Rebecca, you do pop up in the strangest of places.' Karan smiled.

'Quite, first minister. Something about we must stop meeting like this. Ah, I'm pleased you've brought the resident commissioner. Your grandfather and my father knew each other intimately, commissioner.'

'Really?'

Dame Rebecca marched off. 'Yes, my father was one of the few British officers who stayed on after independence. He had spotted that your grandfather was likely to become an important person in free India and, let's say, cultivated him. I remember he had a particular love of—'

'British crime novels.' They finished the sentence together as Dame Rebecca opened the door to a room of turquoise-painted walls decked with Chinese tapestries. An upturned lotus chandelier hung above a wooden table on which one of Dame Rebecca's staff had set up a large monitor. She started, 'First minister, you have become aware that the policing presence across the city was bolstered with support from the military.'

'Yes, Dame Rebecca, and in time I would like to know how that happened.'

'Yes, we would too. But you should also know that further supernumerary troops have been deployed on the streets this afternoon and evening. We believe they came with the governor-general and are Indian military. British soldiers have been given access to high-powered, non-standard assault weaponry. We believe this is being described as an opportunity to test force interoperability.'

'This is just what Manishji did when he was lieutenant governor in Kashmir.' Arun added.

'Precisely, commissioner. As I said, I'm extremely glad you are here.'

'Now the issue is, first minister, we believe that eight disparate protest groups are converging on the city.' Dame Rebecca's staffer pulled up images of the groups on screen. 'We have limited visibility of their actual plans as they are communicating via a Chinese-built app, which I'm afraid to say we cannot intercept.'

Karan scrutinised Dame Rebecca. 'How much of this have you shared with the governor-general?'

'Nothing, first minister, and unless you tell me otherwise, I do not intend to share anything with him. We now believe he is tasking the police and the military directly, orders they have to follow under Indian government constitutional protocol as well as the standard British chain of command. But my service reports to you, and only you. I have taken the liberty of recommending that MI6 also report directly to you for the foreseeable future. Simon, can we go to live images please?'

'Shit,' Karan uttered as they watched images of thousands of protesters attacking businesses across the city. 'Why is the footage so grainy?'

'We have turned our satellites on to the protestors. But the smoke from the fires is now so great it's affecting the quality,' Simon replied.

'First minister, eight separate groups are now converging on the city. It's not just that they are using a Chinese app, we believe they have received funding from Chinese agents. The groups are unlikely to know the source of that funding. But we have been following agents in Little China for some time now and can confidently assess that China is supporting individuals who want to bring down what was the British state. We believe tonight's coordinated disorder is the first in a series of campaigns designed to undermine law and order.'

'Do you think the Indians know this?'

Dame Rebecca nodded. 'Yes, we believe they can intercept the Chinese communications app. We also believe they have allowed the Chinese agitation to get out of hand to lead to an extreme Indian response. It's highly likely you will see the deliberate killing and targeting of English citizens in the next couple of hours.'

'What can we do to stop it?' Karan asked.

'This is the nub of the problem, first minister. We don't think you can do anything. You are not in control of this situation.'

* * *

Hundreds of protesters were crossing London's bridges. Shouting and jeering as they walked over the bascules of Tower Bridge and defiantly chanting at the new Chinese embassy. Picking up cones and trying to free bits of kerb stones on the way to London Bridge. Smashing windows of the Georgian houses unlucky enough to sit at the entrance to Southwark Bridge. And testing the giant dampers on Millennium Bridge as they raced across it under the unwitting protection of the dome of St Paul's. Much younger people, amassed on Southbank, received a message to cycle over Waterloo and Blackfriars. The front of these two-wheeler armies set off fireworks to let the others know they were coming.

Each group's target was the Bank of Britain and anything they could hit along the way. The long lines of protesters were coming together like independent tentacles of an octopus. Messages were being sent to tens of thousands of people to join in, attack, destroy and then liberate the colonised people of England.

The police and military were three-deep at lombard and fenchurch, successfully repelling one of the arms. Projectiles were raining down on them. They had received precise instructions to hold the Bank of Britain at all costs. Security reinforcements were swarming into the city. Mounted support was near too. They could hear helicopters overhead. Twenty-nine-year-old sergeant Ian Kershaw was on the frontline, baton in one hand and shield in another, staring at thousands of people who wanted to kill him. A shadow overhead forced him to look up briefly and see a helicopter remarkably close to them. He asked his senior, 'Has that been hit?'

'No,' came the reply. 'It's landing. We are bringing in the big guns.'

The chinook landed on the lush green lawn of the royal artillery company. An initial deployment of forty Indian parachute regiment and British special forces soldiers jumped out. Royal Marine captain Mark Sutherland barked at his troops, 'Another joint deployment of eighty British and Indians is landing in the next ten minutes. Remember, we are here to provide operational support to the police. I do not expect any of you to discharge weapons in almost any circumstances. Is that understood?' The chinook took off as Sutherland and his team were driven out at speed.

An angry soundtrack demanding the immediate end of Indian rule thundered across the city. Smoke billowed in all directions from the looted and burnt-out buildings. Police cars sped past. Molly's eyes were stinging from the pungent smoke. Jonathan told her, 'I don't know if we'll make it all the way to Whitechapel. Should we try one of the bridges?'

'No,' Molly replied. 'I think the bridges are how they,' Molly pointed at the violence all around them, 'are getting in. We have to keep heading east.' She pulled her collar up and put her head down. Jonathan followed reluctantly.

In his earpiece, sergeant Kershaw heard, 'From our sources in the crowd, we expect the first charge to come at lombard. The helicopters can't see shit.' He felt his legs bend as the earpiece continued, 'Additional support is being sent there. Mounted division also attending.'

Kershaw's senior officer glanced at him. 'Don't worry, son. This will all be over in a few minutes. Mark my words. Remember, just hold the line. We've got your back.'

The protesters' behaviour had hardened. Sergeant Kershaw could see what he assumed were the main organisers marshalling people into formation. Handing out what he thought were guns. Kershaw subconsciously touched his body armour. 'First time out with it and I'm about to find out just how good this kit is,' he thought. He could see people holding lit vodka bottles. 'Molotov cocktails, we used to call them,' his senior added. 'Shitty little things if they hit you.'

Captain Sutherland had arrived at the back of the group and was pushing his way forward, 'Who's in charge here?'

'I am, sir,' Kershaw heard his senior reply.

'I have forty well-trained marines and paras here. We'll be directly behind you. I have told my troops we do not intend to fire. But we will hold the line for your officers to repel the first charge. You're going to go in hard and beat the shit out of a few of them. You do know that, don't you?'

'Don't worry, sir. I served in Belfast. This will all be over in a few minutes. A few broken bones and these little kids will be shitting themselves all the way back to the apartments mummy and daddy pay for.'

Kershaw jeered at the privileged protesters. All the briefings on these groups repeated the same thing. The far left had ample money to fall back on. The far right, though, had been told they were working-class heroes. Caught up in a great struggle for British identity and freedom. 'Well, how had that worked out,' Kershaw thought. 'Here we are fucking Indian. And my arse is covered by forty fucking Indians behind me.' Something crashed around him. Could have been a firework but the smell of petrol told him it was the first of a volley of fiery vodka bottles. Instinctively, he'd raised his shield. 'Training works,' he thought. The rioters were throwing bottles like archers at Agincourt. Kershaw and his colleagues were taking direct hits. 'Officer down. Officer hit' was all he heard on his earpiece. The smoke burnt to the back of his eyes as they heard the noise of a thousand charging feet. The rioters vastly outnumbered them. But then he remembered he had a baton and was expected to use it.

'Wait for it,' his senior shouted.

The mob ran towards Kershaw screaming and throwing whatever they could at him from all directions. Kershaw kept his shield up and watched his colleagues do the same. 'Where are the dogs?' He thought. Then the crack of gunshot. 'Was it our side or theirs?' he shouted and searched around for confirmation. 'Who is down?'

A rioter fell screaming. Blood streaming from his leg. Some of the rioters stopped their charge. One shouted, 'They're fucking shooting at us. With real bullets.' Others retraced their steps. A hardy couple of hundred kept going. Kershaw could see the hatred in their eyes. They were maybe fifty feet away. Thirty. Twenty. He swung his baton and hit as many as he could. Bodies fell all round him like leaves from the trees. Bruised, battered and beaten. Kershaw could hear Sutherland shout, 'Who fired? Who the fuck fired? I did not authorise that.' Then a command on the earpiece, 'Make way for the horses.' Kershaw thought it sounded like 'make hay', and had a smile as they all pulled to the side and thirty mounted horses charged the few rioters who were standing their ground. They were knocked down like skittles at a bowling alley.

'Move in,' Kershaw's senior shouted at them and, as the drills kicked in, his body did exactly as it was told and had been trained to do. They followed in behind the horses and mopped up the odds and sods littering the street. Arrests were made. Sutherland was at the young man who'd been shot, putting a dressing round his smashed leg—a gaping hole where a functioning kneecap had recently been.

Molly and Jonathan could tell something had changed. Hundreds of rioters were heading towards them from both directions. Some were running from something. Heads bleeding. Eyes bulging. Noses broken. 'They're shooting at us,' one shouted. 'Fucking shooting at us.' The thugs and vandals in the crowd had expected this and were waiting for the fight. Others were giving makeshift first-aid to those who'd been hit. The tentacles were starting to gather together all around Molly and Jonathan. Mounted horses appeared at the end of the street. Molly screamed as the sky overhead was lit with burning vodka bottles, which smashed around her. 'Jonathan, I've made a terrible mistake.' They were surrounded by patriots chanting for England's freedom.

Someone grabbed Molly's coat and asked, 'All right, darling. A bit smart for a riot. Fancy a fuck?' Jonathan punched and floored him. The boy jumped up to fight back when his friend told him, 'You deserved that, mate. Leave him and take it out on the pigs.' Molly had never felt smaller. Enveloped. They were being crushed by hate. The pressure on them growing second by second. Jonathan pushed to get them on to the pavement where it somehow felt safer. But the activists kept them in their place in the middle of the melee.

Molly cried, 'I've really fucked this up.'

'Don't worry. We're in no worse shape than they are.' Jonathan could see a few other ashen-faced bank workers. Struggling to work out how best to get out of their predicament.

'No, I may as well tell you.' Jonathan focused on her. 'I'm not a banker. I'm a journalist. I'm probably more one of these people than one of yours.' She pointed around her. 'I'd been sent on a long assignment to uncover exactly where Merchant's got its money after the crash.'

'Fuck sake, Molly.' Jonathan's eyes were wide and his mouth open. 'Is that even your name?'

She nodded, 'Yes, we decided none of you were interested enough to do any actual research on me. So yes, it's Molly. Different surname but what does that matter now.'

'And the fuck on your first night? Was that just to gather more colour for your article? Lascivious banker boss propo-fucking-sitioned me?'

She peered at him. 'No, that's real. We can do it again if we ever get out of this.'

'Fucking hell. Well, you're fired by the way.'

'Thanks.'

One protester shouted, 'Fuck—check the phones.' Molly was searching for a signal. The same protester shouted, 'What the fuck is bharat telecom?' Molly's phone was going wild with welcome messages, adverts for local restaurants, and the one-time opportunity to upgrade to an Indian tv and internet bundle.

'What a fucking time to take over a mobile phone company! They're tracing us,' rioters shouted. 'The comms app has stopped working. Ditch the phones.' The protesters threw their phones down and stamped on them in an oddly coordinated display of communications security.

Sutherland's reinforcements continued to strengthen the back of the police lines and make their way forward. The recent additions wore much more serious kit. Their faces were fully masked. 'Where are your identification tags?' Sutherland asked when the officers reached him.

'We had a request from Delhi to remove all tags,' commanding officer Bajaj told him. 'Now, let's get these little bastards.' Sutherland could hear the smile in his voice.

* * *

The governor-general was by his new standard, showing off the design to all around him. 'Banerjee, the Chinese ambassador is making his way over. Please afford him no more than five minutes. This is a party, after all. Also, Arun Bhai already seems to have disappeared. He was having animated chats with the gay English one. Will you find out what is going on—the PM will be most interested.'

Lu Quan raised his hands together and brought them to his chest in greeting, 'Namaste, excellency, thank you for tonight's reception. Please accept the compliments of the People's Republic of China on India's most recent acquisition.'

'You're most welcome, ambassador.'

'However,' Lu Quan interrupted, 'we do have some concern that Indianisation—'

'You mean integration, ambassador.'

'Yes, integration, what charming doublespeak. My government worries it might result in extraordinarily little collateral for us. India's colony owes China 100 billion pounds plus interest, excellency. Nuclear power, like much else, was an expensive failure for the British.'

'Ambassador, these are matters for the first minister. Britain's pre-integration obligations are not India's.'

'But, excellency, its assets clearly are. And we are all counting.'

'May I give you a tip, ambassador?' the governor-general lowered his voice. Lu Quan nodded in reverential contemplation. 'From one friendly nation to another, I would stop counting England's failures in defunct currencies. I imagine China will want favourable rates and long-term concessions.' Lu Quan nodded again.

'Good. Then I will have the first minister look at this request. It's not our money after all.'

Karan, Oliver and Arun had returned to the party. Karan approached the governor-general, now free of the Chinese ambassador. 'Excellency, might we have a word? I am still concerned about the decision to deploy troops on the streets tonight. It sends a vastly different signal about integration. It's very much at odds with what I told the house today. Can you recall them now and leave the security of the city to our police?

The governor-general was silent for a moment. 'We did it for our safety, for our personal safety, and for the safety of our Indian democracy. Delhi had received worrying intelligence about anarchists infiltrating protest movements across London. In fact, I have had further worrying news from the Chinese ambassador this evening.'

Karan interrupted him, 'Excellency, we cannot have the government of India operating its own intelligence-gathering here in Britain.'

'First minister, we have known for many years that the English state was at risk of attack from deep inside it. You have suffered leftist attacks on your capitalist ambitions. And rightist attacks on your failure to deal with immigration. Populists on all sides wanted to bring your democracy down for many years. You should all be thankful that the government of India will take all and any necessary steps to protect Indian—and what was English—democracy. And to protect me and you, first minister. Anyway, I understand the little altercation in the city will be over in a few moments.'

'Excellency, might you want to share your intelligence with me?'

'First minister, the matter is being dealt with. I am not your nanny or your ma-baap. I am here to make sure your administration succeeds. This is our first test. And one of us is failing. I don't see any need for this discussion to continue further. You can head home safe tonight in the knowledge that your partnership with India is already providing direct results and personal benefits.' The governor-general waved to his wife at the other side of the picture gallery and left Karan standing.

Karan returned to Oliver as Arun was asking, 'I don't suppose there are any good comedy clubs nearby?' Oliver nodded.

Arun asked, 'Do you want to come too?'

Karan replied, 'No, Lord Banerjee is hosting a small gathering after this. Anyway, I'm fairly certain it would be unseemly for the first minister to be in soho.'

Oliver interrupted, 'Well, Leicester Square.'

'Anyway, what do they say, two's company.' Karan winked at Oliver, making him blush.

Isha joined them and handed Arun her business card. 'Arun Bhai, you have to come see me at the store.' And started to take Karan way, 'Are we going to Banerjee's?'

'Yes, briefly for me. He is beyond unbearable.'

After they left, Oliver asked Arun, 'Well, shall we go?' Arun downed his whisky, and they walked through the picture gallery in full view of the governor-general and Banerjee. Both watched them with interest.

Isha turned to Karan. 'Well, looks like there could be something starting there.'

Karan replied, 'I think so too. He is far too young for Oliver. But we both know he has a type.'

Isha teased, 'I think Arun Bhai does too, judging by his private social media account.'

'Really? You Indians are crazy for a good Englishman, aren't you?'

'Yes, let me show you in the car!'

* * *

The police were squeezing protesters into Molly and Jonathan from all sides. Hundreds more angry and out-of-control people had joined the unruly crowd. Both sides were defiantly preparing for one messy last stand. Black-masked reinforcements had been put on the frontline. Molly was shaking with fear. Jonathan felt it too but was trying not to show as he searched for a route to get them out of harm's way. But harm was coming at them from all directions. The rioters knew this was their last stand. Every possible item had been lifted, lit or repurposed for this final battle. A woman protester shouted, 'Charge these bastards! Freedom or death!' Someone let off what sounded like a firecracker and the rioters ran.

Molly scanned all directions. One of the police had been shot. 'Fuck. Fuck. Fuck,' she shouted. Jonathan tried to hold them back from the charge. But they were dragged forward with the crowd. Molly shouted, 'Get me out of there' to anyone that would listen. But no one did.

The frontline of protesters was fifty yards from the heavily protected riot police. 'Fucking scum,' they chanted and chanted, followed by 'All cops are racist bastards.' The shot officer had been lifted up. Molly could see officers moving out of the way sequentially to the back of the waiting police. His colleagues stood menacingly ready. Batons in their hands. They had all the time in the world. Molly and Jonathan could hear the deep growl of police dogs. Both imagined the heads of cerberus were being unleashed. All around them was the regular thud of a drum. It was the only thing able to slow down Molly's heartbeat.

Canisters exploded. They coughed and spluttered as the grey smoke hung in the air, stung their eyes and tore at the back of their throats. Someone shouted, 'Tear gas', and the rioters put on masks. A few handed wet rags round. One told Molly, 'Put this over your mouth and nose, it'll help.' She coughed. Hers was doused in petrol as much as water. The protesters' eyes were streaming. Their throats closing. Jonathan heard another firecracker and studied the police line to see who had been hit. He felt Molly let go of his hand and glimpsed her moving out of the corner of his eye. She was lying on the floor.

A protester shouted, 'They're fucking shooting at us with assault weapons. Get down. It's the fucking army. The fucking army. It's not plastic bullets.' The bullet had torn a hole right through Molly's stomach. Blood was pouring out of her.

Someone shouted, 'We need a doctor or a nurse. This girl is dying.'

Jonathan was at her side and instinctively pressing against the wound, 'We need help here,' he shouted. But no one came. Molly's blood covered the street around them. An incarnadine stain marking the death of English freedoms. Already weak, she tried to speak. Jonathan leant forward. 'Don't speak, love. It will be okay.'

She tried again and he leant beside her ear. 'Take my mobile. My name's Molly Stevens, please.' Her body went limp. As the panicked rioters ran from the police, Jonathan put her phone in his pocket.

'Right back to their mummies and daddies,' sergeant Kershaw thought.

Molly's death took the energy out of the protest. Many retreated. The few who stayed were being manhandled, beaten, or if they were lucky, arrested. Commanding officer Bajaj came up to Jonathan, who was still holding Molly, and told him, 'This is a crime scene. This woman was involved in a direct attack on the police and security forces. Please step away from her now.'

Without lifting his head, Jonathan replied, 'Like fuck she was. You fucking killed her. I'm not leaving her to the likes of you.'

'I'm not going to tell you again, sir. Either you leave now, or I will arrest you.' Bajaj was towering over him. He grabbed Jonathan and pulled him away from Molly. Jonathan watched two officers put her lifeless body in a bag and throw some sand and water over the pool of blood.

'You can't do that. You have to investigate what's happened here.' Jonathan tried to go back but Bajaj was holding him tightly now and leered, 'No, we fucking don't. We are in charge now. We can do whatever the fuck we like. Now fuck off.'

* * *

Police sirens were screaming on the streets as Arun and Oliver walked through the middle of a deserted and pitch-black park. He pulled Oliver towards him and they kissed. Arun ran his hands down Oliver's front, 'You work out too?' He took Oliver's hand but dropped it as they exited on to Pall Mall. The streets all around them were empty. 'A romantic stroll for two is maybe the only benefit of the governor-general's new security policy.'

As they entered Leicester Square, Oliver gasped, 'Every poster is an Indian movie. Have we got some sort of film festival going on?'

Arun shook his head. 'You're all moving far too fast to ingratiate yourselves with us. No fucking British movies. What's happening? You are a great country. Not just some shitty little place we have bought. You're Britain, not Bangladesh!' Before Oliver could reply, Arun pointed at a poster for a Bangalore comic. 'Oh, she's hysterical.'

* * *

Banerjee had joined Karan and Isha as they waited for their car. Karan yawned, 'It's been a day. Would you mind terribly if I missed your party, Lord Banerjee? I'm sure you can look after my wife.' Banerjee's electric Silver Shadow inched towards them.

'Well, I do have some chilled champagne waiting for you, Isha.' Karan kissed Isha just before she jumped in. He watched as they cackled together, and Banerjee poured their drinks. Inside Banerjee exclaimed, 'Congratulations, darling, you've done it!' Outside a flash went off.

* * *

The comedian's set had started by the time Arun and Oliver took their seats. 'People told me to watch my money when I got to London. But shit man, the price of flags in this country is going through the fucking roof!' Arun and Oliver howled. Arun kissed him again. The comedian pointed at them. 'Oh, for fuck's sake, get a room.' Then she returned to her set.

Four

Karan was gently tapping the grounds into his coffee maker and shouted, 'Do you want some?' The hairdryer had been going solidly for almost thirty minutes. The wardrobe drawers slammed again. He was fiddling with the lid when the hairdryer stopped. He tried again, 'I'm making a second pot,' and waited, 'do you want some?'

When Isha was mad, she'd do at least three things simultaneously—shout at him; slam a door; and break something; then disappear into the bedroom to redo her hair. Karan walked over to the kitchen table to survey the green-brown stains her kale smoothie and his first pot of coffee had left on the morning's papers. It had been an impressive swipe. Would have been a strike at the bowling alley they all went to as kids. Every paper led with Molly's death. Most described it as the unfortunate coincidence of a brilliant young banker in the wrong place at the wrong time. One had declared she was an undercover journalist in the wrong place at the wrong time. Karan gingerly picked up the sodden front pages and turned to the tv when Sally announced she was with one of the rioters, 'You were there last night? And you say you saw unacceptable use of force by the soldiers around you? Is that right?'

Karan could hear the seething anger in his reply. The voice of a young man in his twenties, far from the hoarse and croaky voice of one of Karan's peers when they were interviewed in the early morning. 'The murder of this young woman is the first death on our new first minister's watch. He has as much blood on his hands as our corrupt Indian overlords do. Assault weapons were used on London's streets yesterday—not by gun-toting terrorists but by our own armed forces. Public servants there to protect you and me. Not kill us.'

Sally continued, 'Do you feel that your protest had any role to play in her death?'

'No, this woman's murderer is sitting in Downing Street.'

'You fucking little cock,' Karan shouted. 'You don't want to admit you caused it. Crippling our financial centre, causing hundreds of millions of pounds of damage.' Karan examined the images of the wanton destruction across the city on loop on television. He paused when Sally introduced the lord mayor.

'These attacks are a further warning, if any were needed, of the total lack of respect for what was once the financial engine of the UK economy.' Sally asked, 'What do you think being owned by India will do for the economy?'

The lord mayor spluttered, 'Well, I don't think we are Indian-owned, but it certainly will help to be associated with the fourth-largest economy in the world. It puts Frankfurt and Paris in their place.'

Karan smiled. 'At least Oliver has been working this morning,' he thought as Isha returned to the living room brandishing the hairdryer like a gun. 'Who the fuck do they think they are?' She picked up a paper, knocking over her glass again. 'Sanctimonious little shits.' She pointed at the front page and its headline, 'Girl dies while Isha parties,' adding, 'and a picture of Banerjee and me drinking in the back of his car. I look fucking heartless. Like the wicked stepmother. And he looks like a gormless buffoon.'

'Well, in some ways the camera never lies,' Karan ventured.

'You,' she paused, threatening him with the hairdryer, 'you have to stop this.'

'I don't see what you think I can do.'

'You're the leader of the fucking country, aren't you? They are mocking your wife. So that means they are mocking you. Don't you think you should at least offer to do something to protect my reputation, our reputation?'

'I did say that I didn't think an after-party with Banerjee was an absolute necessity.'

'You didn't say you had launched a fucking black ops mission in EC2, though, did you?'

Isha threw the paper back on the table.

'I can't believe she's the first casualty of all of this.' Karan was studying the pictures they'd found of Molly. At university. In her school newspaper. 'What age do you think she is? Twenty-four? Twenty-five?'

'She's the first casualty?' Isha fumed. 'Are you fucking kidding? My reputation is the first casualty.'

Karan checked his phone. 'Where is he?'

'Sorry?'

'Oliver. I've called and texted him about twenty times since I found out about her death. And he hasn't read one message yet. Do you think I should ask the cops to check in on him too?'

'Can you just for once not think about your fucking boyfriend please and put me first? What are you going to do for me?'

Karan put the phone down. 'What do you want me to do? I can give you some advice on how you should react to the story. If that would help.'

Isha, 'Pitaji wants you to close the paper. He says do it right now. Show you are in charge. That India is in charge.'

Karan, 'And does this plan involve selling any of this—or any other newspaper—to your father in the not-too-distant future? We're not doing it. But you are going to have to do something. I think you're going to have to meet her family. Or whoever this is.' Karan pointed to a photo of Jonathan, 'He appears to be running some campaign about her. Or go to a vigil.' Isha had walked out before Karan had finished.

She turned around and returned, 'What's that burning smell?'

'Ah fuck, the coffee.'

* * *

The governor-general was enjoying the vast lawn and mature gardens from the breakfast table at the bay window. 'No, it's still not—how do you say—right. I know chef is trying. Can you take this back and ask him to speak to my wife about how to make the perfect fried eggs for my dosa please.'

Albert sighed.

The table was heavy with cutlery from Albert's family silverware and all manner of plates, serving dishes and glassware. The governor-general had taken an intense interest in one of the delicate sugar bowls.

Albert sighed again. 'It's Minton, each piece personally signed off by me. I had plans for a second set to mark the fifth year of my reign. But ...' Albert trailed off.

Fresh eggs appeared. 'Perfect,' the governor-general declared and began eating noisily. Much to the delight of his staff.

'It's the only service with the green of the Indian—and now the English—flag, your excellency.' Albert continued, 'Are you enjoying life here at the office, as I used to call it?'

'Yes, it's so much better than the rather cramped high commissioner's residence at Kensington Palace.'

'I remember your high commissioner's residence was one of the finest houses in London, excellency. In fact, there are only two homes in London I have wanted to acquire.'

'Really?'

'Yes,' Albert continued. 'Your high commissioner's residence and Marlborough House, just over the road there. My grandmother lived there before we presented it to the commonwealth. You know how much the commonwealth matters to my family, and to me, personally.'

'Really, perfect.' The governor-general was engrossed in breakfast. 'This yolk is perfect. You know we have missed a well-cooked English breakfast. It may have been the only reason the PM was finally able to convince me to take on this assignment. What were you saying, governor?'

'Your move here it's so sudden. Not that I mind in any way. You know how much I enjoy the governor's residence. I would never want to give that up. But you've already heralded so many profound changes to our system. If I might proffer some advice, it might be better to tread a little more lightly. Go with the grain as it were.'

'Yes, yes. Excellent advice.' The second fried egg now fascinated him. 'You'll have seen on your way here this morning that we requested our personal standard be flown. I have also requested that it fly from all the palaces and royal houses. In doing so we are guided by your long-established English protocols. We thought this might give people the assurance you describe. How did you describe it so nicely just then? Going with the grain?'

'I had wanted to address that matter. That particular protocol is about recognising the presence of the sovereign, as monarch and head of the royal family—for whom we are led to believe the English people still have great affection.'

'But that office no longer exists, excellency. You gave it up yourself.' The governor-general set down his cutlery and crossed his arms in front of him. 'We assumed you had done so with full awareness of the implications of the decision on you, your status and your family. The president of the Republic of India is the head of state now. There is no monarch. Your family continues but its role is no more significant than the artificial tree English families decorate each christmas. Power resides in the office of the governor-general, and we are sure people would like to know where we are—and that our constitutional position is secure. We feel sure people would like to know that the governor-general is delivering effective management of what was the royal estate. The full royal estate.'

The governor-general watched Albert twitch and scrape a thin layer of butter on his toast. So thin, and with such force, that more of the toasted outer layer fell on the plate than was added to the spread. Albert took a desiccated bite. 'Over many generations, we have found that the people of this country need a little more than constitutional norms, governor-general, to get on about their day. To be taken from a humdrum existence to the ordinary, maybe even the extraordinary. They need a belief in individuals who can embody their hopes and dreams. That's really what I feel is missing in the great rush to make us all anglo-indians.'

The governor-general inspected his empty plate and his staff. One ran off to the kitchen. 'I think you may be right. This has become fussily legalistic. The people need a symbolic act of coming together.'

Albert's eyes lit up. 'Like a sort of second coronation, perhaps.'

The governor-general agreed, 'Yes, of sorts. I have already made a request to Delhi that the prime minister visit. This could be a useful focal point for it.'

'I could not have put things better myself, governor-general.' Albert added a generous dash of gooseberry jam to the second slice of toast. 'I have to say I thought we might need further sessions to agree to this. But a second coronation to mark my role, nay translation, as head of the Indian imperial commonwealth could be just the thing. I think we could expect the archbishop to officiate, excellency, don't you agree? And even a role for yourself and the prime minister, if she could find the time.'

The governor-general waved his right palm. 'No, no. No need for trinkets. We've already given you that bauble. Or what do you call the thing you wrap around the tree?' He waited to find the word. 'Tinsel! Yes, my children loved it. Creating halos and angels. Highly flammable, I remember. The ceremony should cement our new constitutional arrangements and perhaps the role of governor-general—much like your viceroy was installed all those years ago. Have Lord Banerjee call on me tomorrow, please.'

A fresh egg and dosa arrived at the table. 'Charming!' The governor-general exclaimed, adding, 'You must miss it here', to Albert. 'We should do this more often. Such excellent ideas flow.'

Albert returned to his toast and sighed.

* * *

A half-drunk, open bottle of twelve-year-old whisky stood on the bedside table, sentinel-like. It added a sweet and smoky back note to the sweaty day-after scent of the night they'd spent together. Oliver was drinking water and watching Arun sleep. He felt every day of their fifteen-year age gap. The bottle, and Oliver's hangover, were enough to say it had been a good night. But the abandoned items of clothing strewn from his front door to the bedroom confirmed it.

They'd continued to drink and kiss at the comedy club like college kids. The jokes got funnier and less relevant. When the comedian finished her set, the club management announced that they were shutting early. All London venues had been told to close, for security reasons. They took a back way out on to totally deserted central London streets and kissed under every broken lamp post and in every darkened corner. Eventually, Arun asked, 'Are you taking me back with you?'

Oliver lay back on the bed, staring at the ceiling. Was it just a drunken one-night stand? What would he have to tell Karan? Before he could start to overthink the situation, Arun woke up, leant over and kissed him. Oliver handed him some water. 'My breath is bad?' Arun asked, holding his cupped palm up to his mouth.

'No, but even your young body might need some rehydration.'

'When do you have to leave?' Arun asked. 'I don't suppose we've yet got you tight English boys to adopt a dopahar approach today? Judging by last night you're pretty comfortable going at it into the wee hours.'

Oliver felt his cheeks redden. 'I don't know what that is. But if it means staying in bed this morning, it sounds okay to me.' He switched on the screen on the wall opposite. It was always on twenty-four-hour news. The only thing he was sure about the British media at the moment was that they would take the most contrary position possible to what Karan and his government were trying to achieve. Scenes of the destruction across the city were being shown on loop, with a reporter adding, 'Still no comment from the government on the apparent killing of a young journalist at yesterday's protests in the city. The allegation is that British, or possibly even Indian, troops fired indiscriminately into the crowd.'

Oliver was out of bed, pulling on his clothes. 'Fuck.'

'What is it?' Arun asked. Oliver turned up the sound.

Jonathan was being interviewed on television. 'Can you tell us a little more about what happened?'

'It was a full-scale military operation in the middle of central London. I watched as security forces—not police officers—lobbed tear gas at a terrified crowd of young people just as every mobile phone changed to an Indian telecom provider. So we were left there stranded. At the mercy of these animals. I watched my friend die in front of me and I couldn't call an ambulance. Then they charged and fired on us. People just trying to get home from work. Lots of office workers were caught up in it. I tried to get Molly off the street. But she was pulled away from me. I heard two shots. They weren't plastic bullets. When I checked, Molly was on the floor. I tried to save her, but …' Jonathan broke down and couldn't finish his sentence.

'But your friend had died. Killed, you think, by one of those armed officers on the streets.'

Oliver grabbed his phone. 'Shit, twenty missed calls from Karan.' He read out the last text, 'First casualty. Call me.'

Khalid was on the screen. 'This tragic loss of life is a stain on the new Indian government in England. The state of affairs could not be more serious. It seems to me the new government has implemented martial law on the streets of London without due process or accountability. It's clear this wasn't only a police operation, and the authorisation can only have come from the highest levels. We'll be asking questions in parliament about it today. This is still a democracy, after all.'

Arun was scanning his phone. 'We're reporting that it was rogue British police officers. Do you believe that?'

'Do you? This is a fucking disaster.'

Arun replied, 'No,' as the image shifted to the grey stone of the Edinburgh residence of the Scottish labour prime minister. The black door opened to reveal the prime minister in her ubiquitous red suit. 'My cabinet met this morning to share our concern about the images and news reports of a heavy-handed police response to the demonstration in London yesterday. I've spoken to the governor-general who has assured me that no Scottish citizens have been caught up in the protests. As is usual at times of crises, we have offered the support of the Scottish police force.'

Oliver asked, 'What the fuck would she or they know? Rich, isn't it? She divorced us and has jumped into bed with them.'

Arun replied, 'I think the phrase is "your overlords"? Well, she probably wants to get on our PM's radar. You have to go to Karan?'

Oliver nodded. 'Yeah. Are you okay to fix yourself breakfast and,' pointing to his clothes around the room, 'get yourself out of here?'

Arun smiled. 'I can sort myself out.'

Oliver was already dressed, searching for his driver and smelling himself. 'I should have had a shower. But my car's there.'

Arun was holding Isha's business card. 'I know all hell has broken loose here but I'm going to Isha's factory today. Someone in the party in Mumbai has suggested it is in my interest to check it out.'

Oliver looked at him. 'It's in Little China. So be careful, won't you?'

Arun pointed at the coverage of Molly's death. 'Who's interested in me? She's the story today. Sadly.'

* * *

'Did you see dad on tv?' Jonathan was speaking on the phone from his flat. 'Can you put mum back on? … Are the kids okay? Yeah, I'll stay up here for a day or so. No, you should stay there. The bank has told me to take as much time off as I need.' He snorted. 'Yes, I know they actually mean get back to my fucking desk. But no one is going in today.' He paused. 'No, I won't fixate on this. She was just a colleague. I'll be back tomorrow.'

He slumped as he put the phone down. He could see the still-smouldering city from the bedroom window of his tiny studio flat. He returned to his laptop and hovered over 'Buy now'. He took a deep breath and clicked. An email pinged into his inbox, proudly declaring, 'Thank you for registering a new website with us. ThetruthaboutMolly.org will be available soon.'

All his drawers and shelves were ajar. His clothes strewn over the floor and around last night's takeaway. 'You can't spend the rest of the day in this shit heap,' he told himself. He stood up and started to clear the mess. He contemplated folding the pile of clothes that never quite made their way from the corner chair to the wardrobe. He picked up his running trainers from under the bed. 'What's that?' A small plastic card stuck to the bottom of one hit the floor. It was Molly's Merchant's id card. He crumpled back on to the floor, held her image in his hand and wept.

'Jesus fucking christ,' he told himself, wiping the stream of tears off his cheeks. 'She was only a one-night stand. You didn't cry this much over your own children.' He went back to the laptop. From the cheap website editor package he'd bought, he added a page of biographical information about Molly. He spent the rest of the morning reading news coverage until—'Gotcha you bastard'—he uploaded an image of the Indian officer who'd spoken to him, adding, 'Do you know this man?' on the newly published site. From a blank social media profile, he started to share the website with the protest groups mentioned across that day's news sites.

The phone started ringing. He answered and said, 'Hello.' The ringing continued. He had an old work phone somewhere. He searched in the drawer by his bedside table. It wasn't switched on. 'Molly's phone,' he told himself. He found his bloodstained coat in the washing basket. The phone was still ringing. 'Yes?' he answered.

'You shouldn't be doing what you're doing. This is not your fight. Molly wasn't what you thought she was. And you shouldn't have this phone. We will be back in touch to arrange for you to hand it over.'

'Don't think you can fucking threaten me, you piece of shit. You killed her. I watched you and your friends do it. And I will make sure the world knows about it. Why don't you tell me your name if you're feeling so brave?'

'The world doesn't fucking care. All you need to know is we know who you are, Jonathan Hall. And that you have a beautiful wife and two lovely kids. You can't fit them all into that apartment by London Bridge, though, can you? We can see them right now. What a lovely home you have in Chichester too.'

'Fuck you.' Jonathan made to turn the phone off.

'Keep this phone charged. We'll be back in touch to tell you where to drop it off. Don't try to be a hero. That ends grievously. And it would be a terrible shame if your wife were to find out about your one-night stand, wouldn't it?'

'How the fuck,' he started, but the phone call had ended.

Shaking, Jonathan turned on the kettle. As it hissed to life he went to the bathroom, filled the sink with freezing water and sunk his face deep into it. He stared at his tired reflection in the mirror. And plunged himself back into the sink. An email ping on his computer brought him back out. He took a steaming mug of chestnut-brown tea to his desk and asked the computer to read the latest email:

'Sender, Merchant's Bank HR. Subject, Your disciplinary hearing.' The computer continued, 'Dear Jonathan, we know this is a distressing time for you. But we hope you will understand, the bank will need to launch an investigation into the circumstances which led to you hiring an undercover journalist. At this stage we would like to ask you not to return to work until the hearing commences. We will arrange for your IT equipment and phone to be collected. This will be reviewed, and its contents may be used in any subsequent disciplinary procedure. Should you have any materials belonging to Molly Stevens—or Molly Jones, as she was known to us—we request you hand these in with your equipment.' Jonathan instinctively touched Molly's phone in his jeans pocket.

The computer continued, 'We believe Molly's pass is in your apartment. Its geotag lists it as having been there following her first day in the office. We have attached our standard pre-disciplinary investigation pro-forma for you to complete. Please include any relevant information about the location of Molly's pass. We understand this will be a challenging time for you and recommend you contact the colleague assistance programme.'

'Stop!' Jonathan shouted, followed by, 'What the actual fuck?'

Jonathan returned to promoting Thetruthaboutmolly.org on conspiracy and protest sites. He kept reopening the email and read it like he was picking at a scab. 'These fuckers are going to blame me for everything.'

Molly's phone rang again. Jonathan grabbed it and repeated, 'I thought I told you to fuck off.'

Sally answered, 'You might need to work on your phone manner. Is this the Jonathan who's been on the media this morning? Please don't hang up. My name's Sally. I am ...' she paused. Jonathan heard her take a deep breath. 'Molly was a colleague. We worked on the Merchant's assignment together. Is this a bad time?'

'Well, the last person to call me on this number just threatened my family and me, and my employer wants to sack me for hiring Molly. So, you could say I've had better days.'

'I wonder if you might have time to speak to me. Later tonight?'

'Yes,' Jonathan replied. 'How about a pub in—'

'Don't say any more on here. Text your number to the number I'm calling from. I'll send you the location. Bring the phone with you. And please be vigilant.'

Jonathan sat back, staring at the ruined city over the Thames.

* * *

Arun exited the tube at Tower Bridge. The city had all the hallmarks of the loser in one of those Olympic boxing championships he refused to watch. Black and blue all over. Every surface had been graffitied with 'Indians out.' 'Fuck Delhi.' And every now and again a kangaroo. He felt sorry for the street cleaners power-washing, picking up litter and cleaning the badly mauled streets as police cars raced past. All a little too late.

Heading east, he noticed the vast numbers of security cameras that had been pulled off the lamp posts. He stopped to look at one. It had something on it in Mandarin. The floor was strewn with them. Those that couldn't be pulled off had their lenses covered with spray paint.

He was at the vast new complex with its own giant red flag as large as the anglo-indian one on the Tower of London. Chinese guards and police were demonstrably patrolling the inside courtyard. Arun noticed that everyone walking around outside was of Chinese origin. 'So that's what they meant by Little China,' he thought. 'They've ceded this territory to them.' It was unfathomable to Arun how the Richardson government had allowed the sale of such prestigious national heritage to a foreign government. And not just any government, but the Chinese.

He examined the lamp posts. Alongside the security cameras were all manner of data-gathering devices. Antennae and monitoring equipment had been bolted wherever they were out of reach.

The Indian media had covered the sale and subsequent sinification of the area. Calling it a sign that London was lost while quietly praising the commercial acumen of the communo-capitalist Chinese regime. In anticipation of securing the embassy compound, the Chinese government had bought all the new residential developments around the site. Almost immediately after the deal was signed, five hundred diplomats had moved in. More and more Chinese colonised the area month by month. Arun had read that the Chinese government owned thousands of homes from Tower Bridge to Canary Wharf—part of a debt swap deal with the Malaysian prime minister after the inflation-busting years of the early 2020s.

The east end of London had taken another of its great, migrant-driven transformations. European jews had been welcomed by Cromwell in 1656, returning to England after four hundred years fleeing continental persecution; French protestants had migrated for similar reasons in the eighteenth century; the Irish, and even gay men, Arun read, had found solace and liberty in the east end's dark and deviant lanes. The arrival of the Chinese embassy had ended the greater cultural mix-up these successive waves of migration had created. The original migrant Londoners left, replaced with state-sponsored Chinese businesses. Increasingly, whole streets from the former mint to Greenwich were owned by, and for, the Chinese government. A city state within a city had been allowed to take hold. A state of permanent siege, some thought. They had even been permitted to buy the airport in the east of the city and renamed it London–Beijing.

As Arun had entered the area, alarms had gone off in the basement of the giant Chinese embassy. The screens on the data controllers' desks pinged alerts as the cameras, listening devices and monitoring stations began automatically to follow him. Calls were made from the control station to an army of watchers on the streets around him.

The Mandarin-speaking shopkeepers watched Arun as he dodged driverless auto-taxis to cross into Cable Street, the site of a stand-off between jews and fascists in the twentieth century. Arun's phone was sending him locally targeted Chinese-community propaganda. The shopkeepers were sending their own messages to street-level coordinators who passed them on to the unidentifiable Chinese police officers stationed in each sector of Little China. They sent their reports to the data controllers in the basement of the embassy. Back at the former mint, an intelligence agent had been called to review Arun's presence. 'So an emissary from the Indian government? Get my car ready.'

Arun couldn't read any of the names of the businesses he walked by. All were unapologetically in mandarin. Most appeared to be selling property or offering access to finance from Chinese banks. He recognised the smell of well-cooked Chinese food like he was back in Kolkata. And there was plenty around. A few of the east end's infamous pubs had survived. But with Chinese customers sat in the windows playing digital mahjong for, what Arun assumed, were exorbitant sums of money.

Arun was aware a car had been following him noticeably and slowly. It wasn't making any attempts to disguise that he was being escorted. Instinctively, he turned up his collar and checked his location on his phone. He texted Oliver, 'How's it going?'

He received an immediate reply, 'Shit show. Are you okay?'

Arun stopped and slowly replied, 'Yes. Though Indians appear to be as welcome here in Little China as we are in Pakistan.'

'Do you want me to send my car to collect you?'

'No, but let's have a drink later?'

Arun arrived at the address on the business card. The car had stopped, and someone got out to talk to one of the many shopkeepers doubling up as informants.

'Why on earth would she have a factory here?' he thought as he stood opposite Isha's workshop. Exhausted-looking Indians were coming in and out. Arun surveyed the area and thought, 'Price. She always was cheap.' The high-rise flats that dominated the area were dilapidated. While the Chinese security cameras were still prominent, it was clear these weren't the homes in which its diplomats were living. Most of the people who'd come out of the high-rise next to the factory had been Chinese, but not all of them. Arun spotted an Indian man having a smoke and went over to him, 'Indian ka factory vaha hai?' The man resolutely kept his eyes down but eventually pointed at the building opposite them. He threw his cigarette on the pavement and went back inside the block.

When Arun turned around the Chinese agent was right behind him. He gripped Arun's elbow. 'We don't usually see representatives of the government of India in this part of town. And you don't appear to have your official car with you. It's a strange area for sightseeing. So we assume you are gathering intelligence on your own first minister.'

Arun didn't flinch. 'We know your government is the one with an unhealthy interest in intelligence. I'm here to see a friend. And we don't all need to be ferried around the city like a great panjandrum.' He pulled his elbow away forcefully.

The Chinese agent continued, 'Now you know we know who owns this factory. Not too many people do. If they did, they might find time to complain about the lack of basic rights. It would be a terrible shame if the newspapers continued to report about the abusive first minister's wife, wouldn't it?'

'It sounds to me like you need to speak to her. I'm not sure who you think I am.'

'We know who you are, commissioner. It would be better if you did not come here again. But seeing you are here—and we know you are dealing directly with the Puri administration—we have a message for the first minister.'

'Go on.'

'He might want to ask what his former king knew about all this.'

The agent left. Arun crossed the road and smiled at an older Indian woman entering the car park to start her shift. 'Main manager ka dost hoon. Voh yahan hai?' The woman shook her head. Arun followed her inside.

The noise hit him first. The thunder of the machines was like a military helicopter taking off. Then the heat. Then days of dried-in sweat. It was hot work, and they were working fast. The ceiling was low, and the harsh overhead lights hurt his eyes. Row upon row of women in brightly coloured saris were finishing off expensive dresses. They sat at tiny tables just big enough for their sewing machines. Long tables decked with fabric ran down the middle of the room, cutting it in two. A few young boys in pink and yellow t-shirts were dotted in between them.

A woman in a blue sari and headdress was walking to the door. Arun asked her, 'Aapke yeh factory pasand hai?'

She shook her head, saying, 'Bahut bura', and walked out.

An older man came over to ask, 'Who are you? Some kind of journalist? Fuck off out of here.'

Arun stood outside, blinking in the sun. A cab was driving by. He texted and it stopped to pick him up.

* * *

Oliver continued to sniff himself as the car pulled into Downing Street. He was sure he could smell the mustiness of morning-after sex and hoped neither his driver nor Karan would notice. Oliver had asked to stop at the nondescript entrance to the cabinet office on Whitehall to enter Karan's office without being seen. But they were pulling up right in front of the infamous black door with journalists camped out opposite. They shouted at him before he opened the car door. 'Who's responsible for the troops on the streets, minister?' Oliver feigned he hadn't heard the question.

Seb was waiting for him. 'The first minister is in the cabinet room, minister.' Oliver stopped at the door to the cabinet room. He quickly tried to smell himself again as Seb knocked.

Karan was sat at the large oval table with officials on all the available seats. 'Could Oliver and I have the room, please?' He pointed to Oliver to sit opposite him as people left.

Oliver sat down. 'First meeting in the cabinet room with you as the boss.'

Karan stared at him. 'This is not how I wanted to start. You look like shit.' And then smiled, 'Good night, was it?'

'What the fuck happened?' Oliver deflected.

'Right now, I have no idea. Nor, it appears, does the metropolitan police commissioner or the commissioner of the city of London police. The chief of the defence staff will not return my calls. And I'm supposed to be the fucking leader of this place.'

‘I think we know from last night that that’s not the whole story. Have you had a further update from Dame Rebecca?’

‘She has confirmed they were a mixture of British and Indian officers. She can’t yet tell me which nationality shot the girl.’

‘So what was the chain of command? Who authorised this?’

Karan stood up, opened the doors to the garden, walked out and took a deep breath. ‘I honestly don’t know who we can trust right now. Or whether all our rooms are already bugged. Dame Rebecca has confirmed that the police and military are reporting directly to the governor-general and India. They feel I am fucking superfluous. When I spoke to that bastard last night, he told me he had authorised the military operation and that it would be sorted in a few moments.’

‘How has he managed to achieve all this within hours of arriving?’

‘I need you to find that out.’

Oliver nodded. ‘We didn’t do this to kill our own people.’

Karan said, ‘I told you it wouldn’t end well. It hasn’t started well either.’ He paused. ‘But I don’t think we can let people know what actually happened. The whole project will collapse, and I am sure what would come after would be far worse. We’ll have to try to cover this up for a bit.’

They both went quiet. Karan asked, ‘What about Arun? Do you trust him?’

Oliver replied, ‘Who’s to say? You’ve asked me to get as much information as possible. So I started strong. You’ll meet him again tonight.’

‘He appears to have won over Dame Rebecca. And I assume she, at least, will have done her homework before jumping into bed with him.’

Oliver laughed.

* * *

Isha, Archana and Zarin were giggling as Philippe escorted them to their private dining room. ‘Mrs Puri, chef has prepared a unique menu for you and your guests. They enjoyed the first mouthfuls of vintage champagne as Philippe continued, 'Caviar, dover sole, and then a choice of summer puddings. I will make sure we send you a second bottle too.'

Isha nodded. Every month she brought her most loyal customers together for a lunch curated by Philippe. Today it was just for them. 'Oh, Philippe,' Isha replied, 'you really are treating us like royalty.'

'Vintage champagne?' Archana asked. 'I hope Karan's not covering this on an Indian government salary!' The women roared.

Archana and Zarin glanced at each other, daring one another to ask the question. Zarin ventured first, 'Wonderful to see so much of your new collection last night.' She raised her glass. 'It was a triumph. The whole night.' She stumbled, 'You'll have already secured free coverage in every glossy magazine and newspaper in the world. Your order book will be off the charts by the end of the week.'

'It would have been,' Isha replied, 'if that fucking photo hadn't appeared in today's papers. I mean now they think I'm the wicked witch of the east. Almost literally. It's so unfair.'

'Who cares about the little eco-warrior anyway?' Zarin asked. 'I'm sure when they do a proper investigation into her, they'll find she was trouble.' The women nodded.

'No, I don't think so. Karan says she was genuinely in the wrong place at the wrong time. He wants me to attend a vigil this afternoon. Tells me I have to do it to show some remorse.'

'What the fuck for?' Archana asked. 'You didn't fucking kill her. She killed herself. Greedy little bitch wanted to make as much money as she could for her bank or for her newspaper before Karan pulls the plug on both of them.'

'I can't imagine Sunilji asking you to do that, never mind telling you. Karan sounds like he still has his idealistic specs on. Isn't it time you told him this is deal time? We all need to make as much as possible and get out before the shit really hits the fan.'

The table went quiet. Isha could feel her face tighten. 'It's not like being a junior partner at the bank. Isn't that what Abdul is doing right now? Or VP marketing. Karan's the fucking leader of the country. He does need to have the ideas. How else will we get out of this mess?'

'Let's be honest. No one thinks Karan is going to get us out of this mess. They are all hoping Sunilji has a plan, you'll help us make as much money as possible, and we can head off to the south of France or California before it all implodes.'

Isha watched them. 'Pitaji has a plan. But it involves Karan fixing this mess. That is the plan.' Silence.

From a distance Philippe could sense the tension and sent his waiting staff over with additional canapés before he appeared, announcing, 'I think you ladies need a second bottle. And if I may suggest, from years of training, I never speak about men at lunch with my girlfriends. Never!'

The women chortled. 'Cheers to fucking that,' Archana added.

Isha checked her watch. 'Shit, is that the time? I have to be in the car heading to this vigil.' Seeing a crestfallen maître d', she added, 'Philippe, please accept my deepest apologies. But I did something stupid last night, and now I have to try to make it better. Please entertain my dearest—and oldest—friends.'

Banerjee's car was waiting for her. She sat in the back in silence. After a couple of minutes the driver coughed, 'Shall we go, ma'am?'

'Of course. Thanks.' Tears were welling up inside her. She waved her hands in front of her face hoping that would stop them from appearing. 'Who the fuck do they think they are,' she asked herself, 'questioning what Karan and I will do for this country. And for fucking them. Greedy, indolent jowly bastards.'

She'd felt this way before. This disgusting feeling. Isha closed her eyes and visualised her home in Delhi. Her early twenties. At the bottom of the garden of pitaji's Lutyens' bungalow. Cabinet ministers and captains of industry were daily visitors, asking for advice or if he could intervene to gain some concession or administrative fix to a problem. She'd been allowed to hang hammocks by the water feature that cascaded down three levels to a perfectly manicured lawn.

She was lounging with her friends on the daybed and sipping nimbu pani. They were trying hard to outdo one another's tales of outrageous behaviour at their favourite Delhi nightclubs. Every now and again Isha saw cars arriving, her father welcoming someone else into the house or shepherding someone out. He'd usually come down and see her friends. Share a funny story. Let her tell him a tenth of what they'd been up to. He hadn't come to see her, so she excused herself and found her mother at the steps wiping her eyes. 'It's all gone,' she told Isha before going inside. Isha could see her father in his study. He was remonstrating with this last set of men. Close up it was more like begging. It disgusted her to see her father so desperate. It made her sick. She heard him offer the man sitting opposite him 30, 40 then 45 per cent. They shook hands and the man left. Isha's father had his head in his hands. He saw her. And that's when she first saw her father's total failure. His disgrace. She was ashamed of him. He knew it. She promised herself she would find someone better than him. Someone she could rely on.

She returned to her friends as if nothing had happened. The next day's newspapers reported that her father had been forced to sell half the family business following a series of catastrophic investment decisions. His decisions. He came to her that night and promised he'd win their status back. She hadn't been able to look at him.

'We're here, ma'am,' Banerjee's driver interrupted her. 'The police are saying this is as close as I can get. I'll drive around and wait for you over there.'

'You'll come and fucking get me right here when I'm done.' She slammed the door shut.

'Ma'am, are you in the right part of the city?' The policeman was sure the woman who'd come out of the flashy car must be lost. Then he saw she had a bouquet. 'Do you need me to accompany you? Emotions are running high.'

Isha smiled. 'No, thank you. I'll be fine. I know this part of town.'

People had laid tributes in all directions and on all available spaces. They'd also written graffiti, 'This should have been Karan Puri.' 'Indians must die for this.'

'And so many kangaroos,' she told herself. 'What do they even mean?'

The commissioner of police was waiting to receive dignitaries. 'Mrs Puri, thank you for coming to the city. I'll accompany you,' spotting her flowers, 'I assume you want to lay these?' Isha nodded.

'We've been inundated with mourners. It's reminiscent of the death of Diana. I told my officers we had to direct people off the street. Might I take you to the church?'

Isha was unsure. 'I don't really want to make a fuss.'

'I had to work rather too hard to convince the rector of the merits of this idea. Initially he'd worried about being overrun by squatters. So, your arrival would rather convince him that he'd done the right thing. I did have to cajole him to open the church's conspicuous gates, topped with their gold crown.'

Isha wasn't really listening. 'Oh, well done, commissioner.'

'Well, at the end of it all I told him were he to refuse, I'd make it an order.'

Isha found the strength to smile. 'It's good to have a woman in charge, you know.'

'I'll leave you now Mrs Puri.'

Isha watched a group of young people walking out of the church arm in arm. One of the young boys was sobbing. She moved forward to comfort him. He froze, then focused his stare straight at her and shouted, 'You're his fucking wife.'

Isha stepped back. 'Sorry?'

He continued but louder, 'You're his fucking wife. He did this.' People turned to look at her. He shouted again, 'He fucking did this. You did it.'

The commissioner returned to Isha's side. 'That's enough now.' Her officers approached the young man.

'Now you're going to fucking arrest me for attending a vigil for the woman you killed. Go on then.'

The commissioner turned her back and walked Isha out of the church. Isha was shaking. 'Not to worry, that'll just be the adrenalin. It gets going pretty quickly when they are effing and jeffing.' Isha smiled.

Jonathan watched Isha get back into the Rolls and drive off. He'd recorded the exchange. He went over to the young man. 'Thank you for doing that. I was with Molly when she died.'

'I didn't do it for you either. They said you were some wanker banker. You can fuck off too.'

'Okay. But do you mind if I put what you just said on my website? I want to find out the truth about what happened. To find which of these bastards actually killed her.'

The young man shrugged. 'What's it to me? Nothing changes anyway, mate.' He walked away.

Jonathan uploaded the video as a text from Sally came in asking him to meet her at a pub in Borough Market. He texted back, 'Sure. Mine's a pint of IPA. Then added, 'and a double whisky.' He started walking through the encampment that had now taken over the city. Temporary shelters had turned the walbrook into one of the many gatherings that news reports were calling refugee camps. 'That's not right,' he thought to himself. 'It's hopeful. These people are fighting for their future. For our future.'

He walked past a makeshift stage and saw Khalid speak, 'We are here with all of you. You are starting something here that my generation has,' Khalid paused, 'well, has dangerously fucked up.' The young people watching him applauded. 'When I look out, these tents are like the sunflowers now growing around Chernobyl where the nuclear reactor blew up, sucking all the toxins out of the ground and turning it into something full of life.'

Jonathan was handing out his flyers pointing and asking, 'Have you seen this man?' People stared at him with a mixture of pity and resignation. Every now and again he would tap his coat pocket to check Molly's phone was there. It was like she was with him too. He hoped she'd be proud of him. Soon to be sacked wanker-banker-turned-activist. 'Maybe I can get Sally to hire me on the Merchant's assignment. Whistleblower extraordinaire.'

He was trying to get the attention of an enterprising stall holder who'd spent the last ten hours printing t-shirts with 'India Quit'. 'Why do some have kangaroos on them?' The seller ignored him. Jonathan handed him a copy of the photo. 'Any chance you've seen this man?' The man continued to ignore him. Jonathan picked up a black t-shirt with 'India Quit' in large white writing. 'I'll take this.' He put it on over his shirt.

Every now and again a car door would slam, or something would crash on the floor. Jonathan jumped. His brain would stop. It took him straight back to the riot. To Molly. He wiped the sweat from his brow. His heart was racing. He needed to get out of the camp. But he couldn't remember which way to go. It was as if he was losing his mind.

'Are you on your way?' Sally texted. 'I'm sending a link to the pub.' Jonathan opened it and started to follow the map religiously. He kept his eyes down. He took his earphones out of his pocket and, fumbling, dropped them. He couldn't see where they had fallen. 'These yours, mate?' A guy handed them to him. 'You all right?' Jonathan put the earphones on and turned up his nineties' soundtrack.

'He's a fucking basket case,' one of the men following Jonathan had a thick Irish accent. 'He's a fucking looper. Look at him. If someone drops one more can, he's going to shit himself right in the middle of the street.'

'Let's just wait and see. The journalist has told him where to meet.'

* * *

Sally had chosen a seat at the back of the pub where she could see everything going on. She placed the drinks prominently in front of her. The pint and whisky crowded her vodka tonic. She didn't know the particular people that would have called Jonathan, but she knew the bullying type. Jonathan walked in and she realised he had no idea what she looked like. She waved and pointed to the round. As he sat down, she took his hand, 'You don't look like you've slept much. How are you?'

'Shit, to be honest. I think I'm losing my mind.'

'Have you been to see a doctor?' She was rummaging for a card in her bag. 'You've been through a traumatic situation. If you need to, please contact this guy and say I sent you. We will be happy to cover any costs. It's the least we can do.'

'Who's we?'

'I'm the political reporter on a national newspaper. And a podcaster. We're all podcasters now.'

'Sorry, with two kids and the job, I didn't have much time for podcasts.'

Someone knocked over a drink, and Jonathan jumped. His eyes darted to the bar. Sally watched him intently. 'Look, maybe tonight's not the time for this.'

'No, I need to talk to someone about it and you are as good as anyone.'

'I hate to ask, but do you have Molly's phone?' Jonathan nodded and touched his breast pocket.

Two men at the bar were taking turns to look over.

'Fuck the Indians,' someone shouted from the bar.

'India Quit!' another replied.

Jonathan tensed up again. 'Look, I really don't know what I'm involved with.'

Sally touched his arm. 'To be honest, me neither. It's rare for a political journalist to be pounding the streets. But Molly was working on a story about Merchant's having taken money from a whole host of nefarious characters to get it through the financial crash. And not admitting that to the government or any of the regulators.'

Jonathan nodded. 'I think you'd find most of the big banks did that.' He tried to pick up his coat and continued to look furtively at everyone in the bar. 'I'm really not sure I should be here. I'm not a conspiracy theorist. I'm just a tedious banker. Molly is dead and she's put my life, and my family's life, at risk.'

'We can help with that. Can I get you another drink?'

'Can you?' Can you help me not go mad? I've got to tell my wife in a day or so why I'm probably going to lose my job. Now part of that's on me. Molly and I fucked on her first day. I don't know if she was using me to make me part of the story.'

It took all of Sally's journalist training not to react. She went to the bar and ordered another round and heard a man with a thick Irish accent order a whiskey for the road.

Sally set the drinks down as Jonathan continued, 'I'm a pretty average banker. I've made decent money. Not as much as the top dealmakers or the New York boys who still fly in every couple of months and take everyone out for drinks and afters. You know, down the lap-dancing clubs.' Jonathan stopped himself. 'Sorry, I'm talking utter pish. I could really do with a joint.'

'What about Molly?'

His face lit up. 'She was incredibly special. I mean, she arrived like a good-luck charm, like the pot of gold at the end of the rainbow. What a fucking day that was. I have never seen any of us make so much money. She came in late. I mean she left mine at about four in the morning. We'd flirted the whole of her first day. Who wouldn't be attracted to someone fifteen years younger than them showing some interest? Anyway, it happens. We fucked. And now it's all fucked.'

Sally asked, 'Did she tell you she was a journalist?'

'Yes, in the middle of the fucking battlefield. I fired her. Wish I fucking hadn't now.'

'Can you tell me what happened at the end?'

He had almost finished his second pint. She saw him draw into himself. 'I don't know really. She had wanted to get home. Get out of the bank. She'd spent the day shredding confidential files. So maybe she'd found what she needed. I promised to get her home. I fucking promised. Then we ended up in the middle of the shit. Right in the fucking middle of it. Arseholes and cunts all around us. They shot her. Straight in the stomach. And she told me her real name and asked me to take the phone.' He touched his breast pocket again.

He sat in silence and drank the rest of the pint.

'What do you think you'll do now?' Sally asked him.

'Teach,' he replied, quick as a flash. 'I've always wanted to be a maths teacher. Because if mine had been better, I'd have got into uni. I'm hopeful that I can get those bastards at Merchant's to pay me off. I'll take the money. Go quietly. And study. I'm not some superhero like you or Molly. I just want a quiet life.'

'We'll help. Help me finish what Molly started. And I'll make sure you get a good deal from us and them.'

'Let me think about it. I'll call you tomorrow,' Jonathan replied. 'Thanks for the drinks.'

'All right, just remember. We don't want to live in this world. Of tear gas and people being shot by the police or the army or some secret security force yards from here. They killed Molly and we need to get them. I think the bank is part of a much bigger story. Yes, of a conspiracy. To sell our freedom and our country like they were items on offer on the supermarket shelf. Do this for me and for Molly, and for your children.'

Jonathan shook her hand. 'That sounds like the start of a superhero movie. I'm planning to disappear.'

'Can I ask one more thing?' Sally examined him in detail. She could see what Molly had seen in him. A dependable father, if a bit flawed. 'Molly was also scrutinising Albert. Did she mention anything about that story?'

'The king? No, what had she found out?'

'You know, it's better if you don't know.'

When Jonathan left the pub the night air mixed with the alcohol and hit him hard. He vomited by the door.

'Jesus fucking christ,' the Irishman said. 'He better not do that over me.'

He was lost. His house was round the corner. But which way? He knew he lived near the river so he started walking towards it.

He put his earphones back on and turned his music up. He kept getting flashbacks of the sight of Molly's stomach and all the blood. He couldn't stop seeing the blood.

He was in a covered footpath beside the river. Was this the right way home? The middle of the footpath was dark. He heard a voice shouting, 'Mr Hall.' He checked his phone. But it wasn't ringing. 'Mr Hall.' Someone had grabbed him and pulled him to the back wall.

'No,' Jonathan tried to shout. But a hand smelling of whisky had covered his mouth. He tried to bite it. Then someone hit him. He could feel his cheekbone crumble.

'He fucking bit me,' the Irishman complained, 'He fucking bit me!' A woman screamed as she walked by, and the Irishman said, 'Fuck off, love.' Someone was searching his pockets. 'What's this then? Been busy on your printer, have you?' Jonathan tried to break free. 'Where's the phone?' the Irishman asked. 'I can't fucking find it.'

'Jonathan,' the Irishman was whispering into his ear. He could smell the whisky on his breath. They were pulling his arm behind his back. The pain was intense, as if his shoulder was about to dislocate. 'Jonathan, if you don't give us the phone, we'll have to break something.'

Jonathan managed to turn around to look him in the eye. 'Too fucking late.' They pushed him into the side of the tunnel. Jonathan slumped to the floor and felt something slice across him. 'They've cut my jacket open to find the phone,' he told himself and moved his hand down to feel hot, red blood stream from his stomach. Or was it Molly's stomach. He was lying down. Gasping for breath. He could see Molly's face again.

Someone screamed and shouted, 'Call 999, this man's been stabbed.'

Sally was finishing her drink in the pub when a phone rang. She checked Jonathan's seat. He'd left Molly's phone behind. She picked it up, and answered, 'Jonathan? Are you okay?'

A voice in the same thick northern Irish accent she'd heard at the bar said, 'Not quite, love. You've got something I want. Where would you like to meet to hand this mobile over? It would be a terrible shame for another one of ye to bite the dust.'

* * *

Earlier in the day, Oliver was with his team constantly checking his phone. To distract himself he was counting the number of boats on the river.

'We don't know who put the airport sale into effect,' Alessandra told him while tracking the government's internal websites. Everyone turned to Oliver.

'Sorry, what was that?' He was checking his phone. He that unmistakable twinge of excitement in his stomach waiting for Arun to text. Alessandra repeated it, 'Oh, yes, Heathrow.' He was back to looking out of the window. He checked the phone one final time before returning to the table and putting it screen-side down. 'People on all sides are criticising us right now. From the murder of that young woman in the city, the riots, giving away the actual crown jewels to India, even Isha having a drink in the back of a car.'

'Well, a roller,' another of the team snorted. 'It did look a bit let them eat cake!' Oliver watched as the heads around the table nodded in agreement. Then focused back on their phones and tablets.

'I know this work is uncomfortable for you. It's the same for me. We are all being pushed further and more quickly than we want to. And the governor-general is going to push Karan to go even more quickly. Neither of us wanted the sale. So I do need you to find out what happened.'

'Well, it wasn't a sale. Not by any usual means,' the young man who'd started the whole conversation continued. 'It was expropriated. But none of the directors of the company have spoken about it. So maybe they were in on it too?'

'That's true. Are you trying to tell me something with the phone case?'

He shrugged and held it up. 'It just says "India Quit". That's how I feel. Quit pillaging and murdering. Quit this deliberate display of arrogance and lording it over us. Quit making this so hard.'

Alessandra added, 'I need to know if we are responsible—us here—in any way for her death. The newspapers are saying that it was the changeover to bharat telecom that caused the riots. And the fact that the protesters couldn't communicate with one another after the changeover meant they couldn't coordinate an exit strategy.'

Oliver studied each of their young faces. They'd had their whole civil service lives mapped out; he knew it because he'd interviewed each of them personally and hand-picked them to be in his team. They were his crack troops. 'No, you absolutely are not responsible for her death. It was a tragic accident.' Thinking about it, he added, 'Maybe in time a court will say Karan and I are partly responsible. I feel responsible right now. The first minister does too. We got into this to make things better for our country. When it was at a time of crisis. Not to have British citizens killed.'

Alessandra continued, 'The stories are that soldiers fired on her. Not police. That it was part of some pre-authorised conspiracy for the military to kill people.'

Oliver watched them. 'You've worked in government. Have we ever been able to manage a conspiracy?' That drew a few smiles.

Oliver's phone rang. 'It's the first minister. How about someone take my card and get us all coffee and doughnuts from the shop down the street. That hasn't been appropriated to sell kulfi now, has it?'

'Doughnuts,' Karan teased. 'Don't you have a virile younger man to think about?'

'Yeah, but I just needed to do something to lighten the mood. My little team are at best deflated and probably temporarily defeated.'

'Isha is too. She had a terrible fucking time at the vigil. And has told me I am a fucking idiot for sending her. She got into some sort of altercation with young people, and it's ended up on that fucking campaigner's website.'

Oliver sighed. 'You know it's going to be bumpy. The first casualty, the first mistake. These were always going to happen. We'll get through it. So will Isha.'

'I know,' Karan relented, 'but it's hard when your wife is upstairs in tears. I can't tell if it's tears of embarrassment, hatred or rage. But dinner is still on tonight. So I hope we'll see both of you.'

'Sounds like a night not to miss. Oh, I have a call coming through. Got to go.'

'I wonder who could be more important than your political soulmate.'

I'll see you tonight.' Oliver took a breath before running his fingers through his hair and trying to look relaxed. He practised a few 'hellos' and said, 'Hi.'

'You look sexy,' Arun smiled, 'and tired. But I hope not too tired for dinner. I've received this invitation from the first minister.' He was holding a thick card, the top of which had a golden crest on it. 'So, am I your plus one? You're already putting things in the joint calendar?'

'Ha! You know you've been invited in your own right. And if memory serves me right, your invite says plus one.'

'Now that I look at it more closely, it does indeed say that. Can I ask, will you be there? It does rather affect what I do.'

'Yes, as the most senior member of the first minister's cabinet and his senior political advisor, I have managed to wangle a place. On the first minster's immediate left, I believe.'

'I'm pleased. I was worried we'd have you serving the dinner. And I'm told you've already fixed the seating arrangements. So I will be on Isha's right.'

'You mustn't believe everything you read in the papers.' Arun could see and hear the smile in his voice. Oliver continued, 'What did you find out today?'

'The Chinese know there were Indian troops on the street last night. And Isha runs a pretty dirty business. They raised something else with me, but I'll need to tell you that in person.'

Oliver called Karan back. 'Well, well, well.' Karan smiled. 'You haven't hung up on me in ten years. It must be serious.'

Oliver could hear Isha in the background, 'Give me the phone. Is that Oliver? Give me the phone.'

'They hated me today,' she told him.

'Yes, we should have assumed it was going to be shit,' Oliver replied. 'There were always going to be strong emotions. But I can't believe that's the worst thing someone's said to you on the streets of London.'

'True. And I did jump back into Banerjee's car and buy a new set of jewels for tonight.'

Oliver could hear Karan now, 'What did you say? Give me the phone. When did you have time to go shopping? How much did that cost me?'

'We've both got to go, darling.' Isha smirked as she ended the call and opened the bedside drawer to reveal a red leather box, 'Thank you for these, darling.' She put on a thin strip of brilliant white diamonds with a deep-blue sapphire drop. 'After today, and after seeing Manishji's wife wearing the actual crown jewels, I couldn't bear to be underdressed.'

'Isha, this must have cost more than 25,000 pounds. I mean, you can't be seen to be spending that kind of money right now.'

'But don't I look pretty in them. Plus, those women coming tonight look down on me. Look down on us. I want them to see what we do when we really try.' She dropped her dressing gown and had nothing on other than the diamonds. 'I can give you a present in return,' she told him as she went under the covers. Karan followed.

* * *

After the call, Sally had bought another drink. 'Just to catch my breath,' she told herself. She kept her eye on the door and was racking her brain for the Irishman's appearance. But every time she just about got his face, the image evaporated like a puddle on a hot day. He was about her height. Dark hair. That narrowed it down to a few million Londoners. She checked her messages from Molly; they hadn't fully downloaded, and she didn't know why not. She scrolled back to find the code for Molly's phone. When they had agreed on the assignment, Molly had sent it to her, 'just in case'. Sally had told her, 'Don't be so melodramatic. It's just a little business story about this bank. You'll be in and out in a few days. We'll write it up. You'll get a byline and maybe even a bonus from the bosses.'

She was struggling to enter the pin. Her hands were shaking. 'Adrenalin,' she told herself. Once in she found a series of sexy texts with Jonathan. Molly didn't necessarily mean it to be a one-night stand. Such a cliché, the young woman and the married older boss. She opened the photo gallery. 'They're all deleted,' she thought, 'blank too.' Sally placed the phone back down on the table. Was there nothing else? Was that it? Then she remembered Molly's final text.

Sally's hands were still shaking as she opened up the message to find a password for the storage account Molly had loaded on to her phone. She entered the code, 'Got them,' she told herself. The screen was small, but Sally could make out countries of origin and transfers of tens of millions of dollars into Merchant's from China, Russia, Iran. 'All the top holiday destinations. Thank you Molly.'

Sally wiped a tear from her eye as she continued to review the correspondence. 'Sunilji seems to have made a mint betting against the pound,' she told herself, 'but this looks like Lord Banerjee has too.' She put the phone away, texted the information to her colleagues and left the pub as anonymously as she arrived.

* * *

Karan and Isha were waiting for their guests' car to travel the hundred and fifty yards from the gates.

'Look this way, first minister. This way, Mrs Puri,' the photographers and journalists were shouting. 'Any assessment of who killed that young girl, first minister? Do you regret attending the vigil in a roller, Mrs Puri?' Karan and Isha turned from the press pack as the car pulled up.

'God, I hate these people,' Isha whispered to him.

'Abdul and Zarin, they're some of your oldest friends.'

She raised her hand to her mouth. 'You know exactly who I mean. These jumped-up little shits who think they can tell us what to do. And those jumped-up little fucking eco-warriors too. They can all go to hell for all I care.'

'Let's not give the cameras any more photos, love, eh?'

'This whole thing just makes me think about my father. It's why you have to be a success. And you have to promise me you will give pitaji what he asks. He needs this last win. To show those ugly fucking women here and the Delhiwallahs who we really are.'

Karan moved forward and opened the car door. 'Zarin, welcome to ten downing! I told him to let you sit on the other side so you'd be on the front pages.'

Zarin kissed Karan's cheek. 'Abdul would never miss an opportunity to have his photo taken. You know that!'

Abdul was fixing his tie and waiting for the exact moment to open his door. He led with his orange and red elephant socks, hoping they would make a front-page splash of their own accord. He fixed the shirt on his flat stomach, which he was pulling in with all his might. 'I only hope I look this thin on the way out,' he shouted to the photographers. They took no notice of him.

'So pleased you could make our first little party.' Isha's hand went from Zarin's to her neck.

'Oh my, have you been shopping since we saw you last?' Zarin asked.

'Oh, just a little gift from Karan. These are nothing special.' Isha smiled and walked ahead of them all, going inside.

Karan quickly added, 'Come in, we haven't hosted you for supper in years. It's been far too long.'

'And we have about five dining rooms,' Isha shouted.

'Sir,' a doorkeeper stopped Karan. 'More guests are arriving at the front gate.'

Karan and Isha winked at one another. 'We'll head on up. You can let them find their way to us.'

Arun was about to enter Number 10 when Oliver's car drew up. 'God, he looks good in a dinner suit,' Oliver thought, followed by, 'I'm fucking mad. I could almost be his father.'

He stepped out of his car to hear a photographer ask, 'What is it a resident commissioner does?'

Arun replied, 'I'm not sure either. If you find out before me, send me a note. Will you?' They laughed with him. While turning away he winked at Oliver. 'We've had photographers and journalists basically live with us since before I was born. So we've all had to learn a few tricks.'

'Do you want to see the cabinet room?' Oliver asked. When they were inside, Oliver started to tell him, 'So this is where Churchill and Thatcher as well as Blair—' Arun shut the door and kissed him.

'I've wanted to do that all day.' He smiled.

'Me too.'

Arun put his fingers on Oliver's lips. 'The Chinese believe Albert did a deal with the Indians. What do you think?'

'I wouldn't be surprised.' They kissed again. 'I'll have to ask Karan. But not now. We have to go to dinner. They will know exactly what we have been up to.'

Isha was waiting for them at the top of the stairs. 'Having fun down there, are you?'

By the time they'd made it to her, Karan was in the wood-panelled dining room pouring champagne. The silver candelabras on the table had been lit. 'Such a generous light for old skin, don't you think, Oliver.' Isha clinked glasses and smirked.

'I wouldn't know much about that, my dear,' he replied.

'So I met Arun at a seedy nightclub in Delhi,' Isha confessed to the group. 'He was the best dancer in the place. All the girls wanted to take him home to their parents.' Isha was enjoying the story. Arun less so. 'From the minute he met him, pitaji tried desperately to marry us off!' Karan watched Oliver and Arun look at each other.

'Alas, it wasn't to be,' Arun added. 'Anyway, you've done much better than a south Bombay boy and aspiring politician. You got yourself a real one.'

Abdul interrupted, 'And now a licence to print money, no?' Only Zarin guffawed. 'Come on, 'he continued as Karan poured more champagne. 'Every Indian in London is now on the make. That's what they're hoping from all of you.' Abdul continued, 'They don't expect whatever this is will last for long, but while it does, they expect you to shift as much out of the country as possible. And they are ready to oblige.'

Karan shook his head. 'That isn't why we're in it. None of us anyway.' He pointed at the four of them. 'I want the country to get out of this mess in one piece.'

Arun's eyes went from Karan to Oliver. 'I do too. My father also. We didn't need the stain of colonial misadventure. But you know what, we got through the emergency. And you will get through this.'

* * *

The governor-general was pouring a second whisky. He turned the bottle around in his hand, stopping to savour every smell of its sweet smokiness.

'Lord Banerjee, excellency,' one of his staff announced.

'This bottle is older than the Republic of India, Banerjee!' He took a sip. 'I had the royal vintner produce the inventory of the best of the best. This two lakh pounds bottle is near the top of the lot!'

Banerjee nodded enthusiastically. 'So, you've decided to remain here?'

'Yes, Mrs Pahlkiwala is most happy here. She particularly enjoys the near-private pool.'

'Near-private.' Banerjee was savouring every sip of the conversation and the alcohol.

'Yes, apparently staff can use it. But we never see them in there. So this will do. It means we can host the prime minister when she comes.' 'How is the governor? Is he taking to his new life?'

'He makes himself busy,' Banerjee replied. 'A lot of letters but never any replies.'

The governor-general roared so heartily his leg knocked over a table.

'Thank you, Banerjee. You've already become somewhat essential to our project here.'

Banerjee made to speak but then stopped.

'Go on.'

'It's just a little sensitive, sir. People are asking about Albert's deal with us.'

'Who's asking?' The governor-general put his empty glass on the table and leant forward.

'Karan's rumoured lover, Oliver, and the gay from Bombay.'

'Rumoured lover, Banerjee. The prime minister will be tickled pink, I think is what you say here?'

'You don't think we should be worried? Apparently, the Chinese are spreading rumours. And the journalist may have the story.'

'Let me worry about all this. The gay from Bombay. You are good.' He chuckled.

* * *

Oliver pointed to Arun's bag at the bedroom door. 'So you came prepared tonight?'

'What's with Abdul?'

'He's an arsehole and a drunk. And he's always felt inferior to Karan. Isha loves to have those people around her. And she'll be worse than ever now. She'll have chalked that up as a success. Winding him up so much that he verbally shits himself in front of us.'

Getting undressed as if he lived there, Arun asked, 'And the allegations about Albert?'

'Much more serious, for sure. I'm going to ask to see him in the next few days. Try to flush it out. Now come here.' Oliver put on an Indian comedy channel. Arun jumped up. 'He's from Bangalore. He's funny but they say he's close to the people around the prime minister. Apparently, Sunil uncle books him for all the party fundraisers.' Arun was snickering even before hearing the guy's set.

'The Indians are really making themselves at home in England. They've killed a journalist, put troops on the streets and got rid of the head of state. Some people are calling London "Little Ladakh".'

Arun pointed at the audience, cracking up, 'He is killing it. But people say he runs his more political jokes past the party gundas.'

The comedian continued, 'And the new first lady of the people can't even have a glass of champagne in a Rolls-Royce on the way to a funeral without being gaslighted. She should try the Delhi metro on a Thursday night.

'I have a cousin who works in IT in England. I'm from Bangalore—we all have a cousin who works in IT in England.'

The audience howled, and Arun added, 'That's true.'

He continued, 'The Indians used to come to England for a master's in IT; now they have become the masters of it. That shit's got to sting!'

Oliver watched Arun howling and texting his mumbaikar friends.

'And we read the new anticolonial resident commissioner is enjoying himself in comedy clubs in London. Just watch, sir, the joke may be on you if this whole project collapses like one of your father's construction companies.'

Oliver looked at him, 'They know we were in a comedy club together? You think they're telling us they know we kissed in that comedy club?' Arun was pale, his mouth open. 'Maadarchod. Maad-ar-chod.' He turned to Oliver. 'Mother fuckers, you know what, fuck it. I really don't care. I didn't want to do this job anyway. If they think they can threaten me via some fucking two-bit Bangalore comedian, they have another think coming.'

Five

Karan was still editing his speech as Umesh drove out of Number 10. A brilliant blue flash of light kept interrupting his train of thought. He took a deep breath and made to ask Isha a question, then he paused and returned to the speech. After another run of blue flashes, he breathed in again. Then shook his head.

'What is it?' she tutted.

'Are the flags different? Are they bigger or something?'

'You are obsessed. In fact, you're beginning to sound like the vegan warriors and the India Quit brigade.'

'And what is it with all these kangaroos? Has the Australian prime minister said something particularly anti-Indian again?'

Isha groaned. 'He is such a fucking joke.'

Karan pointed at the giant flags framing the view. 'Look at the spinning wheel. It IS fucking bigger!'

Umesh waited. 'It's bigger, sir.' He pulled up beside an army van whose disgorged young soldiers were performing a series of perfectly timed actions. Karan called Oliver. 'He does have a fucking fetish.'

'What are you talking about? It's Saturday. I know at least one of us is in bed. But shouldn't we both be?'

'Fuck off. I'm watching our highly trained military lower, fold and then raise a new anglo-indian flag. They've got it down to thirty-eight seconds. I've just timed them. It's manoeuvres of sorts, I suppose.'

'You need to stop worrying about this stuff,' Oliver sighed.

'This stuff is what shows the country how far we've lost control.'

'No, it doesn't. In fact, I'm hanging up now. Before you go, how should I go about trying to get an appointment to see Albert?'

Karan continued watching the troops ceremoniously remove flags and unfurl new ones, 'I'll text his office and have them set something up. Do you want me to tell them what it's about?'

Oliver paused, 'Hmm, say it's for his views on how much more we should pay for the important diplomatic and public-facing work of the new office of the governor.'

Karan chuckled, 'That will get you an immediate hearing.' He hung up and counted the number of Indian flags he could see. 'Fifteen at least. What a total fucking waste of time.' He tried to attract Isha's attention. 'At least it's nice to have a day out.'

She stopped reapplying lipstick. 'It's not a fucking day out. It's an inconvenient morning. I had wanted to go early to the workshop and see what that bunch of lazy fuckers had done this week. But no, now I've got to cosplay mute spouse for some God-knows-what shitty little function. Can you promise you'll not speak for long so I can get out before noon, please?'

Trafalgar Square was now home to an encampment of anti-indianisation Indians. All manner of Indian kitchens had been

dotted around Nelson's column and the square's oversized fountains. 'That smells delicious,' Karan declared.

'You're not Indian enough to eat from those grotty little places. You know that. Remember last time pitaji took you out in old Delhi. You were shitting for days.'

Karan groaned. 'It's hardly old fucking Delhi out there. Surely, we're still maintaining food quality standards.'

'Fuck knows. But you're not eating there. That's all I know.'

Karan returned to editing his remarks. When he next checked, heavy, black wrought-iron gates were creaking open for Umesh. 'My god! Flags here too!' He pointed at the vastly oversized anglo-indian banner aggressively flapping from the centre of a nineteenth-century pediment high above them.

'It is bigger,' Isha finally agreed. 'That wheel looks like one of those bindis your aunty Ritu used to put on me whenever we visited,' Isha teased and pressed her thumb hard on to Karan's forehead. 'She'd smudge it around a bit to make it look like she'd been in some sort of battle for your soul.'

Karan chuckled. 'Yes, do you remember the time we went to visit Oliver after seeing her? He opened the door and almost fainted when he thought you had punched me in the head and given me concussion. You only convinced him when he wiped it off with his shirtsleeve. It took him weeks to get the stain out.'

Umesh stopped at a red carpet which jutted out from the middle of the pillared colonnade, like a giant red snake lashing its way down the stone steps. A bespectacled Indian man was checking he hadn't dirtied it. 'First minister, I'm Dr Chandragupta, welcome to the new centre for ayurveda, yoga and complementary medicine.'

Karan shook Dr Chandragupta's hand and deliberately stepped on to the carpet, forcing his host to check the soles of Karan's shoes as they walked. 'From the time I was born, Dr Chandragupta, until about three days ago, this was known as the British Museum. So, you might find it hard to convince me of the depths of your rebranding. Did you need to add the flag?'

'Yes, first minister. The governor-general's office was clear, a flag had to be flown. As you can imagine, it's taken our maintenance crew a few days to do that safely. I've convinced the local council we aren't so much making a striking change to the fabric of the building as building on its narrative journey of "the progress of civilisation".'

'Civilisations, I suppose, Dr Chandragupta. Did they worry just as much about the change of use of the museum?' The director was silent and scanned the area behind him. Karan continued, 'I appreciate the governor-general is the vip today so I will go in and take my seat. But perhaps you could take me to my favourite piece first, the amaravati sculptures.'

'I'm afraid that won't be possible, first minister.'

'I'm sure you can take me there and be back in time for the governor-general. I'm deliberately twenty minutes early.'

'Time isn't the issue. We've sent all objectives deemed to be colonial spoils back to their country of origin or place of relevance,' Dr Chandragupta replied matter-of-factly.

'Colonial spoils.' Karan stopped. 'Country of origin or place of relevance. So what's left in here?'

'Nothing, I'm afraid, first minister. Just some freshly painted rooms awaiting yoga mats.'

They entered the foyer of the once-great institution. Karan peered down empty corridors to his left and right. Nothing. The indentation on the floor where the rosetta stone had stood was all that was left of the 2,200-year-old block of Egyptian rock that had been on almost-continuous display since 1802. 'Where is it?' Karan asked. 'I know it hasn't always been well cared for—the Ottomans took it from a temple, Napoleon's forces took it as part of his Egyptian campaigns; and finally we grabbed it. But where is it now? What's its country of origin or place of relevance?'

'It's on its way to Egypt via Portugal. The Indian ambassador in Lisbon asked for some interesting cultural objects for a show he is putting on at his residence. He is a friend of the governor-general. I was delighted we were able to help.'

'Well, Dr Chandragupta, the stone is a testament to some sort of collective human desire to understand one another. And of a messy past where Europeans took control of other people's destiny and imposed their views and values. So a journey home via Portugal isn't entirely mad, I suppose.' Karan rolled his eyes at Isha.

'I'm so glad you agree, first minister. It also marks progress, innovation and the search for knowledge. The stone's quotidian decree established the cult of the divine new ruler—Ptolemy the fifth in ancient Egyptian hieroglyphic, Demotic scripts as well as ancient Greek. Its real magic was its role in the global competition of the late eighteenth century and early nineteenth century to unlock the mysteries of the ancient world. A race, bolstered by international comity and reciprocity, hindered by churlishness, and won by a Frenchman. In deciphering the code on the face of the stone, he became the first modern human to read and understand ancient Egyptian. He discerned that ancient Egyptian symbols were drawn from elemental forces, agriculture and the land and were as relevant to our understanding of contemporary Egypt.'

'Oh God, get me out of here.' Isha groaned.

Dr Chandragupta missed a step as he accompanied them into the sunlit hall of the great court, pointing out its 3,312 individual glass panels. 'We're not sending them back, are we?' Karan asked, happy to feel the sun's warmth.

'This will be a nice spot for yoga,' Isha told him. 'You see,' she prodded, 'we Indians do know what we are doing.'

Karan was busy talking to the lucky few who had been chosen to attend the morning's event. 'Thank you for your support,' he repeated on loop. 'Christ,' he whispered to Isha, 'every one of the party's top donors is here.' Diplomats and religious leaders had been seated ahead of the funders. Karan could tell the countries whose representatives had received an unexpected call from Dr Chandragupta to take back what they thought was rightfully theirs.

'Most of these countries didn't exist when Britain looted all that stuff,' Isha grimaced as she waved at the commonwealth ambassadors. 'We should have been given first look at this collection. I could have put some of it in ten downing or in next season's collection.'

Dr Chandragupta's staff were nervously directing the press to a pen far from the vips. Two Indian camera crews had been given a prime spot directly in front of the lectern. A British journalist broke free and approached Karan. 'Is there anything you won't let our Indian overlords beg, borrow or give away, first minister?'

Before he could answer, the governor-general's personal swami arrived, and greeted Karan with a heartfelt 'Namaskar'.

'Today is a momentous day for the world, first minister; there has been much evil at the centre of our world cities and here in London in particular. So many reports of violence in these cities. So much stolen from around the world. So many of our gods whisked from our temples have been hidden in cold, dark rooms unbefitting of their sacred status. This marvellous act of Indian generosity will cleanse London and cleanse all these fallen cities. Their people will be pure again.'

Karan wrinkled his forehead. 'Yes, the governor-general is showing real leadership.' He gazed distractedly at the two empty seats beside him on which the flags of Greece and Nigeria had been placed.

* * *

Oliver and Arun were still in bed, browsing through Molly's website, when Oliver's phone rang. 'Hello, Sally. It's a bit early for you on a Saturday.'

'Don't say any more on the phone. Please. Can we meet? We need to. No, we must meet.'

'Sure, let's meet. Shall we go to our usual—'

'No, don't say it. I will text you a time and location. I know I sound crazy. But I met a guy last night. And now I'm worried.'

'Which guy?'

'The guy who set up the website about the girl you killed.'

'Ah.' She hung up before he could say anything else. He glanced at Arun. 'It's going to be a day.'

* * *

Oliver walked underneath the creamy yellow sandstone arch and looked down the tree-lined central avenue of Brompton cemetery. At the far end he could just make out the dome of the chapel. Sally was staring at one of the many elaborate memorials to the 200,000 people buried there. She was laying some purple dahlias as Oliver approached, 'Emmeline Pankhurst's grave? This is a bit cloak-and-dagger, isn't it?'

'I'd like to say it's just two friends meeting. Let's walk.' She led him to a bench away from the families, runners and kamikaze cyclists. Pointing at the graves around them, she said, 'It's a veritable who-was-who of mid-nineteenth-century west London.'

'Yes, you might make it in here if you're lucky.'

'Helpfully, I'm from the east. And I'm not giving them 30,000 pounds for the privilege.'

'Sally, why am I here?'

'I don't quite know where to start. I hired Molly Stevens earlier this year. We agreed she'd go undercover and discover what was going on at Merchant's. She confirmed they'd been funded by a host of dodgy countries to get them through the financial crash. But I think she was going to find out that they also facilitated much of the Indian government's preparation for integration.'

'What?'

'Yes, we think Sunil Grover, acting on behalf of the Indian prime minister, didn't only bet against the pound to push us into India's hands. He, and Merchant's, had been helping Indians acquire all the critical bits of our national infrastructure, the enablers of our whole country, in anticipation of a big payday that actually arrived.'

Oliver took a deep breath. 'Do you have proof of all this?'

'Only what Molly sent me. Have a look.' She handed him Molly's phone. 'You'll also see Lord Banerjee had taken a short position on the pound too, ahead of integration.'

'You know you sound crazy, don't you?'

'Yes, but we have proof of the Chinese, Iranian and Russian money. And that Sunil bet heavily against sterling. And Banerjee. If we'd had a few more days, I'm sure she'd have found what we needed. Really dodgy money is flowing from Gujarat to Mauritius, then via a few former British colonies and Overseas Territories and into Moldova.'

'Why are you telling me another conspiracy theory?'

'Because I met the man behind the website last night. He took this phone off Molly the night she was killed. An hour after he met me, he was murdered. And someone is calling me on this phone threatening me.'

'Indian?'

'No, Northern Irish. But I don't think the accent tells us who the paymaster is.'

'Do you want me to take the phone?'

'No. But I do want you to know all this. I think you also know this is a bad deal. And that Karan's father-in-law is dodgy.'

Oliver stared straight ahead.

'And the reason I think that is you're in a relationship with Arun Deshmukh,' she paused to watch Oliver's reaction, 'and he is in your apartment right now. I know that because I've been outside your apartment for most of the last twenty-four hours deciding whether to speak to you or not. I don't think anyone else has worked it out. But they will. You know that. I think Arun should ask his father's people in Mumbai if anyone suspected financial links between Merchant's and the prime minister.' Oliver nodded. 'I want you to help me expose these people for what they are. And I want to help you and Karan kick them the fuck out of our country.'

'Have you seen how the Indian government deals with traitors?'

'No, but I've seen how they deliver extrajudicial killings on the streets of London. Come on. This isn't why you and Karan came into politics, is it?'

'Give me a few days. I'll text you.'

'One more thing.' Sally took out a bag of nuts and started to attract the park's plump, well-fed squirrels. 'Molly was also working on a piece about Albert's Indian links. She was close to suggesting Albert did some kind of deal to protect his position in the event of a transition.'

'You're trying to tell me you have evidence the king is a traitor? I don't believe it.'

'Well, it wouldn't be the first time, now, would it? But no, we don't have the evidence. I hoped it would be on her phone.'

Oliver got up and left Sally to the squirrels. At Hyde Park Corner a police barricade blocked his progress beyond the commonwealth gates, whose lotus flames were now permanently lit. 'Can you show any identification please?' an officer asked.

Oliver flashed his commons pass. 'What's wrong?'

'Nothing, sir. It's just that we used to keep kids from racing down this road on scooters on Saturdays, whereas now we're holding back these damn protesters.'

Oliver looked all the way down the road by the side of Green Park. Tents, encampments, fires, peace placards had all been pushed to the sides to leave just about enough space for two car lanes. He read the signs as he drove along the side of the governor-general's vast gardens. 'Fuck Indo-British Thievery', 'India Quit Killing US.' All dotted with kangaroos. Or their tails. Or their distinctive legs. Limp and sad union jacks were flying from makeshift flagpoles underneath the giant anglo-indian standards the governor-general continued to deploy.

Bearskin-hatted guardsmen opened the gates to allow the car into the governor's residence. Albert was waiting for him. 'Fighting spirit, governor.' Oliver pointed to a real Union Jack defiantly fluttering from a flagpole on the roof.

'Well, one does what one can. I had never planned for any of this.' As he took Oliver through the building's narrow corridors with shelves rammed full of trinkets from every part of the commonwealth, he added absent-mindedly, 'Yes, best to avoid the spears and shields, minister. And the paintings. We've had to cram quite a lot in these last few weeks. Bit of an enforced move over here, you see.' Every inch of wall space was covered with all manner of art. Mainly of Albert and his forebears. 'Bit of a moonlight flit, once the governor-general decided he was for the big house. I mean, I had always hated that place anyway. But it was ours, so to speak.' Oliver knocked over a watercolour. 'Oh, not that. It's one of my best.' Albert cradled the work like it was one of his children.

'Thank you again for seeing me. The first minister apologises he hasn't been able to call on you.'

'He's been told not to, minister. I've had the same odious little protocol sheet. A sad and destructive little poem in blank verse. As hideous as when bagpipes play pop songs. You get the first note of the tune, but the flats turn it all sour. It's required all the best of my sangfroid to keep going.'

Oliver smirked as they passed a few of the finest Leonardo sketches, exquisite Turners and majestic bronzes. 'Well, you do have a few things to distract you. Anyway, the first minister has been called unexpectedly by the governor-general to attend the opening of the ayurveda and yoga centre.'

'That's today, is it?' Albert moaned. 'My centre. I don't suppose they kept my name on it?'

Oliver shook his head.

'It's all so unfair. I spent decades talking about all this stuff. And befriending every bloody Indian in the country. And all for nothing.'

'Well, perhaps some of it saved the country, sir. Perhaps you had a bigger plan that put country second and self first?'

'What do you mean, minister?'

'I mean you could have ended up like the Romanovs. Or the Nizams of Hyderabad.'

'That may yet happen, minister. I hope you are here to confirm that my privy purse will continue. We can't have it all eaten up by that lodger of last resort over the road.'

Oliver laughed. 'No, quite. You haven't done too badly out of all this, sir. Is it at all possible that you had some forewarning of the Indian government's plan? As you say, you did have a good relationship with many prominent Indians.'

Albert ignored him. 'It is the English people I worry about. Politicians come and go. Even the governor-general will retire. Only my family and the English people endure. Forced to make the best of the beds you force us to lie on.'

'You're also still head of the commonwealth.'

'The Indian imperial commonwealth. Whatever that means. No one calls asking to speak to me. Not even the secretary general. My grandfather invented her bloody job. And not even a card. It wasn't at all what I expected, you know?'

'What were you expecting?'

'Well, obviously, I had heard things. Our country was far more exposed to the whims of a vindictive Indian government than politicians here realised. I made it my business to have open lines of communication, as it were, in case they were needed. I offered both sides my services as a trusted intermediary.'

'And what did the Indians guarantee you in return?'

'Well, let's just say not this, minister. Not bloody this. And I might as well pack it all in.'

'Are you saying there's a limit, sir, to how far you would be prepared to go to make integration a success?'

Albert chose to ignore this. 'Minister, my role was limited. It had always been limited. To advise, guide and warn. Keep the realms connected. Listen to their leaders. Give a friendly nudge. But I cannot act. That is for you politicians alone. And while I fear you will come to regret the choices you have made, I must also think about how this family continues. We represent something far greater than the legal position of the first minister and the government of Britain or state of the Republic of India. We represent the continuously changing, impermanent desires of the English people. So it is for you to fix the political mess and for me to listen to how you plan to do it. But it is as clear as the nose on your face that integration is far from being a success.'

Oliver asked, 'But I do need to know, sir. This inheritance you spoke about. Did you secure it through a deal with India?'

Albert's wizened eyes narrowed. 'I think we are done here, minister.'

* * *

Karan felt diminished and diminutive sitting next to the tall, handsome and slender high commissioner of Nigeria. He scanned the room and wished they'd placed him nearer a more minor ambassador. The Italian was about the right height. Not too tall but not too small. He would ask Seb to consider height charts as well as seating plans in future.

'I received the call last night,' Karan heard the Greek ambassador tell Isha, 'I had been on my annual holiday and only had time to grab a few jars of my family's renowned marmalade before catching the flight from Chios.' His longish grey hair and bronze glow confirmed the governor-general's hastily arranged press conference had interrupted his sun-worship. 'I will make sure to send some to the first minister.'

The governor-general strode in with Dr Chandragupta in tow. The poor doctor attempted to head to the podium to give some introductory remarks. The governor-general ignored all of his exhortations and headed straight for the microphone himself. 'Today, we celebrate the rededication of what was the British Museum with a new purpose; one much more fitting for the twenty-first century.' The governor-general was warming to his theme. 'India has need for neither imperial possessions nor the loot of lost ages.' Karan was struggling to stay awake from a mixture of the heat from the camera lights and the sun streaming in. His head was drooping and nodding. Occasional spasms jolted him back to life. Some of these were being initiated by Isha's middle finger.

'Here.' The governor-general raised his arms and pointed up to the glass roof like a preacher about to condemn the damned. 'In this erstwhile hall of larceny, we announce our new policy of return and renewal.' The audience were murmuring. The Greek and Nigerian ambassadors sitting forward. The news anchors telling their studios to go live. 'Of all of it. From the Benin Bronzes to the Parthenon Marbles, these long-term migrants finally go home.' The room broke out into rapturous applause. The Greek ambassador and Nigerian high commissioner stood.

The screech of metal chairs on the tiled floor forced Karan to jump up. He whispered, 'He's launched a new tv format; I'm a cultural deity, get me out of here.' He sat back down and rubbed his tired eyes. He would shut them for only a minute.

The governor-general smiled. He knew he was about to catch the world's attention. 'With the blessing of the Indian prime minister and her state government here in England represented by its first minister, we also send our gods home. Our sacred Hindu gods. Locked up in dingy basement storerooms for hundreds of years. They too will now find peace.' The governor-general shut his eyes. A whoosh and clatter of camera clicks captured him bringing his palms together on his chest. He stood there like one of the former museum's statues for all ages before adding, 'Namaste.' When the snaps had silenced, he continued.

'But that is not all, with India's Bara North Atlantic Yatra, we are reintegrating a once-great empire. It reminds one of Kipling: I've seen a neater, sweeter maiden on the road to Mandalay.'

Karan's eyes shut as he thought about the last time he had heard those words. He and Oliver had been dancing in their favourite club in Bradford. They'd spent that Friday night like they'd spent every Friday night since turning seventeen. Dancing. Their pocket money saved. New shoes and shirts had been bought. Neither Karan nor Oliver's parents knew where they went. Nor did they want to know. They just asked they stay away from groups of white kids. The news reports of the racist gangs were still growing. Oliver was one of the few white guys who danced in the club, so everybody recognised them. Karan knew it was assumed they were both gay. Time after time he flirted unsuccessfully with all the women around them. It didn't help that Oliver was the better dancer—and had absolutely no interest in talking to anyone other than Karan. As usual, they left around midnight and, with just enough money, waited for a taxi. The taxi rank was a cross between a war zone and the trials for the olympic boxing team. They kept themselves within sight of the club's helpful, but more importantly majestic, bouncers. A couple of white guys were walking up the street. Oliver was in the middle of the road and had finally summoned a car. He turned to see one of the guys nose to nose with Karan. The guy focused on Oliver and spat over Karan's right ear, some of it going down his back, 'You fucking Paki poof.'

Oliver ran between them. 'You're a fucking arsehole, mate.'

The guy stood his ground as the bouncers came over. 'Fuck, it's a gay club now, is it? Even the bouncers are poofs over here, are you?' They both watched the bouncers deliver a nose-cracking blow that knocked him to the ground.

Safely in the taxi, Oliver asked, 'You all right?'

'I mean, it's just normal, isn't it.'

Oliver nodded as Karan added, 'The women think I'm gay so the men might as well too.' But Karan knew what he meant. That was normal too.

Oliver would stay over and the next day the smell of freshly made parathas would wake them up. Mrs Puri's Saturday parathas were legendary. Kids from houses up and down the street would show up for them. Downstairs, Karan's father was reading the *Guardian* while Karan read Oliver's *Spectator*. Karan had devoured his first paratha and was making for his second, adding yoghurt and black pepper. 'Have you heard from Oxford yet?' his father asked. Karan shook his head mid-mouthful. 'An Oxford lawyer in the family. That's all we want.' Karan was about to help himself to a third paratha when Oliver came downstairs wearing a fresh shirt and a prominent Tory-blue rosette. 'Oliver, son, you eat me out of house and home, then you go work for the enemy!'

'Not the enemy, Mr Puri. The party that will keep your family in the life to which it has become accustomed!' Oliver made an exaggerated look around Karan's home. 'This doesn't look to me like the modest surroundings of a normal Labour voter, sir. I think we will put you down as undecided!' Karan howled with laughter. Oliver and his dad's Saturday battles were always good-humoured.

His dad continued, 'But only Labour has been good to our people!'

Karan winked at Oliver. 'Our people, dad. We're British. I'm as British as anyone on this street. You've proved we don't need brown handouts or even Mr Brown's handouts!' Karan stood up and with a flourish pulled his own conservative rosette from his pocket. Putting it on, he added, 'And get rid of Mr Blair!'

Karan's father mocked them. 'Well, you're not going to do Mr Blair any damage in Bradford. So fill your boots, as my old manager used to say!'

'And take some of these for afters.' Mrs Puri had a box of parathas freshly wrapped in foil.

'Mrs Puri, these are the best parathas in England!' Karan's mum beamed.

'Get him out,' Karan's dad shouted, 'before he steals my wife as well as my son!' Karan cackled too and walked from the conservatory past the kitchen, his mother's sitting room on the left, his father's study on the right, a spare bedroom and finally two front rooms either side of the front door. Oliver was grinning like a schoolboy on the last day of term. They jumped in Oliver's little car and pulled out of the double-entry drive. His father was proud of the new red chips he'd bought, 'Just in time for Mr Blair's second victory.' He always called him 'Mr Blair'. Karan didn't know how much money he had given the local Labour party. It was enough to be invited to all their constituency events, which his father attended, having to admit that yes, his son was currently a Tory.

'We're going to Shipley,' Oliver told him. 'Labour lost the council to no-overall control. The ward is green, and we and Labour came joint second. So there's a chance we can pick up some voters here. And who knows, maybe you'll be their MP someday.' Oliver pulled into the petrol station and got out of the car. Karan watched him wandering the aisles. He was still starving and hoped he'd buy a twix for them, with Oliver making some outrageous joke about sharing a finger. Karan checked to see if he'd left anything to eat in the glove compartment. He found a scrunched-up letter with the Oxford

University logo. Oliver had been accepted to Merton. It was the college they both wanted to attend. They'd visited and found the ideal rooms next door to one another. Oliver had even managed to chat up one of the second-years. Karan wiped a tear of pride, squashed the letter and replaced it as Oliver waved the chocolate bar at him suggestively.

Just as Fridays were for dancing, Saturdays were for canvassing. In Shipley they were met by the thirty-something prospective parliamentary candidate and a couple of long-serving councillors. He had the zealot-like intensity of someone trying to get on the central office list of candidates for anywhere other than Shipley. As usual they were the youngest by far.

Out door-knocking, Oliver was trying to replace a gate that was hanging off its post as Karan walked down the path that had more weeds than pavement. 'Why can't they just get out and clean up their own front garden?' Karan whispered. 'Have the council to do everything for them?' Oliver nodded as Karan knocked. The tv was on. A dog barked. Nobody came to the door. Karan and Oliver winked at each other, and Karan knocked again. Their agreed rule was two knocks. Oliver peered in the front window, 'We have movement.'

The door opened, and a forty-something man said, 'Jehovah's Witnesses?'

'No,' Karan replied, pointing at his rosette. 'We're here from the conservative party.'

'You're interrupting the horse-racing.'

'We wondered if you'd consider voting conservative at the next election. We've got a great candidate. He's local and just down there.'

'He's not local.' The man pointed at Karan and turned to Oliver. 'If your candidate's another one, you're not getting my vote.' And slammed the door shut.

'So he knew you were from Wyke then. I told you to watch that accent.' Karan smirked. He was resigned to it. He wondered if he'd have to listen to it his whole life. Oliver had the twix in his hand. 'Time for this now?'

'Time for this now?' was what Oliver would say whenever they opened the cheap champagne they drank as students. On their graduation night he failed to sneak a bottle into their favourite comedy club. Having spent the last of Oliver's student loan on the tickets, they'd been forced to toast their success with tap water.

By the time they sat down the comedian was onto politics. 'Tony Blair was young and cool when he came in. But four years of being George Bush's poodle have aged him.'

Karan groaned before toasting Oliver. 'But tell me again why we decided on King's college?'

Oliver smiled at him. 'Because it's the only place you got into.'

'Do you think we'd have enjoyed Oxford?' Karan asked.

Without thinking, Oliver replied, 'They didn't want us. So, fuck 'em.' He toasted Karan.

'So we've got graduates in tonight.' The comedian's eye had been drawn to them.

'You mean those two,' Oliver shouted, pointing at two well-dressed, thirty-something city-boy bankers. The crowd giggled.

'Tell us you did something useful like medicine or science?' the comedian asked.

'Of course not! Politics and economics.' He dusted off his shoulders. 'Ready for the real world! Were you theatre studies?' The crowd hooted with laughter as Oliver made a show of examining him in detail. 'Hmm. Probably not. Those shoes look more like English lit?'

'So what are you planning on doing when you grow up?'

'I'll be a minister in a conservative government.'

'Not this decade you won't.'

'You'll see!' Oliver replied. He was proud of his repartee and that the crowd were doubled up with him. He turned around to see if Karan was enjoying his heckling as much as he was. Karan's seat was empty. He had moved to the table next to them and was chatting up an Indian girl who was pouring them both some fine champagne. The comedian had moved on too.

Later that summer, Karan and Isha were in Hyde Park with Oliver and David, his cute new boyfriend. As usual Isha had brought a fancy blanket and a basket of goodies. Oliver, head in David's lap, put his book down. 'This Clinton biography is a greater work of fiction than *Oliver Twist*.' He picked up a cheese twist, asking, 'Did you make these delicious things?'

Isha was flicking through fashion magazines. 'No, it's mixture. Some by pitaji's chef. We brought him over. And some from our favourite Chelsea delis!'

'So this is your last weekend of freedom?' Karan asked.

'Yeah,' Oliver replied. 'As of Monday, you're looking at a researcher in conservative central office. David goes to the city. And he had better make oodles of cash.'

David put the *Financial Times* down. 'I bloody hope so. I hope whatever it is I need to do is easier to understand than reading the *FT*.' They fell about laughing.

'You've been especially secretive about your plans,' Oliver said. Karan was quiet, glancing furtively at Isha, who hadn't lifted her head from the pictures of Kate Moss. Oliver could sense that something was coming. 'You're not eloping, are you?'

Finally, Isha grabbed Karan's hand. 'I'm breaking up the boy band. He's coming to Amherst with me.' Oliver widened his eyes to stop the tears from coming. He scanned the park. Groups of boys playing football. Families wandering round with kids in buggies and picture-perfect puppies.

He caught himself. 'That's amazing news. I knew you'd both do it.'

Karan said, 'Yup. Business admin. Who knows what next?'

Oliver raised his glass. 'Any more of Mr Blair and it's the end of freedom as we know it.'

'Pitaji's office has already found us a flat. He's paying for it all on one condition. We move to India at the end of the programme and Karan asks his permission to marry me.' Oliver choked on his drink.

David kicked him out of his lap. 'Are you getting married? That's amazing! We need more champagne.' Isha popped another bottle open as David continued, 'Ha! You're going to meet all those right-wing hindus who believe they'll be president one day.'

'Yes!' Oliver continued in an American accent. 'We know you are really a socialist country. When you get into power you must privatise your socialist healthcare system. Get out of communist Europe. Stop wasting billions on NATO. Let the Germans pay for all of it. Get a trade deal with us and with India. And you'll be fine.'

* * *

True to his word, the month after graduating, Karan was in Isha's home in Delhi. Over the course of a week, he'd met the entire family and almost every member of the Lok Sabha. They'd all been told he was a future prime minister of England. Sunil would see to that. That particular morning chairs had been set up under the mango tree at the bottom of the garden. Karan was waiting. Sunil was running late and in a hurry. He was a man with too much to do. To change Indian politics. And to marry off his daughter. 'Karan,' Sunil said as he walked up to him. Karan stood.

'Karan, I can see that you make Isha happy.'

Karan smiled.

'And I know that you are from an ordinary Indian family in England.'

Karan tried to say something.

'I want my daughter to be happy and to have the best in life. She tells me she will be happy with you. So I will make sure that you both have the best in life. My accountant will talk to you today. There will be Indian funds and US shares as part of a sizeable dowry. But you will make no claim on any of Isha's assets. You'll have a central London townhouse as a gift from me. And I will invest in Isha's business and supplement her income until such time as your businesses take off.'

'Businesses?'

Sunil guffawed. 'Isha's in the business of fashion. You will be in the business of politics. And you'll both do me proud.' Sunil slapped Karan on the back and walked off to his office. Karan watched Sunil issue orders to someone on the veranda and promptly despatch him down to the mango tree.

Isha smiled at the secretaries in her father's outer office and walked past the businessmen waiting to meet him. She knocked and walked into his private office. The walls were covered with his honorary degrees and photos with the leaders of his generation of politicians. Ushaji had pride of place beside her father and grandfather. He motioned her to come in. 'It's done, beti.'

'Thank you, pitaji, but what did you tell Karan?'

'I told him you'd be in the business of fashion, and he'd be in the business of politics. My accountant is dealing with him now.'

'But I told you I didn't want that. We agreed once I was married, I could decide what I would do. That my husband and I would decide what to do. What if we want to have a family and live an anonymous, quiet life in England somewhere? Karan thinks he might want to work in New York. You know I'd love that.'

'No.' He stood up. 'You've had your fun. Now you work for me.'

'No, pitaji. It's our time now.'

Sunil clicked his fingers. 'It can all stop like that. I can send Karan home. You can come here and marry a nice Indian boy like Arun. Is that what you want?'

Isha tried to speak.

'You don't know you are born,' he continued. 'If you had a good Indian boy you'd have no life. That is what I am saving you from. These English boys. You will have Karan wrapped around your little finger. Then when I need him to do something, you can make sure he does. Is that okay?'

Isha nodded.

'You need to find a good business in London. And be successful in your own right. Karan must go into politics. It is all set. Ushaji agrees. And no children until I say so. Concentrate on finding a business. It doesn't matter what it is. I will pay for it. You must be successful too.' He brought some documents out of his drawer. 'Now, I have an additional account at a private bank in London that I want your name to be on. You'll receive private income from this account, but you'll also see a lot of movement of funds. Please don't worry about it.'

'Do you think Karan can become prime minister?'

'I think any son-in-law of mine would. It just happens to have fallen on him.'

'Then I'll do what you ask, pitaji.'

* * *

In late March 2010 Karan was in central London in a low-ceilinged room with four septuagenarians. His expensively tailored dark grey suit was the uniform of a successful investment banker. He was nervous. The selection panel of the Chelsea constituency had modernised in their own way. They had reluctantly agreed to have a woman participant. 'Father's law firm in Bradford, was it?' she asked. 'Provincial clientele?'

Karan's hands gripped either side of the chair and pushed him slightly forward. 'I'm not quite sure what you mean.'

'She means we assume it did a lot of immigration work. Not really much call for him to be at the high court?' the chairman continued.

'British clients, if that's what you mean.' The tips of Karan's fingers were hurting as he pushed them into the underside of the seat.

'It's just,' the woman intervened, 'well, we're quite a homogenous constituency and association. We're just not sure you'll, well ...'

‘Fit in?’ Karan scrutinised the empty scoring sheets in front of each of them.

‘So glad you see the point we are trying to make.’ The panel members closed their folders without adding any comments.

‘I think we’re done here.’

Karan stood up. ‘Well, thank you for your time.’ He was on the phone to Oliver as he walked to the Thames. He slumped into a seat in his favourite sunken garden. ‘Those fucking idiots. The nasty party is alive and well. In central fucking London.’ Karan’s voice broke as he said it.

Oliver was also studying the Thames from his portcullis house office. ‘It was always going to be tough down here. There’s a lot of competition. This was just to get you on hq’s radar. Remember that. You were polite, weren’t you? There’s a seat in Bradford. The MP is stepping down. I’ve convinced him to wait until the last minute so we can parachute in a candidate. You’ll get it. Now stop fucking about and meet me at the house. You owe me a good drink with all that money you make.’

Oliver placed a second call. ‘He’s done the dummy run. He will be our candidate. Yes, I think you’ll have to offer a peerage to get the old fucker to stand down. Look, his father-in-law has put more money in than anyone else. We agreed to this. Just fucking do it.’

* * *

On the tenth of May, Karan, Oliver and Isha were in Oliver’s parliamentary office watching various groupings of British politicians try to form a government.

‘Coalition, then.’ Oliver popped a bottle of champagne. Isha was on the phone to her father.

Karan asked, ‘Are we in government yet?’

‘We will be by tomorrow. Nobody wants the current one to stay. Not even his own party,’ Oliver replied. ‘But who cares? You’re in parliament. Here, drink this.’

Taking her glass, Isha asked, 'What am I going to do now the boy band is back together?'

Oliver smiled. 'Well, interestingly, I know a family in east London who want to sell an old-school fabric workshop. You could turn it into the atelier you haven't shut up about since you got back. I'm sure I can get your father an excellent price.' Isha winked at him.

* * *

'Ow.' Karan felt his side as Isha prodded him back to life. The Greek ambassador smiled. The governor-general was still at the podium. 'I am also heartily pleased to announce a visit by our Indian prime minister to this thirtieth state of the Indian Republic later this year. Through her devotion to our country—'

'Murderers!' a group of young people broke into the great court, throwing red paint at the assembled dignitaries. Police ran in behind them as the protesters screamed, 'Traitors, Indians fucking out!' In their struggle to free themselves from the flailing hands of police and security guards, they knocked over cameras as well as photographers. The protesters took off their jackets proudly to display 'India Quit' t-shirts and threw packets of brown-red dye on the floor, which slowly encircled the vips in a shallow, viscous, bloody pool.

The governor-general's security grabbed him from the podium and rushed him to safety. One of the interlopers shouted, 'You've all got blood on your hands,' as she was pulled down by a well-placed policeman.

Another protester squirted red ink over Karan and Isha, shouting, 'You are fucking roos! Death to traitors.'

Karan's police protection officer knocked one of them over while an enormous policeman pushed another back, saying, 'That's enough now.' More protection officers grabbed Karan and Isha and rushed them out the same route as the governor-general.

The protesters were linking arms on the bloodstained floor. Officers slipped as they walked round them. Some had to take such dainty steps it made Karan snigger. Until he caught the eye of one activist who mouthed, 'Murderer.'

Karan and Isha sat in silence in the car red dye dripping down their hair and faces. Karan's phone rang. 'First minister.'

'Yes, governor-general?'

'We are concerned about today's lapse in security. Obviously, people have a right to peaceful political assembly but a planned attack on the government of India cannot go unnoticed.'

'I assure you it won't, governor-general. I expect to have an update from the police later today on the charges that will be brought. But we will be proportionate.'

'Charges won't be enough, first minister. We will need to consider whether all this so-called freedom of assembly people enjoy here is really necessary.' The governor-general hung up.

Isha glanced at Karan. 'He's right, you know. My father has texted to say the Indian prime minister wants you to take a much tougher line on the right to protest. He also told me they have evidence that Arun's party is making a serious amount of commission on the assets that are being integrated. They want you to look into this.'

'That's bullshit. Let's talk about it later.'

* * *

Isha had been in the shower for over an hour. 'Come on,' Karan shouted. 'You're going to miss the start of Riyaz.' She joined Karan in bed as the larger-than-life comedian came on stage, 'I just needed to wash those people off me.'

Oliver texted Karan to say, 'We're watching, are you?'

'Is that him?' Isha asked.

'Yes, they are watching too.'

'No wonder he's happy. No one is throwing blood over him. And he's making a shit tonne of money out of his Indian fuckboy. It has to stop, Karan. They are making a mockery of you. It was fine when it was just a little one-night stand. But pitaji says they are building their own little nest egg. Millions of pounds already. You have to stop it.'

'No, Isha, you have to stop. This is nonsense. Your father sends one message, and you so far over the edge you can't see it. Plus, whenever there's a chance to attack Oliver, you—'

'I what?' she fumed.

'You just take such delight in taking it too far.'

'Do I?' she shouted. 'Do I? My father has risked everything for what you have now. And if you can't see that, I don't know how to help you. Promise me you'll ask how much money they are making. You'll see.'

Karan turned the sound up on the tv. 'And it turns out the hon'ble prime minister chose the governor-general for his track record. We all thought it was about his considerable diplomatic pedigree. But it turns out it was his running track record.' They showed footage of the governor-general waddling into his car. 'He left his new ayurveda centre this morning faster than the objects he's sending back to India.' They roared with laughter.

Oliver received a text from Sally. 'Please donate to our campaign for a proper investigation into the death of journalist and freedom fighter Molly Stevens.'

Six

Oliver and Karan were in his office, watching Sally on tv. 'Yes, I'm here on college green as preparations continue for the first visit of the Indian prime minister to her thirtieth state.' The camera panned round to show barren, lifeless streets. 'The police have secured this area around Westminster, but the Indian prime minister is likely to travel on a route littered by protesters.'

'Well, that will just make things more difficult,' Karan told Oliver. 'Can't we move them all?'

'More difficult for whom?' Oliver asked. 'People have a right to protest.'

'Do they? Do they have a right to throw fake blood over Isha and me at a fucking yoga centre?'

'Well, you've let them turn our greatest museum into the best-located yoga centre in the world.'

'Who's we and who's them?' Karan asked. 'I don't know any more. Isha's father has made it abundantly clear if we don't get this visit right, the ramifications for all of us will be terminal.'

'Things can't really be much worse than where we are now, can they?'

* * *

Madam speaker was racing from one end of Westminster Hall to the other in her signature grey trainers. A thousand empty wooden chairs covered the ancient floor as far back as the eye could see. She squeezed in between the rows. 'They're as cramped as a budget airline.'

'I know,' her clerk replied. 'We have been inundated with requests to attend. Both houses. Plus, the Indian prime minister's office handed over her final guest list of 350 people this morning.'

'Three-hundred-and-fifty?' Madam speaker blurted, 'It was only a hundred yesterday.'

'Quite.'

'Thank you for doing this.' She was speaking to one of the cleaners who had been fastidiously vacuuming and polishing every row before the sun had come up. A high-backed, studded leather chair was on the platform ahead of them framed by the Indian flag. The state trumpeters were assembling under a giant stained glass window, the sun reflecting on the gold brocade on their uniforms. A fanfare soared to the rafters before crashing on the cleaners who were positioning anglo-indian standards on alternate steps from the throne to the floor. Holding a flag up, one shouted, 'This wheel is even bigger, like the web of a terrifying spider.' A thick red carpet ran from the last flags to the entrance of the hall.'

Under the trumpets' long, brassy notes, a metallic beat, at the speed of a resting heart, was just perceptible and getting louder. The cleaners watched the red-jacketed guard of the honourable corps of gentlemen-at-arms proceed cautiously down the narrow aisle between the chairs. The retired brigadiers and generals, tall and straight, marched like they were at their passing out-day parade. Every available seam was decorated in heavy gold braid. White swan feathers spouted out of their gleaming helmets, making them look half man, half excited parrot. Their long, ceremonial battle axes swung with a heavy clink. For over five hundred years they'd been the sovereign's bodyguard. Today they'd been included for maximum ceremonial effect. The speaker turned to her clerk. 'We're aren't half bad at this, are we?'

* * *

Oliver walked into his office. 'It's six-thirty in the bloody morning. We were here until 2 a.m.' He pointed at the rows and rows of bleary-eyed staff. 'What happened to working from home?'

They all sniggered, with Alessandra adding, 'Big day, boss. We are here with you.'

Oliver nodded. 'Let's get some coffee sorted and go through it all again.'

'Urgh,' the room cried out in unison.

'That's the spirit!' Oliver replied, throwing his jacket on the sofa in the corner of his room and falling into the chair beside it. His team trooped in carrying black ring binders with the fruits of their overnight labour.

'Right, I know we've only had a day to do this. And we might have preferred to delay the big visit.'

'You mean postpone indefinitely,' one replied.

'Quite. But here we are. The big boss is coming. And Karan has given us a job to do. So take me through where we got to. Trains?'

Alessandra opened her binder and replied, 'All the train-operating companies have been transferred to bharat rail and a joint public-private investment vehicle, 10 per cent of whose stock is owned by Sunil Grover. A large chunk has been taken by the Qataris, the Chinese and the rest by the government of India.'

'Okay. Utilities?'

Another binder opened and someone announced, 'The water companies returned to public ownership last night and were transferred at 5 a.m. this morning to pani bharat. A joint public-private investment vehicle, 10 per cent of whose stock is owned by Sunil Grover. A large chunk has been taken by the Qataris, the Chinese and the rest by the Government of India.'

'The airports?' Oliver was going down his list.

A third binder opened and another of Oliver's team added, 'Other than heathrow, which is already fully owned by Grover Industries, the rest of the UK's airports returned to public ownership this morning. No decision has yet been taken on final ownership structure.'

'And,' Oliver asked the team, 'what has this cost the English state?'

'About 350 billion. Sterling rupee bonds, issued by the Bank of Britain, backed by the government of India.'

'And what will this do to interest rates?'

'They'll go up. But who knows by how much?' Alessandra handed a note to Oliver. 'We received this overnight. Do you want us to do anything?'

'All these banks? And what appears to be most of belgravia, chelsea and westmintser?'

She nodded.

'Where has this come from? The governor-general's office? Direct from Delhi?'

‘Sunil Grover’s office is saying Isha had requested this of Karan. And they would both like an update.’ All eyes were on Oliver.

Oliver put the note in the pocket of his suit jacket. ‘Right, I’ll speak to Karan about this. But I need your best options for delaying it. Each item on this larcenous list. And don’t mention any of it now.’ They nodded.

Arun was being escorted into Oliver’s outer office with his team of officials. ‘If you could wait here. I would like briefly to speak to the minister ahead of our formal negotiations.’ The woman behind him pushed forward and said, ‘No, I will come too.’

Oliver was waiting to greet them. Arun opened his eyes as wide as he could, then darted them in the direction of the severe-looking figure beside him. Spotting this, Oliver held out his hand, ‘We haven’t met.’

‘Sunita Sen, head of the commissioner’s delegation and chief negotiator.’

‘Delighted to meet you. Sunita, my colleague will escort you to our ministerial waiting area while I speak to your commissioner.’

Oliver walked into his office and firmly closed the door as Mrs Sen tried to force her way in. He held the handle until he was sure she’d been convinced to go somewhere else.

Arun walked over to the window. ‘Best to look out this way.’

‘Confidential information?’

‘Yes, you do look deliciously handsome in that suit. Would it be terrible to have sex on the table while they waited outside?’

Oliver smirked. ‘With the look on your face, I think the act would be harder for you than for me.’

‘She has been sent from the governor-general’s office. I’ve been told it’s because they want to communicate the success of our negotiation directly to him and the PM. But …’

‘But?’

‘But it’s not that. They want to show publicly they no longer trust me. I’m not sure he ever did. I’m only here to provide cover for

Usha's mad colonial project. But they're making it abundantly clear now to anyone who watches that I'm also on the outside.'

'I think I'm done with all this.' Staring out to the Thames, Oliver stepped closer to Arun. 'Shall we run away now?'

'No, it's your fucking country and we should try to save it. We need a better plan than the one you and Karan have been working to so far. But we need time.'

'Well, then you had better put on a good show. And I have paid for a front-row seat.'

Oliver opened the door and sent a colleague for the delegation. The officials arranged themselves on opposing sides of the table. Oliver's team took their cues from his body language. Today was different from all the meetings they'd had so far. He was formal, serious and immutable. 'Our officials had already agreed that defence and space were out of the scope of this round of negotiations, commissioner.'

Arun tried to intervene, but Oliver spoke over him, 'Can't we settle on announcing the new continental preference scheme? Wherever possible, England will only source Indian imports. From semiconductors to santa hats, they will all be Indian. We'll level a crippling set of tariffs—at least 20 per cent—on all non-Indian imports. That alone should add 0.5 per cent to the Indian economy this year.'

Arun nodded at Sunita. 'Yes, but we are now starting to see the true mess of the English economy. The wanton disregard that became the watchwords for how this country has been run these last few years. And the immediate costs of integration are running at more than 500 billion dollars. Indian families will not put up with any level of hardship to keep England afloat.'

'Well, maybe you can hand it back then?' one of Oliver's team whispered.

'I'm sorry, what was that impertinent remark?' Sunita asked. 'You might be wise to think about the team you have around you, minister. India can decide at the click of a button to leave England to its own devices. But when we go, we take our semiconductors, our IT,' she paused, 'your data, your energy systems, your workforce, and your beloved healthcare system would all be in tatters. Then what have you left?' The room was silent. She continued, 'Nothing. You'll have nothing left. And you'll be bought at 2 cents in the dollar by a much less generous partner.'

Arun nodded. 'Thank you, Sunita ma'am, for spelling out what we are dealing with here. So I'm afraid the agreed list is no longer sufficient, minister. We will also add defence procurement to the announcements the PM will make during the visit. You'll prioritise continental Indian defence supply chains over all your existing defence partnerships. And you will transfer all existing defence IP to our primes. There will be no limits on the export of defence and space technologies from England to continental India and no limits on the manufacturing of those technologies in India.'

Oliver interrupted, 'That breaches a number of international treaty obligations and it's likely to inflame the region.'

Arun shot back, 'You no longer have any international obligations. And nor should you have concern about the region. It has no concern about you.' Arun paused. 'We can take a break for you to speak to the first minister if you'd like.'

Oliver glanced at his team. 'Let's include it.'

Arun said, 'Okay. So I think we're done?'

'Not quite, commissioner.' Sunita handed the list to Oliver. 'The governor-general would also like this list of items included, and he asks for twenty-nine central London properties to be handed over to become state bhavans. Our preference is for all of them to be in Knightsbridge. These will also go on England's side of the ledger, as it were.'

Oliver scanned the list. 'Have you seen this, commissioner?' He handed it to Arun. 'My recommendation is that we stop where we are today. It's a win for both sides for sure. We need to shift to the final preparations for the visit.' He turned the list face down on the table.

Arun nodded, 'I think we should make an announcement about the bhavans. In fact, let's prepone it. That will generate some excitement back home. I can work with your team on that today, minister. But I think we pause on the further transfer of assets. We need to conclude our negotiations now so that the text can be finalised ahead of the signing tomorrow.' Arun focused on Sunita, adding, 'But we will come back to this list.' She nodded imperiously.

'Okay. Let's call it a day.' Oliver stood up as Sunita left, followed by Arun.

* * *

The security guard opened the gates and inspected the car underneath the gaze of the Lady of Justice with scales in hand. The lions beside her had been speedily etched onto the wall, cheering Mrs Justice Elizabeth Linney each day she had come into the administrative court since integration. Most of her male colleagues had been outraged by them. She told them she viewed the Indian lions as extra protection to make sure justice was seen to be done in each of their courts to the best of their abilities. They told her she was idiotic, and it was colonial overreach. Things had become so out of hand she had suggested to the chief justice that he add 'Honi soit qui mal y pense', the motto of the order of the garter—shame on whoever thinks ill of it.

She was struggling with thick files under each arm when the receptionist asked, 'Big case today, my lady?'

'Yes, thank you. I hope it doesn't show.' She continued without stopping and then turned around. 'I'm sorry, how are your lovely grandchildren?' He started to tell her in great detail before she looked at her watch, sighed and took the stairs.

As she turned on her computer another government-issue car pulled into the courtyard outside. Its passenger bounded up the steps and showed his pass. The security guard jumped out of his seat and said, 'Good morning, sir. We don't often see you here.' He continued without acknowledging the guard, taking the stairs two at a time, making his way to Elizabeth's office. He knocked and walked straight in.

'This is a little pokey, isn't it? I hadn't realised quite how administrative we'd made the whole thing—right down to your chambers! Good morning, Elizabeth!'

Elizabeth, deep in thought about the case, had no idea what was going on. 'Master of the rolls! This is a surprise.' Her face lit up. She quickly examined her reflection on the blank monitor in front of her. 'This will have to do,' she thought. 'Can I get us coffee?'

'No time, I'm afraid.' He shut the door and rubbed his back as he sat down.

'Still the sciatica then?'

'Yes, excruciating. Thank you for remembering. How do you sit in these infernal chairs?'

'Well, we take the pain and pray for elevation to higher judicial office!' She smiled and watched him snicker. She remembered how she liked to make him laugh. 'And Lynn and the kids?' His face froze slightly as she asked. They had been in her first chambers together. She would never forget the sex. But it was the speed of his mercurial courtroom mind she'd fallen for. It had broken her young marriage. Elizabeth's husband blamed her devotion to the law and the late nights it constantly demanded. Deep down they both knew; it was her devotion to Nigel that had been the sole contributing factor. While he had soared to high judicial office, she'd made her own way on to the bench—and happily not from his bedroom.

Her court clerk came to the door. 'Thirty minutes, my lady.'

He paused. 'Yes, they're fine.' He continued, 'This the big case then?' pointing at the files on her desk. She nodded as he continued,

'Elizabeth, the chief justice and I handed this case to you. We decided we couldn't send it anywhere else.'

'Oh.' She feigned surprise. 'I didn't think either of you knew where I was.'

'Of course we do. We know where all our little special projects are! But this case, it's important. What you determine and how you do it is important.'

'You're not trying to influence the course of my trial, are you, Nigel?'

He smiled. 'Not at all. This is the first challenge of the new regime under the new regime. The law must hold. It may be the only thing that can hold. But I also have to tell you, the chief justice and I have been told in no uncertain terms by the governor-general that all judicial appointments have been continued on a probationary basis. Yours. Mine. The chief's. Everyone's.'

'I'm not sure if you're telling me that you're seeking to influence this case or not.'

'No, I'm not sure either. Good luck.' He kissed her on the cheek and left.

* * *

Karan was in what he hoped was a temporary waiting room in what had been grand foyer of buckingham palace. Albeit he was sitting in a roped-off section with a sign for vips, dignitaries and ambassadors, it was a far cry from the days when hardly anyone other than the prime minister of the day came up these steps for an audience with the king. Everyone other than Karan was speaking loudly into at least one phone. He sat down and shut his eyes.

On the chairs around him were all manner of Indian business. So much so the constant chatter made it seem more like one of London's busiest streets. He thought, 'There are soon to be more economic migrants inside the palace seeking work than people applying for visas at the Home Office.' The people around Karan had a guaranteed appointment. Many others had turned up speculatively. A third group had been allowed to wait in the courtyard for an impromptu photo as the governor-general departed.

After some time, an equerry tapped Karan's shoulder. 'First minister, he's ready for you. Karan followed the young man up the stairs. He stopped to pray at the image of Lord Vishnu but was interrupted, 'First minister.'

It was a troubled Banerjee. 'No time for symbolic gestures, the governor-general is waiting for you.' He whispered, 'And by God is he in a foul mood. I don't know what you've not done. But it's something momentous indeed.'

On edge, Karan tentatively entered the governor-general's audience room. At its far end, the painting of the young prince Albert had been replaced with a larger-than-life-size image of a regal Usha. Under her sat two rather ordinary chairs on a raised dais and flags, including the governor-general's personal standard. More chairs lined the walls. The painting of Albert in his coronation robes had been replaced with a small photo of the president of India, a seventy-something former Lok Sabha fighter for the PM's party. He'd rubber-stamped every one of her initiatives including integration.

In the remodelling, the antique furniture, the gilded chairs and flourishes had been bunched up at the half of the room nearest the door from which Karan entered. The governor-general watched Karan pick his way slowly through the assortment of antiques. 'Do hurry, first minister. Why are you doing all you can to derail the visit of the prime minister?'

'I'm not aware that we are, governor-general.'

'I need not remind you that nothing must harm the visit. Nothing.'

Karan scanned the room for any trace of the recent past. The photos of Albert with heads of state had vanished. The family ones too. Rather like individuals disappeared from photos in Stalin's Russia. 'Of course, parliament looks forward to welcoming the prime minister. I do too; I last saw Ushaji at Sunil's bungalow about five years ago.'

The governor-general's face tightened. 'That's not what I meant at all. And no need to swap stories about when we last saw the PM. I spoke to her today. She made it abundantly clear to me she holds you responsible for the judicial investigation into the girl's death and her unlawful killing. So you, you must stop this judicial digging—for your sake and for the republic.'

'Governor-general,' Karan replied, 'I'm afraid that's not how the English system—'

'She was a casualty of the change of regime,' the governor-general interrupted. 'As much your problem as anyone's, first minister. Please see to it that the investigation makes no further progress. And have this sorted by the end of today please.' He handed Karan a sheet of paper. 'You may not have seen this list yet, first minister.'

Karan was scanning it. 'No, I have not.'

'Well, I am pleased to say your minister has done an excellent job on the assets for integration, which the prime minister commends him on. But we do also want these matters taken care of. For your father-in-law and your wife.'

'I think the last thing either you or I need is for my wife or father-in-law to be seen to profit vastly from integration.'

'I don't see the public reaction to these changes as any of your concern, first minister. This has been decided on, requested and demanded by your prime minister. Just do it please?'

Once Karan left, the governor-general called out, 'Banerjee, I'm pretty sure the first minister will fail to do his judicial duty. I will need to call for help from our friends.' Banerjee nodded.

* * *

A sea of people in 'India Quit' t-shirts lined the roads throughout central London. Union jacks had been tied to barriers under the anglo-indian flag. The police and security services were happy to have the majority of the troublemakers they had been tracking in one place. In the temporary food stalls, tents, toilets and camps that had been set up, plain-clothes police were gathering as much intelligence as possible on the protesters' intentions. Monitoring devices, antennae and trackers had been fixed to all available surfaces. In addition, soldiers had been stationed every 20 yards of the 15-mile route from Northolt to Westminster.

One group of protesters seeking justice for khalistan and for England had gathered under the statue of the queen mother. 'You've been here twice already,' one shouted as another set of police officers and sniffer dogs pushed their way through them.

'Well, you shouldn't be so fucking interesting then, should you?' Sleeping bags were stomped over, food crushed, rucksacks pawed and pockets emptied.

Once again, nothing was found. 'Sorry about this.' The officer's colleague continued, 'You can't be too careful. It's for your safety as much as anyone's.'

'Fuck off.'

The protesters hung large 'India Quit' banners over the statue. 'Have some fucking respect,' a policeman shouted at them.

'Don't you think she'd be doing the fucking same, you nazi bastard,' they hollered back.

Behind the statue, they'd set up camp with a giant tent in which they held evening discussions covering globalisation as the root cause of England's demise and why getting rid of the architecture of the state would be good for their generation. For the last two nights they'd been joined by a young man, part-anarchist, part eco-warrior. 'Look at that fucking roo.' He pointed to an English Asian policeman keeping people behind the barriers. 'It makes me sick.' This morning he'd told them, 'I've got stickers and badges. I'm going to give them out along the route. All right if I leave my stuff and pick it up on the way back?' No one cared.

* * *

The governor-general was speaking to the metropolitan police commissioner on the tarmac waiting for the prime minister's plane to touch down. 'Well, that's deeply troubling news. I hold you personally responsible. But thankfully I had put the helicopter on standby.' The governor-general walked over to the state bentley and instructed the driver, 'You won't be needed here. Get to St James's as fast as you can.'

He was inspecting the guard of honour for the third time. He had already swapped one of the many deputy lieutenants for Lord Banerjee, telling the poor soul, 'I thought we had done away with you.'

As Banerjee walked forward he told the governor-general, 'I have made sure there will be no press conferences. No unhelpful questions about troops nor about the silly little girl.'

'What is he doing here?' The governor-general was transfixed by the glacial progress of Albert's ageing car. It took the recently vacated prime spot. As the door opened, the governor-general complained, 'Must I do everything myself?'

'I hadn't realised you were attending, governor.'

'Excellency, I thought your office had been briefed.' 'No matter,' Albert continued. 'I'm here now. I'm sure the prime minister won't mind. She does know me rather well.'

'It was only to save the inconvenience of the journey, excellency. But now I do have a most urgent task for you, if you could bear it. It would help me so and I would be in your debt.'

'Name it. Of course, governor-general.'

'I'm afraid the police have been unable to secure the whole 20-mile route to Westminster, so the prime minister will be taking the helicopter.'

'My helicopter?' he asked.

'Yes, the helicopter straight to the barracks. Could you head there now so as to welcome her?'

'I'm sure and certain we won't make it, excellency.'

'Well, I must ask you to try. For England and all that.'

Albert returned to his car and departed just as India One came to a complete stop. The military band struck up 1940s bollywood hits while they waited for the prime minister to take her first steps on her newest Indian acquisition. Pleased with himself, the governor-general took a slow walk to the bottom of the steps. When the plane door eventually opened, she appeared in her favourite turquoise sari. The weather warning she'd received on the plane had come to naught. Both tamed by her mere presence. She waved to the few loyal journalists she'd permitted to attend at a prudent distance.

* * *

Isha was in the bedroom, choosing a necklace and earrings. 'I'm trying to work out what's the greatest number of diamonds I can wear and still come across as English,' she announced to Karan as he walked in.

'What is this fucking shopping list?' Karan asked. 'Have you and your dad gone totally fucking mental?'

She was selecting diamonds and sapphires. 'I don't see what the problem is. Everyone else is getting in on the act. I spoke to pitaji, and he recommended four or five businesses we could have.'

'Oliver sent me your list. I don't need smug fucking texts from him that tell me you want to buy most of Oxford Street, the English insurance industry and a few restaurant chains at knock-down prices.'

Isha stood up. 'Pitaji told me it's our insurance. You won't be here forever.' She had chosen sapphire-drop earrings and a lavish diamond necklace she'd designed and had made by the jewellers to the maharana of Udaipur. 'What else did your boyfriend say?'

'He said you're out of control. Your father is already out of control. And he is clear it can't be done.'

'Did you ask him how much money he and the fuckboy have taken? They are making a joke of you and of me. It's just like all those fucking Indian women and the arse-lickers who tried to ruin my father. Did you ask him?'

'Of course I didn't. I don't need to. I know Oliver better than I know myself. Sometimes I think I know him better than I know you.'

'Oh, I'm sure of that. It's always been you and him plus me. Do you know whom you should be thankful to? Who got you here? It was pitaji.' She paused. 'And it was me. Not Oliver. He let you down at every turn. Made his own way in politics, then only grudgingly got you a seat. Making you go through all those hostile interviews. Every fucking racist one. And even then, not a nice seat—like Fulham or Chelsea. Where we already had property. No, in fucking Yorkshire. So Pitaji had to spend even more money supporting you. You owe him and you owe me. And—'

'And, what, Isha, can you even hear yourself?'

'And it's time you gave up on your self-serving boyfriend.'

'What you're asking for isn't just illegal. It's just plain stupid. We have enough money. I won't do it. But worse, it's now out there. And who knows what damage it will do?'

'Do you know how much money is enough, Karan?' she asked. 'Just a little more. Anything can happen. I saw it when my father was disgraced. I have to look out for him and for us. What damage can it do? Pitaji owns the media. India owns the country. Just shut down whatever comes towards us. Do your fucking job fucking properly. For once.'

He gawped at her. 'Well, you're not getting them. Not from me.'

* * *

'Namaste, prime minister, welcome to your thirtieth state.' They shook hands as she took her first steps on this first Indian overseas territory. 'It really is quite some achievement.'

'Well, we did it for the people here. Not for ourselves.'

'I'm afraid we will have to cut the welcome reception short, prime minister. I have been told that protesters have managed to disrupt part of your route. So I've taken the decision to helicopter to St James's and continue in the car from there.'

'Whatever.' Ushaji was resplendent, like a warrior queen come to survey the spoils of battle. She waved to the press before walking the hastily rearranged red carpet to her waiting chariot.

From the air she asked, 'Do you have the protests under control now? I've seen the intelligence.'

'Yes, prime minister. A few overly excitable individuals led the charge. But we charged back with the full force of the Indian army. They learnt their lesson. Today we are just taking extra precautions. Nothing must go wrong with this visit.'

'I hope you didn't miss the opportunity to take advantage of such a crisis.'

He nodded.

'And Karan?' she asked.

'He is performing as expected. Sunil trained his daughter well. I'm afraid you will be met by Albert on the ground. I did my best to get rid of him.'

The prime minister flicked her wrist. 'No issue. What to do? He has to have some purpose. I will find a handbag for him to hold.'

The helicopter descended into the barracks where red-jacketed bandsmen were playing the Indian national anthem. Usha beamed a huge smile at Albert before saying, 'Governor, how are you enjoying this new position? We must have a meeting on the commonwealth during my trip.'

'Yes, that's a marvellous idea, prime minister.'

'Thank you for receiving me. Now I'm late for parliament. The governor-general's office will arrange the meeting with yours.'

As her car turned, a large section of protesters booed. He had placed military bands at every major intersection. British military tunes of the raj drowned out the worst of the abortive protestations.

Usha caught sight of her governor-general's residence and saw her new anglo-indian flag flying for the first time. 'Well done, Manish. That must really have driven them wild.' She rarely used his first name. He'd been a senior official for so many years now: designations, rank and uniform had taken the place of his individuality. 'Thank you, prime minister.'

Scanning the protesters, she asked, 'Tell me, how much longer must I pretend to like these people?' Before he could reply, they felt the full force of an accelerating rolls royce engine when the car sped forward, pushing them back deep into the plush upholstery. A few activists had jumped the barriers ahead and were being swarmed by some twenty police. Usha observed them. 'So young.' Police batons broke bones and officers hauled limp individuals on to the pavement. 'But they have time to learn.'

'I'm sorry about that incident. I'll have the metropolitan police commissioner send you a personal letter of apology.'

'Not at all. A few bad apples give so much helpful intelligence to our security agencies. Just send me a report of what you know about the various people who are trying to do us down. That will make for excellent bedtime reading!'

* * *

The hum of a thousand excitable parliamentarians, diplomats, dignitaries and hangers-on filled the hall like a children's orchestra. 'Ah, she's here.' Madam speaker had received the nod from her clerk. She stood up and silenced the cavernous room. Enjoying her moment, she walked slowly down the steps and along the narrow aisle to the front door of the hall, collecting Karan on her way. The lord speaker made to follow her, but she pushed him back down. 'Sorry, this one's Indian government protocol. It's just me and him.'

Karan walked with her, smiling. 'You enjoyed that.'

'Yes, the jumped-up little prick.'

Usha's car arrived just as madam speaker made it to the front door. She brought her hands together and gave a warm 'Namaste' to the Indian prime minister. The chatter in the hall was interrupted by the clink of the battle axes of the honourable corps of gentlemen-at-arms slowly making their way to assemble on both sides of the steps at the front of the hall. Great, feathered mascots of what England once was.

The state trumpeters in golden tabards had entered from both sides of the corridor high above them. Part musical. Part theatrical. Fully majestic. The shimmering brass instruments played a lofty anthem. At that, the Indian prime minister, her governor-general, the speaker of her House of Commons and her first minister processed back down the narrow aisle between the chairs.

Two thousand legs screeched one thousand chairs backwards as everyone stood and turned to get a glimpse of their prime minister. The strictures of commons protocol had been shared with the guests, who had been told not to shake hands or delay progress. But Usha took every opportunity to thank and welcome her many Indian friends and supporters. The speaker turned to Karan. 'A bit like the spare prick at the wedding?' Karan smirked.

Oliver had managed to sit with Arun in the front row. 'Shouldn't you be out there welcoming your leader?'

'She's not the leader of my party. That's my father. Who are all these second-rate people anyway?'

'Well, on my side of this horrific, malformed, nightmare wedding we have about eight hundred MPs and peers, then some expectant business leaders and the weird English hangers-on who always get to attend these great occasions of state like gent-of-the-water-closet or something else.'

Arun laughed. 'That's not a real job, is it?'

'It might as well be. If you are going to do any fucking good to this little country, please abolish most of them.' Oliver pointed across the aisle, 'And who did the bride bring?'

'She brought a raiding party of her most senior officials; a retinue of state chief ministers here to devour the fruits of integration like locusts; and then a motley crew of business leaders in need of quick deals. If you thought I moved fast, wait till you see what the people in this room look like tomorrow.'

'Fucked on all fours?'

'Something like that.'

The speaker accompanied the prime minister to her throne midway between the state trumpeters and the vips, then returned to help the governor-general to his seat in the front row. Much to his chagrin. The snare drum marked the start of the Indian national anthem. Karan stood next to Oliver and pointed at the Scottish prime minister. 'Fuck, what's she doing here?'

Oliver replied, 'And, how on earth can she be their guest and in their front row?'

Madam speaker waited until the echo of the last note faded. She made her way slowly and deliberately to the dais. She brought her hands to her chest. 'Prime minister, allow me to wish you a hale and hearty welcome from your parliament in Westminster. Namaste.'

Usha stood and returned the greeting. She walked to the podium and reviewed the scene in front of her with relish. It had taken many years to make good on her promise to her grandfather. They'd rebuilt their lives in India stone by stone. Bit by bit. Rupee by rupee. Vote by vote. The party had taken care of them when neither the British nor the Indian state had any interest. He'd built a power base in Ludhiana and was its first representative in the Lok Sabha. He hadn't thrived there, but he'd been a loyal follower and set the family up for its political dynasty. She'd been proud of her grandfather. Taking the little they had and turning it into something. A path for all of them. She'd watched her father gain momentum and reach the cabinet. But that was as much an appointment to recognise what her grandfather had done as what her father had achieved. His progress stalled. She couldn't remember when she first met Sunil. But when they did, it was clear they needed each other.

Sunil had a flare for marrying politics and business. He'd taken far more risks than her father would. He'd been a constant friend and supporter. Whenever money was needed, Sunil provided it. Whenever volunteers were needed, Sunil appeared with them. Whenever a problem had to be dealt with, Sunil solved it. No questions were asked. Nor was anything sought in return. Slowly, he started to suggest that Usha should have her own political identity. He convinced her to run that first time and promoted her as her grandfather's candidate. No mention of her father. She'd been a runaway success. He'd helped her broaden her political and business connections.

The funding continued. She never asked where from, how or why. Whatever she needed done, or the family needed done, Sunil made it happen. Then the great crash. For both of them. Their mutual disgrace.

Sunil had over-promised. She hadn't seen the change coming. The waves hit them. Accusations of corruption. Sunil lost much of his business and she much of her power base. They agreed to bide their time. The corruption investigations subsided as the new political class took over. Eventually their interest shifted to selling their own narrative and taking down those on their own side. She and Sunil kept out of the limelight, hoping that this new movement would run out of steam. Finally, they saw their opportunity. Continued defeats upset the old hierarchy. Sunil helped her wrest the leadership from its usual suspects. Still, she never asked where the money came from. Their old magic came back. Their unique recipe of politics and business knew no bounds. Success bred success. And now, here she was. Fulfilling a promise she'd made all those years ago. India was now in its rightful place at the top of the world.

'Namaste, and thank you, madam speaker. It is good for one strong woman to follow another.' The audience tittered. 'On the way in I heard someone mention a wedding.' Madam speaker caught Karan's eye as Usha continued, 'That is what this was like for me. Long ago I decided to marry politics. Then I realised I was a bride to the people of India. All of my life has been dedicated in service to that great Indian family, which you are now once again a part of.' The audience applauded.

She knew she wasn't only addressing the thousand or so people in front of her. Much of the west and some hundreds of millions of Indians were watching. Thousands of government analysts were listening to her every word and fashioning them into her policy. 'India's Bara North Atlantic Yatra is a reunification of the greatest empire the world had ever known. Like the emperor Hadrian, our borders stop at Carlisle and in south Asia!' They applauded again.

'We respect the rights of our dear brothers and sisters in Scotland and,' she glimpsed at the Scottish prime minister, 'look to develop our close relationship with their government. They have provided much support to our incoming administration.'

Karan caught Oliver's eye.

'And we welcome its prime minister here today.' There was a rustle of surprise at the back of the hall.

Usha continued, 'Integration reminds us of what our nation shares rather than what divides us. We share a common language, though the development of English is now driven by speakers of English outside of England. We share a love of the food of the Indian mainland—finally, we will bring real khana here.' She heard the polite laughs. 'And of course we share the common law and the rule of law. Principles that have been the basis for trusted trade between our peoples for more than four hundred years and the basis on which England has been fully incorporated into the republic of India. An incorporation that will see this country flourish for many decades to come.'

'But we also share common enemies. Democracies have always been the most susceptible to infiltration and takeovers by extremist ideologies. India will use its new-found position in the North Atlantic to fight for freedom and democracy. Our great empire will beat these malcontents. Be they internal or exogenous. Our hard and our soft power will win the twenty-first-century battles for attraction, influence, land and power. Jai Hind.' She waited.

Those on her side of the room were on their feet and applauding enthusiastically. Usha noted that her English MPs were much more lukewarm, and her first minister decidedly cool. Madam speaker, in what now felt funereal black, accompanied Usha from the platform. They stopped to allow Usha to speak to the Scottish prime minister—a moment of crowning glory for her administration. Karan showed Oliver a text on his phone, 'Judicial review continuing.'

Usha nodded to Karan as she and the speaker made their way at a glacial pace back down the aisle. Oliver whispered to Arun,

'She's just announced the crusades.' Arun nodded. 'And these fucking idiots are applauding their own demise. Unbelievable. They watched Usha speak to everyone who asked. Photos were taken. Grandchildren presented. Businesses promoted. Trinkets received. Aides noted every conversation.

Outside, Usha turned to Karan, 'First minister, hum aapko baad mein dekhenge.' Karan nodded and brought his hands together to his chest. 'Namaste, prime minister. Haan, Ushaji.'

Usha was contemplating Big Ben. 'A good decision, Manish, to invite the Scots. What will the response be to my pronouncement?'

'You heard it, prime minister. The silence was deafening. Integration is no longer temporary.'

Karan watched them both while frantically trying to work out what he could do next. Oliver stood beside him. 'What happened to this-will-all-be-over-by-christmas? Fully incorporated into the Republic of India? This is a lot fucking worse than we imagined. You are not in control of this.'

Karan led him away from the rest of the leaving party, 'Of course I'm not in fucking charge. That was always going to be the case. You said I'd be the saviour. Not me.'

'Albert did a deal with the Indian government. I don't know what it involved. But I wouldn't be surprised if he sold England to keep his crown. And they shat on him from a great height. So what do you think they'll do to us?'

'Do we have any evidence of this?'

'Sunil is using every opportunity to turn this into a massive fucking get-rich-quick scheme. Look around. You can't see what's going on right in front of your fucking face. Isha is doing exactly what her father—and they—want her to do. Take. Take. Take. She's probably been part of the plan from its inception.'

Karan stopped him. 'Enough, Oliver. I asked you to find out what was going on. Not try to destroy my whole family.'

'I wish that was my game. We've got a kleptomaniac in Downing Street. And we're surrounded by thieves and murderers outside.'

'That's enough,' Karan shouted.

Madam speaker came over. 'I don't know what this'—she pointed at them—'is about. But something massive and ruinous is about to happen. And, as they say at my daughter's playground, you started it. So you had better fix it.' She walked away.

Karan lowered his voice. 'You've never liked Isha. Or the two of us together. I can protect you from a lot, Oliver, but not from yourself.'

'And I can protect you from a lot, Karan. But I have never been able to protect you from Isha.'

'You've always had some weird fantasy. That maybe Isha would go and it would just be me and you. That's never going to happen. I mean, look at you and him.' Karan pointed at Arun talking to the Scottish prime minister. 'He could just about be your son. You're trying to relive our youth. But you imagined it. Nothing ever happened. And nothing will.'

Oliver saw a hatred in Karan's eyes he'd never seen before. 'I don't know where this is coming from. It can only be from Isha. I'm sorry for the pair of you.'

'Are you? Or are you just here to make money from me as well as everyone else?'

'What the fuck are you talking about?'

'I've had the reports of the commission your boyfriend is charging and your plans to run away together.'

'Shut the FUCK UP!' Oliver replied.

Karan was on the floor. Had Oliver punched him? Right there in Westminster? There was a buzzing in his ears. He could barely hear anything. But he couldn't feel the impact of any blow. Police and security officers were running towards him. One picked Karan up and told him, 'There's been a series of explosions, we need to get you to safety.'

Karan, on his feet, was scanning the crowd, 'I need to speak to Oliver.'

Oliver pushed his way to Karan. 'It's a bomb. We could be at war. And we have no idea who the enemy is. Let's work out what the actual fuck is going on. And get you to safety.' Oliver turned to

Karan's team. 'Why don't you have the first minister in a car on the way to downing street?'

The officer was listening to an update from his earpiece. 'We don't have an agreed safe route yet. Reports of multiple explosions across the city. One directly in front of the prime minister's car. One over there.' Smoke and debris had filled the air in parliament square and was heading towards them. They could hear screams.

Karan demanded, 'Please can we get some emergency responders out to those people?'

'Not yet, sir. We don't yet know whether it is safe to send people in.' He paused with one hand cupped to his ear, 'And we don't think it's safe to drive.'

'Well, it's certainly not fucking safe standing out here,' Oliver added. 'And keep Karan away from her.' He pointed to the Scottish prime minister, who was remonstrating with officers. Oliver went over. 'Prime minister, there have been a series of explosions across the city. We don't yet know the full extent of the damage or when we will have the incident under control and be sure it is safe for you to leave the area. I'm afraid I have to ask you to remain here and—'

'Oliver!' Karan shouted as he was being made to run by his police protection team. Oliver sprinted behind him. They ran along the connecting tunnel beneath Big Ben and up the escalator into the glass-roofed atrium of Portcullis House.

'Where are we going?' Karan asked as his security team gained more officers.

'Follow us, first minister.' The police officer led Karan and Oliver out of the main entrance. Ahead of them pleasure boats were continuing down the calm waters of the Thames as fire engines, police cars and ambulances screeched over Westminster Bridge. Outside, more officers had joined them. Some were clearing the route ahead.

'It's unorthodox, first minister. But we're going to run to the ministry of defence, and well, we'll show you what to do from there.'

‘All that abortive marathon training finally put to good use,’ Oliver shouted as they ran along the river past the home of the metropolitan police.

Karan heard officers shout, ‘Armed police. Get down.’ They passed terrified tourists and Londoners lying prone on the pavement. Every officer had their gun out. Behind him was a quintessentially British response. Local community support officers speaking to every person who'd been left in Karan's wake and forced to lie face down on the concrete. Inside the ministry, they were in a lift heading deep underground. A notice on the door to the airlock told them all it was ‘PINDAR’. They were all breathing loudly, waiting for the second door to open.

Oliver gasped, ‘Here the hero came. With the head that shocked a royal house, turning King and all into stone: It was long, long ago, if time means anything; Long, long ago.’

‘Have you had a stroke or an aneurysm?’ Karan asked, making the police guffaw.

‘It's Pindar; he was a classical Greek poet. I thought it was an apt quote.’

The click and ping of the door opening allowed the policeman to say, ‘It's also an underground cold-war bunker with a tunnel to the cabinet office. Please take these masks as we're still unsure if we got rid of all the asbestos.’

‘Great,’ Oliver added. ‘If the terrorists don't fucking kill us, 1950s civil service building regs finally will!’

The officer opened a round metal door, like a superhero's shield, guarding the entrance to the subterranean tunnel. He gave each of them torches and hit a switch that turned on a row of strip lights. They peered down the circular tube shaft made of rusty corrugated iron sheets.

‘It's a bit like travelling through the intestines of a giant worm.’ Karan said. ‘Does Pindar have anything on that front?’ Oliver snorted as they were slowly led into the tunnel.

‘There are a few places where the sheets have warped so there’s likely water and rats. I’ll try to make a bit of noise as I go to frighten them off.’ Oliver followed Karan, who stayed close to the police officer. He glanced behind to see the shield door closing with a groan. They were bent over trying to get through the narrow walkway. Their breathing was loud. Adrenalin high.

‘Have we any idea yet of causalities?’

‘Nothing, sir. You will get a full brief in cobra.’

Karan’s right foot made a crunch. ‘What was that?’

‘It’s dead now, sir. Best not think about it to be honest.’

The officer gave a jaunty tap-tap-tap-tap against the shield-shaped exit. It opened with another creak. Seb was waiting at the entrance as they jumped out.

‘First minister, we have cobra ready for you both. Follow me.’

They walked from the deep basement of the cabinet office through a rabbit warren of corridors, Oliver and Karan brushing dust and dirt off their clothes. ‘This was my best suit, by the way,’ Oliver whispered.

* * *

Justice Linney’s clerk watched her as the government’s barrister concluded his case. She was tired sitting underneath a hastily installed glass panel with Lady Liberty and her lionesses, as Elizabeth liked to call her. Elizabeth was surveying her compact courtroom. It was fully of Molly’s family, friends and work colleagues.

The barrister was winding up, ‘This is an application for judicial review into the decisions to deploy police and, it is alleged, members of the security forces, on the streets of London on the night of 14 August 2027. This action, the plaintiffs aver, resulted in the death of Miss Molly Stevens.’

The noise of the door opening forced Elizabeth’s eyes from the file in front of her. She smiled as the master of the rolls entered her court and nodded discreetly. The barrister continued, ‘The government's contention is that the plaintiffs in this case have no standing to proceed. They do not represent Miss Stevens' estate nor her family. Her employer has not joined this action but has allowed itself to be associated with a fundraising appeal on a website.'

Elizabeth was noting all that had been said. When her scribbling ended he was staring at her. 'Anything else?' she asked.

He stood again. 'No, we don't think anything more needs to be added.'

'Motion denied. We will proceed.' The master of the rolls walked out. Elizabeth could hear murmuring behind the barristers. She saw phones being passed and heard a gasp. Just before she started to address the courtroom, her clerk handed her a note. Elizabeth announced, 'As I think some of you are already aware, there has been a security incident in central London. This court will be adjourned until we have more information.' Elizabeth picked up her papers and her clerk rushed her to the safety of chambers.

Nigel followed her in. 'Elizabeth, what on earth are you doing?'

She was reading from her tablet. 'There has been a series of terrible attacks on London.'

'I don't care about that. What on earth are you doing? You're going to bring the whole system down. We can't allow this case to continue. You must find a way to stop it.'

'Are you telling me to interfere in the direction of this case? In the cause of justice itself?'

'Fuck off, Elizabeth. This sanctimonious, holier-than-thou attitude was always your least attractive quality. The freedom of the entire English judiciary lies on what you do next.'

'Is that what they told you?'

'What?'

'Whichever odious master sent you here as a lickspittle little servant of the oppressor?'

'You have gone fucking crackers. Again. Just like the last time. Remember I had to get you out of it then? Well, it's the same now. I'm saving you from yourself.'

'You arrogant bastard. You always were, Nigel. Get out of my chambers.'

He handed her a letter. 'We are taking you out of this court.'

'You can't without the say-so of parliament. Or whatever we call it today.'

'I know that. You've been promoted. You are the first woman to sit on the new court of final appeal that will replace the supreme court. Four Indian judges and four English ones have been appointed. You'll be pleased to know I'm going to be the first president.'

'Congratulations.' Nigel walked out as she tore open the letter.

* * *

Karan pressed his thumb against the scanner and waited for the ping and click of another airlock door. Oliver stood directly behind him. The glass pods opened, and Karan walked out to be greeted by Dame Rebecca. As Oliver exited, he heard her say, 'Multiple explosions and fatalities. A bomb under the statue of the queen mother went off just as the governor-general's car drove past. There's a video on social media being shared by Chinese, Russian and Iranian bots of the governor-general's car in the middle of it.'

Karan interrupted, 'Do we know if the Indian prime minister is alive?' Dame Rebecca shook her head. Karan whispered, 'You are the only person I trust to get us through this.' She turned and walked ahead of him into the meeting room.

Karan was always amazed at how unlike the US situation room his government's national crisis centre was. British humdrum to American hollywood. He sat at the top of the table and pointed for the chief of the defence staff in army fatigues to move down one to allow Dame Rebecca to be at his left-hand side. He motioned for Oliver to sit beside him at the head of the table.

'Right,' Karan asked. 'What do we know?'

The home secretary and the defence secretary both entered the room one after another and took the final two vacant seats. Both were out of breath. 'Sorry, we had to fight to extricate ourselves from the lockdown measures around Westminster. I'm afraid we had to leave the Scottish prime minister to her own devices.'

Karan replied, 'Every cause needs a martyr.' Provoking some gallows humour. 'Also, can we get the television screens on, please?'

They saw images of panic in every part of central London. Emergency responders triaging injuries at both bomb sites. Fatalities everywhere. The most serious casualties had lost limbs and were being rushed to hospitals across the city, which were already starting to feel the strain. Air ambulances were landing in the city's parks to ferry some of the worst casualties further afield. Seated in their secure bunker, they could hear the soundtrack to all this activity with sirens and helicopter engines all around them. They were in the middle of a war zone.

The commissioner of the metropolitan police started, 'We do not yet know if we have contained these incidents, first minister. I'm grateful to the chief of the defence staff for authorising the use of the army's territorial support group which has already been mobilised. Troops are on the streets, and more arrive at Battersea helipad in the next ten minutes.'

'Have we confirmed the present location of the prime minister and the governor general?' Karan asked.

Before anyone could answer him, the screens showed images of a plume of smoke in the city. Dame Rebecca left the room.

'No, first minister. We have not had any contact with the governor-general since the attack.'

'Well, it's only round the fucking corner. Can't someone find out where the car is?'

The room was decidedly embarrassed when Dame Rebecca returned. 'First minister, there are reports of a third bomb near the site of the vigil for the young woman who died in the city. We understand some hundreds of people were in attendance. We're awaiting confirmation on the dead and injured.'

Dame Rebecca hurriedly checked her phone. 'Sorry, it's not the site. It's the bank she worked at. Someone has targeted Merchant's. Apparently there had been a stationary protest there since the girl's death demanding the bank release all its information on its dealings with India. The bomb appears to have targeted those protesters. We believe around forty-five were injured in the first attack and possibly similar numbers in the second. More likely in the third.'

'Do we have any idea of who did this?'

Dame Rebecca continued, 'My initial assessment is that these were serious devices. Expertly made and possibly with explosives that only governments have.' She turned to the chief of the defence staff, who nodded, 'We would like you to authorise military assistance to secure the city and to help contain these incidents.'

Karan observed the defence and home ministers, who nodded their consent. 'Of course, but we need an urgent update on the prime minister and governor-general.'

At that, the governor-general appeared on the wall of screens at the end of the table directly opposite Karan. 'Can we have a sit rep, first minister? I can confirm that both the prime minister and I are safe. However, the car was destroyed.'

Karan started to speak and could see the governor-general being handed a written update. 'I'm sorry to stop you, first minister. We're being told of a possible third attack. Indian government intelligence assessment is that all three devices are the work of a cell of khalistani separatists that has been in London for some time. We do not yet know how far the conspiracy goes.'

Karan glanced at Dame Rebecca who gave an almost imperceptible shake of her head in disagreement. Then at the chief of the defence staff who singularly refused to look Karan's way.

'Governor-general, I am here in Cobra with the whole gamut of the British intelligence state. Our initial assessment is that it is too early to determine who made and planted these devices or why.'

'First minister, I am sharing with you the assessment of what has happened. I am not asking for a first-year essay on the likely causes of terrorism.'

Karan interrupted him, 'I don't know how or where you could have intelligence on which to base that assessment.'

'I'm not at liberty to share with those present where our intelligence assessment has come from, first minister. But you are right; we do not yet know if your intelligence and security services are on top of this incident. We have just suffered the attempted assassination of the prime minister of India. We have credible evidence of further attacks being planned. There is also interest in targeting members of your administration. Therefore, I am declaring governor-general's rule for a period of seventy-two hours.'

'This is unconstitutional,' Oliver interrupted. 'You don't have the authority to do that.'

The governor-general paused. 'First minister, I would recommend that you restrict the attendees of this meeting to those with a direct national security brief.'

Oliver looked at Karan. Karan surveyed the room. Only Dame Rebecca caught his eye. Karan twitched his head towards the door. Oliver walked out.

'Thank you, first minister. As I was saying, governor-general's rule will be implemented for a period of seventy-two hours. Your meeting will confirm its assent to this step.' Karan focused on the junior official noting what the governor-general was declaring.

Parliament will be suspended. All mobile and internet communications in London have already been disabled. Within the next hour I would like your assessment of the ongoing threat from the khalistani cell and for you to provide me with a number of options to neutralise this threat. We cannot have the integrity of the republic at risk.' The screen went blank.

Karan asked, 'Have we lost him? Is he coming back?'

The junior official looked at his monitor, 'No, he has ended the call. His office has told us this meeting has ended too.' Before Karan could say anything, the room emptied.

Dame Rebecca waited. Karan asked her, 'Do you have any evidence this was done by khalistani terrorists?'

'None. I fear what the governor-general has just said presages far, far worse to come.'

'I agree. I need as much intelligence as you can provide on this alleged khalistani cell and its international links. Use whatever back channels you need to.'

'I don't think that it even exists, first minister. I will try to find out all that we have but it is extremely likely that when we don't provide a credible alternative assessment, the government of India will take preventative, peremptory, retaliatory action.'

Karan was staring at the blank screen ahead of him.

'One more thing, first minister.'

'Yes.'

'I am extremely worried about what state of war the governor-general would be happy to take us to. You did not sign up for this and may want to resign. I must request—no, demand—that you don't. We need someone at the top who can lead us through this.'

With that Karan thought about the governor. 'What about Albert? Has anyone briefed him?'

Dame Rebecca nodded. 'My deputy has been in touch with the governor's household. He has been in Windsor for the last few days.'

* * *

Oliver was in the basement watching the rolling news coverage. 'Not in the thick of it?' one of the café workers asked.

'Not this time,' Oliver replied. 'And maybe not for a long time.' He was struggling to hold back tears when he checked his phone and saw fifteen missed calls from Arun. And then text messages. He tried unsuccessfully to send one back and asked as she was pouring his tea, 'Is your phone working?'

'No.' She pointed at the screen on which they both read, governor-general's rule established. All mobile signals blocked. Parliament suspended.' When she turned back Oliver was gone.

Oliver was standing outside watching officials running, into and out of the Foreign Office and into and out of Number 10. The police presence had quadrupled. Emergency vehicles were racing up and down Whitehall and St James's Park. Oliver shouted his driver, 'This is crazy. I'm just going to walk.' He started, then added, 'Thanks for all you've done for me.'

Oliver's pass unlocked the security gate at the now heavily protected exit. Air ambulances were landing and taking off like fairground rides. A crowd thousands of people strong was walking slowly ahead of him. 'This is how you take over a city,' he thought, staring at the empty tents they had left behind.

He took the steps up to Queen Anne's Gate. The last text he'd received contained a surprising address. He pressed the buzzer. 'It's me.'

Arun was waiting for him when he got out the lift. He hugged Oliver. 'Thank God you're alive.'

Once inside his apartment, Oliver told him, 'I'm resigning.'

'What happened?'

'I decided I was going the minute Usha finished her speech. We have been like little lambs. Or schoolchildren. Just so fucking naïve. Now I think they have planted these bombs and killed hundreds of British citizens. God alone knows why. So I've had it. It's enough. This is not what was supposed to happen.'

Arun set a bottle of whisky down and two glasses. 'We need this. You need this.' He poured two large shots. 'But obviously you can't resign. Not yet. Karan needs you. This country needs you. We don't know what will happen next.'

Oliver moaned, 'He didn't look like they needed me. He made his choice. The governor-general over me. And some bullshit from Isha about you and me siphoning off 15 per cent from imaginary deals for some nest egg.'

Arun was pouring a second. 'Okay. So your ego needs this too.'

Oliver was inspecting the surroundings. 'Two bedrooms, a sitting room. A meeting room.' He picked up some of the many pictures of Arun the politician. 'This is yours?'

Arun nodded. 'Yes. This is the family's.'

'Why didn't you invite me here sooner?'

'Look outside.' Oliver went to the window.

'You see that little Indian man in the car.'

'Your driver?'

'No, the governor-general's spy. That day I met you with Sunita they had produced a list of nights that I hadn't stayed here. They'd had people waiting at every gay club and sauna in London. Desperately hoping for a photo. Well, at least now they have one. Wave at him, would you, please? I usually do.'

'So you can see why we didn't use it.' He topped Oliver's drink up. 'The attack on the bank is interesting. I received these papers from my dad's contacts in Mumbai.' Arun handed them over.

'They're bank accounts?' Oliver kept reading. 'This account has the PM's name on it.'

'How on earth did you get this? And this has Isha's. And this Sunil's.'

'And this one has Banerjee's details,' Arun replied, handing over another sheaf of papers. 'And they're all with Merchant's.'

Arun and Oliver watched the rolling news coverage of Karan and Isha, both in black, walking from across the park to the scene of the first attack. He was thanking emergency responders.

'He needs to do a respectable job of gripping this,' Oliver added. 'She, however, can go to hell.'

The cameras followed Karan and Isha's slow progression to the now-dismembered statue of the queen mother. Marquees had been erected along the mall. Oliver assumed this wasn't only to preserve whatever evidence there was. These would be grizzly locations of blown-off body parts.

Karan faced the cameras. 'Our state suffered a terrible attack today. We don't yet know the final number of casualties. Nor do we yet know who is behind these attacks. We do know that many people have been gravely injured and that tragically some who were here to protest, as is their legal right, have been killed. Earlier I chaired a Cobra meeting and tasked the heads of our intelligence agencies and the police to bring the perpetrators of these hideous attacks to justice as quickly as possible.'

'You should just keep walking and arrest that bastard now,' Oliver shouted.

'And pick up Albert on the way,' Arun added before switching to his favourite Indian comedy channel. Riyaz was on. 'Have you seen the explosive welcome our PM received in England today? She's about as popular there as her father was in Ludhiana in the 1990s.'

* * *

The governor-general unlocked the door from his private apartment to the white drawing room, which had been set up to host an elaborate reception for the prime minister. They sat on gilded chairs and ordered drinks. The prime minister waited until the whisky had been served and the footmen had left. 'Well, you've put the cat among the pigeons now, Manish. Did we really need the third bomb?'

He focused on her. 'Prime minister, letting one through is a mistake for the security services. Two becomes a serious error of judgement. The third is a calamity. Your first minister and his intelligence services will be chastened and distracted. We'll have free rein.'

Usha stood up. 'I'm going now.'

Usha and the governor-general walked out to the gardens where her helicopter was waiting. 'Have you confirmed that I can fly out of the Chinese airport in the city?' she asked, and the governor-general nodded. 'So helpful,' she continued, 'to have our friends running their own little city within a city just a mile from here. You've done well there too.'

The governor-general reached the helicopter first. 'I hope you were pleased with the visit, prime minister.'

'Yes, Manish. You are whipping this snivelling little place into shape. This was a lucky country. But it is now a most ungrateful country. We are saving them from ignominy and irrelevance.' She dusted herself down. 'They have permitted an attack on the prime minister of India and on the republic itself. They have brought all of this on themselves. You must now implement all retaliatory measures.'

With that she took her seat. He walked back and the rotors started. Their hum intensified. He waited for the initial airborne jump. A marvel of physics. He continued stepping back on the lush green lawns as his prime minister ascended. Two military helicopters buzzed the palace and placed themselves either side to accompany her on the short journey.

As he made his way back inside, he could hear sirens in every direction. He headed along another red-carpeted corridor towards a room from which he could hear chuckling. He walked in to see Lu Quan. 'About to pot the black, are you, ambassador?'

Lu looked up. 'I hear your prime minister is leaving us. She is happy with all that has been achieved?'

'How could she not be?' Banerjee asked, handing the governor-general a whisky. 'It's been a triumph.'

'Now, ambassador,' the governor-general asked as Lu continued to prepare his shot, 'we will need access to the range of devices you have planted across London. And the AI systems you have set up to control and monitor them as well as inject chaos.'

Lu was concentrating on the pink.

Seven

Overnight, hundreds of Indian reinforcements landed at London–Beijing airport. Rushed along the arteries and thoroughfares of London, they joined British special forces, paratroopers and Royal Marine commandos in a new regiment, the Westminster Pioneers. Commanding officers marched troops in unison across London's bridges and erected checkpoints, choking the limbs of what was once a global city. Governor-general's rule had turned central London into a citadel. The city now stood silent as if in a medically induced coma.

The First Division of the Westminster Pioneers had mustered at Wellington Barracks and marched on Westminster Bridge. The Second Division set their checkpoint at the vast roundabout off Waterloo Bridge. In the process, soldiers blocked its many roads and pedestrian exits while others ran underneath to cajole, beat up, then arrest the homeless who'd lived a speluncean existence for many years. Once visited by a princess, they left in chains. A section of the Second Division was sent to mount barriers at the Old Vic, which sat in dark and dismal solitude like an old man remembering his youth. The Third Division took the bridges of Blackfriars and Southwark.

A young female Royal Marine was staring at terminals in the command centre in St James's Park. 'So this is why you needed a Chinese speaker?' she asked in a Scottish accent.

'What's that, Marine Wen?' her Indian commanding officer asked.

'You're using Chinese systems to control all of London. When I turn the mobile network back on all the traffic will go through this chinese system.'

'Do it,' he told her. Then cut off the power across the city for the next forty minutes.'

Wen's power cut allowed a battalion of the First Division to set out under Admiralty Arch to Aldwych. In pitch-black they passed the ceremonial dragons whose sole purpose had been to remind the monarch to ask permission to enter the ancient centre of London. The battalion needed no such consent. They arrived to find the city's great towers to man, mammon and money empty. They fanned through ancient roads, stopping at the Tower of London and Little China.

Ambassador Lu watched with delight from his penthouse. London was closed. Enchained. Suffocated. Beaten.

Lu Quan surveyed the protestors' retreat. None had the stomach for a fight. Not with these odds. Lines of dejected Londoners, huddled together with their shoulders hunched were leaving the city. They'd set alight great piles of whatever they'd left behind. Now smouldering memorials to what was lost.

Lu Quan was interrupted by Sally's report, 'It's early morning and already thousands of protestors have assembled in parks across the northern and southern extremities of the city, like the one I'm in.' Helicopters hovered overhead as she continued, 'No, it's not quite clear what the protesters will now do. But it's fair to say the mood here is much, much darker than it has been over the last few days. Truly, who knows what state this will all end up in?'

Karan was in the cabinet room reading the overnight intelligence reports, 'What on earth does she even mean with that?' he asked an empty room. Rattling windows told him the military helicopters were low overheard. 'At least she's gone,' he pointed at footage of Usha's speech on the screen.

Khalid joined Sally. 'What the governor-general has implemented is unconstitutional, illegal and fundamentally un-English. Parliament has met in this country since 1215, and it has been the supreme and absolute constitutional manifestation of the collective power and will of our people since 1689 and our bill of rights. There may be little public sympathy left for politics or politicians, but we demand that all politicians ignore the governor-general's piddling little order and come to the Houses of Parliament to demand the restitution of our ancient rights and privileges.'

Sally nodded, 'And if I may, we have time for just one more question, what do you think about the role of the first minister in all of this?'

Khalid exploded, 'He's a stooge of the highest order. A rogue in tight clothing. He's no Englishman.'

Karan turned off the television and returned to his reports. Seb's cough interrupted him, 'The intelligence report from the prime minister's office.'

Karan read the top three lines and shouted, 'Get me Oliver.'

* * *

Oliver was watching Sally's news reports from bed, 'Get away from the window.' Arun was distracted by the heavily armed soldiers marching to St James's Park.

'It's probably already too late,' Arun replied.

'What are you talking about?'

'He's taken over the city. Closed parliament. And he's killed a lot of people. What else is left?'

Oliver's phone rang, 'Of course,' he said into it. 'In a few hours?' Arun came back to bed as Oliver put the phone down. 'It was Sally, she wants to meet me later.'

'You shouldn't go anywhere today. It's not safe for you.' Arun turned up the volume on the news coverage from the protest camps to hear an elderly man in an 'India Quit' t-shirt saying, 'We need our king back. We don't need to be ruled by foreigners. We've never been ruled by foreigners.' Behind him some people were stitching 'India Quit' t-shirts together to form a peace quilt.

Oliver took Arun's hand, 'Interesting but a little ahistoric. We liked our German kings and queens. I'll let Sally break the story of my resignation. I'll tell her the whole lot.'

Arun grabbed Oliver's phone. 'Turn this off. They only turned the network back on so they can monitor us all. Don't say another thing.' It rang again. Arun stumbled for the off button and dropped it.

Oliver scrambled over the bed to answer, 'Yes. I'm on my way.' He turned to Arun, 'Summoned.'

* * *

Banerjee smirked as he waved his pass at the Indian and British soldiers guarding the entrance to Windsor Castle. Heavily armed troops lined his route to Albert's private rooms. 'Thank God you are here, Banerjee. I'm a prisoner. A prisoner in my own castle. Did you receive my letters, and have you been able to forward them to the governor-general?'

Banerjee took time to take his seat. Albert watched his every move furtively, anxiously. 'Might I have some chai. It is a quick drive now from London to Windsor—what with the troops stopping all non-essential traffic. But it does make one thirsty.'

'Of course, my dear friend.' Albert called for tea, continuing, 'So much has happened since I saw you last. I was worried for your safety. But I am so pleased to have a visitor.'

'Oh, you need not have worried for me.' Albert continued to stare at him relentlessly. 'I have spent my time usefully with the governor-general. He is excellent in a crisis. Demonstrates such leadership, don't you think?'

Albert pointed to the television. 'I've seen such terrible scenes, Banerjee. Unimaginable in my time in London. In our time in London.'

They sat quietly as a footman slowly poured a cup. Banerjee brought it to his mouth and smelled it. 'Lapsang. So lovely.' He looked at Albert, 'You were saying?'

'Such terrible scenes. But have you heard? they are calling for me.'

'Who is'

'My people, Banerjee.' Albert pointed again at the television. 'My people want me back.'

Banerjee set his cup down. He made to speak but Albert continued, 'England is far more than an instrument of accession giving some time-limited legal rights to the Indian prime minister. Her generals are standing on a thousand years of civilisation. Of the development of human rights. The rule of law. And of elected parliaments and governments.'

Banerjee took a sip. 'I have been given a message from the governor-general. He would like to see you later today.'

'You think he realises the game is up? And that he will need to call me back into proper service?'

'I don't know, sir. The message is that you have a favour to return. And, Albert, I would prefer if you addressed me as Lord Banerjee from now on.' Banerjee stood up and Albert was open-mouthed.

'What do you mean, Banerjee, I mean, Lord Banerjee? What favour?'

Banerjee smiled and left.

Albert scanned the walls of his apartments. 'It all seems to be closing in.'

* * *

'Oh, for God's sake,' Elizabeth told her driver. 'This is the third one of these we've had to battle.'

An Indian soldier was in front of her car was stopping it from making any further progress. A young British officer was at her driver's door, finger pointing for the window to go down.

'Government plates?'

'Yes,' Elizabeth replied. 'I'm a judge and I have this car for my security from the master of the rolls. I must get to my courtroom.'

'No can do, I'm afraid,' the soldier replied. 'All the courts are shut, ain't they?'

Elizabeth handed him her pass. 'Yes, but I have a case to conclude. Could you please let me get to my office to collect my papers?'

'You see, the thing is, we've been told you judges are planning on trying to keep your courts open even when they ain't meant to be. You trying that, are you?'

Elizabeth neither shifted her gaze nor replied to him.

'Who did you say you were?' the young soldier had her judicial pass in his hand.

Elizabeth pointed to the crest. 'I'm a high court judge. In fact, I've just been appointed to the court of final appeal. Surely I'm not the only one going to work today?'

'We haven't seen many, your honour. As I said, the courts are shut, ain't they?'

Before she could reply, the soldier was on his radio. Elizabeth scanned the area to see an empty road. In the rear-view mirror she saw the sweat on her driver's brow.

'What's your case?' the soldier asked.

'It's about an allegation of wrongful death.'

'Whose?'

'I don't see why that matters.'

The soldier stared at her. Then at the pass. He received another message.

'Not today, my lady.' He handed the pass back. 'Courts closed today. Government orders. Security threat.'

* * *

Oliver nodded at the Indian intelligence officer in the car outside Arun's flat.

'Step to the side, please, sir.' Forty young soldiers filed past him down the steps to the park. Oliver followed at a much slower pace, forced to present his government identity card every 30 yards. Helicopters were taking off from St James's and the barracks like fireworks.

At Downing Street, nervy young soldiers cocked their guns, forcing Oliver to shout, 'I'm a government minister and have been called to see the first minister.'

'Where's your car?' one replied.

'Sorry?'

'We've been told all authorised personnel will approach by car.'

'I didn't take mine. I thought it was unnecessary.'

'Think you know better than us?' the soldier sneered. Oliver watched him look at the pass while he listened to his earpiece. 'You're free to come in. Stick to the middle of the road where we can see you.'

Karan was in his office. 'It's taken you twenty-five minutes to get here from over the park. Did you walk backwards?'

'Now you're getting surveillance reports on your ministers?'

Karan smiled. 'Only on the most pedestrian members of the government. I wanted you to see this.' He handed over the intelligence report.

'I've already been told about it. They're fabricating evidence. And are going to force you to mount an illegal attack. Maybe even a war.'

'How have you already been told about this?'

'Even with all this security, the governor-general's information management isn't as watertight as he'd like.'

Karan hadn't moved from his desk. Nor had he asked Oliver to sit down.

'What are you going to do?' Oliver asked.

'What can I do? I'm stuck here. I can't resign now.'

'I don't know if he's the cuckoo or if you are.'

'What?'

'I don't know if the governor-general is the one who's going to push you out of the nest. Or if your job is to push all of us out.'

'I don't have the luxury to philosophise. Or grandstand. If I go, what will happen to the country?'

'Karan, you're killing the country. Can't you see what's happening? Or are you only reading the intelligence reports they send you?

Suspending parliament—like he's Charles the First. We're not even a banana republic any more. Your administration allowing troops on the streets. Stopping English people from what were inalienable rights to go about their business free from interference. And as for Isha and her father …'

Karan interrupted, 'My administration. I thought we were in it together. Rid of them by christmas. This was your fucking plan.'

'Not any more,' Oliver whispered.

'Sorry?'

'It's not my plan any more. We need to resign. I need to resign. And so do you.'

'You don't get to resign. You are no longer a part of this administration.'

'Thank fuck I don't need to run around any longer watching you in Isha's rose-tinted designer glasses.'

'You're an egotistical prick. You've always been an egotistical prick.'

'People need to know what a fucking mess you've created.'

They stood in silence. Karan continued, 'You could at least have the decency to go once we are through a major national fucking disaster. Put the country first for once.'

'Your administration is the major national fucking disaster.'

'You're an arsehole.'

'Am I? While you are scouring helpful intelligence reports, you might want to look at these.'

'What's this?' Karan asked. 'More conspiracy theories?'

'Take a good look. They're bank accounts.'

'More made-up stories.' Karan threw the papers at him.

'No, the accounts you don't want to know about. The ones Sunil set up to help transfer assets out of India. They're the secret accounts that kept your wife in the style to which she has become accustomed. But also the accounts in which she facilitates the transfer of huge sums of money for Sunil. These are also the accounts that facilitated their scheme to take over our country.'

'This is a new level of crazy. Even for you. Your boyfriend has you involved in some Mumbai–Delhi political bullshit.'

'Karan, look at it. Look at all of it. I can admit I got it wrong. I thought we could ride this Indian thing. That we had enough experience and smarts between us. But they've beaten us. I'm giving you a chance to get out of it. Out of it with me. Right now. Let's resign together.'

'I can't fucking resign. We're under attack. We're about to become embroiled in some international incident. I've got a job to do.'

'You're not saving England by staying. You're signing her death warrant.'

'And what about my wife and family?'

'Look, Karan, you have to make a choice. A real choice this time. Me or Isha.'

Karan walked back to his desk. 'There is no choice.'

* * *

Archana and Zarin were at the table in an empty hotel. Philippe was glum. His staff terrified. Isha's protection officers barged in. One said, Clear, and she entered with five officers around her. She smiled and joked with the men as they settled her into her seat before they retreated to stand directly outside the private dining room. The shadows of their guns visible through the panes of glass in the door.

'Where are all the people, Philippe?' Isha asked.

Philippe shrugged. 'We are closed today, madam. To ensure you have maximum enjoyment.'

Zarin smirked, 'People are too fucking terrified to be around you. They don't know if you'll have them arrested or—'

Isha interrupted her, 'Or what?'

'Or killed.'

'What?'

'Don't you read the stuff online?' Zarin asked.

'No, we try to avoid conspiracy theories and crazies.'

Archana pointed to the champagne and Philippe poured.

Isha put her hand over the top of her glass, 'You're saying that people think that Karan and I are killing English people?'

'No,' Zarin replied.

'Thank God. That would be mad.'

'Only you.' Zarin continued with her champagne. 'Have you seen outside? The city is a fucking war zone. We only got here,' she pointed at Archana, 'because you sent cars for us. I came through eight checkpoints. It's fucking Belfast, Cyprus and Sheikh Jarrah all rolled into one. Have you any idea what's going on?'

* * *

Oliver walked through the creamy yellow stone arch and scanned the cemetery's lime trees for Sally. He laid a bouquet of purple flowers in front of Emmeline Pankhurst's grave, stood staring at its celtic cross and waited. A cyclist careered by shouting, 'Isn't it time you stood up to those fuckers?' Oliver walked towards the domed chapel and spotted Sally by a tardis-like mausoleum.

They walked to the furthest of its four sides and she whispered, 'At some point we have to stop meeting like this. What the actual fuck is going on?'

Oliver smirked. 'Let's walk.'

They sat on a bench between the graves of London's great and good—a hagiography of generals and soldiers, actors and singers—each one attacked by the summer's brambles. Oliver took a deep breath. 'Some years ago, I helped Isha acquire a lovely little business in east London. Her father paid for it, of course. Like he does with most things. You'll see all the financial information you need to in these papers.' Oliver handed them over. 'And if you go into the factory, you'll see the appalling conditions that Isha has created for the skilled workers who earn her millions.'

'Minister?' She was reading the papers. 'This can't be right.' Sally continued to review the pages he handed her. Oliver checked whether they were being watched. 'These are bank accounts. Of someone with the name of the Indian prime minister. And Isha. And her father.' She continued to skim them. 'And Lord Banerjee. This is far worse than the stuff we got from Merchant's. God, they were all at it for decades.'

Oliver scanned the cemetery. 'Don't hang around here much longer. And don't go back the way you came.'

'Now who's cloak-and-dagger? Are you sure you want to do this?'

He nodded.

'Then, thank you,' she replied.

'What for?'

'For trying to save us.'

He watched her walk down one of the side paths and out of view and picked up his phone, 'I've done it.'

Arun interrupted him, 'Please don't say any more. Let's meet back at the flat.'

* * *

Sally was staring at the listening devices, antennae and monitoring equipment hanging off the lamp posts above her and strewn across the road. All had Chinese characters on them. Chinese security guards were stationed every forty yards or so outside the shops and businesses. Military vehicles and police screeched down the roads.

Khalid smiled at her. 'Sally, this was a surprising call. And location.'

'Thank you for coming. I'm not sure why I called you. Probably for security.'

'How did you get here?' he asked her.

'I live further east. We're outside the ring of steel the governor-general has introduced to kill the city. No one gives a fuck about Hackney. I left my press card at home.' She checked the area furtively. 'I never come to Little China. Is it always like this?'

'I don't come here often either. I did about twenty years ago.' Khalid moved away from the security guards. 'It didn't used to be like this. So why am I here?'

'I think we should both take a look at this factory.'

* * *

Lu Quan was watching live footage of Sally and Khalid from deep below his building and leafing through the papers his minister-counsellor had handed him. 'And do we have any images of the exchanged documents?'

'We took these from his phone.' The minister-counsellor was an accredited diplomat with the court of St James as the senior economic lead for the embassy; however, his real role was to head the Chinese mission's covert intelligence-gathering. His staff lived and worked in the bowels of the building. A highly secure area had been excavated, by Chinese contractors, underneath the old royal mint. A miniature AI data centre with feeds from the IOT devices dotted across Little China and the British government's secret network of cables in the ground beneath them. Young data scientists, cryptographers, hackers and intelligence analysts worked in surroundings much like the multi-billion-dollar tech companies in Shanghai.

The work and the area itself were highly classified. Guards of the army of the people's republic were stationed at the bunker's entrance. Sentries had also been placed at a door which only the minister-counsellor and a few undeclared operatives were permitted to use. This was the much-feared interrogation centre which the local Chinese community could talk about in great detail. Its existence ensured they were regular providers of high-grade information.

'What are these photos?' Lu Quan was watching a middle-aged British couple having sex in a Chinese-owned London hotel.

'This is the judge who hearing the case against the government, sir.'

'And him?' the ambassador pointed.

'A man she had been having a long-term affair with. And who appointed her to this role.'

Lu Quan smiled. 'This is excellent work. Recent?'

The minister-counsellor nodded. 'Recent enough.'

'The governor-general has asked for our help. Have these sent to him on the usual channels. And this?' The ambassador opened a manila folder with top-secret markings.

'Sir, these are retrieved private messages from 2004 between the first minister and his political soulmate. They are pretty bland. Sadly, no smoking gun.'

Lu Quan reviewed them, 'Salacious but not explicit' But one of them had been of interest to us?' He asked.

The aide nodded. 'A Chinese parliamentary delegation met young conservative activists. Their cover story was to understand parliamentary democracy. We wanted to collect data on likely future ministers. The white one made what he thought to be a clever speech about one-country-two-systems. He embarrassed our delegation. So we started monitoring him. He joined an app we developed to catch people just like him.'

Lu smiled and pointed to a nineteen-year-old Oliver naked in front of a mirror.

'Yes,' the aide nodded, 'but sadly it seemed our people were not his type.'

* * *

A soldier approached Karan's car as they waited to leave. Karan was looking at the message he had drafted to send Oliver.

'Sorry, first minister. You're being held here until a flight takes off from over the park. Apparently, some military bigwigs were meeting the governor-general. We've been told the new security protocol is to restrict all movement underneath government flight paths. No exceptions.'

Karan raised his eyebrows. 'I think I still am the first minister of this country. I haven't become a terrorist sympathiser, have I? Or a prisoner in own home?'

'Sorry, sir. Orders are orders. I'm afraid we've not had military clearance for your movement, yet.' At that a helicopter soared over them. The young officer pointed and smiled. He moved to the front of the car, put his hand to his ear and then after a while tapped the bonnet and gave Karan the thumbs-up. The gates opened.

'Umesh, let's get the fuck out of here, please.'

Karan spotted the row of houses in which Arun had a flat. He checked his phone and looked again at the text on his phone. This would be just the sort of moment when they'd speak. When Oliver would help prepare him for whatever was about to come next. He deleted it.

Umesh stopped at the checkpoint outside the palace, 'Destination, sir?' the soldier asked.

'We are the only car on this road. It's perfectly clear who we are and where we are going. What can possibly be stopping us now?'

'You don't yet have clearance from the governor-general's office, sir.'

A cavalcade of heavily armoured vehicles raced out. Karan watched them speed through every barrier on the road. 'Fuckers.'

A footman was waiting at the portico, 'I'm sorry, first minister. I hope you were not inconvenienced. The governor-general had a high-classification meeting in the main house. A few of the military bods left by helicopter. The governor-general's office asked that we take you to his private apartment.' The footman was attempting to rush Karan up the steps. Karan watched another three-car military convoy speed the heads of the armed forces out of the courtyard.

'You have had a busy morning, haven't you?' Karan asked as the butler left him in the yellow drawing room.

The governor-general walked in. 'First minister, the prime minister of India was subject to a vicious attack under your watch.

What more do you know of the international terrorists who plotted this heinous crime?'

Karan tried to respond, 'Well, the heads of the agencies have assured me they are doing all they can to answer that question.'

The governor-general remained standing. 'This is simply not good enough, first minister. English security forces were completely unprepared for this.'

'Governor-general, I came to discuss how long you intend to continue governor-general's rule for.'

'First minister, it will run for as long as it is needed to protect this country from itself.'

'You will have seen the news reports. My own MPs no longer support this course of action. What you've done is being called unconstitutional. It is likely to be challenged in court.'

'It will not succeed.'

'How can you be so sure?'

'I do not intend to let the former courts try new cases. I have asked the master of the rolls to set up a new court of final appeal staffed with British and Indian judges. Appeals from it will flow to the courts in Delhi. The only ones in which we have total faith.'

'That's preposterous. And smacks of corruption and desperation. What next?'

'First minister, the benefit of governor-general's rule means it is not legally possible for the head of this state to be corrupt. But you have distracted me. What progress have you made on the attacks and the international terrorists behind them?'

'Cobra continues to meet. We are bringing the assessments of the Six-Eyes community together.'

'That must stop immediately, first minister.'

'Why?'

'We have reason to believe that one of the partners is complicit in the attack and is feeding you compromised intelligence.'

'Excellency, our assessment is that there is no evidence to point to international terrorism. It is most likely to have been opportunistic attackers from within the UK. Individuals who wish to challenge the authority of the newly established order.'

'We have shared our assessment with you?' The governor-general handed Karan a set of papers.

'Yes, excellency. But, as I say, our agencies have come to a remarkably different conclusion. And I must take their view over others. That is my constitutional duty.' Karan set the papers on the side table between them.

'Your constitutional duty, first minister, is to the territorial integrity of the republic. Your agencies have forgotten what it is like to live with the constant drumbeat of barbarians at the door. India has not had the luxury to develop a four-day week at the expense of proper policing and thorough investigation.'

'What are you saying?'

'We have human intelligence and intercepted evidence that confirms that this was an operation of the global khalistani movement. And that its perpetrators, its decision-makers, are currently in Canada. And they acted with the tacit support of the government of Canada.'

'What is this human intelligence? You mean you're interrogating khalistanis and muslims in questionable jails? Torturing people does not create credible, verifiable evidence, sir. It tells us exactly what we want to hear.'

'I will ignore your baseless allegations, first minister. We also have intercepted evidence. Of members of the Canadian government.'

'You cannot surveil our six-eyes partners. That's the whole point of the partnership. Who else are you listening to?'

The governor-general was silent.

'Excellency?'

'We do not intend to answer to our temporary political appointees, first minister. India has been subject to constant attacks and the constant threat of attack. We have learnt to give up some of our individual freedom for the good of the republic. You should see that too. We know what an attack on sovereignty looks like. And we know how to respond. You will prepare all military options against the khalistani threat, wherever it is based.'

'I won't give those instructions.'

'I already have, first minister. These were a direct command from the prime minister.'

'You are asking me to prepare attack plans on a member of the commonwealth? This is preposterous. And illegal.'

'You will consider the plans the heads of the armed forces present to you. I will then review them. First minister, an attack will be launched. And you will be the one announcing it.'

'Excellency, I won't do it. You will have my resignation later today.'

'First minister, you are all that stands between England and its annihilation. The prime minister has a fondness for Sunil and his beti. She does not wish to do anything that would humiliate them. You are uniquely placed to save what little there is left of this island's dignity. But be assured, should you resign, governor-general's rule will never end. We will turn this green and pleasant land into the sort of colonial factory serving the republic that of which only your east India company would be proud. And history will show it was all your fault.' The governor-general paused, 'And the attack will still go ahead.' With that he made to leave.

'One more thing, I have asked that your security and Isha's be reviewed. I have received reports of plots against you. And against Albert.'

'I hope that doesn't mean house arrest, excellency.'

'These measures are for your safety. You might also speak to your cabinet. And its former members. Pernicious briefings to the media might seem harmless but will be treated as sedition. A capital offence in the republic.'

The governor-general handed Karan the note he had been carrying. 'There are further orders from the PM. She finds the BBC distasteful. And believes it to be generating a great deal of negativity in this state. You are to privatise and sell it. The PM believes that

Sunil will be best placed to help with its transformation.' With that he walked out.

* * *

Back in his office, Karan rubbed his eyes to stay awake. He'd listened to four hours of briefings from Seb, Dame Rebecca and his national security advisor, Vice Admiral Rachel Moore, a forty-something two-star officer.

'Well, this isn't what you all signed up for,' Karan pointed out matter-of-factly. 'I've had hours of briefings from a series of people I no longer trust. Many in my own cabinet. And now the chief of the defence staff is too busy to meet me.' On the screens above him were charts and maps under the title 'operation aquiline'.

Karan was leafing back through one of the many folders. 'We don't want to invade Canada. Or do anything to Canada. Who ever wants to do anything to Canada? I mean no one has since the early nineteenth century.'

Rachel smiled. 'It's not madness, it's hubris.' She continued, 'What's madness is that the chiefs have already presented full attack plans to the governor-general. Something about them only recognising the legality of the chain of command. And that once the civilian authorities had made the decision to amalgamate with India, they had no other option.'

Dame Rebecca added, 'We are on a path to war.'

'No, we fucking are not.' Karan slammed the binder shut. 'What is the bare minimum we can be seen to do that would look like a proportionate response?' Karan had typed Oliver's name into his phone again. This would be the time for one of his brilliant suggestions.

'We could refer the issue to the UN,' Seb replied. 'It will take a day or so to get on to the agenda of the security council. We can tell the PM that this is her first chance to sit in what was the UK's seat. To drive an international consensus against terrorism. And ...'

'And what?' Karan asked.

'Once we are in the UN system, we'll never get out. Like Jason and the minotaur.'

'I think it was Hercules. And I think he did kill it,' Karan replied.

'It was Theseus who killed it. And led the athenians to freedom,' Dame Rebecca replied. 'But I don't think she will buy it.'

Another of Karan's private secretaries came into the office and put the television on. 'He's addressing the nation.'

The governor-general was speaking from the music room at Buckingham Palace. The flag of India and the governor-general's personal standard were lined up behind him. As were the chiefs of the armed forces.

'What the fuck is going on? Get me the defence secretary,' Karan shouted but nobody moved. They were all focused on the television.

'I wanted to speak first to Londoners and apologise to them for the changes we have made to their city. I hope they will understand that the safety and security of the people of this state is our paramount responsibility. And for those reasons alone, we have sealed off the political centre of the capital until we are sure that the attacks have stopped and the perpetrators brought to justice.'

Karan surveyed the transfixed stares and the slow draining of power from him and the people around the table.

'I instructed the first minister to continue his efforts, and those of the police, to uncover those criminals and terrorists who planted yesterday's bombs. But it is now clear that these attacks were not by lone wolves. Indian intelligence confirms that this was a cold-hearted attack on the Indian prime minister herself, initiated and orchestrated by Canadian khalistani separatists hell-bent on destroying India's sovereignty and territorial integrity. Worse, this group have been given succour and support by a friendly government.' The room was silent. Downing Street was silent. No one could believe what they were hearing.

'We cannot stand idly by as these terrorists use the levers and freedoms of democracy to attack the republic of India. So I have given orders to launch operation aquiline—a joint military response. The Indian strike group in the North Atlantic will be joined by Britain's carrier strike group. Together, this awe-inspiring force will make immediate preparations to sail for Canada. This show of resolve will, we hope, encourage the Canadian government to hand over these terrorists and separatists to the government of India whereupon they will undergo a full criminal trial for their seditious and murderous acts.'

Karan's phone was ringing. 'I have the defence secretary for you.'

Karan put his phone down, 'He supports this necessary course of action.' He examined each one of them. 'What the actual fuck just happened? Is this a coup?'

No one could answer. He picked up his phone again. 'Get me the Indian prime minister.' Everyone turned to watch him.

'Her office have instructed you to speak to the governor-general.'

'Tell them that her governor-general is on English television declaring world war three with her own ships.'

There was silence. For some minutes. No one wanted to speak. Or to voice an opinion on what might happen next.

'They say she supports the actions the governor-general is taking and expects the first minister to implement them fully.'

'Sweet fuck.' Karan ended the call and dialled Oliver, who was in his bedroom with Arun.

'Take it,' Arun suggested.

'No. I can't help him and anyway the story is about to break.'

The phone stopped as Arun asked, 'Surely they won't run it now.'

Oliver had been refreshing the BBC site. 'It's up. "Isha's secret sweatshop".'

Arun read the story. 'I wish you hadn't done this. They're on a war footing. And there will be plenty of casualties.'

Karan called again. Oliver ignored him and kissed Arun.

* * *

Isha stormed into Number 10 threw the door to the cabinet room open and marched into Karan's office. She announced, 'Your boyfriend just shat on me all over the BBC.'

'Everybody out.' Karan stood up and ushered them to the door to his private office. 'What are you talking about?'

'Don't you give a shit about me? How many press officers do you have here? Hasn't one of them come in to say Isha's in trouble?'

'No, we have been dealing with a world war and the sort of coup you might find in Burkina Faso. What are you talking about?'

'The factory is all over the fucking BBC. Oliver is quoted. The fucking lazy bitches who don't work there are quoted. They must have taken a translator. They never speak to me in English. And I'm portrayed as some kind of creative devil-master.'

'We can fix this. Also, it will blow over. This is not the story to worry about today. It's just not big enough.'

'It's big enough to me, Karan. And it will bring in pitaji. And then the PM.'

'How can it do that?'

'You know how. These people love to smear lies. And fuck knows what Oliver is going to say.'

'I can't deal with this today.'

'Yes, you can.'

'What?'

'Pitaji told me you've been told to sell him the BBC. Do it now and he can stop this.'

'I'm not selling the BBC to Sunil so he can save your embarrassment.'

'You're such a self-righteous prick,' Isha screamed at Karan and walked out.

* * *

Albert watched what was once his helicopter land on the lawn. The windows of the 950-year-old castle shook. Its norman architecture was holding up better than he was. The retinue of government cars that made up the governor-general's lengthy cavalcade headed to the castle. High above Albert, the governor-general's personal standard was being raised on the ramparts.

'It was good of you to join us, governor-general.' They were sitting in Albert's private apartments overlooking the garden his grandfather had established.

'You travel with a far greater number of soldiers now.'

The governor-general savoured his whisky. 'It is why I am here. We have intelligence that you, as well as the first minister and his wife, and I, are the subject of extensive and detailed terror plots.'

'Why should anyone be interested in me, excellency? I am in semi-retirement.'

'We are all targets now, governor.'

'Now that you have declared war on Canada. That was a rather novel decision, excellency. I had thought you had come here for some advice. Yes, the last time we had a battle on Canadian soil was the war of 1812. George the Third was regent at the time. I had the archivist find some of the relevant papers. You know that our personal papers are kept here.'

The governor-general took a deep sip of whisky. 'That has been the great success of your family.'

'Sorry?' Albert had cocked his head like one of his spaniels awaiting a treat or instruction.

'To hang on, governor. Hanging on is your remarkable success. You appear to be the unbending foundation of justice and mercy. The manifestation of all that only be right. But of course, the truth is, you flex and bend.' The governor-general was demonstrating with his wrist. 'Your trick is that no one sees you do it. Yet it's done in plain sight.'

'I really don't understand the point you are making.'

'If your public were to find out just how dirty a little deal you had done to keep your palaces and personal wealth, the people might finally jettison you.'

'That wasn't the arrangement, Manish. We did it together. I would stand by you—and you by me. I think you are the one who has failed to abide by that bargain.'

'I think it would be wise, Albert, for you to adopt a period of quiet reflection. Maybe even total retirement. Lord Banerjee here can help you make the necessary plans.'

Banerjee was neck-deep in the royal whisky cabinet. 'I think I will try this one.' He brought out a 1978.

'An excellent choice, Lord Banerjee. Don't you agree, Albert?'

* * *

Oliver and Arun were in the kitchen of Oliver's flat finishing dinner. Arun opened a bottle of red wine, 'Just in time for Raksha,' and turned on the television. 'I miss that place,' Arun told him.

Raksha was in the middle of her Mumbai comedy-store routine. 'So now the khalistanis are the problem? Seems like they are running out of people to blame for our colonial misadventure. How many Indians does it take to plant a conspiracy theory?'

Eight

Karan was in the cabinet room looking out at the military encampment engulfing him. A clock chimed half past five. 'Fuck, I need coffee.' He told himself as he walked into his private office. Seb, on the phone, pointed his finger at him to wait.

'Who was that?' he asked as he sipped from a steaming mug.

'The *Portsmouth Courier* asking for a quote.'

'How did they get to you? Don't we have press officers working twenty-four seven right now?'

Seb nodded. 'Yes, but you'll want to hear this. They asked what we plan to do with the Canadians.'

'What?'

'Canadian ship *Yukon*, a Halifax class frigate, slipped anchor sometime in the last twenty-four hours, leaving fifteen of its crew on shore. The remaining crew were arrested by the military police last night. The *Courier* wants to know if they're prisoners of war.'

'Fuck. It was part of our combined carrier strike group?'

Rachel walked in. 'I'm getting details on the ship's progress now. I'm also getting reports of new orders going to HMS *Sutherland* from permanent joint headquarters.'

'The *Sutherland*?' Karan asked.

'Yes, the *Sutherland*'s a Type 31 frigate. The fastest in the fleet.' Rachel handed him photos. 'If he asks her to, the *Sutherland* will outrun the *Yukon* and sink her.'

'You think that's what he will ask?' Karan was studying photos of the young company on both ships.

'I do, sir,' Rachel replied. 'He's going to order the *Sutherland* to sink the *Yukon*.'

Dame Rebecca had also arrived. 'First minister, don't comment on the Portsmouth story.'

'Which one?' Karan asked.

'Either. The first sea lord is implementing all the orders received from the governor-general's office. Without question.'

Karan led the four of them back into the cabinet room. Dame Rebecca shut the door. 'I don't know if there is anyone you can trust, first minister, other than the people in this room. The first sea lord is taking a punt that the governor-general will make him chief of the general staff.' She tutted, 'He always was an odious little shit.'

Rachel interrupted, 'The *Sutherland* sets sails in the next couple of hours. The commander of the strike group has been given orders to sail as soon as possible after that. They'll try to reach the *Yukon* and then make their way to the Canadian eastern seaboard.'

'We need to find someone we can trust at the admiralty,' Karan said.

'I have someone in mind,' Rachel replied. 'My old boss, the second sea lord, admiral Nick Brannick.'

'You trust him?'

'I do, sir,' Rachel replied. 'With my life.'

Karan asked Dame Rebecca, 'Do you?'

'I don't know. After last night's television parade, I certainly don't trust the chiefs. Nick is the best option we have. In the meantime, you are going to have to attend some cobra meetings on this and pretend to be implementing all the governor-general's orders.'

'First minister,' Rachel's face was serious. 'From here on in, what you decide could lead to charges of war crimes.'

'Or worse,' Dame Rebecca replied. 'Sedition in the republic. And that carries the death penalty.'

'Let's take one step at a time.' Karan turned to Rachel. 'Get me Brannick.'

* * *

Elizabeth was already in her office. A late-night call from her clerk had told her to be ready at 6.00 a.m. Neither of them knew why. There was a knock on the door and her clerk came in. 'Brought you a fresh cup, my lady. It's a godawful time to be at work.'

'Yes,' Elizabeth replied. 'I was last at my office desk at 6 a.m. about twenty years ago. I thought I'd given early starts up when I gave up commercial law.'

Nigel opened the door. 'May I come in?'

She was surprised. 'The master of the rolls. At six in the morning. Whatever is going on?'

He shut the door and stood against it blocking anyone from seeing in. 'Have you thought about our offer to elevate you to the court of final appeal?'

'I have, Nigel, and I don't want it. It smacks of all that is wrong with the current situation. I am happy to see this case through. And if need be, you can retire me.'

'Elizabeth, you mustn't. There are other considerations to take into account.'

'Nigel, it sounds decidedly like you and the lord chief are trying to have a direct bearing on the administration of a particular case. And that is not permissible.'

'Elizabeth, we've had an instruction from the governor-general. Make this application go away. Or they close the courts. For good.'

'That's nonsense. We've had judges administrating justice in this country since the twelfth century. You know it. I know the lord chief justice knows it. Indians believe in the law. Hell, they've turned it into a national industry. Tell the governor-general to get back in his constitutional box. Someone needs to.'

'Elizabeth, it's not like that. He can shut the courts. For good. He can take away liberties. For good. He's already closed parliament. With no real desire to reopen it. The lord chief justice wants you to make this application go away. Dismiss the matter. And we will elevate you to the court of final appeal. You will fight for justice from there. It will give us all time to fight for parliament. Fight for this country.'

'Fight for our rights, but just not right now. Look how low they've driven you, Nigel. Begging me at six in the morning to break not only the law, but our constitutional rights. The one thing you and I actually believe in.'

'Elizabeth, don't be an idiot. They killed this girl. They'll kill others. Maybe even you.'

'Nigel, it doesn't work like that. I don't work like that. You of all people should know it.'

He handed over a manila file. 'I have been the one negotiating with the governor-general's office for days now. First it was judicial pensions. Then junior courts. Then jury trials. Then this made up court. Then someone couriered this file over at four o'clock this morning.'

Elizabeth was holding pictures of her and Nigel naked. 'How did they get these? Where were they taken?'

'The hotel. The last hotel.' Nigel's body crumpled. 'You told me we shouldn't, and I begged you to. I knew this would all come back and destroy us someday.'

'Us? You fucking imbecile. So now you want me to kill off my integrity. My career. So that yours, and your empty fucking marriage, can survive.'

He was silent.

'Ignore this. Tell whoever sent it politely to fuck off.' She handed him the papers. 'We haven't done anything legally wrong. Morally, perhaps. But nothing to stop me from being the judge the people in that courtroom expect me to be. I'm delivering my verdict tomorrow.'

* * *

Oliver was on the phone to Arun. 'I'm going to park under parliament. It's the safest car park in London. It always has been.' He was waiting for the checkpoint to open, staring at Big Ben with its blue dials and the bright red of St George's cross.

'Well, it hasn't,' Arun replied. 'Just be extra careful today. Both with what you say and what you do.'

'Don't worry. It's going to be a wonderful day. The first day of the rest of my life. Our life. See you later.' Oliver left the car park deep underneath parliament and headed to college green. He spotted Sally and her television crew.

'Are you sure you want to do this?' He nodded as one of her team put a microphone on him.

Sally turned to the camera. 'I've got the deputy first minister with me right now. Why has the government declared war on Canada?'

Oliver said, 'I might correct you, Sally. I'm no longer the deputy first minister. I met the first minister in the course of the last forty-eight hours and resigned from his administration. I could no longer remain silent and supportive in the face of egregious decisions by the governor-general, which the first minister has been forced to implement.'

'So why are you here?'

'The ancient rights and privileges of parliament have been denied to MPs and peers. I'm here today to call for the speaker to reclaim these rights and recall parliament today.'

'Don't we need the consent of the governor-general to do so? Isn't that the legal position that you yourself created when you worked with the first minister to have England become a colony of India?'

'Sally, there is nothing in our agreement with India that supersedes the rights of our MPs and the rights of parliament. So, I am asking the speaker to recall parliament today. With or without the consent of his excellency the governor-general.'

Sally smiled. 'We've only got time for one more question, I'm afraid. You are remarkably close to the first minister and his wife. What do you think they are talking about this morning?'

Oliver smiled, 'I'm not really here to answer hypotheticals, Sally.' Oliver stood and waited to see the operator switch off the camera.

Sally was taking off her own mike, 'So you think she'll recall parliament?'

'Well, it's for the speaker to decide. And she has been a great supporter of Karan's through thick and thin. I don't hold out much hope. More importantly, I have a date tonight.'

She leant into Oliver and whispered. 'Are you sure you want me to run the other story?'

Oliver focused on her. 'Totally.'

* * *

Isha threw her hairbrush at the television, narrowly missing Karan, who'd just walked in. She screamed, 'About your fucking treachery.' She retrieved it and continued brushing. 'He's such a smug little prick. How can you ever have liked him?'

Karan drank his coffee and leafed through the newspapers in front of him.

'Karan?'

After a while he replied, 'He has a point. You shouldn't have been running a sweatshop.'

She threw the brush at Karan and stormed out. He heard the hairdryer. Then the stomp of her feet heading back towards him. 'You have never once taken my side over him. Never. Pitaji says not to worry. He's getting the BBC and all this will go away.'

Karan was attacked for launching an illegal war on the front pages. The flight of the Yukon led the next. Somewhere between pages three and seven were the stories about Isha. The east London factory was universally called a sweatshop. Sunil bankrolling her lifestyle. And much about how Karan had been nothing until he'd married her. He smiled. At least the pictures of their wedding were flattering.

* * *

Commander Singh was on the bridge of the *Yukon*, staring at satellite images of the British carrier strike group, its aircraft carrier and their brand new Type 31 frigates last seen some 10 kilometres off the coast of Portsmouth.

In the early hours of the morning, Singh had told his crew, 'Take us out of the channel as slowly and quietly as possible. Our best hope is that the noise in the shipping lane confuses them. And,' he ordered, 'We're going EMCON Silent from now. Turn off all radars and transmissions. Keep your eyes on them for as long as you possibly can.' Commander Singh had been full of pride as his bridge swung into action. He knew each of the hundred-strong crew on the lower decks was putting their individual preparations into place.

They raised the anchor and held their breath. The *Yukon* was taking slow steps to freedom.

The ship, having succeeded in leaving undetected, was now underway. Singh's executive officer was reiterating their last message. 'From, headquarters, sir.' Singh looked at him as he continued, 'Indian intentions now clear. Return to Halifax. I can't believe they will follow us,' his executive officer continued. 'We've spent the last nine months with them. It'd be like being taken out by your brother or sister.'

Singh's officers were watching him. After looking at the charts he said, 'Our job is to assume the worst and secure the best.' Like them, he worried his thirty-five-year-old ship was no match for the British fleet's newest Type 31 frigates.

The handset beside him rang, interrupting his thoughts. 'Captain, will we signal Halifax about the crew we've left behind?'

Singh sighed. 'Let's not risk it. Halifax will find out soon enough.' He hung up and turned to his executive officer. 'With a twelve-hour start, we have a chance of outrunning them. Just depends when they send the *Sutherland*.'

Singh's executive officer was looking at the last satellite imagery they'd been able to download. 'Looks like nothing moved quickly, sir. Maybe someone in the British Admiralty is trying to play for time.'

Singh nodded, 'Keep the comms off. We need to remain silent. And you'll need to run us as fast as you possibly can. From here on in, we're on our own.' Not for the first time Singh was regretting the political delays and shenanigans that meant he was sailing one of the oldest ships in the fleet rather than one that could guarantee his crew would make it safely home. 'What's the best possible range of our harpoons?' Singh asked, knowing the answer.

'70 miles, sir,' his Warfare Officer replied, 'and the Type 31s have maritime strike tomahawks with a thousand-mile range, sir.'

Singh silently felt for the picture of his family in his top pocket, 'You have the bridge.' As he walked out, his executive officer continued their course for Halifax at full speed. Singh's tour of the ship forced him to catch the worried glances of his young and trusting crew. In his cabin he took the photograph out from his pocket and gave his wife and children a kiss.

* * *

Khalid was giving an interview to Sally. 'This judge has been subject to state harassment. The governor-general is not content with declaring war on one of our oldest allies. He has also decided to mount an assault on our judicial system. Judge Elizabeth Linney is being pressured to recuse herself from this case and become one of the first justices on the governor-general's kangaroo court. A foreign court that will be introduced into the English system packed with Indian judges. I for one don't want it. And I'm here today to stand by this brave woman.'

Sally interrupted, 'Thank you, Mr Khan, and now we are going to Edinburgh to hear from the Scottish prime minister.'

She was on the steps of bute house. 'I have spoken to the offices of both the first minister and the governor-general to make plain the fervent opposition of the government and people of Scotland to an attack on Canada. I have also made clear that sovereign Scottish bases and ports will play no part in this act of aggression. We have made a request via the UN that the security council meet on this issue today. I can only hope that sensible heads in Delhi rein in this extraordinary action before any lives are lost.'

While that was airing Sally asked Khalid, 'What do you think happens next?'

Khalid replied, 'God alone knows. How about we have a coffee this afternoon?'

* * *

Inside the courtroom, Elizabeth was leafing through the thick pile of papers which had been presented to her this morning. The barrister was continuing, 'The media is reporting that this court has been subject to illegal interference and that this case will be sent to the court of final appeal for determination.'

Elizabeth looked out at a court full of Molly's family and friends, journalists and those fighting for their own truth as much as Molly's.

The barrister continued, 'We are making an additional application to the court this morning. We submit that the most recent decision by the governor-general to effectively declare war on a sovereign nation is illegal. But it is relevant in determining why there were troops on the streets of London on the day on which Molly Stevens was murdered. Our contention is that all this is connected. And that this court needs to take a view on the illegal declaration of war as well as the extrajudicial killing of a British citizen.'

Elizabeth interrupted, 'Counsel, I will need to take advice on the competence of this court to address the additional issues you've raised.' Elizabeth left for her chambers.

Her hands were shaking as she reviewed the additional bundles.

'May I come in?' Nigel asked.

'I really don't think this is sensible. People may not have seen you at six o'clock this morning. But there are plenty of folk around now. And no one will expect to see the master of the rolls in my chambers.'

'Elizabeth, don't talk nonsense. You're the only person in the country who doesn't realise the interplay between politicians and judges. We need you to get this right. I need you to get this right. Please don't let our personal history get in the way of doing the right thing.'

She scoffed. 'Nigel, it is our personal history that is getting in the way of doing the right thing. You are here to plead for your own reputation far more than the reputation of the law and the judges in this country. You want me to make all this go away. To give you a few more days to work out whether you need to tell your wife about us or not. And how many times have I heard you give that speech? The "I'm going to leave her tomorrow" speech. I don't know how many hotel rooms I've waited in. Or how many phone calls I've waited on. All for naught. This time, let's just let the law do the talking.'

He knew it was the last time he'd speak to her. She knew that too. Whatever she decided on the case, she'd decided on him. This wasn't the Nigel she fell in love with. This craven, power-hungry toad was about as attractive as last week's rubbish. She returned to the papers on her desk and only let out her breath when he left.

* * *

In Portsmouth, commodore Matthew Hughes was checking final preparations on the bridge of the Prince of Wales, the strike group's flagship. The aircraft carrier was accompanied by four frigates, a supply ship and a nuclear submarine. All to exert maximum pressure on the Canadians.

Commodore Hughes was speaking to captain William Arthur, commanding officer of the *Prince of Wales*, and the other captains in the group. 'We deploy in six hours. Carrier strike group is the greatest projection of our naval power since the Falklands war. Some of you may be confused at the nature of the mission and worried about the legality of the threat of force against a commonwealth realm. Our political masters have decided that the khalistani movement in Canada has killed innocent men, women and children on our streets. We should need no greater requirement to act than those factors. I know you will lead your ships with glory and honour. Captain Hadwell will leave now, interdict the *Yukon* using all necessary force and turn her back. The rest of us will catch her up and then continue to Halifax. By the time we arrive, we hope our political masters will have been able to use our presence to secure the necessary political outcome.'

Hughes turned to captain Arthur. 'I hope I'm right. Can you get me commodore Savarkar on the *Vikrant* please?'

The signals officer replied, 'He was listening in, sir. He's on the line now.'

'Ranjan?'

'Commodore Hughes?' a crackling Indian voice asked.

'Ranjan, we sail in six hours. Jai Hind.'

'Jai Hind.'

'Captain Hadwell?'

'Yes, sir?'

'You will lead a difficult mission. You and your crew will do it well. Find the *Yukon*, stop her and turn her back. It's imperative we show we mean business. What information do you have on her current position?'

'Sir, the *Yukon* went EMCON silent and turned off all radars and transmissions when it entered the Channel. At the moment we still don't have a fixed position for her. But we'll find her and catch her.'

Captain Hadwell turned to her bridge on HMS *Sutherland*. 'Well, we know what to do. Find the *Yukon* and stop her.' She looked at her colleagues. They'd just spent the last eighteen months on deployment with the *Yukon*. Her sailors and officers had partied with them in every port from Guam to Cyprus. Beds had been shared. And now former shipmates and hunters had become the hunted.

'Let's get to 34 knots. She must be on the way to Iceland from Ireland.' Captain Hadwell tried to make it sound convincing before announcing to the whole ship's crew, 'Attention. We are now on active operations. We've been given a critical mission for our country. I know you will do your duty with expertise and professionalism.'

Twenty metres below the *Prince of Wales*, captain Payton, a thirty-five-year-old sailor in charge of HMS *Assurance* had been listening in to the exchange on the bridge. 'New instructions from

PJHQ. Request to decode these, sir,' his executive officer handed him a sheet of paper. Payton nodded and they headed to the safe. Payton watched the young man he'd been sailing with for the last five months search for his key. He opened the box in the safe and took his code book. 'Me, now XO,' Payton used his key to open a second box, taking out a small leather book on which was written 'HMS *Assurance* captain's validation'.

Captain Payton waited while his executive officer performed the mental arithmetic that would turn the encrypted codes from London into a target that could change the fate of his country. 'Validation, sir.' Payton's executive officer handed him the sheet without flinching. They both stood silent as he entered that information into the monitor in front of them. Payton took a deep breath and waited. 'It's the *Yukon*, sir.' Payton nodded.

'Prepare torpedo bays,' Payton instructed and waited. At the front of the ship, two missile technicians initiated the standard loading procedures from beneath the torpedo bay while another waited to line it directly in. 'Ready.' With a flick of the switch, the drone slowly nudged into the chamber. Shutting the torpedo bay, he grabbed the nearby handset to call the bridge, 'Bay One loaded.'

Captain Payton announced to the ship, 'We've received our orders. And are now going dark.'

At that his executive officer dimmed the ship's lights and said, 'Dive to 75 metres and take us to 35 knots.'

* * *

'First minister?' Rachel was at the door of Karan's office. 'May I bring in admiral Nick Brannick?'

'Of course.' Karan stood up to shake his hand as Rachel and Dame Rebecca walked in. 'Thank you for your help, admiral Brannick. I need it. What is happening at the ministry of defence?'

'Legal advice has been taken,' Brannick placed his hands behind his back as he spoke. 'They believe they have to follow all decisions issued by the governor-general until parliament or the courts intervene. Some of them are saying that this way they remain in operational control of the nuclear weapons and submarines. But …'

'But what, admiral?' Karan asked.

'A small group of us think they really want this to go ahead.'

'An attack on Canada?'

'Not that so much as a projection of who we are. And who we plan to be this century. And a much more ruthless set of rules of engagement.'

'Do you think they'd listen to me?' Karan asked. 'If I instructed them to stop?'

'No, sir. You're no longer in that chain of command. They would listen to parliament and probably the judges. So they're watching this hearing at the administrative court.'

'What hearing?'

'The judicial review into the protester's death. They're trying to extend its remit to look at the legality of the governor-general's orders to attack Canada. If I were being generous, they may be trying to protect you, sir. The actions they take may well be referred to the Hague. But I don't think my colleagues are that well intentioned. The truth is, the first sea lord sees this as his big opportunity to lead the transformation of this country. He'll do whatever the governor-general asks of him.'

'I need to know what we can do to stop that,' Karan said.

'To be honest, sir, there isn't much. They have legal authority for their actions. And operational control.'

'Nick, I think there are two things we must do.' Dame Rebecca had been reviewing the reports in front of her. 'You must speak to your opposite number at US naval forces Europe. Get them to mobilise the sixth fleet. They will be happy to sit this out. The Indians must think that the fleet will intercept them in the north atlantic.'

'Can you do that?' Karan asked.

'That would be insubordination, sir. Probably sedition too. A court martial and maybe a capital offence.' Nick paused and then put on a broad grin. 'But I'll try.'

'Thank you, Nick.' Karan turned to Dame Rebecca. 'Two things?'

'Admiral Brannick?' Dame Rebecca urged.

'The *Sutherland* is our fastest surface craft. But …' He stopped himself.

'But what?' Karan asked.

'We have an undisclosed submarine programme, sir. A small, fast nuclear submarine, which has not been declared to parliament, to you or your government.'

'What?' Karan wasn't surprised. 'Oliver always told me to look at your budgets in detail. I told him he was a fantasist.'

'You wouldn't have been able to find this, sir. We're exceptionally good at hiding things in plain sight,' admiral Brannick replied.

'So what's so important about this secret programme?'

'We've been able to optimise the nuclear reactor in two ares class submarines, achieving a much better power density ratio. Meaning it can reach 35 knots. It can launch a long-range, nuclear-powered drone we developed called *Ceirean*.'

'*Ceirean*?' Karan shook his head.

'A Scottish sea monster so large it fed on seven whales and could disguise itself as a small silver fish. When fishermen landed it, it changed back and destroyed them.' Brannick continued, '*Ceirean* can travel at 100 knots and has a range of 10,000 kilometres. It operates at a depth where it can evade detection.' He paused. 'It has the capability to reach and sink the *Yukon*. My assumption is that the chiefs will offer it to the governor-general. And are using the *Sutherland* as a distraction. To lull the *Yukon* into a false sense of security.'

'What can I do?' Karan asked.

'You're going to have to keep meeting the governor-general and play for time, sir. I will need some time to convince the Americans, and we need to keep the secret options off the table.'

'I'll need a cobra with the chiefs.'

Dame Rebecca nodded.

* * *

In the palace's blue drawing room, Karan blinked from the enormous glass chandeliers as the governor-general continued, 'We have barely any time, first minister.'

'You've seen the criticism of the Scottish prime minister?'

'Irrelevant.'

'We expect more governments and world leaders to follow her.'

'Also irrelevant. These separatists have been planning the disintegration of India for decades, with the help and generous assistance of their Canadian hosts. It's time we dealt with them properly, once and for all.'

'So,' Karan said, 'this is just an excuse for you to deal with the problems of your own backyard? You're throwing my government and this country's reputation down the drain so that you can take out a few noisy malcontents?'

'First minister, you have two options.' The governor-general had come so close to Karan's face he could see the sweat on his upper lip. 'Continue to oversee the running of your state or resign. There are plenty of others in the wings. Your military advisors are most pleased with the present course of action. While some would be surprised by your resignation at this moment, most would see it as an act of treachery. A contemptible act when we have English men and women in the atlantic right now. Striving to defend our freedoms.'

Banerjee entered the room. 'Governor-general.' He bowed his head. 'First minister.' He reserved a slightly exasperated tone for Karan. 'Governor-general, I thought you might want to know that the speaker has recalled parliament.'

'Hmm,' the governor-general grunted. 'And now thanks to your former deputy, you will have to answer for our actions there too.

We are watching him closely. He should be aware that sedition is a capital offence in India.'

'I will answer for the actions of my administration, governor-general. But only if I am to have full authority for them. The prosecution of the fleet's progress should be through a first minister–chaired subcommittee of the cabinet. I will report to you on progress. But I must now insist that I am responsible for the next steps. I will let the chiefs know.'

The governor-general thought about this. 'You can have as many committees as you like so long as you do what I ask.'

Karan bowed his head at the governor-general and walked out.

Banerjee waited.

'Yes, Banerjee?'

'That was surprising, sir.'

'Not really. We may all end up being tried for war crimes. I thought it better if he had his hand on the tiller,' the governor-general stopped. 'Now I have some further insurance to put into place, Lord Banerjee.'

* * *

Oliver was on the phone to Arun while checking his car. 'Yeah, someone has smashed the lights at the back. They probably reversed into me.'

'I don't think so,' Arun replied. 'It's a warning. Because of your stupid interview.'

Oliver smiled. 'Did you see the interview?'

'Yes, I wish you hadn't done it.'

'But you've seen the speaker has recalled parliament?'

'Yes, I wish you hadn't done that either.'

'I've told her to release the next bit.'

'And I really wish you hadn't done that. I'm worried about you. My side doesn't play straight.'

'Luckily, nor do we.'

'The car is a message. Please will you come home?'

'No, I've got to go to the office and say bye to the team after the chamber. Can we meet for drinks later?'

'Sure. Usual place?'

'Usual place.'

* * *

The governor-general and Lu Quan were watching the latter's statement on the BBC, 'The people's republic is concerned by the actions of the Indian government in England. But we are equally concerned by the attacks on the territorial integrity of India by state-sponsored terrorism. We have called for an emergency session of the security council.'

'Well done, ambassador. Our prime minister is delighted with the tenor of the statement by your government.'

'Thank you, governor-general. It's our understanding that the emergency session will take some days to organise. Your relationship with Russia is also proving most fruitful to you.'

'It is true we have friends in a number of places. I understand your president has set out some conditions for our ongoing relationship. You wish to have further concessional access to England's energy markets. I have been told to review these demands favourably.'

'We would never make presume to make demands on the government of India. But we hope that our intelligence-sharing will continue to be of assistance to you.'

Lu Quan pointed to the folder he had handed over to the governor-general.

'Thank you, ambassador. The photographs are most revealing.'

'Yes, someone has already sent them to the master of the rolls. We believe it will have the desired effect.'

'Excellent, and this afternoon's plan is all set?'

He nodded.

* * *

Admiral Brannick had entered Karan's den. 'Any luck with the Americans?'

Brannick shook his head. 'Not yet. They don't believe the Indians have the balls to see it through.'

'Do you?'

'I don't know. I'm unable to account for one of the fast-attack subs. If that gets to the *Yukon* and fires, we are in a whole different ball game.'

Dame Rebecca had come in. 'You have to chair cobra now, first minister.' She led Karan through the desolate corridors of the cabinet office. Room after room was empty. Even the usually cheerful communications team were nowhere to be seen. The receptionist opened the pods to the secure area without acknowledging them. Karan sat at the head of the table and gazed at the collection of ministers and intelligence and defence chiefs. Other than Dame Rebecca and Brannick, who had been relegated to chairs on the back wall, Karan trusted none of them.

'Where are we with operation aquiline?' he asked.

'We will wait for the governor-general to join, first minister' the chief of the defence staff said with a tone of superiority.

'No, CDS. At the governor-general's request, I have taken strategic and political command of the operation. I'll be advised by Dame Rebecca and report to the governor-general. You will answer to me.'

The room was silent. Karan quickly worked out that none of them were with him. He continued, 'CDS, let me be clear. British citizens were killed in three separate attacks by terrorists housed in Canada. You have been instructed to prepare for a proportionate response and to interdict the Canadian ship *Yukon*. I would like to know where we are with the operational plans.'

CDS cleared his throat and took Karan through the high-level plans for the operation. Setting out the size of the British carrier strike group, the joint nature of the mission with the Indian strike group whose flagship was the *Vikrant*, and the method by which a successful interdiction would be sought.

‘It will be the *Sutherland* and the *Sutherland* alone that will strike the *Yukon*?’

‘Sorry, first minister?’ the CDS asked.

‘I want to know which ship of the fleet launched as part of operation aquiline will reach the *Yukon*. Is the *Sutherland* the only one with the capability to reach her?’

‘It is hard to say for sure.’ The CDS surveyed the room. The politicians were surprised by the answer.

‘CDS, are you asking that we reduce the size of this meeting to enable you to share greater operational specificity?’

The CDS was silent. He was staring at admiral Brannick. The only reason Karan could be asking this question was if he had shared the most highly classified information with him.

‘Yes, first minister.’

‘All right. Could everyone not code-word-cleared on Aquiline please leave the room.’

The dynamics in the room had shifted. And everyone could tell. Karan had somehow obtained some advantage. The politicians left the room unclear what was going on. But something was afoot. Karan knew the corridors outside would be rife with speculation.

‘And can the secretariat turn off all the recording devices in the conference room, please?’ Karan's steeliness impressed Dame Rebecca. And Brannick.

‘On present rates, which ship is likely to reach the *Yukon* first, CDS?’

The first sea lord cleared his throat. ‘First minister, it appears you are referring to *Assurance*. The ares class are still in prototype. We have secretly optimised their reactor and achieved a much better power density ratio. They have the speed and capability to deal with the *Yukon*.’

‘Thank you, first sea lord. Can I ask why this programme hasn't yet come to the defence expenditure committee or the subcommittee, which I alone chair?’

'Sir, it has been a long-established agreement that those committees discuss expenses which must be reported to parliament. The programme is off books in all ways.'

'Does it have any political oversight?'

The first sea lord shook his head.

'Well, it does now. I want a full briefing on the ares class on my desk in half an hour.

'Gentlemen, I also want a briefing on the legality of an attack on the *Yukon*. My understanding is that we could be dealing with a warship leaving the field of battle. And that we might well be in breach of a number of conventions on the laws of war if we were to attack.'

'We don't agree, first minister.'

'Sorry?' Karan asked.

'The *Yukon* may appear to be leaving the immediate place of battle, but she has the capability, and likely intention, to attack our forces in future.'

'When will Assurance make contact?'

'In about six hours, first minister.'

'I want the decision to fire on the Yukon to be mine alone. Is that clear?'

The room was silent. No one moved.

'CDS? First sea lord? Am I making myself clear? I will give the order to fire on the *Yukon*. You will see that Dame Rebecca receives all the necessary briefing ahead of that decision.'

Karan walked out and headed back to his office.

* * *

Bruce Woodward, Canada's prime minister, was standing with the five Sikh members of his thirty-five-strong cabinet. 'Right now, our thoughts and prayers are with commander Singh and the crew of Canadian ship *Yukon* who are being chased by British and Indian ships. Ships they have been training with until only some days ago. We understand the *Sutherland*'s orders are to take all necessary steps to stop the *Yukon*. All we want is for commander Singh and his crew to reach our eastern seaboard and to return home safely. I repeat my message to the Indian prime minister, theirs is a peaceful mission.'

The prime minister continued, 'We have seen reports that suggest the English and Indian carrier strike groups will proceed to Canada. It may well be that the Indian government in England has declared war on Canada. This would see the government of India attack a fellow commonwealth nation. We are calling on the UN security council and the president of the United States of America to intervene.

'We Canadians are proud of the diversity of our country. We have welcomed people of all faiths and none, and many Indians are prominent in public life. We refute any and all unproved allegations that the government of Canada played any role in the recent atrocities in London. But let me be clear. Canada will not allow itself to be unilaterally attacked and subsumed by a bellicose India. The Indian prime minister should be aware we are not England.'

* * *

Karan was standing outside the chamber behind the speaker's chair. MPs and ministers were avoiding him. Only his civil servants stood nearby. His phone rang. 'I think you've dialled the wrong number.'

Arun replied, 'No, I'm worried about Oliver. If you can do anything to keep him safe, please do it. And please remember why he's done the things he's done.'

Karan hung up and entered the commons. Madam speaker announced, 'Statement from the first minister.'

Karan stood. MPs' phones went wild. One of Karan's ministers gingerly handed a phone to him. He scrolled the headline of the BBC's next story about Isha, Sunil and the Indian prime minister as he continued with his statement. He turned the phone over and set it down on the despatch box.

'The house will be aware that some time ago, Canadian ship *Yukon* deserted its designated role and place within the carrier strike group off the coast of Portsmouth. The commanding officer, Commander Singh, is at present somewhere in the north atlantic. Concerned about commander Singh's intent, the *Sutherland* is in hot pursuit of the *Yukon*, and we expect to have visual contact soon.'

MPs around Karan, even on his own side, were shouting, 'Shame.' One added, 'What's the going rate for treachery today?'

Karan continued, 'In addition, the continental Indian government has intelligence that—'

MPs shouted, 'Bring it to the house. We've had enough dodgy dossiers. If you can't show us it, don't rely on it.'

Karan focused on his statement and tried again, '... has intelligence that sets out an unequivocal case for action against those shielding the terrorists who committed atrocities on the streets of London in the last few days. Madam speaker, I need not remind the house that 137 people were killed or injured when improvised devices exploded in the centre of our city. One some moments from this seat of democracy.'

'It's a seat with broken legs,' one MP shouted. 'You should be ashamed of yourself.'

'Madam speaker, this house does not have the competence to view intelligence from the government of India. The house's new powers are restricted to the actions that I and the ministers in the state cabinet make.'

Oliver stood up and madam speaker called, 'Oliver Benjamin.'

The house quietened. 'Madam speaker, I rise briefly to say that I am as disappointed in the first minister, his decision-making and the course of action he has settled on as the leader of the opposition. I had hoped that he would show the leadership I know he is capable of, but instead all we have seen is a family on the make and on the take. Grifting of the highest order. And it is time for him to do the one thing available to him: resign.'

MPs on all sides of the house attacked Karan. Madam speaker, who was no fan of her now diminished role, took the opportunity to read that day's order paper and let the unhappiness grow.

Karan shouted, 'Madam speaker,' and tried again, 'Madam speaker.' Still, his colleagues did not quieten. Finally, 'Madam speaker, the house knows that the first and paramount duty of a government is the safety and security of its citizens. It was with great sadness that I had to instruct our forces into action. Cobra will remain in constant session, chaired by me, until this action is concluded.'

Khalid jumped to his feet. 'Madam speaker, we were promised the brightest politician in his generation. Someone whose unique skills and temperament would navigate us through stormy waters. He wants to justify his decisions to take us to the brink of war. But first we have to ask about the news story that has just broken. A story that alleges his own former deputy shared details of secret bank accounts in his wife's name, his father-in-law's name and the name of the Indian prime minister. These documents show tens of thousands of pounds regularly shifting from one account to another. The first minister's family appear to have made tens of millions of pounds out of Indian politics and have already stolen millions out of England.'

Karan was reading the story as Khalid attacked him.

Khalid went on, 'Isn't it the case that this whole fabricated attempt to attack Canada was to distract us from the lies and larceny in his own family and at the heart of downing street? He must resign.'

Karan leapt to the despatch box. 'My former deputy was a fantasist. He'd started to hang around with conspiracy theorists. I wouldn't be surprised if his next story was that he'd met aliens on a secret military base. He was sacked for his ever-growing paranoia. And these baseless allegations are no better than the gutter in which his mind now resides. The right honourable gentleman opposite might also take his head out of the drain and focus on the safety and security of our citizens.'

* * *

Oliver had left the chamber and driven to his old office. Sitting outside, he asked himself, had he really not known what Isha's father was capable of? What Isha was capable of? And now they were all staring at a nightmare scenario: a paranoid and delusional governor-general whom Karan was unable to thwart. It would be the end of England.

'Minister?' Alessandra had been trying to get his attention. Finally, she opened the car door.

'Sorry about that. Lost in my own thoughts.' Oliver jumped out. 'Is the gang inside?'

She nodded. Her eyes were already tearful. 'Are you sure you want to do this?'

'Which bit? Lunch or the scathing resignation?'

'Both. But probably the latter?'

'I think it's a bit late for a change of plan, don't you? Lunch is easier. Take this.' He handed her 100 pounds. 'That should cover it.'

Alessandra led him back inside. Oliver chatted briefly to the security guards and the receptionists. He remembered the cleaner's son who had been about to graduate. He had time for everyone he had spoken to every morning. Finally, they made it to the ministerial floor with the best views. Oliver's private office staff were waiting to greet him. He looked around at the empty desks and darkened ministerial offices.

'People were called to an urgent meeting in the cabinet office.'

Oliver nodded.

'It was to do with the fallout of the—'

'Of my disclosure about Isha's sweatshop. And now I'm pretty toxic.' Oliver watched each of them in turn. 'You poor sods have drawn the short straw and been told to make it look like the department cares about me. But also make sure I don't take anything I can later give to the BBC that might damage departmental—or worse, senior civil servants'—reputations.'

There was nervous laughter as they walked into his office. Alessandra shut the door. 'You're right, erm.'

'Call me Oliver now, please.'

'You're right that no one else in the department wanted to be seen with you. But we're not here from some sense of obligation. We're your team.' The other four nodded. 'And we were proud to work with you. And now …'

'And now … what happens next?' Oliver asked.

Luke, the head of Oliver's outer office, replied, 'Now we're terrified. Who's going to take on India?' A graduate in his early twenties and at the start of his career. He managed all the correspondence the office received. He caught Alessandra's glare, with the puppy dog eyes she tried to ignore, hoping she had an answer.

Oliver smiled at each of them in turn. 'You are.'

'What?' Luke asked.

'You are. You all are. India won't get away with what it's done in the last few days. The international system will correct these excesses. You need to keep doing your job. Do what Karan needs you to do. If you do that, you'll be taking on India.'

'How can you say that? You've just called him a delusional liar.'

'I'm going to let you in on a secret. I love Karan like a brother. More than a brother really.' The four squirmed and tried to look away. 'He's making a mess of it right now. But he won't keep making a mess of it. He'll find a way out. And, when he does, he'll need all of you.'

'What will you do?' Luke asked.

'I think I'll have to sit out for a bit. Then I'll be on the sidelines. Maybe in prison.' Alessandra grabbed his hand. Oliver wiped his eye. Thinking about what he and Karan could have achieved together. 'Right, enough of this maudlin stuff. Let's get your lunch started and my packing finished. I have a hot date!'

Arun texted Oliver, 'Are you sure you wanted the financial story to run? Couldn't it have waited another day? See if Karan does get out of the mess?'

Oliver replied, 'Too late. They raised it in the house. We need to exert maximum pressure on the Indians. Yes, Isha and Sunil are casualties. But there's not much I can do about that. See you later. x'

Oliver packed up and watched them eat. They were in stitches at the many gifts he'd acquired. 'Almost as dubious as Albert!' Oliver snorted when he'd found yet another luxury watch gifted by a Gulf sheikh. 'Please make sure the accounting officer records all of these, will you.'

Oliver opened champagne and poured each a glass, 'To accompany these elaborate cakes Alessandra has bought. She's already gutted my redundancy pay!'

She gave him sparkling apple juice. 'Because you're driving. And probably already a fugitive.'

He chuckled. 'You think I've gone too far?'

Oliver took Alessandra's hand. 'Thank you. Now I have one final thing to say.' They were waiting expectantly. 'Alessandra, Luke has the hots for you. He always has. For the love of God, please go out on a date with him.'

Alessandra leant in and kissed him. 'Thank you,' she whispered. 'Look after yourself, won't you?'

Soldiers were standing round Oliver's car when he left. 'You can't park this here.'

'I'm taking it away right now.'

'I'd watch yourself if I were you, sir.'

Oliver ignored them and started the engine.

One of the soldiers knocked on his window and smirked. 'I hope we'll not see you here again. sir.'

Oliver put his window back up and turned on whatever music was at the top of his playlist. 90s brit-pop blared from the speakers. He enjoyed the sun and empty roads the length of his drive to the restaurant. When he made the final turn into a Mayfair side street, he spotted Arun. They waved to one another. He drove on 300 yards to avoid the embarrassment of attempting to reverse park with an audience. He turned off the engine and opened the door. He smiled as Arun walked towards him.

* * *

Khalid walked out of the chamber and over to central lobby where Sally was finishing her live interview. 'We have already heard strong words from the leader of the opposition that it's the death of liberty, of British justice and this Parliament.'

Interview over, he asked. 'Shall we go for a coffee?'

He took Sally through Westminster Hall, over the plaques that marked its hundreds of years of history. Below Big Ben. Up the escalator. They stopped under the vast glass roof of portcullis house. Khalid looked up at the cloudless blue sky. The atrium buzzing with MPs, journalists and young staffers. They'd all found a way to come in for this illicit gathering. Khalid's team had two coffees ready for them and left them to sit beneath the summer sun.

Sally asked, 'So you think any of this will do any good?'

Khalid's phone rang before he could answer. 'I've got the governor-general for you.'

Khalid mouthed, 'Governor-general?'

'Mr Khan, I wanted to thank you for your performance today. It really was memorable. Now could you do me a favour? Do look up and think of all that damage your people did in Kashmir.'

As Khalid tilted his head, the first drone released its payload, shattering the domed roof. Glass flew in all directions. The building's design forced some of the initial blast upwards, like a giant chimney. Thick shards of metal struck people as they screamed and ran from the giant steel structures falling around them. Trainers and shoes crunched shards in every direction. Before Khalid knew what had happened, or had time to react, a second drone dropped its payload directly above the table at which he and Sally were sitting. He watched the little dot get closer and closer, shouting, 'Run,' as it exploded above them. The once-gleaming white floor tiles were smeared with blood. A deep, dark red river was forming from the islands of victims dotted around the atrium. Khalid and Sally lay motionless.

Karan saw the blast of the first explosion rise like an erupting volcano, then watched the second plume emerge. Police officers were running towards him. 'Not again,' he shouted.

'We need to get you into the car, sir, run.'

Karan followed his protection team through the corridors of the commons. MPs, staffers, cleaners, tearoom ladies and visitors all jumped out of his way. Everyone who saw him knew the look in his eye. It was the fear of death. The courtyard under Big Ben was already full of injured parliamentary staffers huddled in groups of twos and threes. In the car Karan asked, 'Can you tell me what has happened please?'

'There was a bomb. We think the leader of the opposition has been killed. Multiple casualties.' The officer went quiet.

'What else?'

'It's Oliver, sir.'

Nine

Karan was scanning the exponentially growing numbers of social media comments to find out what had happened to Oliver. 'Take me to him.'

'Sir, that would be a breach of our standard operating procedures. Plus, the governor-general has made it clear—'

'The governor-general has just tried to kill my best friend. I want to go there right now. 'Jumping into the back of his car he leant over and said, 'Umesh, as fast as we can go.' Karan shouted at the officer, 'Where is he?'

'Mayfair. Sir, we really don't recommend this.'

Umesh saw the look in Karan's eyes. The outriders were already on the move and heading to downing street. Karan shut the door, leaving his protection officer in the square. Umesh ignored the police motorbikes and raced down St James's Park, towards Hyde Park Corner. The police had closed the checkpoint. Soldiers had raised their guns and were signalling for Umesh to slow down.

'Keep going,' Karan shouted.

Umesh accelerated, sending them in all directions. While trying to text Arun, Karan asked, 'You know where to go, don't you? My favourite restaurant?' He fell back in the seat as Umesh sped down Park and barely braked until they reached Mayfair. Karan got out by the door of Oliver's car. It was 30 feet away from the car itself. He ran towards the thick, deathly smoke bellowing from it. Karan's protection team arrived in an unmarked car behind them.

The street was littered with barely distinguishable glass, plastic and metal chunks from the parked cars and vans next to Oliver's. A few passers-by were sitting on the pavement, trying to work out what had happened. Arun was crouched in the middle of the street, cradling Oliver's lifeless body in his arms. A trail of blood connected him to the car like dots in a children's colouring book. For a moment Arun caught Karan's eye. His face was bloodied. Lost. Helpless. He returned to Oliver.

Karan's protection officer ran over and pulled at his shoulder. 'The ambulance is here, sir. This area isn't secure. I need you to get back in the car.'

He couldn't move.

'Now, sir,' the officer tried again.

Karan was rooted to the spot. It was the end. The end of everything.

* * *

The *Sutherland* was battling 12-metre-high waves in the North Atlantic. 'Signal PJHQ,' Hadwell instructed her officer of the watch, 'tell them we know the *Yukon* is ahead of the storm and 1,100 nautical miles from us. We expect to be within range of our tomahawks in the next two hours.' Turning to her crew on the bridge, Hadwell added, 'Keep on this course, let me know the response. Let's be ready to fire in two hours.'

Unknown to Hadwell, some 150 miles ahead of the *Sutherland*, HMS *Assurance* was being tested to the maximum of her capabilities. 'We're approaching the firing location, sir,' captain Payton's executive officer told him.

'Bring us to 10 knots.' Payton watched the dials in front of him show the slow reduction in speed as the engines went into reverse mode. Not one of Payton's team had questioned the orders they'd received. They knew the lethal drone they were about to release would do enormous damage, possibly even to their reputations, but they had been trained within an inch of their lives to carry out their political masters' instructions.

Payton watched his executive officer move to the firing station and turn his key. A red light told them the torpedo bay was armed. His executive officer turned to Payton, who nodded, unlocked the firing safe and took out the plastic firing pistol—a cross between a children's gun and a walkie-talkie handset. He pulled the black trigger and they heard a click as the drone left the chamber.

* * *

Elizabeth was addressing the court, 'I've had an opportunity to review the application that counsel has made. I am refusing the application to extend the scope of this judicial review. If the plaintiff, or her barrister, wishes to examine the legality of the government's decisions to deploy English forces, then they will have to make them to the court of final appeal.

'However, on the balance of probabilities, this court finds that military forces were active on the evening of 14 August 2027 and that those forces were not under the command of the civilian administration headed by the first minister of Britain and of the Republic of India.'

Journalists were rushing back into her court with phones in their hands, sharing her judgment live on various social media channels.

Elizabeth continued, 'We find that those forces received orders to deploy from the office of the governor-general of the Republic of India in England. Not the first minister or ministers delegated to coordinate security and intelligence matters. This court finds that these additional orders materially affected the chain of command expected of a policing operation; and that this confusion, in part, resulted in the death of one of the protectors, Miss Molly Stevens.'

The protesters in the court erupted. Elizabeth smiled and left for her chambers, Nigel running behind.

'You fucking bitch. You know what you've done. You've ruined both our reputations now. They'll release the story. I'll have to resign. But I'll make sure you resign too. And, what's worse. The ships are already at sea. So all of this has been of no consequence. Why couldn't you just hear the case until they blew up the frigate?'

Elizabeth's clerk came in. 'I need you to look at this, my lady.' Social media reports were leading with 'Master of the Bedroom' and sharing photos of Elizabeth and Nigel.

'The lord chief justice wants to have a call with you, my lady. Shall I tell him you're free now?'

'Yes, he's basically God.'

* * *

Karan was in his office. Dame Rebecca, Rachel and admiral Brannick had been speaking at him for the last ten minutes. But he hadn't heard a thing they said. He glimpsed over at Dame Rebecca, who was trying again.

'I have to ask, first minister; do you really think you're up to the next meeting? No one could criticise you if you wanted to spend time with Isha.'

'That's not what he would have wanted,' Karan snapped. 'Oliver always wanted me to be better than I was able to be. He wanted me to fix this. So that's what I have to do.'

They sat in silence. Karan couldn't work out if Dame Rebecca was undertaking a psychological assessment of him. Or if admiral Brannick was about to confine him to quarters.

'I will need to speak to the Americans, won't I?'

Dame Rebecca and Brannick nodded.

'I know what I need to say.' He shouted to Seb, 'Can you request a call with the president of the United States?'

Karan walked to cobra. In a daze. The last time he'd done this, even his team had avoided looking at him. This time people stopped him. Stroked his arm. Told stories about first meeting Oliver or when he'd helped them convince Karan to take another course. They all knew—and it turned out, loved—Oliver. They wanted to share. A funny quip. A story. A cherished memory. Each reiterating his loyalty to Karan.

In the corridor just before they walked in, Karan said, 'They know what we're up to now. We may all be resigning by the end of the day anyway.' Karan paused. 'It's not much of a motivational speech, I grant you.'

Dame Rebecca nodded as Brannick opened the door, 'It'll do, sir'.

Karan took his seat at the top of the table. Dame Rebecca had only called the chiefs. Brannick was now indelibly linked with them, so Karan pointed for him to sit on his left.

The chiefs walked in, and Karan asked, before they sat down, 'Operational update, CDS.'

'The *Sutherland* will be within striking distance of the *Yukon* in ninety minutes. She is battling a storm in the atlantic.'

'She sailed straight into a major storm?' Karan asked.

'Well, they are pretty hard to miss, sir,' CDS replied, dismissing Karan's question.

'Where is Assurance?'

'It's now within 150 nautical miles, sir.'

'CDS? Have we any intelligence on the attack I have just witnessed? Have any of our agencies, police forces, any member of your own team given you evidence that links these attacks to khalistani terrorists?' The room was silent. 'Can someone fucking answer me?'

'None at all, first minister,' Dame Rebecca replied. 'In fact, it's much more likely that portcullis was attacked by drones. Drones made by the Chinese government, flown into Britain via London–Beijing airport run and managed by the Chinese government. And operated by pilots in the basement of the former royal mint.'

'Anything to add, CDS?' Karan asked before returning to the papers in front of him. 'In light of this, I have reviewed the plans and rationale for this operation. At the present moment I do not believe we have sufficient evidence to merit an attack.'

CDS cleared his throat. 'We feared you may make such a suggestion, sir. So we briefed the governor-general ahead of this meeting. He instructed us to proceed with aquiline. Assurance released its drone about thirty minutes ago. It will strike the *Yukon* in the next ninety minutes. We expect all souls will be lost.'

Karan erupted, 'How could you have unleashed such evil? What the fuck are you doing here?'

'Following orders.'

'Sorry?'

'The governor-general asked that we meet you to give him time to prepare a speech to the nation.'

Seb burst in. 'Put the television on.'

The governor-general was addressing the nation, 'In the last hour we saw a cruel, cowardly and fatal attack on a former government minister and member of parliament. We have also suffered a grievous attack on what was the mother of parliaments. We do not yet know how many MPs and their staff have been killed. This is further evidence of the failure of this state to protect its citizens. I have instructed security forces to undertake an immediate and thorough investigation into these attacks.'

'You fucking killed him.' Karan glared at the screen with disgust.

'The security situation in England remains volatile. For this reason, I am extending governor-general's rule across the country for a further forty-eight hours. From here on, parliament is dissolved to be replaced by the state assembly. The foolish attempt by parliamentarians to use a defunct legislature to rally against the Indian government gave the terrorists the opportunity to maim and murder once again. We cannot afford to allow cold-blooded murderers to exploit our weakness to attack our way of life or the Republic of India. We had expected our first minister to establish the state assembly by now. In light of his inaction, we will fix this deficiency. I have informed the speaker that former parliamentarians will meet under the guise of her current speakership as members of the state assembly. But I will not hesitate to revoke these privileges.'

The governor-general paused, 'We now have extraordinarily strong reason to believe that Canadian ship *Yukon* is harbouring the khalistani operatives who detonated the bombs on the former deputy first minister's car and on Parliament.'

'No, you fucking don't, you lying piece of shit,' Karan shouted.

The governor-general continued, 'Signals were picked up between the *Yukon* minutes before the bombs detonated here in London. I am demanding that Canadian ship *Yukon* stop where it is to allow our ships to board her, catch those criminals and bring them to justice. Finally, I am taking the necessary decision to ensure greater access to information at this time. As of midnight, the BBC will become the bharti broadcasting corporation. A privately run entity. With a new mission to promote cohesion and the communication of government information across the thirtieth state. Jai Hind.'

Karan scanned the room. The faceless security state had bet against him. 'I think we're done here.' He walked out. Followed by Dame Rebecca, admiral Brannick, Rachel and Seb.

* * *

Captain Hadwell addressed the crew. 'Update?'

'We are within range of the *Yukon*, captain.'

'Have they turned on radar or transmissions?'

'No, and they haven't detected us.'

'Prepare to fire.'

Hadwell watched as her officer turned his key to arm the firing mechanism. The light on the panel in front of him went red. He turned to Hadwell.

'Fire.'

He pressed the large button in front of him. In the torpedo bay, the missile's turbofan engine ignited, sending it straight into the air. The trail behind it told them it was going to reach sub-sonic speed and head 1,000 miles to strike the *Yukon*.

* * *

The three of them watched the rolling coverage of Oliver's life from Karan's office. Lord Winston now appeared to speak for the nation, his Northern Irish brogue soothing Karan, 'He really was head and shoulders above all the other politicians in his generation. We would most definitely not be in the mess we are in today if he'd remained in Karan's cabinet. Of course, we all expected that he would have been made chancellor as well as deputy first minister. Many of us realised that the wheels would come off the Puri administration the day he wasn't. It became clear that Karan was unable to reward friendship and loyalty. These really are our most fundamental conservative values. And I suppose it means that Karan is not our kind of conservative at heart.'

'Turn that Northern Irish gobshite off, please?' Before Seb could turn it off a call came in. The White House situation room was on the screen. President Hinkle was in her third year in office. She had focused much of her time on international affairs. Keeping a belligerent China in its place. A proxy war with Russia started in Ukraine and continued in Africa. And a new deal with Latin America. But she had shown too little interest in Europe. And even less in England. She came on the screen, 'First minister, it looks like a war zone over there. We send our deepest condolences to you and the people of England.'

'Thank you, president Hinkle.'

She continued, 'We are reporting that maybe as many as thirty of your MPs have been injured in the portcullis house attack as well as the targeted assassination of the leader of the opposition. And, of course Oliver. Whom I know was dear to you.'

'Thank you but I think we have to do that another day. I need you to send the sixth fleet into the North Atlantic to protect the *Yukon* and to head off own our ships.'

'Karan, the *Sutherland* is behind the *Yukon* in a huge storm. We know the *Sutherland* has fired a tomahawk but we have confidence captain Hadwell knows it won't make it and that the *Yukon* will reach home. We've been sitting this one out. Because we know what the final score would be.'

'Madam president, you're wrong. The *Sutherland* has fired a missile, and it may well hit the *Yukon*. Our chiefs are eager to show our overlords their willingness to do the Indians' bidding as well as their capabilities. But the *Sutherland* isn't the issue. We secretly optimised the reactor in our ares class submarines. We haven't disclosed this to you. I am authorising my national security advisor to share all the details of this programme, which I have only been told about now, with her opposite number. *Assurance* has released a nuclear drone which is on track to blow up the *Yukon* in the next sixty minutes.'

The screen went black.

Karan shrugged his shoulders and gestured at Dame Rebecca and Brannick to ask, 'what's happening?' He rested his chin on his hands and focused on the screen.

President Hinkle returned. 'I have ordered the sixth fleet into position. We're communicating this directly to the Indian prime minister's office. I will demand that the drone is dealt with and the tomahawk aborted. My team are drafting a public address for me to make now.'

'Thank you, madam president.'

'Karan,' he leant forward, 'you need to get yourselves out of this. We are too tied in with India to be of any more assistance to you.'

'Yes, madam president.' The screen went blank as Karan asked, 'What the fuck happens next?'

Dame Rebecca started, 'Well, we are still Indian. You've really pissed off the chiefs. They didn't get a battle. They didn't get to win. And now they don't even have any authority for their own kit. I expect we'll have an Indian defence minister sent here. To whom they will all answer.'

'Oh, and you've outed our most top-secret programme to the Americans,' Brannick interrupted.

Karan asked them both, 'What do you think happened when the screen went blank?'

Dame Rebecca tittered. 'I imagine president Hinkle was bollocking my oppo. I hear she has a foul mouth and a terrible temper. He had no idea we have this capability. We're going to have to give them all the plans. It will become an American project until ...'

'Until?' Karan asked.

'Until we're free of these bastards,' Brannick replied.

'I don't know how we do that now. Oliver had a plan. But I have nothing. I'm not even sure I want this job. I've already tried to resign twice in the last seventy-two hours.'

Damc Rebecca looked at Brannick.

'What is it?' Karan asked.

'It's highly likely they will court-martial Brannick. He failed to follow the chain of command. He gave up military secrets.'

'No, he fought for his country. This can't be right, Nick. Can it?'

'Afraid so, first minister. I've already had my first summons from the adjutant general's office. It's part of how we do things. Nothing you can do. Especially not now we report straight to Delhi.'

* * *

The lord chief justice was speaking to Elizabeth. 'I have a note-taker on the line. Are you comfortable with that?'

'Yes.'

'Are you having an affair with the master of the rolls? The former master of the rolls.'

She sighed. 'No.'

'Did you have an affair with him?'

'Yes, for five years. It ended about eighteen months ago.'

'Did either of you declare this?'

'No, and I don't think it would have been necessary or appropriate to do so.'

'Why not?'

'We were not having an affair when I received my judicial appointment. I was appointed through a fair and open competition. And ...' She paused.

'And?'

'It's none of your damn business. Can we please dispense with the note-taker now?'

'All right,' the lord chief sniggered. 'This is all true. But Elizabeth, Nigel did push this case to you. And he was under some pressure. I put him under some pressure, to have the case shifted to the court of final appeal. Following a request from the office of the governor-general.' He paused. 'Now that you've done the exact opposite of what we recommended, I need you to join this new court and try any appeal against your case with the Indian judges who will try to stop you. And to stop British justice. Will you do that for me?'

'Of course,' she replied. 'And Nigel?'

'He has resigned. If I have my way, you'll become the president of the court.'

* * *

The Indian prime minister was in her office with Sunil, watching president Hinkle.

'We cannot allow aggression, intentional or otherwise, to go unchallenged. The sixth fleet has been instructed to take position in the north atlantic and ensure the safe passage of Canadian ship *Yukon*. The fleet and US law enforcement and intelligence agencies will work with the Indian prime minister and her first minister in England to determine whether any threat exists from the khalistani movement in Canada. We expect the Indian prime minister to instruct her carrier strike groups to return to England.'

Usha turned off the television. 'How has this happened, Sunil? You promised your daughter would never let her father down.'

'It may be that Karan is not quite the boy I thought he was. I will speak to Isha later.'

'There is only one thing for it.' Usha left the room and walked to the Lok Sabha. The opposition was baying for her blood. She could sense it. She launched into her speech without waiting, 'I want to thank the president for her assistance in bringing those who have repeatedly attacked India to justice. I have instructed the governor-general to await the return of the carrier strike group. The precipitate action of the first minister to use might rather than right and to send our ships into harm's way was a failure of policy. State governments do not have competence in foreign and defence policy. We will rectify this anomaly in

England now. From here on, the foreign and defence policy of England will be reserved for union cabinet ministers here in Delhi.'

The PM sat down and prepared for the onslaught.

* * *

Karan walked into cobra with Dame Rebecca, Brannick and Rachel to be greeted by the chiefs of the armed forces.

'Update, CDS?' Karan demanded.

'The *Sutherland* fired its missile about forty-five minutes ago and it will strike the *Yukon* in about the next thirty minutes. *Assurance* fired her drone and we expect that to hit at about the same time, if not a minute or so ahead.'

Karan stared at them. His eyes narrowed. 'Seb, please turn on the television.'

They watched reports of president Hinkle and then the Indian prime minister's speeches.

'CDS, abort that missile and turn the drone around.'

The chief of the defence staff and his chiefs stared backed at Karan indignantly. 'We have no intention of following orders from the US president. We'll await instructions from the prime minister of India.'

'CDS,' Karan sighed. 'Either you turn that drone off and abort the tomahawk, or I will put you and the other chiefs into police and military custody as war criminals.'

At that, Seb walked in and handed a note to the CDS, who sneered, 'We've received instructions from the PMO. We will raise the drone to sea level, where it will be tracked by the US, Indian and Canadian systems as well as ours and the Chinese, no doubt. It will be brought to an agreed location on the eastern US seaboard and collected by the United States. The missile will be aborted.' The CDS paused.

Karan asked, 'Yes?'

'Declaring this capability is by far the stupidest thing you've done yet, first minister.'

Karan turned to Seb. 'Get them out.'

* * *

Karan came into the flat as Isha was on the phone, 'Pitaji, you didn't need the BBC. You can't make it right just by closing things down. That's not how it works here. And you know it.'

Isha looked at Karan as she continued, 'There's already terrible press about all of us. And the money. You told me the accounts were dividends from the company. But it was a slush fund. A filthy stinking slush fund to keep Usha chachi in power. I want all of them stopped.' She waited and replied, 'All of them,' before hanging up. She looked for Karan, 'You want to chat?'

'No, not yet.'

She got up. He closed his eyes and listened to her prepare a drink. Ice cracked against the crystal glass. She unscrewed the whisky bottle. The predictable glugs hitting the waiting cubes soothed him. 'You brought this back from your mad trip round Scotland to save the union.'

'Oliver's favourite,' they both repeated in unison. They held one another's gaze. Karan returned to the glass. Isha found a comedy show for them to watch.

Riyaz was wearing a black 'India Quit' t-shirt. 'India Quit' was in giant letters on the backdrop behind him.

He spoke directly into the camera, 'Tonight, there's nothing left to say. There's no one left to kill either.'

Karan smelled the whisky. He was remembering their soapbox tour where they'd been heckled in villages and towns across the country. They'd turn up at whatever hall they could find and debate with whomever would turn up. They'd found supporters from Orkney and Stornoway to Edinburgh and Cumnock—just not enough. The independence campaign's terriers were always at their heels, and they had the better arguments. Identity, freedom, sovereignty meant different things in Scotland. They knew Karan and Oliver were on the losing side of the argument. In hotels and bars, nationalists charmed them. They were treated like curiosities from a bygone era. In the small moments he'd catch himself glancing at Oliver. On the tiny private plane that shuttled them around. On the coaches that took them into the villages. Waiting for the reporters to arrive. He always had a story. A funny line. A desire to connect. They walked the streets of Ayrshire, and stopped off in Patna, the only Scottish town named after an Indian city. It was in Cumnock. Near the conclusion of the campaign and tour. They'd had a long day. And a long night of drinking. The locals had been merry too. They'd known the campaign was over. Karan had asked, as usual, that the connecting door be unlocked. He invited Oliver in for a final nightcap and to read the papers' assessment of the culmination of their campaign. They'd had too much good whisky and Karan kissed him. Their first and only time in twenty years. And their last. They'd promised each other it didn't mean anything. In his death, it meant everything. If he'd made him chancellor, he'd still be alive. He'd have been protected. Immersed in the suffocating security Karan lived with.

'Karan,' Isha interrupted him. 'Karan, I don't want this any more.'

He took her hand. 'I don't want this either. I loved him. I wish I'd told him.'

She was startled but caught herself. 'He knew … he knew you were best friends.'

He dropped her hand. 'I think we both know it was more than that.'

They sat in silence. Isha heard Karan finish his drink. She tried to speak but each time failed to find the words. Finally, she said, 'Karan, whatever we are will have to wait. Oliver's dead. This has become a killing field. And we are in the middle of it. We need each other to get out of it.'

He nodded.

'I'm going to bed. Do you want to join me?'

'No, I think I'll take the spare room for a bit.' He picked up the bottle and poured another.

* * *

The next morning, Karan was dressed standing by the window and searching for something hopeful in the cloudless blue sky. Isha walked in and asked, 'Are you sure you should wear a black tie?'

'Why?'

'Well, you should reserve that for the funeral and the memorial. Wouldn't he want you to wear something colourful?'

He ignored her and continued to stare out of the window.

'Have you heard from Arun?'

'No. The Indians aren't saying anything about him. I assume he's gone back to consult with his father. What about your dad?'

'We're not talking.' She looked at him. 'Do you have a plan to get us out of this?'

He couldn't answer. 'I'm going now.' He knew that Seb had kept everyone from contacting him, and if he were honest, he was somewhat grateful for the transfer of the BBC to Sunil. It had stopped another day of constant attacks. Of course, England was less free because of it. But it was one less thing to worry about. He couldn't believe Oliver was gone. Killed. And that he had to go on. And worse. That he had to go on with the people who had murdered him.

'We're here, sir,' Umesh told him. Seb was waiting for Karan outside a battered and bruised portcullis house. Madam speaker was there too. They walked together into the roofless atrium. The floor had been cleared of glass and debris but the smell of burnt human flesh lingered.

Karan was numb. As if on autopilot, he asked, 'Where was Khalid killed?'

The speaker replied, 'Over there,' and pointed to a spot on the far wall with a growing collection of bouquets. Karan walked over, laid his wreath and bowed his head. They walked in silence to the chamber. Members of parliament came over to tell him how much they missed Oliver. Karan had worried they would all blame him. They just wanted to say they were sorry he'd lost a friend. His best friend. In the commons, madam speaker announced, 'Statement from the first minister.'

Karan was on his feet. He read out the lines Seb had prepared for him, 'Thank you, madam speaker, for all you have done to maintain and protect parliament's ancient rights and privileges.' Karan scanned the opposition benches, expecting Khalid's, 'Hear, hear.' But there was nothing. An ashen-faced deputy whose name Karan couldn't remember was sitting in his place. Karan continued, 'Members on both sides of this house will have been aghast at the decision to deploy British forces to attack one of our oldest allies. I am grateful to the president of the United States of America, whom I spoke to last night and whose steadfast support helped the Indian prime minister admit that the intended course of action was misguided.'

'Hear, hear,' Karan's backbenchers uttered. He turned around as if to see Oliver sitting watching him. He could hear him at least, urging him to finally do the right thing..

'The judge in the initial review into the death of Molly Stevens has found that the presence of troops on the streets following orders that had not been issued by my cabinet led to her illegal killing. The case will no doubt continue to the new court of final appeal. This will, we hope, mean a proper review of the events before and during the protests in London. My government is committed to undertaking any further review that case demands. I would like to thank Judge Linney for her work and congratulate her on her appointment as first president of the new court.'

Karan surveyed the chamber. 'And now, madam speaker, I wanted to take a moment to remember the servants of this house.

There has been too much death and despair these last few days. And too much of it visited upon the good and decent members and staff of this house. The opposition benches will follow me to speak about their leader. I know we have lost a great man in him. We have also lost a great public servant with the assassination of Oliver Benjamin. The best politician of his generation and a superb statesman. The initial investigation has confirmed the explosives were military grade. Our agencies will do all they can to bring the perpetrators to justice. But today, madam speaker, on the last day of the parliament of Britain, I simply wanted to mark the loss of my best friend.'

Karan sat down. The house was with him. He could tell that. He hadn't experienced it for many weeks. Perhaps for any weeks of his time as first minister. He sat silently as the opposition benches spoke about Khalid. He had agreed with the speaker that another member of the government would remain in the chamber as the debate continued around him. As he walked past her chair, she stopped him. 'I think I saw today the young man I first saw in this house many years ago. He has been missing these past few months. If you have found him, don't lose him again. We need him. Now more than ever.' She held Karan's hand. 'Do this for me and for Oliver.'

Isha was waiting for him. 'You need a break. I've arranged with your office that we'll go away.'

'I can't. I have a country, a state, a something to run.'

Isha eyed the small group around Karan. 'They all agree you need a break.'

Karan smiled at them. 'You do?' Seb nodded. Isha took his hand and led him through the house. 'I've packed weekend bags. They've let me take a helicopter.' As they got in the car Isha directed, 'Battersea, Umesh, please.' With their outriders, Umesh raced down Embankment and over Vauxhall Bridge. 'Why aren't we using the one at the barracks?' Karan asked.

'I don't know. They told me to leave from Battersea.'

Umesh drove through the heliport checkpoint and stopped the car on a giant number 1. A black Agusta A109S grand was on heliport 3, the take-off and landing zone over the Thames. Isha was giving the bags to the porters and supervising their loading on the Agusta. Seb was waiting as the blades started to turn. Isha asked, 'Karan, where are your phones?'

'What?' he shouted.

'Your phones. Give me your phones.'

Karan went into his inside pocket and brought out both his mobiles. 'You mean these? We have to turn them off? They don't usually ask that. Are you sure we shouldn't take a government heli?'

Isha handed them to Seb and winked. 'We've agreed no contact this weekend.'

Karan was worried as she ushered him into the helicopter. The porters shut the doors and the captain explained how to work the headset. The rotors increased in speed. Karan could feel the Agusta make its little leap and then they were airborne. They climbed to the height of the nearby chimney stacks to make their way along the river. 'Where are we going?' he asked but Isha had shut her eyes.

* * *

The governor-general was in his private office. He picked up the phone on his desk, 'The first minister, please.' He returned to his papers and waited for the phone to ring. He allowed three minutes to elapse, then picked up the phone again, 'Get me the first minister right now.'

'Yes, sir. We are trying to locate him,' his private secretary replied.

The governor-general returned to the papers on his desk. Another three minutes elapsed, and he picked up the telephone again. 'Tell Number 10 this is urgent union government business.' He hit the table as he emphasised the last three words.

His private secretary knocked on the door. 'Come in.'

'I'm sorry, your excellency. We haven't been able to find the first minister.'

'You can't find the first minister. Are you telling me he's missing in action?'

'No, sir,' he paused. 'He's on holiday.'

'He can't be. Call his mobile.'

'Message from his wife's office, sir. They've gone away for the weekend. He needs the rest.'

The governor-general hung up and called Banerjee, 'Our first minister thinks he can evade me. I know where he is headed, and we are going to get him. Get the jet ready.'

'Certainly, sir,' Banerjee replied.

* * *

'First minister, we're about to land. Welcome to Scotland.' Karan stared at the mountains of the Scottish cairngorms. Lush green pine forests as far as the eye could see. He spotted the clear, fast-flowing rivers beneath him and his stress began to dissipate. He had fond memories from every one of his visits to Scotland. His father had once driven them to Loch Ness for a week's holiday. All Karan could remember was the journey. It was one long drive. No breaks for service stations. His father disliked them. And then that second independence referendum in 2023. They had all known for some time the nationalists would win. He couldn't think of Scotland without thinking of that tour with Oliver.

He suddenly remembered a particularly messy night in an Edinburgh whisky club and smiled. Oliver had told him not to worry about Scotland. He'd repeatedly told him, 'Scotland is going to be fine with independence. It's England that's going to be fucked.'

The helicopter landed. A top-of-the-range black SUV was waiting. Men in kilts loaded the bags while Karan thanked the pilots and asked, 'Isha, where are we going?'

'It's a surprise.'

They had landed in a farmer's field. The driver didn't speak to either of them. Karan assumed they'd found one of the many dour

Scots he had spoken to during the campaign. They drove through the rich, arable lands of the mearns with every hue of green and yellow. The journey took them past castles and farmsteads with auburn Highland cows ready to fight them. Finally, they came to a narrow stone bridge over a crystal-clear river and across to a set of cast-iron gates. The gates opened to reveal another glade of Scotch pines. Signs promised red squirrels. The turrets of a grey baronial castle peeked through the canopy. At the end of this arboreal driveway, more kilted staff were waiting. 'Isha, this is beautiful,' he told her.

She smiled. 'Just wait.'

A man in a dark green tartan kilt opened the car door. 'First minister?' Karan got out and the footman headed off. He glanced at Isha. 'On you go then, follow him. I'll deal with all this.'

Inside was an explosion of navy blue and dark green Scottishness. Tartan carpets ran the length of the narrow corridor ahead of him. Mounted stag heads were hanging from either side of its tartan walls. Tartan cushions sat on tartan chairs at the far end, which he was fast approaching. The footman must have been 6 foot 3. He was well ahead of Karan and had no intention of slowing down, which Karan was surprisingly happy about. He was terrified of Scottish accents. He had come to realise they were decipherable. It was just that by the time an English brain realised it was listening to penetrable Scots, the speaker was generally on their third paragraph and had no plans to stop. The footman knocked on a heavy wooden door and opened it without waiting. 'The first minister.' Karan walked in and was momentarily blinded by the light from the full-length windows. It took his eyes a moment to adjust. The view was spectacular. Over the peaks of the cairngorms. He took in the watercolours before spotting the small figure at the writing desk.

'First minister?'

He blinked and thought, 'It couldn't be.' He heard himself say, 'Your … Majesty?'

The queen stood up and walked slowly over to Karan. She held out her hand. He bowed. 'No, none of that here, please. You've banned it. Don't you remember?' She kept walking. 'No royal family. No order of precedence. Union government protocol to be followed at all times.' She had taken a seat in one of two floral chairs in front of an elaborate marble fireplace. 'Do sit down, first minister. And close your mouth. It's a most hospitable place for the Scottish midge.'

'But how are you here?' Karan asked.

'Well, we own Balmoral. Our great-grandmother built it. We have made some small alterations. And we have always loved Scotland. But that's not what you mean?' She had a glint in her eye.

Karan smiled. 'No, ma'am, it's not.'

'My son wanted to be king to the exclusion of all else. I did not want him to be regent. And nor did I want to die. So we came to an arrangement. I moved to Scotland. And slowly people just stopped talking about me. After Scottish independence we agreed I would live here—I have always loved Scotland—and Albert became king. I have become queen emeritus. We learnt that from the Pope. We hosted him at Holyrood, you know. We could feel John Knox turning in his grave.' She smirked. One of the footmen brought in a tray brimming with treats. She checked her watch. 'Excellent timing, first minister. I do love afternoon tea. You must try chocolate biscuit cake. It is my favourite. It's my only real pleasure.' The queen emeritus poured tea. While Karan took his cup, she prepared a small plate. He hadn't realised how hungry he was. It was as if he was in a dream. He knew that any minute he would wake up. And be back in the awfulness of Westminster.

'You have made rather a mess, first minister.' Karan was grateful his mouth was full. 'I have seen many men, and a few women, crave power. It consumed them and generally ended badly.' She drank some tea and took a bite of cake before continuing, 'As sovereign I had little opportunity to appear—or act—tendentiously. But as a former queen, I find that I have much more up my sleeve. Come with me, first minister.' The 101-year-old monarch was sprightly. She had the energy and enthusiasm of someone half her age. She avoided the many pitfalls of her study. The evidence of a life of global service and of a life well lived. She reached a pair of heavy, sliding wooden doors and waited for Karan to open them. He obliged with a small heave. They walked from the wood-panelled festival of tartan to walls of computers, sleek desks and a retinue of young people working at laptops and on screens. The queen was ahead of him. 'You'll see some former chiefs of the general staff and chiefs of the defence staff and young recruits. Admiral Brannick, if I might hand over to you.'

Karan scanned the room. Elderly and retired generals mixed with twenty- and thirty-something tech wizards and smart young soldiers. More a family christmas than a council of war.

'First minister.' Nick was standing erect. And on parade for his sovereign. 'We have been working here under her majesty's protection and guidance.'

The queen tutted.

'We have assembled the beginnings of a task force to take back England.'

'And we want you to join us.' Karan knew the voice. But it couldn't be. Oliver came out from behind Brannick. A broken arm in a home-made sling, the other arm holding on to a crutch. Karan ran to him and held him. He couldn't let go.

'What's taken you so long?' Arun was standing in front of him.

Tears were steaming down Karan's face.

He saw Isha in the doorway behind the queen. She was staring at Oliver. Eyes wide.

'We don't want you simply to join us, first minister.' The queen held Karan's gaze. 'We want you to lead us to our freedom.'

An equerry coughed. 'Ma'am? We've been told the governor-general landed in Aberdeen about seventy-five minutes ago and is now at the castle gates. He has continued to demand to see you.'

'Oh to be popular. Well, then,' the queen continued, 'we had better let him in.'

The equerry slid the doors shut behind the queen. Karan asked Oliver, 'What happened to you?'

Oliver, holding Arun's hand, replied, 'We knew we would both have to disappear. And that India was going to continue to try to kill me. So they needed to think I was already dead.'

Arun continued, 'I received some strange intelligence from vice admiral Moore.'

Rachel appeared. 'Hello again, first minister!'

'Rachel's intelligence told us we could find a way up here on the freedom express.'

'The what?' Karan asked.

'The freedom express,' Oliver replied. 'A specially kitted-out carriage on the sleeper train. We hide fugitives who board on the last stop before the Scottish border. Arun and I took it here. And were as surprised as you.'

'And you, Brannick?'

'Well, sir,' Brannick coughed. 'I decided I didn't quite fancy five years in military prison in India. So, Moore gave me a train ticket for the freedom express too. Could I introduce a few more of the team, please?'

'This is Royal Marine Wen. A brilliant Marine commando and Mandarin speaker. She's been invaluable to us decoding the exchanges between Ambassador Lu and the Indian government.' Wen turned around from her screen, took off her headphones and shook Karan's hand.

'And this is Leon Smith, an MI5 intelligence agent suggested by Dame Rebecca. Smith won't want me to say, but he's the most senior black British officer in MI5. Dame Rebecca says he's her best—and that she's not sure what she'll do without him.'

Smith's cheeks reddened and he looked down at his oversized 1930s Indian watch.

Karan surveyed the team one by one. Oliver and Arun. Nick and Rachel. Wen and Leon. Behind them was a legion of former generals and soldiers. All staring directly at him. 'You have been busy, haven't you?' He grabbed Isha's hand and pulled her into their circle.

A footman walked in. 'Sir, the queen asks if you might all keep quiet for a few minutes. She is about to receive the governor-general.'

The queen was waiting in her sitting room when the governor-general entered with Banerjee. She stood up. 'Governor-general, I don't think we have met. But I do know Lord Banerjee.' She shook their hands and sat down. 'Now, to what do I owe this pleasure?'

The governor-general fumed, 'You have taken my first minister and are keeping him hostage. I have come here to have him returned.'

The queen moaned, 'Governor-general, I am over one hundred years old with a fondness for small dogs and horses. I have neither the strength nor inclination to take your first minister hostage. What is this all about?'

'Indian satellites tracked the first minister's helicopter to a landing strip near this castle. I am reliably informed he took a car here. And is in hiding with you. I demand you hand him over to me.'

Footmen arrived with trays. 'Would you like tea?' She waited while hers was poured. 'I can understand why the first minister would come to this part of Scotland for a holiday, governor-general. I came here every year for more than ninety! And often sailed around the islands, which I thoroughly recommend. It sounds like you need the benefit of a good break too.'

'What do you mean?'

'You have reached an independent country. You can't make any demands of me here. I'm a private Scottish citizen. In fact, a European one too. I will make enquiries about the first minister's whereabouts. And if I find something I can share with you I shall. But I'm sure you're Chinese-Indian satellites might find him quicker than I can.'

The governor-general stood up. 'Now listen here, old woman. The days of your family lording over us are gone. You are right, I can't do anything to you here. But I could just as easily put Albert in jail.'

The queen ignored him. 'Well, I think we've come to the end of this little show. Thank you, governor-general.' With that she rang for a footman and stood until they'd both left.

* * *

Brannick was showing Karan the nascent plans they had developed for bringing down the Indian administration. 'But we would need you to return as first minister, sir.'

'Really?' Karan asked.

'Yes,' Oliver replied. 'We will need time to build and train an army. To secure supplies. We'll need to run some counter-insurgency programmes. But all of that is predicated on you and Isha returning to London and acting as if everything is normal.'

'And it will be dangerous for you both, sir.' Rachel said. 'Let me handover to Leon.'

Leon stood up from his computer and handed Karan an intelligence report. 'This report says that the Indian government considered abducting Arun and Isha and holding them hostage in India. Going back will put your wife at some personal risk.'

'Yes, we are going to place a burden on both of you, first minister.'

The queen had returned. 'Admiral Brannick, I was told it was time.'

'Yes, ma'am.' Brannick stepped forward. 'we've been tracking the governor-general's plane with a drone. They are still in Scottish airspace. We can't identity any defensive measures and they are about to fly into some wet weather.'

'Typical.' The queen added, making them smile.

'And, first minister,' Brannick added, 'We would like you to give the order to blow it up.'

The room was silent. All eyes on him. He turned to each of them. Oliver and Arun nodded. Brannick and Moore too. Leon and Wen were waiting at their stations to give the instructions to the drone.

'Well, first minister?' the queen asked.

'Blow it up. Now.'

They watched Leon and Wen send the coded signals to the drone. The plane's radar signal disappeared.

'Just what they deserved,' the queen declared before walking out. 'Now, tea?'

About the Author

Alan Gemmell spent six years living and working in Delhi and Mumbai. He travelled India meeting activists, artists, business people, policymakers and politicians in twenty-six states. He has a particular connection with the North-East of India and an interest in India's second-tier cities. In 2022 he undertook a thirty-city tour of India's second-tier cities to see the people and places who will drive India's growth for the next twenty years.

In July 2024 Alan was elected Labour member of Parliament for Central Ayrshire, the Scottish constituency where he grew up. Alan was His Majesty's Trade Commissioner for South Asia and has a unique perspective on the UK–India relationship and the key political and business leaders behind it.

30th State is his first book.